The Black Throne

The Black Throne
Book one of The Black Throne trilogy

To the morally grey and twisted

Content Warning:

This trilogy is meant for mature audiences.

If you cannot handle or do not like the following: gore, blood, death, off-page sexual assault and cannibalism, torture, LGBTQ+ representation, and sex stop reading here.

For everyone else, enjoy.

Character Index

Rulers

Anselm Oakens—Former King of Oakens Region, father of Leontios, retired, barbarian

Basia Zeldine—Queen of Zeldine's Region, close friend of Violet, followed tradition by slaying the previous ruler, orc

Caroline Boon—Queen of Jared's Region, eldest ruler, close friend of Thorn, created and hosts the Celebration of Peace, elf

Decimus Cain—King of Cain's Region, tenth generation of rulers, friend of Surin, human

Holister Castine—Former King of Alucard's Region, father of Magnus and Padma, husband of Vesh, angel, deceased

Ko Wolfgang—King of Wolfgang's Region, eldest of four siblings, close friend of Yoon Woo, wolf beastman

Leontios Oakens—King of Oakens Region, his tattoos represent his rulership and accomplishments, barbarian

Magnus Castine—King of Alucard's Region, Malice's lover, son of Vesh and Holister, older brother of Padma, half human half angel

Malice Reap—King of Hordes Region, Magnus's lover, son of Nyx and Karlisle, elder brother of Juno, younger brother of Kiran, demon (?)

Surin Raelle—King of Raelle's Region, friend of Decimus, strategist, fishman

Thorn Maziar—King of Maziar's Region, close friend of Caroline, second eldest ruler, dark elf

Valentine Ezhil—Ruler of Florence's Region, third eldest ruler, pacifist, fairy

Vendetta Claymore—Former Queen of Hordes Region, mother of six children and Malice, wife of Emil, demon, deceased

Violet Yeager—Queen of Yeager's Region, close friend of Basia, dwarf

Yoon Woo Braxton—King of Braxton's Region, father of three children, close friend of Ko, giant

Royals

Alec—Older brother of Kai, Royal of Alucard's Region, barbarian

Ahenobarbus (Barbus) Narine—Member of Unit One, Royal Knight, ex-mercenary, Helen's lover, angel

Amos—Instructor, Royal Knight rank A, specialty is regeneration, Howard's lover, fishman

Arthur—Instructor, Royal Knight rank S, specialty is close combat, barbarian

Barren—Instructor, Royal Knight rank B, specialty is defense, lion beastman

Corgan—Royal Knight rank S, friend of Gareth, Magnus's guard when Gareth is not, human

Eunice Baklav—Malice's First Sword, Royal Knight, wife of Helle, bear beastman

Edith—Instructor, Royal Knight rank B, specialty is long-distance, fairy

Gareth Birch—Magnus's right-hand man, instructor, leader of Unit One, Royal Knight rank S, has been the right-hand man for three generations, dark elf

Howard—Instructor, Royal Knight rank A, specialty is magic, Amos's lover, dwarf

Ida Ravish—Close friend of Laci's, Royal Guard rank A, Malice's disciple, raised by her grandmother, giant

Isaac—Instructor, Royal Knight rank C, specialty is teamwork, human

Laci Holigan—Close friend of Ida's, Royal Guard rank D, barbarian

Lucas Knightridge—Eldest son of Elena and Cesar, elder brother of Joseph and Maryjane, Royal Knight rank A, member of Unit One, elf

Lycn Grove—Pich's lover, Royal Knight rank B, member of Unit One, half human half coyote beastman

Marris—Instructor, friend of Barbus, Royal Knight rank S, specialty is hand to hand combat, angel

Pich Conwrath—Royal Knight rank C, healer, Lycn's lover, member of Unit One, fairy

Taryn—Instructor, Royal Knight rank A, healer, elf

Vinney—Instructor, assassin, Royal Knight rank S, orc

Voidents

Cas—One of Zephyrus's subordinates, a 'master'

Lazarus—Second commander of the voidents on Vinyamar

Valken—One of Zephyrus's subordinates, a 'master'

Zephyrus Laska—Former Royal of Hordes Region, a commander of the voidents, half demon half fairy

Akatchi—?

Others

Cadmus Locke—Professor at Everest Academy in Ivory's Kingdom, taught both Joseph and Lucas, widow, retired underground fighter, angel

Cesar Knightridge—Husband of Elena, father of Lucas, Joseph and Maryjane, retired royal knight, craftsmen, elf, deceased

Charles Bilgen—Blacksmith, wanted criminal in all regions, involved with voidents, human

Darinka Locke—Wife of Cadmus, botanist, dark elf, deceased

Elena Knightridge—Widow, wife of Cesar, mother of Lucas, Joseph, and Maryjane, retired royal knight, elf

Helen—Alucard's Kingdoms castle doctor, Barbus's lover, associated with Yahui, orc

Hyacinthia Valor—Former Noble of Ryzion in Hordes Region, friend of Hordes Reap, grandmother of Malice and Juno, demon partial human

Joseph Knightridge—Younger brother of Lucas, older brother of Maryjane, son of Elena and Cesar, student at Everest Academy, artist, elf

Kai—Younger sibling of Alec, Joseph's bully at Everest Academy, barbarian

Kiran Pretorius—Older brother of Malice, son of Tendai and Blodwen, healer, witch doctor, Malice's former regent and advisor, bison and cow beastman, deceased

Kuro Mantis—Cesar's killer, criminal, involved with voidents, seer, partial dark elf

Maryjane Knightridge—Only daughter of Elena and Cesar, younger sister of Lucas and Joseph, painter, elf

Padma Castine—Younger brother of Magnus, youngest son of Vesh and Holister, half angel half human, deceased

Vesh Castine—Mother of Magnus and Padma, wife of Holister, ex-prostitute, human, deceased

Yahui—Craftsman, associated with Helen, demon

Founding Rulers

Alucard Castine—Killed by Coatliris, angel

Amori Oakens—Killed by Coatliris, barbarian

Bilge Cain—Killed by Coatliris, human

Dieu Maziar—Killed by Coatliris, dark elf

Florence Ezhil—Killed by Coatliris, fairy

Hordes Reap—Killed by Coatliris, demon

Hyeon Braxton—Killed by Coatliris, giant

Ikram Yeager—Killed by Coatliris, dwarf

Jared Boon—Killed by Coatliris, elf

Kamen Zeldine—Killed by Coatliris, orc

Lior Raelle—Killed by Coatliris, fishman

Slava Wolfgang—Killed by Coatliris, beastman

Species Index

Angel—Angels are an immortal race. It is rare for an angel to be born without feathered wings or to be born wingless. Angels are descendants of Archangels. One bloodline is a direct descendent of Archangels: the Castine bloodline.

Barbarian—A barbarians lifespan is one hundred twenty to one hundred fifty years of age. Barbarians are the sister race to humans. Barbarians are physically superior to humans. Tattoo's hold a significant meaning to the barbarian culture.

Beastman—Beastmen are a humanoid race; beasts with human-like features or vice versa. Beastmen are land mammals such as wolves, bears, rabbits, and so on. The human characteristics vary per person. Beastmen's lifespan is fifty to ninety years of age.

Dark Elf—Dark elves are an immortal race. The complexion of a dark elf stays on the desaturated purple to blue spectrum unless mixed. Dark elves are the sister race to elves. Ears are shorter and pointed downward. Dark elves are descendants of High elves.

Demon—Demons are an immortal race. A demon's appearance varies per person. It is rare for a demon to be born with feathered wings. Demons can control certain aspects of their appearance such as horns, wings, tails, or claws. Demons are descendants of Devils. Three bloodlines are direct descendants of Devils: the Reap, Valor, and Apostolov bloodlines.

Dwarf—Dwarves lifespan is one hundred eighty to two hundred years of age. A dwarfs height will not exceed one hundred fifty centimeters. Dwarves are descendants of Trolls. Worship toward different deities and their ruler is a significant practice in the homeland of Yeager's Region.

Elf—Elves are an immortal race. Ears are long and pointed upward. Elves are the sister race to Dark elves. Elves are descendants of High elves. Elves live off and respect the land. Most villages and communities in the homeland of Jared's Region are deeply connected to one another and often come together for song and dance.

Fairy—Faires are an immortal species. Skin tone varies per person, but it is rare for them to have vibrant skin like a demon would. The majority of fairies have wings, said wings mirror that of an insect. Faires are a naturally androgynous and intersex race. Faires are descendants of Nymphs. Wearing clothes in the homeland of Florence's Region is seen as restrictive.

Fishman—Fishmen are a humanoid race; sea creatures with human-like features or vice versa. The human characteristics vary per person. Very rarely will a fishmen be born without gills even if they are mixed. Fishmen's lifespan is eighty to one hundred thirty years of age.

Giant—Giant's lifespan is one hundred forty to one hundred eighty years of age. A giant's height will not exceed two hundred fifty centimeters and will not dip below one hundred ninety-five centimeters. Giants are descendants of Titans. Respect and tradition are significant values in the homeland of Braxton's Region.

Human—Human's lifespan is eighty to one hundred ten years of age. Humans are the sister race to Barbarians. Humans have adopted numerous ways of life from the other races. In the homeland of Cain's Region, hunting for game is a significant part of human culture.

Orc—Orc's lifespan is one hundred to two hundred years of age. Orc's skin tone stays within the green spectrum. The size of an orc's tusks vary from person to person. Orcs are descendants of Ogres. Warriors and battles hold a high significance in orc culture.

God—Gods are an immortal species.

Voident—Voidents can resurrect so long as their god is alive. Creatures of darkness.

N
NW
NE
W
E
SW
SE
S
ALUCARD'S REGION
CYTOR
IVORY'S KINGDOM
WOLF
HOWLERS FOREST
REDCOL
KINGDOM OF PHOENIX
ANDDULIA
CAIN'S REGION
NTESAL
LIOTKIN
MAZIAR'S REGION
YEAGER'S REGION
BRAXTON'S RE

VINYAMAR

Oakens Region
Jareds Region
Raelle's Region
Zeldine's Region
Bextierther
Estera
Hordes Region
Mondlesgrave
Mutuwa
Ryzion
Florence's Region

Prologue

Gods don't bleed.

Tushuni, the god of fertility, was nothing like Malice had imagined. Not that he knew what to expect when he confronted the god. It was massive, larger than Hordes Kingdom, and paler than he was. Every trail of magic coursing through its body was visible, glowing veins of pulsing white underneath a thin layer of skin. With fleshy wings triple the size of its body, Tushuni would have little trouble making its home among the clouds. What made Malice's stomach lurch, however, was the god's head. As if two hands had been welded together by the wrists, finger-like appendages cupped and surrounded hundreds of eyes, its mouth at the center.

Warmth radiated through Tushuni's body. Something akin to a heart pounded at a steady rhythm. Its ribcage expanded and deflated as if its lung-less body had the capacity to breathe. Without a brain or a nervous system, Malice thought its death would be a painless one. That was not the case.

When Malice tore its magical core from its body, the god cried in pain. The sound was a mix between the ghastly screech of a howler, the bone-chilling laughter of an onyimyth, and the wail of a babe. Tushuni's scream made the clamor of war seem like a whisper. Eventually, all of Forli fell silent. Like all living things, Malice had expected the god to lie there and decompose. Instead, magic oozed into the atmosphere, embers of light spiraling toward the heavens, the body of Tushuni no more.

A breeze swept through his hair. He tilted his head back, nostrils flaring, taking in the foul stench of rot and the metal tang of blood. No matter how often he smelled it, he didn't think he'd ever get used to the stench of death. Below the pillars of mountainous rock Malice sat on, the mists of Forli were crimson from the ceaseless killing the war had brought. Bodies of all races littered the ground, covering the earth in rot and decay, and crows circled above the scattered trees of what was once a magnificent forest.

Northeast of Vinyamar, across the vast ocean, the continent of Forli was foreign to Malice. It was the land of mountain pillars, thick greenery weaving between them, masking the ground, while civilization thrived at the peaks. Their tongue was not his own, but he had learned it quickly; he had little choice if he wanted to gain the trust of Forli's people. Their customs and culture mirrored a few regions of his homeland, though only vaguely.

The wind, low and mournful, rarely died this high above the earth. Rising from the ledge, Malice walked through the carnage. If he breathed too heavily, he could taste the sulfur. Homes and buildings made of wood and plaster were destroyed, their skeletons smoking or fully collapsed heaps of debris. Like the forest floor, festering corpses were abundant. Swarms of bugs created buzzing clouds of grey. Dirt and soot streaked his clothes and skin. Dried blood—none of it his own—stuck his linen shirt to his skin, made the blotches of it on his pants stiff, and made his leather boots dull.

He knew more than anyone how he *should* feel right now: disgusted, hollow, angry, guilty, even. He lost that ability some time ago, or perhaps he had unknowingly abandoned it.

The call of home was a lullaby that steadily became more difficult to ignore. Overwhelming, it was a sense of accomplishment, a lightness in his limbs and chest. Malice had come for a reason—to kill Tushuni—and now he could leave.

Beyond a pile of blackened lumber, shriveled vines, ropes, and plaster, Malice eyed the small body of a child, the skin alive with writhing maggots. Then he stopped beside the bloated corpse of the village chief. Jingyi was an orc in her forties, her hair braided and adorned with feathers, beads, and jewels to represent her status, her skin now the color of rotted beef. Malice was the one who killed her, ran a blade through the center of her being, her magical core.

Slowly, Malice had killed too many to count over the past two years. Jingyi was simply one of the last. It was like a hunt: Malice, the predator; the people of Forli, his prey. Yet, it was like a royale: Malice killing every soul in a village or province. With the trust of Forli's people and no survivors, pinning the blame on another clan was easy. Conflict spread like wildfire soon after.

Jingyi's white-fogged eyes were open. He crouched and stared at what were once deep brown eyes, vibrant with life and defiance. He watched the vibrancy leave her as his blade met the resistance of flesh and bone, betrayal a bitterness that contorted her face. And despite the pain of Jingyi's demise, death was the better of the two.

When Malice stood and continued south, his boots smacked against the sludge of excrement, blood, and pulpy organs, bugs pestering him. Behind him, there was the crack of wood breaking and a boom from another home crumbling. It was autumn, winter not far off, so the air was crisp—not that it helped with the putrefying bodies strewn about—and the sun was warm on Malice's face.

Tushuni may not have bled, but the twelve races did, and it made war that much easier to wage.

Heart of Innocence

I

His heart thumped, a single beat that reverberated through his chest into his skull. Joseph's name had been the only sound for an instant, bouncing off the brick walls that surrounded him. Dryness hugged his mouth. He glanced at the royal guard near the edge of the courtyard, his silver armor polished and branded with the Alucard's Kingdom sigil. Behind Joseph stood his peers and professor, watching him, judging him.

A hunk of metal, a few logs of wood, water, a bowl of fire, and other elements lay about the stone floor. Joseph stopped at the center. He knew his magic was that of earth and eyed the various-sized rocks beside the flames. Sniggers reached his ears, no doubt from Kai and their band of miscreants. Taking as deep of a breath as his lungs would allow, Joseph closed his eyes and focused. A subtle twinge tickled his sternum, his magical core. He opened his eyes and lifted his hand, willing the smallest of the rocks to move, to tremble, to twitch.

The rock remained still. Joseph concentrated, his brow furrowing. *Just move.*

It did not.

"Enough," the guard said. When Joseph turned toward him, he waved his hand dismissively.

Joseph bowed at the waist and rushed to the edge of the courtyard, underneath the shade, with the rest of his class. Those closest to him shuffled away. Heat flared in his chest and face, but it quickly dissipated. *It doesn't matter if I can't use magic. It has nothing to do with me.*

Thirty students were called upon before the royal guard stepped back and allowed a beastman to take over, paper in hand. She was old, her skin a few days from becoming tan leather. Her legs were slender and covered in short auburn fur. Around her hooves jingled silver, copper, and gold anklets, matching the jewelry around her neck and in her ears. Unlike the guard, the woman didn't make a grand speech about who she was and why she was here. Instead, she called the first name on her list. Then the second and the third.

"Joseph." The deer beastman squinted at the document. After a time, her eyes went wide. "Knightridge? Sir Lucas' younger brother, huh?" Her gaze sliced to Joseph. He flinched.

The dread from earlier had lessened. How much more of a fool could he make out of himself, anyway? Stopping a few meters from the old woman, Joseph gulped. She looked at his core, the center of his being for a moment, and grunted.

"I'd stay in that little village of yours," she said.

Joseph's blood ran cold. He bowed once more and walked to his original spot, trying to keep Kai out of his sights. They were staring at him though, their pale skin almost grey in the shade, their hair jet black. He snapped his head away, eyes falling to the stone.

Not so long after Joseph, the woman called out Kai's name. Hardly five seconds had passed before the seer smiled at their core.

Seers were those able to see the flow and amount of magic within someone's body, an innate talent from what Joseph knew.

"I hear you want to become a royal," she said cheerfully.

Kai nodded. "I do. I want to one day join my brother."

"I can see you becoming a fine royal, Kai, and I wish you the best of luck."

Shoulders proud, a grin on their face, Kai strutted into the shadows, their friends punching their arm and whispering encouragement.

Take what the seer and royal say with a grain of salt. It only has as much weight as you give it, Professor Cadmus explained the day before. Joseph peeked at the professor, who stood a head above the students near the edge of the courtyard, a hoard of bodies between them. His long, light brown hair swept past his waist, the breeze pushing strands out of place. The sharpness of his clothes accentuated his slim, lanky figure. Briefly, their eyes met. At least Joseph thought they did. It was difficult to tell with Professor Cadmus, his eyes completely white like all pure-blooded angels were.

He was right, though. Joseph took what the seer and royal said and let it go. What bothered him, a sense of foreboding sinking in his gut like lead, was Kai. Their threatening glances pestered him throughout the rest of class. *Please, just leave me alone.*

Professor Cadmus went over the basics of magic after the students returned to his classroom around high noon. Joseph paid loose attention to the lecture, having already known about the main elements, their sub-elements, and how magic was used. Bits and pieces, however, caught his attention. The properties of emit, pressure, pacify, and intimidation; formless magic that was extremely hard to control—deadly as well—and therefore rarely used.

Joseph was one of the last students to walk out of the classroom when someone grabbed him from behind and slammed him against the wall. He gasped from the impact as an arm pressed into his neck, making it hard to catch his breath. Kai pushed him further against the wall, their brow creased and their nostrils flaring. They were lean, stronger than their appearance let on, and taller than Joseph. He choked and gripped Kai's arm, squeezing against their impossibly powerful hold, air refusing to fully inflate his lungs.

Kai moved their head, their slightly minty breath hitting Joseph's face. "A weakling like you should have just stayed home," they hissed. Their deep, indigo eyes almost shared the same intensity of hatred as their voice did. "You're pathetic, an eyesore, a parasite. Why are you even here? I mean, if you enjoy being my practice dummy, by all means, stay. Otherwise, why not run away? Just like your brother did." Kai spat in his face.

How do they know about Lucas? "Because," Joseph struggled to speak, "I actually… want an education… I wouldn't want… to become like you… after all." Sucking in a sharp breath, Joseph held Kai's gaze, a bit of regret forming at the foremost of his mind.

They brought their free arm back and punched his gut as hard as they could. His vision sparked with darkness before Kai released him. Joseph collapsed to the floor, hacking violently like he'd taken a drag off some mugwort. While he was on the ground, he hoped they would walk away. He hoped Kai had had their fill. As if luck would favor him on a day like this. Kai retreated a few steps and swung their leg, kicking Joseph's face. The tip of their shoe caught the bottom of his chin, flinging his head and body against the wall.

"You're lucky we're being watched, or I would've made sure you did more than spit red." Kai glared for a moment longer, eventually joining their friends down the hall, their insults and snickers echoing.

A metallic taste filled Joseph's mouth as he wiped the spittle from his cheek. He must've bitten his lip or tongue, not that it actually mattered where the source was. Pain pulsed through his gut and face—throbs that made his eyes water. Over his shoulder, he spat ichor onto the ground. Just then, something dripped from his nose like a raindrop hitting the floor. It was bright red. Taking his thumb, he pushed against the nostril that wasn't bleeding and blew. Blood splattered his clothes, and the floor, followed by a clot. *I should have kept my lips sealed.*

Out of the corner of his eye, he saw a figure standing in the doorway, leaning against the frame, watching in silence. *So, Kai went easy on me because of him.*

"Why didn't you step in? Stop them? You're a teacher, aren't you?" he asked bitterly, his voice hoarse. He ran his tongue along his teeth to make sure they were still there and secure.

Professor Cadmus pushed himself off the frame and sighed, "Are you not old enough to settle such squabbles on your own? Conflict has many ways to reach a resolution. You just have to be willing to try them."

Joseph could tell he was disappointed—his glum tone expressed that much—and he was old enough; would be seventeen by the end of spring. It was frustrating, but true, which made it even more frustrating. Using the wall, Joseph heaved himself up, the change in elevation causing his lower face to throb.

The few that stuck around in the halls gave him quick glances before exchanging whispers with their friends. While cradling his gut, he hastened his pace, his cheeks flushing. Joseph spat at the thought of Kai as he walked out of the academy.

The paddocks were behind the main building of brick, beyond the headmaster's little cottage. Joseph's feet smacked against a slurry of dirt and snow. He glimpsed the old stable master tending to a donkey. Animals waited patiently for their owners to retrieve them—mules, horses, even a pig half the size of a grown giant.

Joseph entered the paddock and Finbar, his colt, poked his head out of one of the middle stalls. Hurriedly opening the gate, he was relieved to see the stable master had left Finbar's saddle on and guided the horse out of the paddock. The stable master fed the donkey some barley stalks as Joseph re-tightened the straps of the saddle, hopped onto his horse, and placed his feet in the stirrups. He kicked Finbar's side; the horse neighed and set off into an impatient trot until Joseph spurred him into a gallop.

Around the western building, Joseph crossed Everest Academy's campus within a hundred heartbeats and sped through the iron gates into the streets of Ivory's Kingdom.

It was a straight shot southwest from the kingdom to Redcol. He wouldn't get there till evening, not that Joseph minded. Gently tugging on Finbar's reins, he slowed to a canter. He didn't want to go home. He didn't want to have to talk about his day. And he didn't want his ma to see his bruises and blood-stained clothes.

The winter air brought a crispness into his lungs that refreshed his mind. Joseph gazed at the horizon to the southeast, admiring the snowy peaks of the mountain range that went into Wolfgang's Region. Then, east of Ivory's Kingdom, was the Lake of Ishier, a white canvas covered with shining crystals. The scenery was never something he could capture on paper like his sister Maryjane could, but it always eased his worries, blowing them away like dandelion seeds in the wind.

As he continued down the path to Redcol, reality sank in again. Joseph didn't need an education to sell his artwork at his village's trading festival. Still, his pa had one, Ma did too. Lucas had gone to Everest Academy before he became a royal, and so would Maryjane when she was old enough. He wanted to learn, but Kai dampened his desire for knowledge a while ago. *Should I... let it go?*

Everest Academy was one of six in Alucard's Region and Joseph's village wasn't particularly close. His family was well enough off that he could go to school all year round if he wanted, thanks to his parents being retired royal knights. That money had nothing to do with Joseph, though. He had to earn his own coin. So Elena allowed him a few absences to work around the village.

Early in the evening, Joseph came home to Maryjane sitting on the front porch, her hair a mass of leaves, twigs, and grass. He approached the little girl, his thighs and calves burning from riding Finbar and trekking up the hill. His footsteps alerted her, making her jump to her feet, her expression bright. Then it dimmed as her blue eyes followed the dark red, almost brown splatter down Joseph's clothes. Maryjane put her hands behind her back and dug her foot into the ground.

"What did you do?" Joseph asked, knowing that if he didn't strike up a conversation first, Maryjane would ask about his injuries.

She pouted her lips. "All I did was roll down the hill," she said woefully.

Joseph sighed and considered asking Ma to simply chop off all her hair, so it wasn't such a hassle. But Maryjane loved her long, tight curls that were the color of a golden daisy. Loved doing her hair up in all sorts of ways to impress Grams, Elena's mother.

"Do you want me to help clean it up? Before Ma comes home and skins you?" It would help take his mind off that morning and afternoon.

"Really?" Maryjane beamed.

"So long as you don't tell Ma about this—" He gestured to his face and shirt, although he could change his garments while Maryjane gathered the supplies for her hair. The bruises throbbing on his face and torso, on the other hand, he would be lucky if they faded to a nice dull shade of yellow by the time Elena got home.

Grunting and holding her chin the way Cesar had while deep in thought, Maryjane nodded determinedly. "Deal."

Time slipped by as Joseph teased stubborn snarls from Maryjane's head, picking out dead leaves, twigs, stalks of weeds, and hay, and eventually braided her hair to keep it out of her face. She hopped to the attic to change out of her soiled clothes.

If there was anything Joseph's magical energy could do, it was regenerate the minor cuts and bruises Kai would give him. When Maryjane bounced into the kitchen and dining room, most of the bruises had diminished, their tenderness easing. They cleaned the debris left behind from her adventure of rolling down the hill, a weariness gradually sinking into Joseph's muscles. His pitiful amount of magic used more energy to regenerate his injuries than it did to make a stupid pebble move.

Elena came home later that evening with two baskets in hand. One had food—meats, bread, cheese, fruits, and vegetables— and the other had presents for Maryjane's tenth birthday. It reminded Joseph of the Trading Festival that started on the morrow. It was as much a bother as it was an escape.

Maryjane trudged down the steps, arms full of supplies, before she slammed everything on the dining room table. Joseph sat at the counter, watching his ma chop some vegetables for rabbit stew. He and Maryjane caught the rodent yesterday, helped skin it, too. Glancing back toward the table, paints, brushes, and papers were spread across it. In seconds, she came thumping down the stairs once more, carrying notably less, but it was Joseph's art supplies—his sketching pad, charcoal, and a small sharpening blade. He frowned, *she went through my desk... again*, and rolled his eyes.

After putting his materials down, Maryjane turned to Joseph, a hopeful little smile on her face, her blue eyes big and round. With a sigh, he joined her at the table, somewhat grateful to get away from the potent onions Elena was cutting. His eyes had started to sting and water. He gave Maryjane a pointed look as he pulled a chair out; the legs scraping against the wooden floor. She nodded at him, a single, deliberate bob of her head. *You promised*, he mouthed to which she squinted her eyes with a slight teeter of her head. She started sketching on the parchment in front of her.

"How was your day? Anything interesting happen at the academy?" Elena asked as Joseph collected the knife and charcoal. The hunk of black was dull. He walked into the kitchen beside his ma, where the compost bin was halfway full of scraps from the meat and vegetables.

"A seer came in today," he said and carefully carved a point in the charcoal, shavings fluttering into the bin.

"So, how did it go?"

He sighed. "My flow of magical energy is weak." He expected as much before Professor Cadmus announced the seers' and guards' arrival. Elena had earth magic while Cesar had had fire magic. Maryjane inherited Ma's earth, and Lucas inherited Pa's fire. Joseph tried using either element, discovering he could make a pebble, the size of his pinky nail, hop. Once.

"The seer said I should stay in Redcol... I don't particularly disagree with that."

Now that the charcoal had a sufficient point, Joseph returned to the table, hoping he would actually stay seated till dinner, and sketched the first face that came to mind. Elena's. She had an angular face, a small chin, and soft eyes with slight wrinkles at the corners. The tips of her high pointed ears poked through her wavy hair no matter how wild it was. Soft freckles covered her face like stars covered the night sky.

"Does that bother you?" Ma asked without turning around, scooping up the pile of chopped vegetables on the counter and tossing them into the big pot.

"No," Joseph answered hesitantly.

"Yes, it does," Maryjane chimed in while bobbing her head from side to side. Open jars of paint sat about her, the smell of oil wafting about him, the paintbrush in her hand sliding across the paper. She was painting sunflowers, as always.

"Why would it bother me? I don't plan to use my magic for much. I had hoped to use it for mundane tasks." That was true, though he didn't know what earth magic would aid outside of heavy lifting and construction.

"It is nice to have around when you need it," Ma admitted. "But there's more to it than that, isn't there?" Elena stopped chopping and turned to face Joseph, wiping her hands off on her apron as she did.

Joseph met her unwavering stare, her sky-blue eyes almost as bright as Maryjane's. *I hate that look.* He swallowed and averted his gaze. "I don't know if I should continue… my studies."

"Oh? And why is that?"

"Because he got beat up again," Maryjane said.

"Maryjane!" Joseph shot up in his seat, a cold chill running down his spine. "You promised!"

"Joseph."

"Ma, it's not an issue," Joseph said pleadingly after glaring at Maryjane, who stuck her tongue out at him. "It's just—"

"It's just what?" Her tone was harsh, resolute.

Joseph couldn't speak, his mouth refused to open. Underneath the table, his nails dug into the palms of his hands. With an inhale and exhale, he managed to say, "Just some rough sparring. The others got a little too carried away while the professor taught us self-defense. It would have been nice to have a bit more magic for that." He chuckled awkwardly, trying to resolve the tension between him and his ma.

Maryjane still bobbled her head, feet probably swinging under the table, her painting of a meadow—full of sunflowers— near completion.

"You don't have to follow in our footsteps," Elena said, a bit of hesitancy in her voice. "Magic… can be fussy sometimes and you got the short end of the stick."

Clearly. He fought the urge to roll his eyes.

"Your talent lies elsewhere, son," Elena sighed. It took a moment, but her expression softened, and she crossed the room. "You're good with your hands and your brain. Take a few days to decide what you want to do next. I'll support you no matter what."

She stopped beside Joseph's chair, his head turning. She caught him by the chin and guided him back. "All right?"

Finally meeting her eyes, Joseph nodded. "All right."

Brushing his hair out of the way, smiling, she kissed his forehead, then returned to the kitchen. He knew she meant well, but her words of encouragement weren't all that encouraging. How could they be? She had talked throughout his childhood about how her children would become mighty royals. Eventually, she had dropped the topic when Joseph reached the age of eight, maybe nine, and he still couldn't use magic. At least around him, she had.

Maryjane and Joseph cleaned off the dining table soon before dinner was served. The smell of rabbit stew was thick in the air, causing Joseph's mouth to salivate and his stomach to grumble. Maryjane babbled on about her day, which she usually spent with Ma around the village or at home, Ma checking in on her often.

"Would you like to join us?" Elena offered when she mentioned that she and Maryjane would go to Cesar's parents on the morrow.

"No," he said. Elena pursed her lips, a slight frown creasing her forehead, but she didn't push.

Maryjane, glancing between the two, whined, "If he's not going, then why do—"

"You're going," Ma said. "Your grandparents want to see you for your birthday." None too happily, face sour, Maryjane gave in.

After helping Ma clean the table and wash the dishes, Joseph and Maryjane retired. With every step, the floor cried faintly, like it was tired of being walked on.

A black divider in front of their beds split the attic, their desks just beyond them. Rounded windows displayed the dark, starry sky. Maryjane ran and jumped onto her squeaky bed. Crickets chirped outside, the wind a hushed whistle.

Joseph went to his armoire on the right side of his bed, got out his nightclothes, and changed. The ceiling was pivoted but tall enough for him to stretch without touching the wood above him. His bed also creaked when he climbed under the covers. The little energy he had drained from his body like water from a splintered bucket. Between dinner and the injuries he'd gotten from Kai, it was difficult for Joseph to stay awake, not that he fought the slumber.

Heart of Innocence
"The Trading Festival"

A little after dawn, Joseph stood on the porch and recounted his coins. Five bronze, two silver, and two gold coins. Months of doing odd jobs around Redcol and saving, and this was what he had to show for it. Still, it was enough to get Maryjane a gift or two for her birthday. Shoving the coins back into his pocket, Joseph headed toward the bustling village.

Redcol was established in the saddle of multiple hills, a paddock off the village's edge. Joseph glanced over his shoulder. On top of one of those hills, overlooking the village, was the house Elena and Cesar had built decades ago. It was made of wood and plaster, while the roof was thatch, a raised garden bed on its side.

The Trading Festival was a three-day event held once a year as winter melted into spring. People from nearby kingdoms and holds crowded the main street. It was a cacophony of ear-ringing sounds—chatter, laughter, arguments, and the thud of shoes on cobblestone. Booths, tents, and tables filled either side of the street, going well past the northern edge of Redcol. Why an event this big was held in the little town of Redcol was beyond Joseph.

A booth to the left was selling clocks of all sizes, most made of wood, but a few had a metal frame. The one to the right sold fruits like apples, oranges, grapes, and weird round, hairy, brown things he had never seen before. Joseph stepped in closer, squeezing himself in between people.

"I went and handpicked these myself!" the vendor proclaimed, teeth missing from his wide grin. "These here are called coconuts! They only grow in Florence's and Hordes Regions."

Joseph peeked over someone's shoulder to watch the vendor break the coconut open, the crack loud enough to be heard over the crowd. A watered-down milky fluid splashed out. The vendor, with a curved, jagged knife, started shaving the insides and white strips fell onto the table like fresh snow on the ground. He wasn't here for strange fruits, so Joseph turned and ventured further into the festival.

Eventually, around late morning, something caught Joseph's eye. An older woman sat on a stool facing a canvas, paintbrush in hand, and jars of paint on the table beside her. He maneuvered his way around people to her setup and gazed at the paintings displayed on easels. Most were landscapes of places he didn't recognize. He assumed they were from other regions. One was a waterfall surrounded by a forest, a stream flowing from the edge of the canvas that had bright orange, red, yellow, and white fish swimming in it. Another was a deer standing in a beam of golden light in the middle of the woods.

"Looking for something, lad?" the woman asked without taking her eyes off her painting. Her voice was soft and accented, meaning she was not of this region. She was small and stout on her stool. Her skin had a light green tone to it, giving her a sickly appearance. He could tell her hair was once as vibrant as a pumpkin, but age had softened it and added grey. Her face had many soft lines around her mouth and on her forehead. Two small tusks poked through her lips; it was clear she was part orc and part dwarf.

"I'm just admiring your paintings," Joseph said.

The woman dipped her brush in dark blue paint, then brought it to the canvas. "They're all for sale if you'd like one."

The colors were rich—deep green like a forest at night, blue like that of an anemone, sunflower yellow with hints of orange. He felt every brush stroke under his fingertips, ripples telling how this woman created scenery from nothing.

"Do you also happen to sell paint?"

"No lad, that I don't." Her tone was level. "I can, however, tell you how to make it." She peeked around her canvas.

"Really?"

The woman dipped her head once. "Aye, but for a price."

Joseph stared for a moment to see if it was a joke. "How much?" he asked hesitantly.

"Hmm…" She rubbed her chin, smearing blue paint across it. "One gold coin."

"A gold coin?" he repeated, his voice much louder than he intended it to be.

She shrugged and went back to her painting. "Aye, lad. Paint is an artist's way of giving a piece of their soul to something blank and lifeless. Besides, everything comes at a price, including information."

After a moment of silence, he sighed, reached into his pocket, and dug around for a gold coin. The lady stretched her free hand out. He placed it in her palm, her fingers encased it, and her hand slipped into her paint-stained smock.

"A minute, please."

Though she couldn't see him, he nodded and returned to the canvases. A different painting caught his attention. It was beautiful. A meadow at high noon with a stream running through the right side and trees gathered on the left. There was a single sunflower facing him amid many wildflowers. It reminded him of Maryjane and her sunflower obsession.

"It's not something I'm proud of, but if you like it, take it," the lady mentioned as she handed Joseph a folded piece of paper.

"I think I will." Over the front-most paintings, he grabbed the meadow and slid it under his arm, so he could unfold and read the paper.

Mix refined walnut oil with pigment and then use a muller to disperse the paint on a flat surface.

You can get jars of paint pigment made from charcoal, vermillion, daisies, pomegranates, carrots, and much more.

There are two tables down the way with what you'll need.

A smile grew on Joseph's face as he dipped his head. "Thank you." Shoving the paper inside his pocket with the coins, Joseph turned back to the crowd and went on his way.

Maryjane had mentioned making her own paint after hearing Grams talk about it. Grams had even lent her a book on how to do it. Until her paint was gone though, she refused to make her own. Maryjane said it would waste the paint Ma had bought. Trying to explain otherwise sent her into a fit, so Joseph and Elena let her be. Now that her paints were running low, at least her favorite ones, it was the perfect time to get them.

Food, metal, wood, and sweat filled the air as Joseph neared the end of the booths. The sun, a few hours from dipping below the horizon, blared, flushing his face. He still couldn't see the end of the festival over all the people, but he knew he was getting close. His stomach growled and started to cramp from hunger while the soles of his feet ached. With so little left to see, he decided to continue and ignore the hunger and his feet for now. Or maybe he wouldn't have to.

The smell of freshly baked bread floated toward him for a split second. He followed the scent the best he could while keeping an eye out for a baker's tent.

On the right, there was a pudgy woman with high-pointed ears—much like his own—and dark hair drawn into a bun, moisture sticking flyaway strands to her forehead. A customer placed a coin or two in her outstretched hand before she relented a loaf wrapped in brown paper. Both smiled at one another, then the customer disappeared into the sea of people.

When Joseph pushed his way through the crowded street, there were four golden brown loaves of varying sizes left.

"What can I get ya?" the baker asked, her hands on her hips and her smile friendly.

He dug into his pocket and retrieved two bronze coins. "Your smallest loaf please." He pointed at the furthest loaf on the counter and offered coins with the other hand. The longer he stared at the bread, oats sprinkled on top, the more his mouth watered.

She took one coin, "Of course. You want that wrapped?" and dropped it into the front pouch of her light pink apron as Joseph put the other back in his pocket.

"No, thanks." He didn't think his hunger would allow him to wait much longer. Ravenously, his stomach rumbled loud enough for the baker to hear since she giggled.

"Well, have at it!" she said, gesturing to the loaf he picked.

He quickly snatched the bread and smiled. "Thank you."

The lady's shadow moved to the left as she moved to the right, catching Joseph's attention. *What was that? Am I seeing things?*

A loud guttural laugh pierced the noise of the festival and Joseph stopped short of sinking his teeth into the bread.

"Leave! Leave at once!" an old haggard voice shouted as something slammed against a table from the sound of it.

Joseph turned. A person, tall and shrouded in darkness, walked across his path, their cloak fluttering behind them. Others had stopped briefly to check on the sudden commotion. Moving backward, he took a bite of the bread and peeked around the corner at the booth next to the bakers.

Necklaces with big and small pendants, earrings that looked too heavy for an ear to hold, bracelets, anklets, and cuffs made of copper, silver, and gold filled the tables.

Behind the front tables of jewelry were weapons. None appeared to be for actual combat. Instead, they seemed better suited for resting on a mantel or shelf. Daggers, knives, and there were a few long, thin-bladed swords with intricately designed sheaths. In the rear was a small furnace, empty at the moment. Beside the furnace was an old man bent over a table covered in the same tools his pa's forge had. He muttered something as he worked.

The weapons didn't appeal to Joseph, so he returned his gaze to the jewels. *Neither Ma nor Maryjane would like this stuff. I don't think even Grams would.*

"Found nothing of interest, boy?" the old man called out as he moved and shoved what he was working on into the front pocket of his leather overall. The old man hobbled to the table and wiped his hands off on his sides. His face sagged at the jaw, long, wiry, white hair sprouted from his chin and upper lip. Brown lopsided spots dotted the old man's bald head. He was short, his back hunched like a scared cat.

Joseph swallowed a hunk of bread which almost caught in his throat, but he choked it down without coughing. "No… but you have a fine touch for craftsmanship from the looks of it." If he could avoid it, he'd rather not get screamed at for insulting the old man's collection.

"Not buying for yerself, are ya?" The old man leaned against the table, propping himself up with a muscular arm. He peered up at Joseph, his eyes so dark they were almost black.

"How did you know?" Joseph asked as he avoided the old man's eyes. Something about them made him uneasy, like spiders crawling up his spine.

"Maybe I can be of some help. Who is it fer?" He caught his long, bristly beard and stroked it.

"My sister, she's turning ten on the morrow."

The old man nodded, grunting in a contemplative manner. "What does she like? Big and bold? Perhaps something small? Is she one fer color?"

"… She likes flowers. More like loves them," Joseph said with a bit of hesitancy. Glancing over the old man's collection again, he was not one to make floral pieces.

The corners of the old man's mouth curved, making his mustache and beard twitch. "I've got just the thing."

From his pocket, he pulled out a gold-chained necklace. "I've been meaning to add more… nature-inspired jewels and decorations fer a while now." A pendant dropped from the old man's calloused paw of a hand. Yellow petals caught the light while the brown seeds in the center created a bumpy texture. It was simple and not too big, the size of a coin at most.

After staring at it for probably too long, Joseph smiled and held his hand out. "It's perfect. I know she would love this!" He set the painting in his opposite hand down, letting it rest against his leg and dug around in his pocket.

"Wait," the old man said. "It's free. Take it and leave. I'm sure ya need the money fer other things." He wiggled his mustache like a rabbit twitching its nose and looked away, as if embarrassed.

Frozen in place, wide-eyed, Joseph said, "Really? Are you sure of this? I can pay." He started digging around in his pocket again for a silver coin.

"No!" he yelled, his eyebrows furrowed. "Now get! Before I change my mind!" The old man waved his hands in a shooing motion. He spun, gimping back to his table of tools.

Joseph glanced between the necklace in his hand and the old man. "Thank you, sir."

The old man grunted. Joseph set out onto the street, feeling a little silly for being nervous about an old, kind-hearted blacksmith.

The painter was right. Two stalls at the end of the way sold oils and pigments. He convinced the oil merchant to sell him two bottles for two silver and two bronze coins. However, the young fox beastman wasn't too happy about the exchange, considering the original price was three silver per bottle. Joseph reached his final destination in the late afternoon, his neck prickling as if eyes were on him. He shook the feeling off. Of course, eyes were on him. Redcol was as packed as the dirt beneath his feet. The vendor allowed Joseph to take ten jars—his pinky finger in height—for the rest of his coin and threw in a free sack to carry his belongings.

When Joseph reached the eastern side of Redcol, he stopped and plopped onto the cold ground, so he could take a breath. For some reason, constantly avoiding ramming into people was more exhausting than last year. He reached over and absently rubbed his stomach; maybe he hadn't fully healed yet, and that was why he was so tired. There were no bruises, though. Kai raced to the forefront of his mind, and he scowled.

They'd met a little over a year ago on Joseph's first day of class. Kai had been there only a few months longer, yet played ruler over the students—Joseph—or tried to. He ignored them, which pissed them off and earned Joseph a slap to the face. Even still, Joseph refused to play along, furthering Kai's antics.

A salty breeze swept through his messy hair, pushing it out of his face and blowing Kai away from his thoughts. *Is a storm coming?* So far inland, the only time the wind grew salty was when a storm was on its way. The chirping of birds and crickets mingled with the chattering village. He found himself relaxing and forced himself to his feet, so he didn't accidentally fall asleep.

Corruption

II

The wind howled and chilled Joseph down to his bones. He continued on the dirt path to his house, a single tree ahead. Bird song and muffled chatter from the village faded as an unease settled in his stomach. The hairs on his nape stood on edge like they had on the streets. Had someone followed him? It wasn't like he had anything worth stealing, but Joseph glanced over his shoulder. He sighed; no one was there. *Maybe I need a nap.*

Turning around, Joseph froze. A dark figure propped itself on the lone oak's trunk, its branches hanging over the path creating patchy shade. The figure was tall and obscured by a black, travel-stained cloak.

Joseph stepped away. "Who are you?" He recognized the cloaked person. They were the one that stormed off after the old man had yelled at them. "Reveal yourself or else…" Joseph paused, knowing he could do nothing if the person truly wanted to hurt him. Except run back to Redcol and hope to lose them in the crowd, assuming he was faster than them.

The figure chuckled as they stepped out of the shade. "I didn't mean to frighten you." The deep rasp of his voice startled Joseph. The cloak concealed the man's body, his face perfectly hidden by deep shadows, but Joseph could tell his shoulders were somewhat broad and that he was taller than his ma.

"I won't be stealing your things, either."

Joseph took another step backwards. "Then," he said, trying to keep his voice steady, "what are your intentions?" He eyed the mysterious man.

"To warn you."

"Of?"

"The man you got the necklace from."

Joseph's eyebrows twitched. "What of him?"

The man raised his hand and beckoned him closer, his long black nails wagging to and from. Joseph refused to move, just narrowed his eyes. The man shrugged and spoke, anyway. "His name is Charles Bilgen, a wanted criminal in almost every region."

"Criminal?" Joseph spat and frowned. "What could an old man with a foot in the grave do?"

"I was getting to that," the man said dryly. "He has kidnapped, beaten, and raped children under the age of twelve for decades. His bouncing between regions has kept his head on his shoulders."

At his side, quiet clinks started coming from the sack. He glanced down, realizing his hands were shaking. Joseph was overly aware of how hard his heart was pounding, but played along. Obviously, whoever this was, was insane. "I'm much too old to be his target." Maryjane popped into his brain, and his veins crystallized with ice.

The man tilted his head. "Yes, but you know someone young enough, don't you?"

There was a long uncomfortable silence filling the air between them before Joseph spoke sharply. "What is your point in telling me this? Why go through the trouble when it has nothing to do with you?" Bringing the sack closer to his person, Joseph held it tight.

"I have a feeling this will be his final stop, so why make you or your sister his last victims?" The man gestured loosely to Joseph.

Joseph reeled, disgust like a roach scurrying under his skin, making him shudder. "What is that supposed to mean? You just said he targets children. I'm too—"

"You *are* too old for his sexual desires, but he hunts siblings for a reason."

"What are you—" A new wave of disgust washed over Joseph. The bread he had eaten earlier raced to the back of his throat, then plummeted into his stomach. He couldn't imagine what someone could do to another person, nor did he want to know.

"Let's hope you don't have to find out," the man said. "As for what I would suggest you do next, toss the necklace and keep a close eye on your sister for the next few days." The man's tone was serious, not harsh, just level and absolute.

"Why should I believe you?"

"You don't have to believe me. Nevertheless, I think it will be in your benefit to heed my warning." The man took a step forward and Joseph flinched, his heart jumping into his brain, giving him an instant headache.

"My name is Joseph Knightridge," he blurted, and for a moment, he didn't know where he was going with that and neither did the man in front of him as his head tilted up. "You've watched me ever since I left the old man's—Charles' stand, right?" That was the only way he'd know about Maryjane.

The man nodded.

"Show me a reason to keep your words in mind. All you've convinced me is that you're a loon looking for a good laugh!" The instant the last word left his mouth, Joseph regretted asking for more.

The man stood quietly, his gaze sending pricks of ice down Joseph's spine, before laughing. He bent over slightly, holding his gut, and straightened himself, bringing the hood of his cloak down as he did. "My name is Malice Reap."

Joseph startled. The man's voice didn't match his face… at all. His features were striking and regal, soft yet masculine. The man had snow-white hair and plump pink lips. Joseph suddenly felt heat flush his cheeks, yet he couldn't look anywhere else.

His intense green eyes locked onto Joseph's. "That necklace is how he marks his victims." Malice's face was calm and cold, matching his tone. "He gives them something of his creation, then finds them later."

Joseph glanced at the pocket he had put the sunflower necklace in.

"You may do what you wish, Joseph Knightridge. I can't and won't force you to do anything." With that, Malice pulled the hood back over his head. As he walked past, Joseph noticed his boots left no imprint and made no sound.

He waited until he could take a deep breath and look behind him. Malice was gone. Feeling his shoulders drop and his knees buckle a bit, Joseph rushed home.

There was no sign of Maryjane or Elena when he opened the door and peeked inside. Joseph darted upstairs and stuffed the sack of oil and pigment under his bed after setting the painting against the wall. He flopped onto his creaky bed, the necklace shifting in his pocket. He took it out and held it above him.

Perhaps that feeling of unease Joseph got wasn't unfounded. He stared at the necklace, slowly rotating, catching the sunlight from the window. He scowled at it. Charles was simply being kind and understanding. What reason did he have to doubt Charles and believe Malice? Tossing to his side, letting the necklace fall to the bed alongside his arm, Joseph wondered how seriously he should take this. Maryjane's life could be in danger, but… how true was that?

On his back again, the subtle headache grew to throb against Joseph's skull. He rubbed his forehead, sat up, and tucked the necklace inside the cubby of his nightstand, feeling the key he found the other day brush against his fingertips. *I'll have to give that to Ma when she gets home.*

Elena was a frequent victim of headaches, so there was always chamomile in the cupboard. Padding into the kitchen, Joseph grabbed out the teapot from a lower cabinet and placed it on the counter before grabbing the tea down from the shelf. Behind the chamomile was a bunch of black tea, green tea, jasmine tea, and others in labeled jars.

The dried blossoms trickled into the teapot, then he filled it with water and set it on top of the oven. He grabbed the fire starter from the closest drawer and sparked the wood. Hand cupped over his mouth, Joseph blew until an ember grabbed a hold of the wood. If Lucas or his pa were here, they could have started the fire with a flick of their finger.

Cesar used to put on shows on clear nights. In front of everyone, as if he were on a stage, he would make animals and people out of his flames. Joseph always laughed because they never resembled the animal he was envisioning, and the people didn't look like people. Not to mention the voices he'd use were too silly not to laugh at.

As the kindle sputtered, Joseph spun and grabbed a red clay cup from the open cabinets next to the window. The outside was smooth and on the bottom of every cup, bowl, and plate in the house were the initials *E.K.* Elena made all the dishware. She would even sell a lot of her creations. The most popular were the vases and pots. More often than not, dried clay cracked her hands and soiled her clothes. But that was years ago when Cesar could walk into the house and put the brightest smile on Ma's face.

Maryjane burst through the front door, startling Joseph as the teapot whistled. He quickly took it from the heat. She stomped to the kitchen, dragged out a stool, and climbed into it with a huff and a puff. Elena was soon to follow, closing the door behind her, sighing heavily.

After turning to the counter, Joseph poured the yellow liquid, his hands trembling a bit as steam hit his face until the cup was full. He gingerly blew over the surface, making it ripple, while his ma took her shoes off and walked to the cupboards on the opposite side of the kitchen.

Maryjane groaned, put her chin into her hands, and folded her fingers into her inflated cheeks.

He took a small sip, the tea burning his tongue, and asked, "Did they hound you or something?"

Maryjane's expression worsened.

As Malice's words flooded his ears, he averted his eyes.

"Ugh! Of course, Grandmother did!" She pushed herself off the counter and, with another huff, crossed her arms. "I hate seeing grandfather and grandmother!"

Joseph wasn't surprised. Every time they visited, Pa's parents always found something to chastise. There were a handful of times they had lectured Joseph about his lack of magical energy, as if he had any control over that. He hadn't seen them in a few years because of it, although he knew he would have to, eventually.

Grabbing a few spices from the cabinet and taking a pan from a hook on the wall, Elena said nothing for a time. Joseph didn't think she was too fond of Cesar's kin either.

"Enough of this complaining, you hear?" She turned to look at Maryjane, her brow slightly creased. "They both love you in their own way, and it's not like you have to see them very often."

Maryjane peered at the stairs, tears swelling in her eyes as her bottom lip quivered. She always got emotional whenever Elena's tone became short. Especially if that shortness was directed at her.

Joseph stood against the counter and took another sip of tea. He couldn't talk much since he wasn't a fan of his grandparents. He understood where Maryjane was coming from, but Ma had a point, too. Sometimes, Joseph wondered how Cesar came from such stuck-up people.

Pain struck his head. Joseph winced and set his cup on the counter. The necklace painted the back of his eyelids, Malice's voice an obnoxious hum in his ears. He peeked at Maryjane, who was still upset but refused to leave the kitchen. Then glanced at Elena, who had gotten a cutting board, a knife, and a few thick cuts of steak from the ice box underneath the floorboards next to the sink. She slid her foot over and pushed the handle into the groove, so no one tripped on it.

"I'm going to rest for a bit," he finally said as his head throbbed again. "I think I got too much sun today." Maybe that was true, but Charles and Malice were proving to be quite a headache.

"All right. I'll call you down when it's time for dinner," Elena called after him.

Maryjane took the opportunity to leave as well and jumped down from the stool. She stomped her way up the stairs and yawned.

He crawled into bed, yanking the covers over his body. Maryjane threw herself onto her bed, which creaked as she bounced. The squeaks of their old frames annoyed him, like mosquitoes pestering him in summer, until he finally drifted off to sleep.

Elena called Joseph and Maryjane down for dinner far too soon. He woke, grumbling, and shuffled downstairs to find dinner spread out on the dining table and plates were already full. He managed to eat half of his meal before his appetite disappeared. He didn't have much of one to begin with.

When his ma asked how his day went, his heart skipped a beat. He told her everything, save for Malice, in as joyful a tone as he could muster. After he was done, she stared for a few seconds, nodded, and said, *'Good, I'm glad.'* Plate, cup, and silverware in hand, Elena went to the sink, Maryjane following with her own dishes, handing them over.

"How about you go on up to bed," Elena said and pet Maryjane's head.

"But—"

"No buts." Ma bent down and kissed her forehead. Maryjane pouted but listened and hurried upstairs. Each step made her golden locks spring. He always thought it was a bit funny.

Joseph sat for a moment longer, staring at his food, his hands becoming clammy. Eventually, he scraped his plate off into the compost bin and handed his dishes to Elena. She placed them in the sink as water filled it. Joseph tried to make his escape.

"You stay," she demanded, "and tell me what the problem is."

He sighed. *Should have known I wouldn't be able to get away so easily.* He scratched the back of his head. "I promise nothing is—"

"Don't lie to your mother, Joseph," she snipped and shot him a glare. Mothers have a way of seeing through their child; Elena would use that phrase to get information out of Joseph or Maryjane. Grams would too.

He didn't know what to say. How could he say anything with no evidence? He didn't want to cause his ma to worry if it was nothing. Malice continued gnawing at the rearmost of his mind, though. His headache returning with vengeance, Joseph squeezed his eyes shut.

"Someone at the festival… insulted Pa and I… wasn't able to do or say anything against them… is all." That wasn't entirely a lie.

A year ago, as Joseph came around a corner, he heard two men talking about Cesar. Nothing good, of course. Too scared to do anything else, he listened and clenched his fists. They were twice his size and double—maybe triple—his age. They weren't close, Joseph and Cesar, but he was still Joseph's pa, his family. He felt responsible for keeping his name unsullied the best he could in Redcol, yet he couldn't do anything. Or maybe that was just what he was telling himself to make up for his lack of action.

Elena sighed and turned around, wiping the suds off her hands from the soapy dishwater. "You don't need to defend your pa's name or reputation. Those without honor are the people who ramble on about a dead man because they have nothing better to do."

He smirked.

"Besides, you chose to stay silent for a good reason, I assume."

Not wanting to get beat sounded like a good excuse at the time, but it didn't feel like one.

"And there is nothing wrong with that. Not everything has to become a battle with words, fists, or otherwise. You understand?" She grabbed and tilted Joseph's chin up, bringing his eyes up to meet hers. Her eyebrow jumped.

"Yes." He couldn't hold her steady gaze.

"Good. Now you go to bed too, you seem exhausted." Elena kissed his forehead before returning to the dishes. Sluggishly, Joseph got up and went off to bed.

Maryjane was fast asleep, her mouth gaping open, drool pouring out and everything. She hadn't even changed out of her day clothes yet. Joseph didn't want to wake her though and fell onto his bed. The smell of his blankets and sheets filled his nose as he took a deep breath and crawled up to his pillows.

The day went from good to bad in a matter of a heartbeat, but he was used to that with Kai at the academy. Swinging his head away from his pillow, he stared at the nightstand his pa had built. The nightstand had been there longer than Joseph had been alive, so the exterior had plenty of scratches now.

From what he knew, Cesar had made most of the furniture in the house. The dressers and counters, the tables, chairs, even the couch in the living room, and the bed frames they continued to use. Constantly having the things Pa had made all around him didn't make him feel any closer to him. To Joseph, they were just pieces of furniture. Lucas would probably get upset if he heard Joseph say that out loud.

If Maryjane doesn't get the necklace till after The Trading Festival, wouldn't that solve the problem?

His eyes opened wide. If he could keep the necklace from Maryjane for a few more days, then he could kill two birds with one stone. Keep her out of harm's way and still give her a present she would love. There was no way he could keep that necklace from her forever. He didn't have the heart to toss it or keep it to himself. That shouldn't be too hard considering Maryjane would be gone most of the morrow and he was sure he could keep her busy the day after, too. *I'll move the necklace before Maryjane wakes up.*

Corruption
"Nightmare"

Morning crept up on Joseph like a spider moving toward a fly caught in its web. He felt heavy and exhausted from a restless night. The same nightmare haunted the little sleep he got.

In the meadow closest to his home, wildflowers burst with color and their fragrance filled the air. The breeze was gentle and warm, causing the long grass to sway against his legs and the trees to rustle in the distance. Maryjane was ahead of him, plucking a bloom every now and again, sniffing it and either putting it in the bouquet she started or tossing it aside. She was as happy as could be, giggling, hopping from spot to spot, admiring everything around her.

Suddenly, the sky became dark and stormy, the wind cold and harsh. Maryjane stopped giggling, her back turned to Joseph. He ran after her. The grass transformed into vines that gripped his ankles like icy, clammy hands. The dirt became mud, sucking him in. He called out to her, but no sound left his mouth, not even a gasp. A sunflower sprouted and bloomed behind Maryjane. As she turned, it wilted and blew away with the wind. Her face was unrecognizable. Her clothes and hair were bloodied and dirt-stained. She mouthed something before the earth swallowed him up.

That was when he would wake, out of breath, sweat dripping down his face into his hair. Joseph glanced from one side of the room to the next, the sun shining through the window. He squinted and yanked the sheets off him, throwing his feet onto the chilly floor. With a stretch and a yawn, he got up and shuffled to the edge of the black divider. Maryjane was nowhere to be seen, but at least her bed was made. *Must be downstairs already. So much for getting up before she did.*

Joseph fumbled to his bedside, grabbed the necklace out of the nightstand's cubby, and moved it to the drawer. After a breath of relief, he made his way to the armoire between his bed and desk. It opened with a high-pitched squeak, revealing his clothes. He chose a white shirt, a brown pair of trousers, and undergarments.

Lazily, he changed. He knelt and slid out the tan sack of pigment and oil. Joseph used the bed to pull himself up, his eyes glimpsing the canvas leaning against the wall on the other side. He'd forgotten about it altogether. There was a suitable space just beyond his desk, perfect for the painting. He decided to hang it up after breakfast.

Elena stood on one side of the counter, a cup of tea still steaming in her hands while Maryjane sat in a dress Joseph had never seen. It was white at the top and faded to light blue, with sunflowers at the bottom of the skirt. Her hair was up in a loose bun, untamed curls bouncing as she moved her head around. That must've been Ma's gift.

Joseph gently placed the sack in front of Maryjane, the glass clinking as he put it down, and joined his ma to watch.

"Is this for me?" Maryjane asked an obvious question, trying to sound polite but couldn't hide the excitement sparkling in her bright blue eyes.

Joseph nodded before turning around and grabbing himself a cup. "Is it someone else's birthday?" Elena jabbed her elbow into his arm. "Ow!" He rubbed his now tender arm. "Yes, it's for you. Open it."

She wiggled in her chair and undid the drawstrings, reaching inside. Confusion struck her face as she grabbed a jar of pigment, then another and another until her strained expression melted.

"Are these to make paint?" she asked eagerly, practically beaming.

Joseph poured a cup of black tea, a slight earthy bitterness wafting to his nose. "I met an artist at the festival yesterday and she gave me the recipe for the paint she uses."

A jar of sugar cubes sat in front of his ma. He grabbed one. It plunked into his drink, and he swirled it around, dissolving the sugar cube. Ma always liked a little tea with her sugar.

"Really? Was she good?" Her eyes darted from color to color, taking them all in. The red was as bright as a poppy, and the orange was like a pumpkin. Two bright golden yellows sat alongside two different shades of green. The color of the sky was beside the color of a delphinium. Snow white powder and charcoal filled another set of jars in front of the oil.

"Sure was. She even gave me one of her paintings for free. It's upstairs next to my bed if you want to see it." Blowing over the top, Joseph took a long sip, enjoying the rich, sweetened flavor of the tea.

She got down from the stool and carefully put all the pigments and oil back into the sack. Then she dashed to the stairs, the sack pressed against her person.

"Wait," Joseph called out when she was halfway up the stairs. She turned. "Can you grab the key from my nightstand for me?"

She grunted, nodded, and continued up the stairs, the sound of her heavy footsteps thumping into the attic.

"That was awfully kind of you, Joseph," Elena said in a soft voice. She leaned over and kissed Joseph's bedhead. "So, how much did it cost you?" Her voice was still quiet, so Maryjane wouldn't hear through the floorboards.

Joseph shrugged. "All of it, but it's not like I can't make it again." The older he got, the more people were willing to pay him for his services. That didn't change the fact that people were stingy with silver coins, even more so with gold.

"True enough." Elena refilled her cup, but hesitated before it reached her lips. "What key are you talking?" she asked, glancing at Joseph. As if she smelled that her tea wasn't sweet enough, she dropped a few more cubes into her cup.

"Oh, I found a key lying on the floor a few days ago. I put it in my nightstand but forgot about it till just now. I meant to give it to you."

"Hmm… I don't recall losing a key…" she said into her cup and took a sip. She flinched backwards, the tip of her tongue sticking out. The steaming tea wasn't as cold as she thought it was, apparently.

Maryjane's feet pounded against the wood as she rushed down the stairs and stopped at the bottom with a grin she was so desperately trying to hide.

She held something up for them to see. "Is this for me?" It dangled and twisted, the gold chain and sunflower pendant catching the light, the necklace sparkling.

Joseph gulped hard against the nerves bound to come up once he spoke. *She looked in the drawer.* He swayed a bit and firmly gripped the edges of the counter to steady himself.

No! Tell her no! Even if it makes her upset, be the bad guy. It doesn't matter if what Malice said was a lie. Tell her no!

Nodding, he propped his elbows on the counter, his spine slightly hunched, hands gripping each other. "It is," his voice cracked. "I forgot about it. Out of sight, out of mind." He hoped his tone sounded calmer than what his ears told him. Shame gripped his chest, his eyes now on the floor. He may not have any other choice but to tell Elena.

Maryjane lit up, bouncing all over the floor, giggling, running over to Joseph, and squeezing him with all her might. "Thank you!" she squealed and peeked up at him, a grin on her face that spread from ear to ear, a black hole where her front tooth used to be.

He tried to give a smile that didn't seem forced, but Maryjane didn't notice as she swayed and spun around him.

"Here! Put it on!" she demanded while shoving the necklace in Ma's face.

"Why not do that later? After you come home from Grams and Grandmas?" He had pushed himself off the counter and started spewing words before he could gather his thoughts. The protest sounded silly. The necklace matched her dress perfectly, and she loved dressing up for Grams.

His ma gave him a questioning look, her eyebrow raised, when she took the necklace from Maryjane. "Why? It'll take not even five seconds." She was right. In a breath, the necklace was unclipped then re-clipped around Maryjane's neck. Giggling, Maryjane danced around the kitchen and ran about the living room.

"Is something wrong? You're pale." Elena pulled a face.

He nodded. "Yes, no, I'm fine. It's just—" he hesitated, trying to produce a good reason.

"Just?"

"It's just… I don't know. I guess I'm out of it. I didn't get a good night's rest." The nightmare was as clear as day in his head. He observed Maryjane's happy-go-lucky expression, and his chest ached, his gaze forced elsewhere.

Elena's shoulders loosened. "Then how about you go back to bed?"

He plastered on a smile and shook his head. "I'm good. I'll see the two of you off first." *What am I so worried about? It's just a necklace.*

Her face relaxed. To catch Maryjane's attention, Elena gestured to the door and shortly after, gave Joseph a bear hug.

Joseph picked at his cuticles while Maryjane anxiously tapped her feet and Elena slid into her shoes. Unable to wait any longer, Maryjane bolted out of the front door, letting it slam shut behind her.

"Are you sure nothing is wrong?" Elena stood, her hand resting on the doorknob, her sky-blue eyes trained on Joseph.

"I'm just worried," he said in an attempt to sound reassuring. He still contemplated whether or not he should tell Ma about yesterday. Time was running out and he couldn't catch his breath. *It's just a necklace.* "Since the festival is so hectic, I don't want anything to happen."

"Honey," she sighed with a comforting smile that wasn't so comforting to him. "We do this every year. You worry too much."

She was probably right.

"I know, but I have a bad feeling so just," he kept his eyes glued to the floor, "hold each other's hands. Stick close to one another." Jerking his hand, a small, thin strip of skin ripped from his nail. He looked down to see an instant dot of red appear and he quickly tucked his hands behind his back.

"If it will ease your worries, I'll stick to Maryjane like sap on bark." She waved her hand and closed the door.

Although muffled, he heard Elena call out to Maryjane. They left. They would walk to the paddock where Elena would chat with the stable master. Maryjane would give Elena's horse some loving pets, but she would quickly grow impatient. Saying their goodbyes, Elena and Maryjane would head off to Gram's and Grandmother's cottage near Anddulia. Everything would be fine. *It's just a necklace. Everything will be fine.*

Unease grew in Joseph's stomach, clawed at the lining, and tried to climb up his throat, only to slip and fall into the pit. Questioning if the tea would come up, he needed to keep his mind off Maryjane and cleaned. He needed to dust and wipe the counters and shelves off before sweeping and mopping the floors. As he lifted the corners of the rug in the living room, there was a dent from the first time Maryjane used her magic.

Almost four years ago, on a bright summer day, Joseph woke up late. Maryjane woke up too early. She was playing outside when he came down from the attic. Not long after he did, she stomped into the house with a big rock floating in front of her. She was as proud as could be as she showed it off despite the struggle painting her face bright red. Her strength left in an instant and the rock slammed into the floor. Elena had rushed out of the bathroom, hair dripping from her bath, and checked Maryjane over. She was gloomy for a while after that, especially since Ma had scolded her for bringing a rock of that size into the house.

Then he ran across the scorch marks Lucas had left the first time he used his magic. Joseph hadn't been born yet, but Cesar told him the story plenty of times. Lucas and Elena had gotten into an argument over him being too fussy about his vegetables. Out of anger, Lucas bunched his hands and flung them toward the floor. Fire shot out of his fists, burned the floor, and surprised all three of them.

Joseph stared at the marks. Magic came so easily to Lucas and Maryjane that sometimes he wished it would come easy to him, too.

After the floors were cleaned, he made his bed and tidied his and Maryjane's desk. Yard work was minimal—weeding the gardens, sweeping the porch off, and collecting firewood. With hours of spare time until sunset, Joseph headed for the paddock to take care of Finbar. Keeping his body busy kept his mind busy. Although he found himself repeating those words in his head, *it's just a necklace,* as if it actually calmed the growing chill of dread that settled in his bones.

Joseph had called Finbar *boy* or *buddy* when Elena gifted the colt to him for his fourteenth birthday. Then he walked around Redcol and heard someone say the name *Finbar*. Initially, it sounded like any other name, but he used it on his colt, anyway. Finbar, for the first time, had listened just a little. The horse decided on his name before Joseph could produce anything different, and he was all right with that.

As a newborn, Finbar neighed and scoffed at practically everything. If that didn't work, he tried to kick anything that was near. Joseph thought it was for attention, but it was because Finbar was a prick. He didn't like much like an old, cranky man. Joseph learned patience through Finbar and for that, he was grateful. However, every now and again, Finbar liked to test the waters, seeing just how feisty he could get.

After grooming Finbar and taking a stroll to the lake of Ishier in the west, Joseph returned his colt to the paddock and went home.

The sun was setting as he trekked up the hill, and clouds were moving in from the northeast off the coast. The chilly breeze made Joseph shiver. *Wish I had brought my cloak.* It had been a while since he had the house to himself, yet he spent most of the day away from it.

Despite his brain being preoccupied with Finbar, his thoughts drifted to Charles and the ever-fleeting sense of comfort whenever they locked eyes. Then Malice and his deep voice echoed in his ears alongside the beauty he had never seen a man have. Remembering it still caught Joseph off guard. It was like observing a wolf from a distance. Its beauty was bewitching, but he knew not to get any closer.

On the porch, Joseph plopped into his ma's rocking chair and reclined, tilting his head to rest on the wood. He closed his eyes briefly, not realizing how much the day had drained him. His eyelids became lead as he tried to peel them open. They fluttered closed. It wouldn't be long before Elena and Maryjane came home, so what harm would it do to close his eyes for a moment? Just for a short while.

The rumble and growl of his stomach woke Joseph from a dreamless slumber. When his eyes adjusted, he looked around. He wasn't outside anymore. Joseph threw the blankets off, his eyes raking his body. *Same clothes as yesterday.* He flopped back, assuming his ma carried him up after she got home, then glanced out of the window. The sky was dark and gloomy. He rolled out of bed, stumbled to his armoire, sniffed his shirt, and crinkled his nose. A change of clothes was in order, as was a shower, but he was too tired to shower. He could do that after he saw Maryjane was fine.

The smell of toast and freshly ground coffee beans floated through the floorboards. He walked to the door, stole a look at

Maryjane's bed, and left. The biggest of the blankets covered two fluffy pillows on the bottom, while the edges of the second peeked out underneath the top blanket. He felt relieved, like a boulder had been lifted off his shoulders, knowing he had just been overthinking things. Even if what Malice said was true, it was silly to believe Charles could pinpoint Maryjane all because of a necklace.

Still groggy, Joseph came up to the counter. There was an open teapot with cheesecloth tied around the rim and a heaping amount of coffee grounds. The house was tranquil. The doors to the bathroom and Ma's bedroom were closed, and the couch seemed like it hadn't been sat on since yesterday. However, the front door was open, letting in the sound of songbirds and the smell of rain.

His eyebrows twitched. "Where's Maryjane, Ma?" A bit of worry clawed at his stomach, taking the edge off his hunger.

Elena turned, a kettle of steaming water in her hand. "Not even a good morning?" she asked and raised an eyebrow as water poured from the thin long spout onto the grounds. Water instantly soaked into the grounds, but the more she swirled the kettle around, making sure to get every bit of dry coffee, the more the water rose.

"Good morning," Joseph corrected himself, taking in the smell of brewed coffee. The aroma, compared to the dark brown, bitter drink, was scrumptious, especially in the morning.

She nodded. "That's better." The kettle emptied and the cheesecloth could handle no more as the teapot filled one drop at a time. "But what a silly question. She's upstairs in bed, isn't she?"

He slowly shook his head. "Could she be in the bathroom or outside?"

"No, she would have come out if she were in the bathroom and I would have called her in already if she was outside." She gestured to the two pieces of toast slathered in strawberry jam on a plate next to the empty wooden bowl.

Joseph looked at them with disgust, his stomach churning. The strawberry jam turned bright red and oozed off the sides onto the plate. He slid his foot backward, frazzled, and glanced up at his mother. She was unbothered, rubbing the sleep from her eyes. When he checked the toast, the jam was jam again. *It's just from the lack of sleep.*

"We came home last night and found you asleep on the porch. As I was picking you up, she realized she'd dropped the new earrings Grams gave her and hurried to retrace her steps." She sighed as if trying to keep a yawn at bay. "I must've fallen asleep waiting for her to come home after I put you to bed."

"You promised you would stay close to her! You said you would stick together!" He snapped and a sick feeling wrenched and squeezed his chest, which made it hard to focus; hard to breathe. It was a mistake not to go with them yesterday.

Silence filled his ears and the realization of yelling at his mother forced Joseph out of his mind.

"I may not know why you're this upset, but I suggest you keep your temper under control. There will not be a next time. Am I understood?" Her voice sent a shiver down Joseph's spine. Her calm anger was more frightening than when she yelled. She leaned over the counter, both hands on the edge, a deep scowl creasing her brow and nose.

"Yes, ma'am," he said in a lower tone, eyes on the brown clay teapot.

"Tell me why you are so concerned about your sister. Did something happen at the festival? Did someone threaten you or her?" As always, his ma's guess was almost spot on.

Joseph explained everything from the painter to the baker to Charles, and lastly, Malice. Usually, when he unloaded all of his worries like this, his ma listened, read his expression, then offered advice or stayed quiet and it was relieving. Not this time. This time, he could barely hold eye contact. He had stuttered more times than he cared to admit. It felt like his palms were dripping and his stomach had been wrung out.

Once Joseph finished, his throat was dry, and a heavy silence filled the air. It was almost suffocating. He brought his head up. Elena's hand connected with his face, and he stumbled sideways. His cheek instantly stung as tears swelled in his eyes.

Neither said anything for a long while. The pain blooming in his cheek reminded Joseph of all the time he had spent worrying over Charles, being torn up by the decision. He should have thrown it out after hearing what Malice told him. A necklace could easily be replaced.

"Put your shoes on," Elena finally said after what felt like an eternity. Her voice was shaky; Joseph could tell she was struggling to suppress tears of anger and fear. "We are going to search for Maryjane, and you are not leaving my side." She glared over her shoulder at Joseph, tears turning her eyes red.

He had already put his shoes on when his ma walked out of the kitchen and headed toward the front door.

"If what this Malice person says is true, Charles will be after you next." She spoke as if she already knew Maryjane was lying dead in the dirt somewhere and it hurt more than the slap.

Joseph rose and moved to the side, so Elena could get to her shoes. A gentle knock came to the door before she could slide her foot in.

With a curse under her breath, she opened it. "Who—" She froze.

At the door, pale golden locks similar to his own glowed in the light, and sky-blue eyes regarded them. Lucas. He was much taller than the last time Joseph saw his brother, more muscular, too. He wore a white blouse with ruffles tucked into a pair of black trousers and a winged sun and eye brooch pinned to his left breast. Three brown belts on his waist holstered a long sword in a leather sheath.

Lucas' solemn expression moved from Elena to Joseph. "I need you both to come with me," he said in a gentle tone.

"Where?" Elena scanned him up and down, her eyes wide. She frowned. "We need to find Maryjane. She's missing, so if you'll excuse us." She bent down and grabbed her shoes.

"That's why I need you to come with me." Lucas paused, glancing away as if hesitant to say anything more. "It's been too long since I've seen Maryjane." He'd left soon after Maryjane turned four.

"So?" Elena seemed repulsed, like she was looking at a criminal instead of her son.

"So, I can't confidently identify her." There was remorse in his voice, but he felt detached. Lucas wasn't family anymore; he was a stranger.

"He's right," Joseph said as he peeked at his ma, his eyes probably as red as hers from holding back tears. "We should hurry. If it's not Maryjane, then it would be best to look for her in daylight. If it is..." he didn't finish his sentence, the words like poison on the tip of his tongue, slipping down his throat, sinking further.

Elena rose as Lucas stepped from the door's entry, allowing Elena and Joseph to walk out before he closed the door behind them.

He guided them to the southwestern edge of Redcol, where the entire village gathered around a wall of earth between two buildings. Upon seeing the mass, Lucas turned and went around the rear side of a house and store. A royal guarded the alley but quickly let them through at the sight of Lucas. There weren't many. Ten, maybe fifteen royals stood next to one another, whispering as they waited for Lucas's return.

Joseph followed quietly, or at least he thought he did. He couldn't hear anything over the sound of his blood rushing to his ears and his heart pounding against his ribcage. The dampness of his palms dissipated. Now they were dry and cold. His nausea grew as he got closer, like his stomach was doing somersaults down a rocky, uneven hill.

Lucas quickened his pace, then stopped in front of a tall dark elf in clothes the color of night. They exchanged a few words. The dark elf nodded, shifted toward the royals, said something, and stepped aside. The other royals did too, leaving what they were surrounding open for Joseph and Elena. Gloom, disgust, and anguish were all Joseph could see. Perhaps it was the dark, looming clouds that made everything dim and lifeless, forcing time to a halt.

Stopping in her tracks, Elena crashed to her knees. Her trembling hands went to cover her mouth as tears ran down her pale cheeks.

A vile smell filled the air—blood, urine, rot—it was enough to make him gag. Glad he didn't eat anything, Joseph moved toward the small body lying in the street. Each step was like walking into the ocean from the shore. Freezing water surged and crashed against his legs, then his chest until his head was underwater. The world vanished around him when he stopped.

White and light blue shreds of cloth barely covered the body while the rest of the dress lay scattered on the ground beside it. Dark red streaks and splatters masked freckled skin. There were two other fluids. One glistened, and the other was milky white. Underneath the bodily fluids and dirt, her skin was black and blue. Dirt and blood matted long, golden curls. Her face was so beaten it was unidentifiable until Joseph noticed a pendant resting on her exposed chest. A thin gold chain went around her neck, a flower of bright yellow petals with coarse brown seeds at the center.

He knew that little girl. He had watched her grow, after all. He had helped do her hair more times than he could count. He drew alongside her and admired her paintings.

Something grabbed and squeezed Joseph's heart, making his mind fuzzy and his ears ring. One of the royals to his left moved to put a hand on his shoulder. Were they saying something too? He evaded their touch as Charles, his smile, his shy behavior, his false kindness flickered in his head. He was right to feel uneasy around the old man. Malice was right to warn him.

Cesar had offered Joseph advice one time. He was young, though, too young to grasp what he meant. *Never betray your gut,* he told Joseph. Joseph didn't understand because he always listened when his gut told him how hungry he was. Cesar laughed and ruffled his hair, telling him he would eventually understand. He did now, but it was too late. He should have listened to his instincts, to Malice. Maryjane was dead because Joseph couldn't get over himself.

Run. A voice—Maryjane's high-pitched voice—said to him. *Run away. You don't deserve to stay here after what you've done.*

Looking up from his sister's body, he turned and marched past Elena, who tried to reach for him, but his strides were too fast. Joseph stalked past Lucas, who averted his eyes, agony painting his face. No one called after him, not that he could hear.

Joseph clenched his fists and started running, the frigid wind like ice picks hitting his face and stinging his lungs.

Guilt

III

When Joseph came to his senses, he stood in front of Everest Academy's gate. The courtyard was empty as the trees rustled in the wind. Three red-brick buildings stared back at him, the belfry in the middle ringing, the stained glass arched windows vibrant from the evening sun. Without moving their head, the guard in front of the gate eyed Joseph but remained silent. Of all places, why did he bring himself here? There was nothing for him at the academy besides a headache.

He walked down the stone path, disappointed the guard didn't stop him, and suddenly remembered his brother. Lucas and Cesar were ecstatic the day they toured the academy. Both had the opportunity to meet the headmaster, a madwoman from what they described, and Lucas's professor, Cadmus Locke. The first thing Pa noticed was the professor's cauliflower ears. He said it meant that he used to fight a lot, or that he still did.

Joseph hesitated at the big oak doors, then pushed them open. A few torches on the walls illuminated the empty corridor. He walked through the smell of paper and chalk, his shoes echoing on the marble floors.

Joseph had only caught glimpses of the other professors but never got the chance to meet them; he didn't even know their names.

In front of his classroom door, he reached to turn the knob and open it when the door swung out. He reeled, and the professor gasped, quickly grabbing Joseph's arms to help steady him.

"Oh!" All six ghostly eyes widened. "You startled me, Joseph."

Shrugging his hands off, Joseph stepped away. Cadmus's eyebrows jumped. "What brings you here so late?" he asked, closing the door behind him.

Now that he was here, Joseph didn't know what to say. He looked down at the floor, the professor's pointed shoes creased from years of use. "Help me," he said in a low tone, almost a whisper, his gaze moving up to the angels.

"Are you all right?" Professor Cadmus's voice was unusually frantic. "Did something happen? Are you hurt? What is wrong?"

Pain stabbed Joseph, radiating from his chest, the world swaying like long grass in the breeze. "Please," he grimaced. "Just help me." Tears stung his eyes, threatening to escape, but he forced them to stay. *Don't cry.*

The professor nodded before he rushed toward the other end of the hall and placed the metal cup hanging from the holsters on top of the torches. The hallway darkened one torch at a time.

Cadmus was the only person he knew that wouldn't force him to return home, return to Elena. Or somehow alert her to Joseph's whereabouts without his knowledge. His grandparents would have done that out of concern and love, but Joseph didn't give a damn about love right now.

Why are you helping me? Is it because of Lucas? He'd heard whispers from Kai that Lucas was close to Cadmus during his time at the academy. Perhaps Cadmus felt obligated because of it. Joseph was curious, yes, but not curious enough to ask.

"Follow me, Joseph," he said.

Joseph trailed a few paces behind. His feet ached. Each step was like walking across a bed of jagged rocks. So long as Cadmus was in sight, though, it didn't matter.

The streets of Ivory's Kingdom were unfamiliar, at least in the north. Not much was different; metal lamp posts lined the brick roads, houses were almost stuck together, and shops were at least two stories tall. They passed a lively tavern, and an inn overgrown with creeping vines. Every now and again, the professor glanced over his shoulder as if he had something to say, but, just as quickly, turned his attention forward. Having a clear view of his back, Joseph wondered if the professor had flown to the academy or walked. He assumed Cadmus walked based on how small his wings were compared to his body.

It was completely dark when Cadmus and Joseph reached the edge of an oak and maple forest.

The professor waited, allowed him to rest a moment, then said, "Take hold of my wing." The bottom of two wings stretched out beside Joseph. "It is too dark, and I do not want you getting lost." Cadmus's tone was gentle, sympathetic.

It made Joseph's stomach turn.

Taking hold of the tip of his smooth wing, they started into the forest. Moss dampened their footsteps as their feet sank into patches of it. Dead leaves and twigs crunched and snapped beneath them otherwise. The path was small and narrow, but straight for the most part. An owl hooted high above, thunder a low grumble in the distance. Joseph kept his eyes moving from his feet to watch his step and Cadmus. Soon the dark mass ahead of them lightened and the professor's strides sped up. Joseph nearly lost grip on his wing from the sudden advance.

Once they reached the clearing, however, Joseph let go of the professor. He tried to keep the same pace as well, despite wincing when he put too much weight into his step. Something was beside the cottage, rectangular and slightly raised, perhaps a garden of some sort. Opposite the garden, a small silhouette of a shed or an outhouse barely stood out against the blackness of the trees. Crickets chirping in rhythm sounded all around the glade. Joseph breathed in the smell of wet, cold moss and soil.

The professor opened the door and hurried inside while Joseph stayed at the doorframe. With a few clicks, a tiny flame burst, and Cadmus lit a candle, going around to light the rest of the long white candles and lamps. The house wasn't too big, so the professor finished in no time and placed the first wax stick back in its hold. Joseph, watching Professor Cadmus, shivered at the gust of wind that hit his back.

The professor nodded inside, his six eyes closing slowly, a gentle smile on his lips. Joseph stepped in and closed the door. Wiggling and rubbing his fingers together helped bring some warmth to them.

"Come. Sit down while I prepare dinner." The professor pointed at one of two chairs at the round table as he walked to the kitchen.

Joseph took his shoes off, shoving them to the side with his foot. A thick layer of dust blanketed the chair closest to him; he brushed it off. Across the table, the other chair's seat was faded, deep scratches disrupting the grain of the wood.

As the professor clinked and clunked in the kitchen, Joseph took in the cottage. The living room was right off a stairwell, plants all over the place. On one windowsill, a heartleaf philodendron wrapped around the edges. He recognized it from a botany book he read in the library a while ago. Two pots hanging from the ceiling had pothos spilling over the sides and creeping onto the window, intertwining with the heartleaf while the other rested on a bookshelf against the wall. The shelves bowed as they were, it was a wonder they hadn't snapped in half yet.

Many pots had big, leafy green plants on either side of the couch, near the bookshelf, and around the entrance. In the dining room, close to the table, a curio cabinet had three shelves—wine filled one, chalices the other.

At the opposite end of the living room, there was a big pot between two doors. Thick, dark green leaves surrounded a white cup-like bloom with a bright yellow spadix in the center. Joseph had never seen the beautifully simple and elegant flower before.

"It is a calla lily. It was my wife's favorite flower," Professor Cadmus said.

Joseph whipped his head around, but the professor had gone back to what he was doing. *Was?* Sympathy twinged in his chest, a sensation similar to pinching the skin of his hand.

"I apologize it is nothing special, but I hope you enjoy it." Professor Cadmus smiled and placed a plate of food comprising a thick piece of lightly toasted, buttered bread, steamed and seasoned vegetables, and seared meat in front of him.

The smell hit Joseph, and his gut grumbled loudly. He hadn't eaten since yesterday's festival. His stomach told him to, but his brain reminded him of the odor of rotting flesh, and he lost his appetite. Still, he forced himself to eat everything on his plate, gobbling it up much faster than he thought he would.

When he looked up from his empty dish, Cadmus had barely finished half his meal. Joseph sat quietly and slouched in his chair, keeping his head down.

Professor Cadmus chuckled softly. "If you are hungry yet, there is plenty on the counter. Feel free to eat your fill." He gestured toward the counter, taking another bite.

Joseph shook his head, but his stomach had other ideas. It grumbled and gurgled, making his face turn bright red.

"Thank you," Joseph said quietly before he stood, chair skidding, then walked into the kitchen, and served himself a second helping. He left more than enough for Professor Cadmus in case he wanted more as well.

Joseph ate slower this time, matching the professor's pace. As delicious as the food was, he felt guilty for enjoying it even just a little.

By the time he was done, so was Professor Cadmus. He grabbed the napkin beside his glass and wiped his mouth clean, even though his face appeared spotless beforehand. Shadows danced over Cadmus, pronouncing his angular features as he pushed his chair out and crossed his legs.

"What happened? You have never directly asked me for help like this," he prodded.

Waves of nausea pulsed through Joseph, he continuously swallowed them down. The events of the past two days repeated in his head so many times that if he were to get amnesia, he was sure he wouldn't be able to forget what happened.

"My sister," the words caught in his throat like a hunk of dry bread, "was killed."

"I am… I am so sorry." The professor's voice was brittle, almost weak. His worry felt like a jab for some reason, peaking Joseph's annoyance for a split second.

"What can I do?"

Joseph's jaw twitched, and he mumbled something.

Cadmus asked, "What was that?"

"Revenge," he heard his ma say a few nights after Cesar's death. "The person who killed my husband wanted revenge, I'm sure of it!"

Joseph couldn't sleep that night and tiptoed down the stairs, stopping at the platform. He had never heard such scorn in his ma's voice. Until yesterday, that was.

"Elena," Grams said with disappointment. "He was in the wrong place at the wrong time. You know this."

"No!" Elena shouted as she got up and started pacing. "I don't know that and neither do you! He was a royal knight for decades! It's more understandable that someone sought Cesar out and killed him for throwing them in a cell to rot than it is that his death was a twist of fate!" she huffed.

Joseph had made his way back upstairs after that. He hadn't seen his pa's body. One day, Elena had just come home, her eyes red and swollen, her voice shaky as she explained what had happened. Lucas was already gone; he learned about Cesar's death long before even Ma did.

Something curdled in his gut, something vicious at the thought of hurting Charles. He shuddered when the idea of warm blood pooling outside the old man's body, leaving him cold as ice—just as he had done to Maryjane—entered his mind. Screwing his eyes shut, Joseph considered that coming here was a mistake. On the morrow, he would return to Redcol and to his ma.

You can't, not after what you've done, Maryjane's voice resonated through his skull.

"… Revenge," he muttered.

The air in the room went frigid. Professor Cadmus's expression hardened as he adjusted himself, like his clothes were suddenly uncomfortable. His stare sent prickles down Joseph's spine.

"Revenge?" he repeated. "Revenge is a dangerous path, Joseph. It will swallow you whole and leave an empty husk of who you used to be."

"What do you know?" His bottom lip and chin quivered, his eyebrows furrowed. Fists clenched and trembling, Joseph felt his nails dig into his palm.

"More than you think," Cadmus sighed, rubbed his face down, and looked away. His face soured as if he had recalled a bad memory. "My wife," he said solemnly, "disappeared almost a century ago. I searched for decades to find nothing at all. I knew she was never coming home. She was dead."

"I could not bear her death; I did not want to face it and turned to underground fighting." Joseph glanced at his cauliflower ears peeking beyond his brown hair, then at his troubled expression. "Nothing helped ease the pain, Joseph."

"You don't know a thing about what happened!" He glared at Cadmus. "Charles didn't just kill my sister, he tortured her." Each word shook, a quake of emotions Joseph desperately tried to contain.

The heavy silence rang loud in Joseph's ears. He stood abruptly, causing Cadmus to snap his head toward him in surprise. The nausea he thought he had suppressed came back tenfold. He rushed to the kitchen sink and vomited over the edge. Everything he had just eaten splashed into the metal tub. Tears dripped from his eyes. Bile burned his throat and nose on the way up. He heaved and gagged, then spat. From behind, Cadmus had walked over and rubbed in between Joseph's shoulder blades, his touch tender and soothing. He gripped the edges hard enough to turn his knuckles white.

The wind outside picked up and beat the side of the cottage, whistled through the trees as lightning flashed white, followed by the crack and boom of thunder. Inside was dead calm, the steady candle flames providing ample light for the kitchen.

"If you will put in the effort," Cadmus said after a long while, catching Joseph's attention, "starting tomorrow, I will train you."

Joseph pushed himself off the counter and faced Cadmus, bewildered.

"One month. I am giving you one month to show improvement, or you will return to your mother."

His eyes swept over the professor, trying to read into anything he could, but that was Elena's thing. "You were so opposed to it earlier. Why the change of heart?"

"It is… against my nature to leave a child asking for help alone." He crossed his arms, leaning on the counter. "I do not want to see you go down this path, but I have a feeling that if I do not help, you will do it yourself and die in the process," he admitted.

Joseph wouldn't have. He wasn't like Lucas. He would have crawled home to Elena with his tail tucked between his legs and lived in a tomb of self-pity. But he let Cadmus think what he wanted and nodded.

"You need to realize." Cadmus uncrossed his arms to place his hands on Joseph's shoulders. "Once you have spilled blood, there is no going back. You will never be the same, understand?"

"I understand," he said with simple directness. By now, it didn't feel like they were talking about death or revenge. The edge of disgust and worry had slightly worn off. Instead, there was a numbness coating everything from the top of his head to the tip of his toes.

Cadmus retreated a bit and asked, "Do you at least have a plan?"

Joseph gulped and fiddled with the bottom of his shirt. How ridiculous. Where Charles was hadn't crossed his mind. In his defense, it was too much of a mess to think about much of anything.

"Um..." Malice had said it would be the last time Charles struck. "He was arrested..." He thought. "So, I..." Cadmus raised an eyebrow, watching Joseph fumble over his words. "Can find him in Alucard's... Kingdom?" *How stupid can I be?*

The professor stared, his eyes narrowed, his mouth drawn in a thin line. After a moment, he spoke, "If he was arrested for the crimes he has committed, he will most likely be sentenced to the Games."

"The Games?"

He dipped his head. "Alucard's Kingdom holds the Games of Retribution once a year. It is an execution, and a show of skill wrapped in to one event."

Joseph wiped the sticky sweat off his face from vomiting his guts out. "Will he be tried for all his crimes?" he asked as he cleaned his hand on his pants.

"That depends on where they were committed."

"Everywhere." Joseph shrugged. Charles made his head spin all over again. "Malice said he had been all over the continent killing children and..." He tried to focus on the sink and keep whatever was left in his stomach in there. His legs were gradually losing feeling, and he started swaying on his feet.

"If that is the case," Cadmus took a step closer, his arms tense at his sides, "then I doubt it. Crimes from other regions do not carry over due to the *Crime of Region* law. The rulers can take them into account, but they cannot punish based on crimes committed in other lands."

"That makes little sense," Joseph snapped.

"It is a long-standing law." Professor Cadmus sounded exasperated as he massaged the bridge of his nose. "It has been efficient, thus far. I have yet to hear otherwise."

He took a deep breath before walking to the table and collecting the dishes. "Your best shot at revenge will be at the Games in a little less than three months, during spring." Stacking the plates and cups on top beside the silverware, Cadmus carefully came back to the kitchen, looked inside the sink, then put the dishes on the counter. He ran the tap, using his hand to disperse the water around the metal sink.

Joseph watched, feeling sorry the professor had to clean up his mess when he was standing right there, fully capable of doing it himself. After the sink was cleaned out, Cadmus put the dirty dishes inside and faced Joseph again. There was something about the way his mouth twisted downward that made him seem mortal, showing his age through the lines and creases on his face.

"I have agreed to help you, but I want you to know that I think you are too young to devote yourself to a path that will end in tragedy. I want you to sleep on it tonight."

What else is there to think about? "Okay."

Giving a halfhearted smile, Professor Cadmus gestured to the living room. "I will show you where you will be sleeping."

Past the counter, across the dining room, and into the living room, Cadmus stopped near the stairwell. Joseph followed, and he opened the door to a stagnant room. A bed sat in front of a small round window with a nightstand on either side. The long dresser against the wall had a candle on top. Stale linen flowed into Joseph's nose; not a terrible scent, but not a good one.

"It has not been used for quite some time, but I try to make sure it does not get too dusty."

Joseph entered the room and gazed at the bare walls and plain sheeted bed. It reminded him of the blank canvas leaning against Maryjane's desk. He glanced down at his charcoal-stained fingers and rubbed them together, remembering the feel of smooth charcoal between them. The urge to sit down and draw hit Joseph like a boulder, his fingers twitching.

"There are some spare clothes in the dresser for you to change into," the professor added in an awkward tone. His head swiveled as he tucked strands of hair behind his ear. "If you need anything, I will be upstairs… I will let you get some rest. Good night, Joseph."

"Good night." He turned just when Cadmus closed the door. The room went dark and soon the orange light flooding in from underneath the door died too. Footsteps creaked up the stairs, then silence.

Joseph ran his hand over the dresser's surface, it coming back dusty. He brushed it off on his trousers and opened one of the drawers. It was empty. He tried the top three, which all turned up empty. Two of the bottom drawers had sheets, one had day clothes, and the last had nightwear. He grabbed a pair of thin, loose cloth pants and a white shirt, throwing them on the bed. After digging around some more, he turned to the one beside it in search of underwear. There were none and he cringed, thinking he would either have to go without or wear them for another night.

Joseph stripped his dirty clothes off, tossed them on the floor close to the wall. Something clinked from his pants pocket. He bent down beside his bottoms and shoved his hand into the pocket. He pulled out a sunflower pendant. Joseph jumped back, landed with a thud, and dropped the pendant, the metal clanking on the wood. The cold floor shocked his body.

When did I take this? Was it when the royal put his hand on my shoulder? This morning was a haze, a blur of overwhelming guilt and sadness. So many things blended together that he couldn't pull anything apart. He reached and picked the pendant off the floor. There was blood, dried and brown, staining the flip side. The gold chain must've slipped off before he shoved it into his pocket.

You don't deserve to cry, remember?

Multiple deep breaths later, Joseph finally got to his feet, placed the pendant on the dresser, and moved to the bed.

Stench—his own stench—made Joseph's nose crinkle as he put the pants on and drew the shirt over his head. He flopped onto the mattress, dust rising like fog all around him, and sneezed.

He tossed over to his side as tears swelled and flowed from his eyes, and he sat up, wiping them away. He didn't want to cry. Didn't have the right to cry since everything was his fault. Biting his lip, he hoped to keep from sobbing, so Cadmus wouldn't hear, but they escaped, anyway. He bent forward and wailed into the sheets, balling them up in his fists.

The world was cruel; Joseph knew that, but why to someone so innocent, so young? She had so many years ahead of her and all of it was taken just like that. How could he ever apologize? How could he face his mother now? Nothing made sense. Every inch of his body ached and burned. It was suffocating, the guilt and sorrow adding fuel to the fire, smoking him out.

A Dim Light
IV

The morning sun painted dew drops on the window while roosters squawked to no end. It was strange waking up in an empty house, even stranger knowing that it wasn't his house he was waking up in. Reluctantly, Joseph wriggled out of bed, stiff and exhausted from crying himself to sleep. Outside his room, it was quiet. The professor must have left near dawn to arrive before the students and other teachers.

On the table in the dining room, there was a plate of oat pancakes sprinkled with berries and a drizzle of maple syrup. Beside the plate was a fork and a dull knife. On the other side, an empty cup had a note underneath it. They were probably cold, but he didn't mind. Food was food. He sat in the same chair as yesterday. The food reminded Joseph of his ma and her home-cooked meals… and how he left her behind.

When Joseph finished his plate, he moved the cup, slid the note toward him, and flipped it open.

Joseph,

While I am gone, go to the shed behind the house. Inside there will be a few weapons; acquaint yourself with them, then choose one. Once you have chosen, start swinging to get used to the feel and, if you want, take a few stabs at the training dummy. After we eat, I will start training you properly. This is to get you familiar with the idea of training. I will return in the evening. Do not forget to eat.

C.L.

Joseph crumbled the note and shoved it into his pocket. Although he wished the professor would have mentioned something about where he could take a bath, if he were about to get sweaty and dirty from training, he supposed that taking a bath right now was pointless.

Hurried to his room, he searched for clean clothes. He cringed as he put his dirty shirt and pants back on, but they were better than being constantly distracted by baggy clothes.

Joseph's feet squished in the mud on the way to the rear of the house. Trees surrounded him for quite some distance. It was the perfect place, with no one else around, to… well… commit murder. The quiet was serene, small animals rustling in the foliage and breaking twigs. Rain, wet grass, and soil mixed with the scent of wildflowers all around the glade. He took it in and breathed it out. For a moment, he thought the calm of the woods would help ease the dull ache through his body, make him feel a little less miserable, yet too many memories flourished to let that happen.

The shed he saw the night prior was shabbier than he imagined. Many planks were uneven and old, and he could tell that mold or pests had made themselves a home within the wood. Rusted nails poked out everywhere. Joseph was amazed that the thing was still standing. The door swung open, creaking. There were scuffs and streaks from where it scraped against the floor for the longest time.

On one side, there were gardening tools such as hoes, scythes, and shovels. The other side had six weapons. Three of which were swords, one was thin bladed, a long sword, and the last one was a common sword he had seen too many times to count at the Trading Festival. There was a dagger, a spear, and a bow with an arrow-filled quiver beside it. His gaze lingered on the dagger. Retired royals in Redcol talked about the use of a dagger in combat. Most said it was a dirty way of killing.

The long sword was heavy, the leather handle worn in the shape of a hand, the blade itself scratched and chipped. Attempting to raise the sword over his head ended with him and the sword on the ground. He tried the bow next, facing the dummy as he nocked an arrow to the bowstring. When he pulled the string back, it didn't budge. A few grunts later, arms burning, he released it. The arrow had ricocheted off the wooden dummy and Joseph dove to the ground for cover. In the ground a hand's width away from his head, the arrow embedded itself.

The spear was light but awkward to use. It didn't help that the only thing Joseph knew how to do was jab at the dummy. Feeling as ridiculous as he did, he was glad no one was around to see him fumble with the spear. The thin-bladed sword was light, easy to wield, and the grip felt nice. If he remembered correctly, once he got a closer look, it was a sword from Braxton's Region called a Jingum. Joseph used it, left a few slashes on the dummy too, but something was off. He couldn't think of why. It was like a shirt that fit perfectly, yet the material was prickly against the skin.

Joseph tried the common sword. It wasn't as heavy as the long sword, yet it made his arms burn after a few swings all the same. His hands were sore when he put the sword in its place on the wall in the shed.

Close to high noon, Joseph grabbed the dagger. *If it can kill Charles, it doesn't matter how dirty the weapon is.* It was about the same weight as the Jingum, but its reach was much shorter, more personal. He swung it in his hand, causing the straight edge to kiss his forearm before swinging it forward. His eyes glided down the blade, the weapons displayed on tables popping into his head, Charles grinning behind them.

He jabbed at the air a few times, twisted on his heels, ducked, and swerved. Sprinting at the dummy, he thrust the dagger up into the left side of the chest where the heart would be. The tip was barely embedded in Charles' chest. It certainly wasn't deep enough to kill him.

A smirk teased his lips. The dagger was easy enough to wield. The grip felt right. His left hand was free, which he liked, and he could conceal it easier than a sword. His attention snapped to the dummy.

Are these my thoughts? Joseph's own mind was becoming a foreign thing to him.

The ground slowly dried as the day went by. He had slipped and fallen on the wet grass and mud so many times that he was well acquainted with the ground, perhaps too acquainted. Many places all over his body ached because of it and if his clothes weren't filthy before, they were now. Sweat soaked through Joseph's shirt, staining it further. He panted heavily, unable to remember the last time he did anything so fiercely and for so long. Open blisters stung on his right hand more than his left, and his arms ached. He looked back at the dummy, a dagger sticking out of its chest. It was still early. The professor won't be home for a while yet. Joseph walked to the wooden target and wrenched the dagger out.

Foot slipping behind him, Joseph rocked, then rushed forward, striking the dummy left and right. He noticed the slashes he left were deeper, barely, but it was progress. He moved behind it, shoving the tip of the blade into the target's ribs, jerking it free.

In ways he had seen others attack their opponents, Joseph assaulted the wooden dummy until he was out of breath again. He aimed for the joints, neck, head, kidneys, and chest, thrusting the blade in as deep as it could go.

Applause erupted from the quiet. Joseph jumped and spun around, dagger in hand but at his side. The professor smiled delightfully. He relaxed and fell to the ground as Professor Cadmus walked over.

"I see you fancy the dagger," he said and held his hand out for Joseph to surrender the weapon. "I would not have guessed this to be your style. I thought you would have gone for the bow and arrow or spear. They are not so… intimate."

"So… did… I," Joseph panted, using the back of his hand to wipe beads of sweat off his upper lip.

The professor gave an impressed look while turning the dagger over in his hands. "You do have a talent for fighting. It has nothing to do with magic, is all. Speaking of—" He handed the blade to Joseph and waltzed around him to inspect the dummy. "How is Lucas? He left so suddenly after Cesar's death."

Joseph bent his knee, so it touched his chest, frowning. "He's fine, I suppose. Seems healthy and all." He played with a long blade of grass in front of him, twirled it around his fingers. "He's a royal knight, even part of a Unit."

"Really? That is quite an achievement for someone as young as he."

Joseph grumbled as he rolled his eyes and tore the blade of grass before getting up.

"Why ask about him out of the blue? Looking to use him as a comparison?" His tone came out more bitter than he intended. Joseph averted his sights, confused as to what he was mad about. No one had ever compared him and his brother besides himself.

"… No. That was not my intention. You both have your strengths and weaknesses. It would not be fair to compare the two of you." Cadmus turned to face him. "I was asking out of curiosity. He was my student at one point, just like you."

"I apologize, Professor Cadmus, for snapping at you like that." He peeked up, but couldn't hold his gaze. Somehow, his underwhelming reaction made Joseph feel worse.

"It is all right, but no more 'professor.' I doubt you will return to the academy, so just Cadmus is fine." He smiled dimly.

Unsure whether he should say anything else, Joseph nodded.

"Now, get into the stance you have been using," Cadmus said.

Joseph assumed his position, his legs somewhat spread and sore. His left hand was awkwardly up but ready nevertheless, the dagger in his right hand, and his back slightly hunched. Cadmus walked around him, probably eyeing every inch of his body. He couldn't tell with those stark white eyes.

"Keep your left hand in a loose fist and keep it slightly tucked behind the other." Joseph followed his instructions intently. "Spread your legs out a bit more. Make sure one foot is always in front of the other. Relax your shoulders. Keep your heels hovering above the ground." He stopped. "Go ahead, attack."

Joseph pushed off the ground with a burst of speed. He swung at the neck, leaving a thin line across it. Behind him, Cadmus grunted. Not one of disapproval, it was more like one of contemplation. Joseph returned to the spot he had formerly been in and waited for input.

"You will use the target for basic practice and to get used to holding the dagger but for actual combat…" Cadmus paused, fixing on Joseph inquisitively. Examining the scuffs of dried mud on his clothes, sun-kissed skin, and strands of hair tangled together by wetness. The puffy dark circles under his eyes, and the sweat staining his shirt. Joseph knew he looked horrid.

"We will spar tomorrow. As for today, you will bathe while I fix us some dinner. I assume you have not eaten?"

"No, I haven't. I've been focused out here."

"I know you have." He placed a hand on Joseph's shoulder and spun him around. "While you are scrubbing away your filth, I will put some clean clothes on your bed." Cadmus guided him to the front of the house.

"Where is your bath, anyway?"

"In the room opposite of yours."

As they walked in, Cadmus shooed Joseph into the bathroom. Joseph slid his shoes off and closed the door, then gladly hurried to the door on the other side of the living room.

Inside was a huge wooden tub surrounded by smooth rocks, a faucet beside it, and a window on the outside wall like the one in his room. In the corner to his right was a table, a lamp, and a fire starter on its surface. Then a shelf with three stacks of white towels, two per stack, and another for hand cloths. Pushing the lever to the faucet, water gushed out and filled the tub. The water was icy and crisp. Putting his hand underneath the stream made his entire body shiver. Joseph grabbed the fire starter, clicked the flint and steel into the hole where a rock was missing, and waited until he could feel the heat pouring out.

Joseph scrubbed his body, wincing at the open blisters on his hands from the soap and cloth. The scent of fresh grass and flowers caused his mind to wander. Ma had packed a basket of food and drink one day, closed it up and put a blanket over the lid. While Cesar, Lucas, and Joseph ran around and roughhoused throughout the meadow, Elena stayed with Maryjane, playing, making faces, or wiggling her small limbs around. Most of the memory was fuzzy. Anything that was said was a murmur, and his family's expressions were blurred.

When Joseph snapped into reality again, he stepped out and grabbed a towel. Shuffling around the tub, he opened the window to allow the steam to flow out before drying his hair and body. He wrapped the towel around his waist, wondering how Cadmus emptied such a big tub himself. Maybe he was stronger than he seemed.

Joseph opened the door just enough to peek out of the crack. Cadmus faced the counter, his back turned as his wings danced to the melody of his hum. Now was the time. He dashed over to his room and shut the door behind him. Even if they were both men, he didn't want the professor to see him naked. Mostly naked. Joseph's cheeks flushed at the thought of it.

On the foot of the bed, neatly folded, were the clothes Cadmus got out for him. A white frilled shirt was on top, underwear, a balled up pair of socks, and a pair of bark brown trousers. With someone else's clothes on, he realized how skinny he was. The garments were ridiculously baggy, uncomfortably so. His pants fell off without him even moving. Embarrassment coloring his cheeks, Joseph held his pants up and walked into the dining room.

"Did you enjoy your bath?" Cadmus must've heard Joseph's footsteps over the sound of sizzling. He glanced over his shoulder.

"Do you… um… have a belt I could borrow?" Joseph asked timidly.

Cadmus stared for a second, then burst into laughter. Joseph's face turned into a beet. "Of course I do!" he laughed, stirring something in the skillet. "Can you wait until I have finished cooking? I will get you a belt afterward," he chuckled some more as Joseph sat at the table.

Half an hour later, steaming on clay plates, dinner was served. Cadmus hurried upstairs and returned with a long black belt in hand. He handed it to Joseph before he sat, an apologetic look on his face.

"It is the smallest I own."

Joseph stood and slid the belt through the loops of his trousers, stuffing the excess into the circlets. He took his seat and dug in. Lamb chops cooked with wine and other spices and herbs, carrots, broccoli, and peas. A slab of toasted bread had a smear of garlic and olive oil, cut tomatoes on top. Cadmus offered him some red wine, which he accepted. As he poured Joseph a chalice, he explained how he made the wine himself and that it had been fermenting for years before he finally started drinking it. Joseph took a small sip. It was sweet and somewhat bitter and had a slightly sour aftertaste. The flavor was better than what Elena had described to him—she wasn't a fan of red wine. And Cadmus was right. It paired well with the food, although he figured just about any drink would go nicely with lamb.

"How do you empty that tub by yourself?" The dirty water sitting in the vat would be a hassle to drain and Joseph was dreading it.

Cadmus, glancing up from his plate, raised an eyebrow. "You do not know?" Joseph shook his head and took another drink of wine, the dark red liquid warming his gut and chest. "I have wood magic. I collapse the tub and let all the water out at once."

"That means I don't have to help, right?"

"No," he chortled, the lines at the corners of his eyes deepening. "You do not have to help. It will be easier for the both of us if I did that myself."

Joseph sighed and finished the rest of his wine in a gulp, then stood, collecting his plate, and walked to the sink.

"But," Cadmus followed suit, "you can help do the dishes."

Once the dishware was cleaned, dried, and put away, Joseph retired early. Cadmus didn't take long afterward to head up to bed as well. They didn't talk much. Even if he had something to say, Joseph felt he would have kept it to himself all the same. The atmosphere was a little awkward. It was clear Cadmus wasn't used to having someone else in the house, let alone one of his students.

Crawling into bed and pulling the covers over his body, Joseph told himself it didn't matter. Cadmus was willing to train him and give him sanctuary for the time being. He couldn't ask for much more. A part of him was still in shock that Cadmus agreed, despite thinking it was a bad idea. Joseph was grateful, nonetheless.

The next day, Cadmus left a note explaining the importance of strength-building. A strict routine that Joseph would complete in the morning before training with the dummy ended the note. He understood the importance of it, yet Joseph groaned at the list Cadmus left him. Sit-ups, pull-ups, pushups, swinging the longsword, running, and squats until Joseph couldn't do anymore. Sighing, he figured he should start running around the tree line.

White and grey fluffs heading westward clouded the sky. Joseph had built up a sweat, his muscles aching from the morning workout. He dove into training with the target a little after high noon. His limbs felt ready to fall off. Sometimes he wished they would. Pain stabbed his ribs when he tried to control his breathing and slow it down, but that only made him lightheaded.

Cadmus strolled around the house, his clothes simple, the edges of the sleeves and pant legs frayed. Even his shoes were worn, and mud-stained. His long brown hair was tied up in a bun, wild hairs flowing in the breeze. A small distance ahead of Joseph, he rolled his shoulders, then cracked his neck and knuckles.

"Whenever you are ready, I want you to attack me as if I were Charles," he said, and got into a stance where his fists were in front of his face and chest, legs spread apart, heels hovering slightly above the ground.

Joseph looked at him, perplexed. He knew he had no right to think this, but how could he attack an unarmed man? It didn't feel right, even if the difference in their abilities was like night and day. He inhaled sharply and assumed his stance, ignoring the throb of his muscles.

He didn't want to rush in. He never had the luxury of seeing Cadmus spar. Step by step, he moved closer. Cadmus shifted a bit and Joseph charged.

He swung the dagger up and across his forearms. Cadmus slid back, using Joseph's momentum against him, pushing his arm away. Joseph spun and Cadmus connected his fist to his gut just enough for Joseph to feel the professor's fist dig into his skin. Thankful he didn't go full force, Joseph was annoyed that Cadmus didn't at the same time.

Disengaging, Joseph didn't stay put for long. He ran around Cadmus, slashed at the backside of his knees. The angel crouched. Swinging his long leg out, he swept Joseph off his feet and knocked him to the ground. Joseph gasped and winced. After he stood, Cadmus extended his hand out to help Joseph up; he took it and was hoisted to his feet.

"We will spar until sundown," Cadmus said. "Are you good to go again?"

He knew he was asking out of concern, but that only riled Joseph up. "I can go well into the night if I must." They both knew it was a bluff.

He tried his damnedest to keep his legs from shaking and his arms from giving out. Still, if it meant getting stronger, to get revenge at the Games—the best opportunity lying in front of him—then he would go without as many sleepless nights as it took.

Joseph swiftly fell into a routine.

The dagger became more comfortable to hold, easier to manage and maneuver. That was why Cadmus wanted Joseph to swing the longsword around. He got better, faster, stronger; he could feel it in the way his muscles grew accustomed to morning training and how the blisters on his hands turned to calluses.

In the evening, after Cadmus came home, they would spar and eat dinner. With each day, they talked more about mundane topics like alcohol, lessons, books, and so on, the awkwardness fading. Most nights, his sleep was dreamless, but when it wasn't, Maryjane's corpse and Charles haunted him. He counted the days to the Games of Retribution, restlessness seeping into every fiber of his being. Charles filled his mind more often than Joseph liked; it disgusted him and kept him focused.

79

A Tale For The Weary

V

The outside world was calm, peaceful, unaware of the misfortune that had taken place over a month ago, but that was how the world was, oblivious to one's suffering. Cadmus knew that better than most, he thought.

He sat at his dining table, reviewing a stack of book reports from his students, a chalice of red wine calling his name from the table's surface. A call he could not resist as he took a savoring sip.

It had been interesting to bring Joseph, a child, into his home. Yet, it dredged so many memories Cadmus wished had stayed buried deep within the archives of his old mind. He and his wife, Darinka, had tried to conceive, but, as immortals, bringing a child into the world was not as easy of a feat as it was for mortals. The pain it caused both of them was of a physical nature, a tearing at his heart, a pressure around his airway, a pang of guilt that never truly went away.

A quiet, high-pitched squeak disrupted Cadmus's concentration as Joseph opened his door and shuffled out. His pale blonde wavy hair was chaotic, dark circles under his half-closed eyes, his thin eyebrows knitted together. The boy wore Cadmus's nightclothes—a white shirt and loose trousers, both cotton—which were far too baggy for Joseph's thin frame, but they worked.

"Cannot sleep?" Cadmus inquired while Joseph approached the table, nodded, and sat across from him in his wife's chair. A subtle twinge tugged at his heart. He had never thought he would see someone sit in her chair again. He didn't think he ever wanted to, either.

Nightmares had plagued Joseph since his first night here—Cadmus assumed, from the look of him—though this was the first time he had come out to the living quarters to find a reprieve.

Cadmus set the reports down and shifted in his seat. "Have you heard of the founding rulers?" Perhaps a lesson would bore the young elf to sleep.

Joseph nodded, his hair moving with him.

"Shall I teach you a bit more about their history?"

He thought for a moment, his lazy eyes lingering on the table before he nodded once more, settling into the chair and giving Cadmus his attention.

There was much to tell, but Cadmus would digress. The founding rulers were divided over six hundred years ago, all fighting for glory, for land, for power. Language and culture helped to fortify the solace of the twelve races. Constant feuds created bloodshed further dividing the races. Until one man started gathering those who were like-minded, those who would help him change Vinyamar for the better.

Cadmus paused briefly. Joseph was still awake, his head now resting in his palm, his eyes fluttering every so often. *Just a little more.*

This man was Hordes Reap, the second son of Oumar Reap, the fearsome leader of the demons. Hordes gathered one person from each clan—no matter their social class or status, so long as they had the heart and will to aid in his cause—and opposed those like his father, those too stuck in their ways to see what the war of species was doing to their people. Together they ended the centuries-long war, created laws that would protect the people and keep their fellow rulers in line, and shaped the regions that were now known.

Most of what Cadmus said was common knowledge if one read a little into the war, save for King Hordes' father's name. He admired the courage of the twelve founding rulers and, at times, wished he too had that same courage.

Slouched in his chair, breathing deeply, mouth slightly parted, Joseph slept soundly despite how uncomfortable that position must be. Cadmus chuckled softly under his breath, the first night Joseph was here coming to his mind. The boy had wept late into the night. Cadmus thought to comfort him, thought to embrace him the way Darinka would surely have done to comfort Cadmus. The pain, the agony, the gut-wrenching gasps for air Joseph desperately tried to take brought tears to Cadmus's eyes, brought a deep, unsullied pain to his body. He could not face Joseph that night or that morning, his heart would not allow it.

Taking a deep breath, Cadmus rose, stepped toward Joseph, and carefully brought him into his arms, hoisting him up. He was light, much too light for a growing boy, but he lacked both muscle and fat. He breathed a slow, steady rhythm like the waves lapping the shore on a beautiful summer day.

In his room, Cadmus gently placed Joseph on the bed, pulled the blankets up to cover his legs and torso, then stared at him for a few heartbeats. Joseph resembled his father more than his mother— though only marginally—had his slightly down-turned eyes, a strong jawline, and tanned skin. He had his mother's blue eyes, blonde hair, freckles, and thinner frame, his shoulders a bit broader. Lucas, on the other hand, took after his mother. That might have changed since the last Cadmus had seen him.

The door clicked shut behind him. He looked across his empty, quiet home, to his chalice of wine not yet finished and reports not yet gone through. The breath he took in had no hint of his wife's floral yet earthy scent, no matter how many plants he put in his home.

After re-stacking the papers against the table, Cadmus poured out the rest of his wine, placed the dull metal chalice beside the sink, put out the candles, and made for bed.

What it Takes to Kill
VI

At the dining table, Cadmus and Joseph sipped on wine after a long day of training almost three months after Maryjane's death. They were talking about future lessons Cadmus had planned when a knock, hard and fast, came to the door.

"I'll get it," Joseph said as he stood, pushing out his chair with his legs.

Cadmus held his hand out, "No," and rose, his expression serious.

Joseph cautiously followed and stopped once Cadmus reached the entrance. He opened the door, Joseph peeking beyond him. A young man stood there, skinny and soaked from the rain. His clothes were tattered and stained. A single twitch ran through the young man's body. The skeletal demon with pale orange skin, a single pointed horn growing from his forehead, and small bat-like wings sprouting from his back, gazed at Cadmus. He pleaded for a place to stay, just for the night, and perhaps some bread and cheese.

"No," Cadmus said bluntly.

The demon's eyes darted past Cadmus to Joseph before he turned to glimpse the outside. "Please," he begged and licked his cracked lips, his tone different.

"I have already given you my answer and it will not be changing."

Joseph looked between the two, confused by Cadmus's harshness.

Cadmus closed the door, but the demon forced it open, a knife in his off-hand. Cadmus reeled, then winced and fell to his knees with a thud, doubling over. The demon cackled, the knife slick with red. Joseph couldn't move. His legs felt as though they were knee deep in mud. His heart pounded in his ears, his mouth as dry as sand. The man lurched forward. The words that left his mouth sounded alien.

A single stake pierced the demon's sternum, his core, forcing him to stop dead in his tracks. The stake retracted, leaving a rectangular hole, and the man collapsed to the ground, a pool of crimson instantly spreading. It was over as quickly as it started. The breath Joseph had been holding escaped, and he fell to his knees in front of the corpse of a stranger. Cadmus dragged himself over and shook Joseph out of his daze.

"Joseph! Joseph!" Cadmus yelled. "Are you all right? Did he hurt you?"

"Why are you worrying about me?" Joseph mumbled, his eyes coming back into focus. "You're wounded! You were stabbed yet you're worrying about me?" His voice trembled, the pendant pressed against his chest like ice.

"Of course I am!" Cadmus grimaced. "You cannot regenerate like I can. See?" He pulled his forest green shirt up to show that there was only a thin line, like a scratch, where he was stabbed. "It is almost completely healed but Joseph." Cadmus sat and brought one knee up. "You froze."

Joseph's eyes went wide. *Is that what I did?* He didn't realize, more like he couldn't comprehend the situation in front of him enough to act. The man appeared innocent. How could he have known he was a bandit?

Joseph glanced at Cadmus's solemn expression, a mix of relief, pain, and disappointment. He swallowed. What excuse could he even come up with? Almost three months of training, sparring, going to bed with aching muscles and bones, and sores and blisters. For what? It was the perfect opportunity to put the training to use, and he let it slip through his fingers. Freezing in fear at the sight of a knife held by a liar, a thief, and probably a murderer.

*

Cadmus sighed and used his knee to help get himself off the ground. It was rare to have uninvited visitors in the middle of a forest. The few he had had were bandits. The first of which he and his wife let stay the night. They had fed the young orc, let her bathe, made sure she had the warmth of a blanket and bed, only for her to take as much as she could carry while they slept. The orc was gone the next morning, and many things had vanished, only their imprint left behind.

"I do not think it would be wise for you to join the Games, Joseph. You would not be able to survive long enough to get revenge. You... do not have what it takes to kill." He held his hand out for Joseph, but he slapped it away.

Cadmus brought his stinging hand close to his chest, a dull ache throbbing behind his ribs.

"I—" Tears glistened in the boy's eyes. "I know I have no excuse for what just happened, and you're probably right. If I enter, I'll be killed." His tone hurt Cadmus in a way he did not think hearing the truth would.

Joseph got to his feet, fists clenched, knuckles turning white at his sides. He said, "I didn't know what I wanted when I came to you."

Cadmus's foot slid across the floorboards. "What are you getting at?"

"I decided a while ago that even if I must die in the process, Charles' death will be by my hand." Turning on his heel, Joseph went to his room. "The first day I held that dagger, I knew if you told me to leave after the first month, I would be fine by myself."

Cadmus listened, his heart pounding in his ears as he inched toward Joseph and tried to keep his breath under control. He remembered that feeling, a sensation to which he was too accustomed.

"But it's as you said," Joseph called out shortly before stomping into the living room wearing the clothes he had arrived in. Although now they were a bit tight. "I have a talent for fighting, so I picked up on things rather quickly, right?"

"I beg of you, Joseph, do not let this hunger for revenge consume you. Your life is far more valuable than you think!" he said, taking one stride at a time closer to the living room. "You are too young to throw it away like this!" The necklace hanging off Joseph's collarbone shimmered in the orange light of the candles.

One night, Joseph had placed the sunflower pendant in front of him, asking if he had anything he could use as a chain. The only thing he had was thread for sewing up clothes. After grabbing a few colors, Joseph measured three pieces. Two were the length of his arm, while the third was double that. With the ends under a cup of water, Joseph weaved the string and knotted and singed the ends together. He threaded the cord through the pendant loop, tying it around his neck. All the while, he had explained the sunflower's origins, disgust and sympathy twisting Cadmus's gut.

"Just stay one more night." Cadmus stood in his path toward the door. "Please, Joseph," he pleaded, hoping he could convince the child in front of him to avoid such a thorny path. He did not want Joseph to become like him, a shell of the man he used to be and filled with regret, piled on top of more regret.

He did not want Joseph to end up like his wife.

"No," Joseph said bluntly as he walked around Cadmus.

"Why not?" He whipped around, following Joseph to the door.

"Because the Games of Retribution are in a week. If I'm going to make it in time, I need to leave tonight."

Cadmus blinked at Joseph.

"What's the matter? Did you think I'd lose track of time just because I wore a smile?" Joseph spat, bitterness hanging off every single word.

Cadmus ground his teeth and looked down at Joseph, who had started to put his shoes on. "I can hope, can I not?" He bent down, placing a hand on Joseph's, stopping him from grabbing the other shoe. "You can leave on the morrow. I will even bring you a horse. Stay for the night. It is pouring outside, and you do not know the route to Alucard's Kingdom."

"So?"

Cadmus recoiled in shock, expecting something along the lines of *You're right* or *Fine, one more night.* But to be met with such coldness, it felt like an icy pick stabbing his heart. *Not again.*

"I can always find a map; I'm not half bad at reading them." Joseph shrugged as he grabbed and put his shoe on. "I know how to hunt and build a shelter. You—" Joseph rose alongside Cadmus, holding eye contact. "You were a means to an end. A tool to help me reach my goal. If you're no longer of any use, why should I stay?"

His harsh words cut deep. Cadmus winced, anguish and regret a mix of turmoil within.

Joseph went on, "So, I can wallow in my defeats? So, I can constantly dwell on my own weaknesses and shortcomings? To be constantly reminded of my sister who's dead! Dead! Because of a single person! Because of me!" He gestured to himself. His eyebrows were furrowed, face burning with anger, a vein throbbing on his neck.

"I got my sister killed! The only way I can atone is to kill him! And if I must kill myself along the way, then so be it! It's the least I deserve!" His eyes were bloodshot, tears glistening, his lips and body shaking.

A dense, heavy sorrow weighed on Cadmus, suffocating him. He reached to stop Joseph from leaving, to stop him from walking to his death, but the door slammed shut. *Not again!*

Silence filled the open space once more. Rain and wind beat furiously against the house. Cadmus trembled. He bit his lip, trying to hold his tears back. *Why am I so hurt?*

On a night just like this one, dark and stormy, Cadmus and his wife had gotten into an argument. She marched out of the house looking to calm herself down with some fresh air and a stroll. She never returned. Cadmus searched for days. Nothing but her bracelet was found. Darinka had vanished into thin air.

His hunger for revenge left a bitter metallic taste on his tongue. He understood, more than anyone else, what it felt like. Yet he could do nothing to ease that feeling. He could do nothing to help Joseph. The dim light in Joseph's eyes, growing brighter by the day, was nothing but Cadmus projecting his own hope. The smile he thought was genuine was a trick that worked flawlessly. The simple cheerful conversations they had had given Cadmus hope Joseph was letting the idea of revenge go. How could he have been so wrong about everything? He had let his wife go all those years ago and now he let Joseph, a child, go running to his death.

It all went wrong so fast. It was hard to gather his thoughts. He slammed his fists into the floor, the only sound that echoed in his hollow house. He wanted to go after Joseph, but he hadn't the will to do so.

*

Joseph stalked across the glade, then ran into the forest. He was furious, just as he was hurt and ashamed. Everything he passed was a dark blur until he made it out of the woods. Very little was recognizable. He chose the direction he knew the kingdom was in, south, and walked as rain soaked every bit of clothing.

Unfulfilled

VII

The night was relatively young when Joseph walked the streets of Ivory's Kingdom. The rain had let up, but the roaring thunder slowly closing in told him it would only be for a short while. Street lamps around stores and other establishments were still lit, allowing Joseph to navigate his way around the kingdom.

A tavern door swung open, and a man stumbled and swayed to the road. His face was delirious from alcohol. Laughter and slurred sentences drifted out as the man waved his arm, and the door closed. The man whistled on his way to the alley, a sword resting on his hip. Joseph huddled close to the shadow of the building beside it. He didn't know why he hid. If he had continued walking, he was sure the drunkard wouldn't have bothered him.

Before he knew it, Joseph had followed the man, ducking behind the corner as he went deeper into the alley. The man had taken his sword and propped it against the wall, so he could relieve himself—though it made little sense. Joseph assumed one could piss with a weapon on their hip. Not that he was complaining. Joseph snuck as fast as he could to the man's sword. The drunkard groaned, spreading his legs wider with a hop.

"C'mon now," he grunted. "I didn't drink that much!" His voice was hoarse, probably from laughing and talking much louder than he should have.

Joseph snatched the sword and turned to leave. A big, clumpy hand grasped his shoulder, holding him in place. Every bone in his body told him to drop the sword and run. Run as fast as he could, but the man's grip was tight, and his legs were frozen in place. Again.

The man swung Joseph around, knocking him to the ground. He landed on his back, hard, taking his breath away. The man shouted words Joseph couldn't understand over the ringing in his ears.

Step by step, the drunkard came closer and closer. Not feeling the sword in his hand, Joseph looked from side to side. It was right there, just a few inches. He stretched his arm out as far as he could, and the drunkard quickened his pace. Joseph pulled it closer with his finger until he could grab it. Hands trembling, he yanked the sword out of its sheath. The drunkard wrenched his fist back and lunged, his face scrunched and red. Joseph turned his head, shut his eyes, thrusting the sword upwards.

It went silent. The man was no longer screaming and the ringing in Joseph's ears had stopped. Something warm trickled over his hands. He peeked at the drunkard. The sword had disappeared into the man's sternum—his magical core—and blood flowed down the blade onto the hilt and handle, then his hands and arms, dripping onto his torso.

Blood seeped from the gaping wound, staining his tan shirt bright red. He stumbled backward, dislodging the sword before he dropped to his knees. Joseph, wide-eyed, pushed himself up, fumbling to get away. After what felt like hours, the man fell forward, hitting the ground with a wet thud, his eyes open. Joseph waited breathlessly to see if the drunkard would move or make any sound. He didn't. Instead, blood drained from his body at an alarming rate. Joseph didn't know blood could flow so quickly. Magic had been the only thing keeping the man alive.

Joseph grabbed the sheath, put the bloodied sword into it, and got to his feet. For a brief moment, he was fine until his tongue seemed to retreat to the depth of his stomach. Vomit spewed from his mouth as he hit the ground, pain racing through his knees. The smell of urine, ale, and iron didn't help. When he glanced at the body, it twitched. Joseph flung himself back, bile painting his chin and the corners of his mouth. Blood stained the hand he went to wipe his mouth with, crimson spreading along the fine crevices of his skin. His stomach twisted again.

Gathering enough of his bearings to turn and grab the sword, Joseph darted off. He sped down one street, then another. Lightning flashed above as he struggled to breathe, the air seemingly as thick as molasses. His quivering legs felt like they would give out any second.

Once he was near the heart of the kingdom, Joseph ducked into an alley, leaned against the wall of some store, and slid to the cold, damp ground.

I killed him.

He examined the leather sheath in his hands and held it out in front of him. There were scuffs and scratches, signs that it was well used but not well taken care of. Bloody handprints had more shine than the leather.

No matter how many deep breaths he sucked in, he couldn't calm down. Adrenaline ran through his veins like a hare running from a fox. Still in a bit of a daze, Joseph got up and started down the street, hoping to find a canopy of some sort before the rain returned. Constantly glancing over his shoulder,

Joseph quickened his pace when a light mist started spraying his face.

Further down, he noticed a bakery where the roof leveled out over the sides. He hurried to the side of the brick building just as the rain became heavy and the wind picked up. As long as the wind didn't change direction, Joseph would be dry for the rest of the storm. He hunkered down, bringing his knees to his chest, the sword in between his thighs, and angled away from his head.

A metallic tang mixed with the scent of rain, stone, and bread. The blood on his shirt stuck to the skin underneath. He didn't mean to kill the man, but that meant nothing since he was the one holding the sword and he was the one that got to walk away in the end. Cadmus suddenly derailed his thoughts, the devastation on his face clear as day in his mind. His teeth ground, the world around him fading to black despite the street lamps glowing a soft orange.

Now look at what you've done. Killing me makes you no better than Charles… murde—Ding!

Joseph blinked, confused and sore from sleeping upright in a crouched position. A door clicked shut and the sound of a bell chime made him flinch.

Barely above the horizon, the sun warmed the dark blue sky. The street was bustling with people so early in the morning, preparing goods for their shops, delivering products, or walking to the academy. He got up, brushed the dirt off his pants, and noticed just how much blood got on his shirt and arms. He cringed, the drunkard's face flashing behind his eyelids. Since there was nothing he could do about it right now, he walked into the street, pacing as fast as he could without running. Some narrowed their sights on him, disgust or confusion washing over their faces, but didn't bother confronting Joseph. Relieved yet concerned, he thought it best to keep his head down.

Nearing the southwestern edge of the kingdom, Joseph went up to a stranger and asked for directions to Alucard's Kingdom. They grunted as if it were a hassle to say, but informed him, anyway. When he asked about a trail and time, the stranger hawked and spat at his feet, then growled, "Just keep going west from here and you'll be there in a few days, maybe a week, if you're slow."

Joseph nodded and left. People were not as friendly here in Ivory's Kingdom as he initially thought. Or maybe they wanted nothing to do with a blood-stained boy. On the trail leading to the grass plains, Joseph asked a few others, all of which said the same thing. *Head west and you'll be there in a week or so.*

Many wildflowers were already in bloom, their bright colorful petals easy to spot during the day, their scent saturating the breeze. It rained often. Most of the time it was a drizzle, and Joseph's clothes would only get damp. When it poured, he stopped wherever there was cover, which was usually a tree, and his clothes would get wet anyhow. The warm sun had dried them as he marched onwards, though. He passed a couple of abandoned holds and watchtowers of stone overgrown with moss and vines. It made him wonder if they were from the war of species over six hundred years ago before the founding rulers put an end to it.

The war had lasted centuries and the regions he knew now didn't exist. Instead, there were territories constantly fought over, conquered, then fought over again. Joseph didn't dare go too close; their old, battered and partially collapsed stone made his skin crawl.

In the middle of the night, Joseph's breath fogged in front of him. Sitting beside a small fire that didn't want to stay lit was barely enough to keep him from shivering all night. Most sticks were damp by nightfall, making it difficult to start and keep the logs aflame. It was pointless trying to cook food in such conditions, despite how good rabbit sounded. Joseph stuck to a diet of wild berries, nuts, and plants his ma had shown him were safe to eat. Thanks to the rain, his hands were mostly blood-free, though it took an effort to get them clean. As for his shirt, the stains remained.

On the nights he couldn't sleep, he went through the exercises Cadmus had him doing. It helped clear his mind, kept him focused on his body as he tired it out, so he could get some rest. At times, he would look at his surroundings and the darkness would come to life, whispering in his ears. *Killing me makes you no better than Charles,* the night would tell him. *Yes, but you know someone young enough, don't you?* Malice's voice came like a punch to the gut.

Otherwise, he continued to walk westward, the atmosphere increasingly saltier, his feet sore and achy.

In class, Cadmus had talked about Alucard's Kingdom with great fondness. The entire city was on an island connected to the mainland by stone bridges. People from all over the region and continent kept the streets busy. He talked about how big the kingdom was and yet, despite its size, the castle could be seen towering over buildings and homes. Patrol was strict, so crime was low. Joseph assumed most wouldn't want to commit a crime in the king's backyard. Unless they were brainless, of course.

Sun setting, Joseph peered down at his hands. The greyish stains on the inside of his fingers from charcoal were gone. He made a noise half between a grunt and a laugh. The feeling of holding a hunk of charcoal in his hands eluded him. Sketching the guidelines of a face then scratching in the details while being inches from the paper did too. His ma had caught him a few times and told him to fix his posture. Joseph *would* straighten his spine. In minutes, however, he would be hunched over the desk, face inches away from the paper again.

As he pushed a swaying piece of long grass out of his way, he wondered if he would even remember how to draw. Would the memory return in a flood, or would it filter in? Not that it mattered now, but it was relaxing to think of what could happen after the Games. If he survived.

Five days had passed since Joseph left Cadmus's house and almost three months since Joseph had last seen his ma. Elena's features weren't crisp in his memories anymore, and neither were Maryjane's.

The early morning sky of pinks, purples, and oranges faded into blue, the clouds small and rare. A subtle breeze wafted briny air and something else, something Joseph couldn't recognize.

By noon, Alucard's Kingdom crested over the horizon, sending a rush of excitement through Joseph. For some reason, he wasn't nervous about the Games of Retribution. Perhaps it was because he had already killed someone. Blood stained his hands, whether they were clean or not. Sometimes the strange sensation of warm, thick blood flowing over his skin would come back to him, a shudder raking his body. Then the drunkard and his dead eyes staring up at Joseph would strike his vision like a bolt of lightning.

Killing Charles, an old man who had been sitting in a cell rotting for three months, shouldn't be difficult. That was assuming Charles would be his first opponent. Although eager, the feeling of hatred grew like a parasite feeding off the petals of a sunflower.

It sickened Joseph, made his gut churn.

He tried to think of other things. When nothing came to mind other than the Games, he swallowed the growing nausea and pushed onward. The kingdom was so close; it was within his grasp. *Just a little bit more, a little bit longer.*

White stone bridges stretched across a wide strait. The blue water glistened in the sunlight. Joseph peered over the edge, squinting until he saw brightly colored fish swimming around. Straight north, the figure of another bridge and two more to the west could be seen. People of all races walked beside him, both coming and going. On the left side of the bridge, a wagon went by, then a dark green carriage with gold rims and accents trotted past Joseph. A castle towered over the city in the distance, just like Cadmus said it had.

As the day settled into evening, Joseph walked through the southern district of Alucard's Kingdom. Blossoms, meat, bread, wood, salt, and more filled the air—a dizzying amount of scents. Houses, big and small, and all sorts of shops, lined the cobblestone streets. One sign had 'brothel' written on it. A dwarf smoking a pipe, wearing too much makeup and burgundy silk robes, and a demon wearing only a loincloth, stood in front of the dark brick building. He didn't know what a brothel was, but when he locked eyes with the dwarf, she wagged her finger at him and winked. He looked away instantly and hurried along.

Joseph stared in awe at the many who wore clothes he couldn't even dream about wearing himself. But that was only a handful of people. Most wore attire only slightly nicer than what he would find at the shops in his village. After glancing down at his filthy garments, he was sure people thought he was a bandit or a beggar. Though that wouldn't be too far from the truth.

In the east, a chapel peeked beyond the mass of buildings. Near the heart, there was a roofless, circular sandstone structure. Cadmus had said something about the coliseum where the Games were held. Royals trained there while the prison was underneath the arena. If a criminal were to escape, they would be met with a horde of royals itching to test their skills.

The closer Joseph got to the coliseum, the more he heard talk about the Games. Plenty of the people he passed talked about someone they knew—a lover, their child, a friend—entering. Some talked about how it was the tenth anniversary of the king's coronation, and they bounced ideas of how the king would celebrate off one another.

Conversations shifted slightly as the streets crowded even more, the atmosphere becoming stuffy. Instead of talking about others, people talked about themselves. More like bragged. Slowed down by the crowd, Joseph overheard two people.

One man proudly proclaimed, "I swear on my family's name, I will kill every last one of the criminals in the Games!" He shook his fist toward the sky as he spoke.

The man to his side laughed. "Only if I don't get to it first!" Then they both cackled and blabbered about booze.

Joseph couldn't forget his reason for joining the Games, disheartened or otherwise, nor did he want to. Pride had nothing to do with it, and he didn't care about his family's name. Lucas could be the pride of the Knightridge line. Joseph was sure many others were there for revenge, but he knew a good chunk was there for the thrill of the hunt.

What if someone gets to Charles before I do? Cold sweat collected in his palms, his brows furrowing. Joseph started thinking of what he should do if that happened, how he could escape without being noticed. Easier said than done.

The coliseum's walls were as pristine as any other newly constructed building. Columns, at even intervals to the top, were carved with scenes of battle. A lot of diligent work was needed to keep such an enormous structure pristine like it was. He felt bad for the people taking care of it.

The flow of bodies carried Joseph to a small wooden stand, the darkness opposing the creams and tans of the sandstone. Upon seeing the booth, he pushed his way through. People griped and cursed as he passed, but eventually, he made it.

Two beautiful women stood inside the booth, each wearing blue, white, and gold blouses and various jeweled trinkets. The taller and fuller-bodied one of the two had white wings, the edges tan, four white eyes, and her light auburn hair was up in a braided bun. Joseph remembered trying to do something similar for Maryjane, but her curly head of hair made it difficult, so he stopped, opting for something much simpler instead.

The other's white skin was tinted purple, as if she had been in the cold for too long. Her wavy hair was a few shades darker than her skin and her eyes were as yellow as a butterfly flower. She also had wings, only hers resembled a bat's.

The two were chatting, not paying attention to who walked by until Joseph stopped and cleared his throat.

"Where can I sign up for the Games?" he asked in as loud of a voice as he could muster, but it was much quieter than he expected. To his surprise, they stopped their conversation and glanced his way.

The demon stepped closer to the table in between them. "I'm sorry but..." she hesitated and looked back at the angel, who nodded. "We can no longer accept new participants. All the spots have been filled." Her eyebrows twitched closer together as she considered Joseph.

He just stared, wide-eyed, unable to comprehend what she said. "You… can't make an exception?"

The demon shook her head. "No, I'm sorry, but there are only so many people who can be in the Games. There's always next year though," she tried to console, a small smile on her orchid lips.

His eyebrows knotted. "I can't wait that long."

He glanced down at his shaky hands and the crude strap he made of vines and leaves from the forest, keeping the sword on his waist. His hand always hovered beside it, just in case the belt broke. "I've been traveling for a week to get here and you're telling me I can't participate?" he breathed.

"Listen, kid." The angel stepped forward, her expression impatient and irritated. "There is no more room for you. You're too late. There is nothing more we can do." She eyeballed him before adding, "Besides, you don't appear old en—"

"Then why are you here?" Joseph asked harshly and weathered the urge to scream at them; to scream in general till his voice could give nothing more.

"We're waiting for the guards to come and take the stand down so we can leave."

"What about…" Joseph's head dipped, and he slid his hand up, placing it on the hilt of his sword. In his nail beds, he could still see the drunkard's blood, dried and black. "Criminals? Can they be put in the Games?" He glanced at the ladies, unsure if he said that aloud or was just thinking about saying it.

The angel held her arm in front of the demon, pushing the demon behind her. "I… don't know."

So, he had spoken.

"If we test it out, will someone answer and let me in?" It was like hearing someone else talk with his voice. It didn't feel like him, but it was.

"I'm sure if you wait a bit longer the guards will tell you more." The angel also put a distance between her and the table, a bead of sweat forming and dripping from her temple.

Joseph ground his teeth, his gaze darting between the women and his sword. He closed his eyes. A cold rush of anger washed over him. Charles and Malice entered his mind, both laughing at him in their heinous voices.

With no sense of urgency, he drew his sword, pointing the tip at the women who had backed themselves up against the wall.

This is no different from the bandit Cadmus killed or the drunkard. Kill them in one strike and it's over.

Joseph raised his arm, placing both hands on the handle, and took a step. Someone grabbed his wrists. The grip wasn't hard, but it was enough to prevent Joseph from swinging.

He turned to look over his shoulder. A tall, broad-shouldered, dark elf, a patch of white in his hair and a scar across his face, glared down at him. He wore almost all black beside his gauntlets of leather brown, the silver chain on his hip, and the holster going across his chest for the blades jutting behind him. A little beyond the dark elf, seemingly concerned, was an angel. His hair was the color of red brick, freckled skin, and eyes the color of a lilac. He wore a small black corset with a shirt of red lace underneath tucked into white pants. The cloak of black fur over his shoulders just barely kissed the ground.

In an instant, the dark elves' expression changed after his eyes moved from the necklace on Joseph's collarbone to his face.

"Joseph?"

Joseph recognized the elf and snapped his arms away, then turned on his heel. "You're that elf my brother talked to that day. Are you his Unit leader or something?" he said bitterly.

The dark elf nodded, a little frazzled. "Gareth Birch... What are you doing here?"

"Isn't it obvious? Or are you just oblivious?"

Gareth scowled. "You will die before you even have the chance to avenge your sister."

The man at Gareth's side eyed Joseph but remained silent, his expression passive. *Who is that? He looks too nice to be a knight.*

"You will not be able to enter the Games of Retribution. You are too young. We would make you wait another year or two. So please, go home," Gareth said, his demeanor softening.

Every inch of Joseph's skin felt like it was on fire. His head throbbed so much he could barely make out what Gareth was saying. If he couldn't get into the Games, no matter what he did, what was the point? He knew, didn't he? Cadmus knew Joseph couldn't enter the Games because of his age. Betrayal, like a heavy blow to the gut, took Joseph's breath away.

Charles smiled and handed him the necklace with the very sunflower that hung around his neck. Maryjane lying mangled on the street caused his stomach to wrench and curdle. The unbothered voice of Malice echoed in his ears. Cadmus took care of Joseph, gave him food, shelter, a bed, clothes, then trained him only for it to be thrown back in his face. The drunkard's warm blood flowed down his hands and arms, staining his shirt and skin so that he had to scrub for hours in the rain.

He had killed someone. The feeling of it overwhelmed his senses. He shuddered.

Everything flooded his mind like the sea wreaking havoc on the shore, leaving nothing in its wake.

Joseph stumbled forward, clutching his chest, his eyes screwed shut. Gareth caught him by the arms and steadied him. It was hard to breathe, hard to think.

"What was all of it for?" he said, his voice trembling and cracking. "What was the point of this if I can't kill Charles? Tell me!" Joseph abruptly brought his head up, tears streaming down his face, an immense pressure on his chest.

Gareth winced, his arms twitching when a man spoke, breaking through all the noise.

"Is this where I can sign up for the Games?"

The world stopped. Joseph's breath caught in his throat and his heart pulsed in his ears. Peering over his shoulder, he stood up straight and turned, feeling Gareth's hands squeeze, then hesitantly release him.

"Ah, I remember you," Malice said, "but it seems you didn't heed my warning." His voice was deep, a melody of amusement and mockery. The cloak concealing the man's appearance was the same as in Joseph's memory, travel-stained, and sun-kissed.

"What a shame."

"Who are you?" Gareth stepped defensively in front of Joseph, holding his arm in front of him as a shield.

Joseph shoved Gareth's arm out of the way and lunged, sword above his head, ready to be brought down. Behind him, Gareth growled a warning, but he didn't care. Malice was right in front of him. He did nothing. He could have saved Maryjane. He could have prevented her death if only he had acted sooner. If he had turned Charles in sooner. If he had killed Charles himself, then Maryjane would still be alive.

No, Joseph knew Maryjane's death was his fault. He had no right to blame anyone else, but this was his chance to force his way into the Games.

The edge of Joseph's blade stopped a fingertip in length above Malice's head. His lungs were suddenly empty, deprived of every bit of oxygen. His grip loosened, the sword dropped and clanged against the ground. Malice hadn't moved an inch. Joseph's foot slid back. His mind went blank as he gasped for air that refused to come.

Gareth bolted to his side and helped him to the ground. His vision started fading to black, the world becoming fuzzy. The ability to speak fled. It was like his head was underwater. Curling over, his chest getting heavier, he pressed his forehead against the cool stone of the street—it was nice, barely ebbing the heat of his skin.

Gareth was shouting at Malice, but it sounded like a murmur from a different room.

The strength in Joseph's body left him. It was hard to keep his eyes open, so he closed them. Everything hurt inside and out. He had felt this once before, the night he heard Cadmus come down the stairs and stop in front of his door. He was about to knock, apparently thought better of it, and sighed, his footsteps trekking up to the second floor. Joseph had cried himself to sleep with the image of Maryjane's lifeless body painting his eyelids.

Walking along the path to their house from Pa's funeral, Joseph kicked a pebble a few meters ahead of him while Maryjane swung her legs up as she walked. Elena was a little behind them, talking to Grandmother and Grams. All three wore sad expressions. It was cold out, snow lightly sticking to the ground and their breath a white cloud in front of them. They wore heavy, fur bear hides to keep warm.

"If I die," Maryjane said in a casual tone, "bury me in an empty field."

Joseph raised a suspicious eyebrow and looked down at her. "Why an empty field? I would have thought you wanted to be buried with a bunch of sunflowers."

"I do!" she exclaimed and pouted, which lightened after a second. "But I don't. I want you to bury me with a bunch of sunflower seeds, so I can start a sunflower field, a huge one!" She extended her arms out as wide as she could.

Until then, she had never talked about death. Joseph thought she was too young to understand what she was saying and what it meant, but he played along.

"Hmm." Joseph brought his hand up to his chin, something he saw Cesar do when he was deep in thought. "Only if you bury me with paper and charcoal, so I can draw in the afterlife." He held his pinky out, a wimpy smile across his lips. If it made her smile on such a gloomy day, even though he didn't understand the concept of an afterlife, one promise wouldn't hurt.

Maryjane grinned and in return, locked her pinky around his. "Promise!"

It had been the only promise Joseph ever made to his sister, one that he had forgotten about. Now, of all the times, he remembered and was ashamed. Blinded by rage and sorrow, the only promise he made was left unfulfilled.

If anyone were listening, Joseph prayed they would give her a field bigger than she could have ever imagined and fill it with sunflowers till it couldn't be filled anymore. Maryjane deserved all the sunflowers in the world.

... I don't want to die yet.

He wasn't ready to be buried alongside paper and charcoal, not with so many regrets looming over him. He wanted to see his ma one last time, apologize, and feel her warmth as she embraced him and told him everything would be all right. He wanted to thank and apologize to Cadmus. He was a wonderful professor and didn't deserve the harsh treatment he received. He wanted to congratulate Lucas and tell him he wanted to become a royal too, after all this was over. He wanted to plant thousands of sunflowers in that empty field near the house. He wanted to learn to paint just so he could make use of the new pigments he bought. Joseph wanted to make himself into someone *he* could be proud of.

I'm sorry. I'm sorry Maryjane. I'm sorry Ma. I'm just... I'm so sorry.

*

Gareth clutched Joseph in his arms as a final breath hissed through his teeth, and his body went limp.

The Games of Retribution
VIII

Gareth gently brushed loose curls from Joseph's forehead. He certainly held a resemblance to Lucas—blue eyes, blonde hair, sharp features. Shifting the boy in his arms, Joseph's body gave no resistance, it did not twitch nor stiffen.

He was dead.

From the crowd, two royals pushed their way through, one gasping and rushing toward the stand. The other stayed put, head surveying the space around Gareth. Eventually, he took a breath and looked up in time to see the first guard guide, the two women Joseph held at sword point, into the crowd. His eyes fell on the cloaked man, the murderer. To kill a boy in broad daylight was something *bold* could not quite cover.

"Your orders?" the second royal guard said while glaring at the man. She must have pieced everything together. Her silver armor caught rays of sunshine, creating blotches of light on the man's cloak.

"Arrest him and throw him in a cell," he said coldly, his gaze never leaving the man.

"Yes, sir." The guard quickly went to the man's backside, grabbing one arm, then the other, and pinning them between his shoulder blades.

"Wait," the king said. The guard halted as he approached, his cape fluttering around his legs. The king walked in front of the man when Gareth reached out to stop him.

"It is too dangerous, your majesty," he cautioned. "We can do that later."

The king lifted the murderer's cloak, ignoring his right-hand man. He was fair-skinned, jawline sharp, hair the color of snow, grey under his green eyes as if he hadn't had enough sleep. The two of them stared at each other for a moment. Gareth watched the two men, both as stoic and unmoving as a statue.

"Take him," the king ordered.

As the guard yanked the man around, he smiled at the king. Gareth ground his teeth, and the guard carried him into the coliseum. Out of the corner of his eye, Gareth noticed the first guard staring off into the crowd and frowned.

"You!" Gareth barked, making the guard flinch and turn toward him.

"Yes?" he shouted and stood at attention.

"Take that damn stand down before anyone else comes." Gareth did not have time to babysit a royal who should know how to do their job.

The guard glanced down at Joseph. "What about the body, sir?" he asked in a low tone as he glanced at Gareth.

"We will take care of him," the king stepped in with a neutral expression, his voice gentle. "You just need to do your job." The guard nodded, spun on his heels, and started dismantling the stand.

*

Cadmus rode his stallion hard across the plains of Alucard's Region, so he would make it in time. He knew he ought to get down, let his horse rest, but he came to a decision too late, and now time was working against him. It was times like these he wished his wings were big enough to carry him anywhere.

It took three days for Cadmus to go after Joseph with the hope of bringing him home. He regretted not having told Joseph that he was not old enough to take part in the Games. If he had, maybe he would have given up the night he came to Cadmus. What would have happened if the boy had returned to his mother? The only thing he could envision was Joseph succumbing to the never-ending sorrow and withering away. He cringed and pressed his horse harder. Alucard's Kingdom was close, he could see it in the distance.

The stone bridge was full of people and carriages. Cadmus could not get through on horseback. Dismounting his stallion, he made a run for it. Amid the crowds bumping into people, heart racing in his ears, lungs stinging with every breath, Cadmus could only plead.

Please.

Three days before the Games, every slot ought to have been filled, no matter the number of participants.

Please let Joseph be too late, please.

Cadmus frantically searched for Joseph. He burst past the front line of a crowd surrounding a partially built booth. Out of breath and sweaty, his eyes fell upon a knight kneeling on the ground. Joseph lay still in his arms. It felt like he had taken a blow to the sternum. Cadmus teetered on his feet, his head spinning and his gut twisting. The dark elf looked up at him—Cadmus recognized him from the times Gareth had visited the academy—his silver eyes grim, and rose, Joseph's limbs dangling from his arms.

"Did you know him, Professor Locke?" Gareth asked.

All Cadmus could see were the dark circles under Joseph's eyes and the dirt caking his skin. Something shimmered on his collarbone.

"Yes," he breathed. "I was… also his teacher." His tone was so hushed that he could barely hear himself. *At least I was able to see you.*

Gareth spoke while Cadmus reached forward, grabbed the necklace, and pulled it over Joseph's head. He placed his hand over the boy's left breast and pressed down, waiting to feel a heartbeat that never came. Cadmus rested the necklace on his stomach.

"Please, give this to his brother, Lucas Knightridge." He turned, unable to face Joseph's corpse any longer. *I must tell his mother.*

*

The crowd swallowed Cadmus. Gareth glanced down at the necklace he had placed on Joseph's stomach, questioning if he should give it to Lucas. In Redcol, Lucas made it clear that his relationship with his family was as thick as a strand of hair.

He turned toward the king, a glum expression darkening his features. As Gareth walked to him, the king unclipped his cloak with a shrug and placed it over Joseph's body. Since Joseph had no family to collect his body, he would be buried outside the kingdom in the sepulcher to the northeast.

"Malice"

A single wide staircase, thirty meters deep, led to the prison under the coliseum. The cell system had fifty rows of fifty cells and each cell was three meters wide, three meters deep, four meters tall. Rock and earth walls created good insulation, keeping the prison cool or slightly warm. Torches spaced every three chambers lit the hallway and cast dark shadows into the cells. Inside the compartments was a wooden bucket with wads of paper beside it and a bed of hay in the opposite corner, a stained pillow and blanket neatly folded on top. Feral prisoners were somewhere within their box of earth.

Malice had been thrown into the forty-seventh cell of the fourth row to the left of the stairs. He counted each one on the way. He had nothing better to do since the guard refused to utter so much as a curse.

The guard that took him was young, seemingly a rookie. She was tall for someone who looked barely seventeen and her freckled skin mirrored the king's—though much lighter in complexion. Her sandy tan, thick locks came just below her eyebrows, each eye a distinct color. One was blue like a forget-me-not and the other was as brown as tree bark. Despite the hungry or angry looks from the inmates reflected on her armor, she walked calmly with her head high, Malice's arms in hand, until they got to his cell. Another guard, to which she had motioned for them to follow behind, opened the metal bars by jerking their hands apart. She shoved him in, and the guard instantly brought their arms together, closing the bars.

"Sir Gareth will most likely come to question you later," she said, utterly disgusted, and turned to leave. Her footsteps resounded off the walls while the guard she summoned stayed, standing in between Malice's cell and his new neighbor.

Malice undid the string to his cloak before pulling it off and tossing it onto the bed. He chuckled to himself, thinking of the last time he had been thrown into a cell. Eight years didn't feel like long.

He went to sit on the edge of the mattress and wait for Gareth when a battered, adenoidal voice penetrated the wall.

"I recognize that cloak ya wearin' newcomer," Charles said.

"Is that so," Malice replied, resting his elbows on his knees.

"Malice." He paused. A second later, he slammed his hands against the bars. "The bastard that put me in here!" Charles shouted. Gasps echoed in the corridor from nearby inmates.

"I don't recall putting you in here." Malice sat up, already tired of the conversation, as he pushed his fingers through his greasy hair. "I warned you, didn't I? And what did you say after? Wasn't it something like, *If they can catch me sure, but they won't?*"

Malice continued to mock, "If they didn't catch you, what are you doing here? Relaxing?" A smirk teased the corners of his mouth.

"Shut yer mouth, ya wretched bitch!" Charles snarled.

Malice leered, "I do truly wonder what happened. Did your friends betray you? Or did your luck finally run out?" *They wouldn't have saved you, anyway.*

"You!" he fumed, fists pounding the wall. "How did you make them—"

"Quiet!" the guard said, slamming his sword against the bars of Charles' cell. Startled, he fell to the ground, a heavy thud. His teeth chattered as he cursed and crawled to his bed of straw.

"Another word out of either of you and I'll get a knight down here!" All that heard the threat fell silent. A pin drop could be heard as the flames blinked and danced.

Malice lay on his cloak, closing his eyes.

Heavy footsteps made their way closer and closer to Malice's cell until they stopped in front of the metal bars. Gareth crossed his arms, a scowl on his face. Malice got out of bed and walked to the barricade. Gareth was quite a bit taller than Malice, his frame broad and muscular. The scar on his face had faded a little over time, but was deep in its pale purplish color. With features as sharp as a knife and stern as a rock, one glare could probably send an adult crying to their mothers.

Others had joined Gareth; a woman aged with wrinkles and grey hair, and a few guards.

"Begin," Gareth commanded.

The woman next to him held her hands out, so they were almost touching the metal rods, her eyes closed. She breathed in... and out. Immediately, she struggled. Her posture became stiff, and a frown accentuated her wrinkles. The growing tension caused sweat to bead on her forehead as her breathing got heavier. Still, she pressed on. *It won't work with so few.*

Dropping her hands and stepping away to catch her breath, it had been no more than a couple of minutes. Gareth stared at her for a heartbeat, then looked at Malice.

She wiped the sweat off her forehead. "Sir Gareth... I... cannot do anymore," she said in between pants.

"You say that as if it is a bad thing." He studied Malice, his eyes raking his body. Malice shrugged at his inspecting gaze.

"It is." She shook her head. "We need more people. I can't do anymore because I'm at my limit."

They were trying to drain his magical energy, a sensation similar to pulling a stitch from a wound.

Gareth clicked his tongue and waved his hand. "Gather as many as you think you will need to drain him. Just be quick about it." His silver eyes stayed on Malice while the woman bowed her head and darted down the hall.

Absorbing another's magical energy was like pouring one half-empty glass into another. The glass could only hold so much. Now that Malice was thinking about it, a glass of wine sounded exemplary—he hadn't had a glass since he couldn't remember when. To fully drain someone of their magic, the person draining it needed to release the excess magic that was absorbed. If they didn't, it could cause permanent damage to their core. Malice heard that it wasn't a difficult skill to learn, but it was best that a seer, someone who could see the magical energy within someone's body, did it. He knew a similar technique, one that hurt a hell of a lot more, but did the exact opposite of what was being done to him.

After half an hour or so, the seer returned with five people: a giant, a demon, a fairy, an orc, and finally an elf. The six of them lined up before the metal bars when Gareth took a step back to let them in. Malice remained close to the barrier, waiting patiently for his magic to be drained. *Such a tedious process.*

"Begin," Gareth gave the command. Again.

The fifth person finished, exhausted, and sweat-dampened, allowing Gareth and the seer to step forth. The woman focused on Malice for a time, then released a haggard breath and nodded to Gareth. Quickly bowing, she left, taking those she had brought down with her. The guards Gareth had brought followed the seer and her party on his word. He glanced to his side, waving his finger at the prison guard. They swiftly got a wooden stool and placed it behind him. From in between his legs, he dragged it forward and sat down.

"You are quite troublesome," Gareth said as Malice returned to bed. "But now that it is over, I expect you to answer me. Honestly." His voice was deep and gruff as it had always been.

The informant next to him, the only person he permitted to stay, grabbed a piece of paper on a thin board and a stick of graphite from their satchel when Gareth spoke. They were nervous, glancing between the cells in front of and behind them. Their nose twitched often, pushing their glasses up a bit followed by a wiggle of their mouth.

"Of course." Malice propped his head up on his hand while lying on his side. "Ask away."

Gareth grunted. "What is your name?"

"Malice Reap."

"Your real name." Gareth furrowed his eyebrows.

"I do believe that was the name I was given as an infant."

Gareth inhaled sharply. "How did you know Joseph, and why did you kill him?"

"I didn't know, Joseph." Malice started playing with a stalk of hay. "We met once for a little chat. I killed him because I'd like my head to remain whole."

The informant was scribbling every answer Malice gave while Gareth clicked his tongue—a habit, Malice assumed, since the dark elf did it often. That had not changed from the little time he'd spent with the knight as a child.

"Claiming self-defense," he muttered. "What did you *chat* about?"

"I warned him," Malice said.

"Warn him of what? Charles?"

Malice inclined his head. "Yes, I warned him of Charles, told him about his," he glanced at the wall to his right, "habits with children." Hay rustled before quiet footsteps walked to the bars and stopped.

Gareth's eyes darted to Charles' cell, then narrowed on Malice. "You knew of Charles, how exactly? Were you the one helping him?"

"No." His lip flared, revulsion writhing in his stomach like maggots. "I stumbled upon him a few times in the last six months."

"You expect me to believe this is just a coincidence?" Gareth asked, a slight growl at the back of his throat.

"Believe what you want."

Gareth sighed. "How? Explain to me how you stumbled upon his habits."

"The first time was when I was walking on the outskirts of a village in Raelle's Region," Malice said, his tone level. "Noticed Charles over his victim out of the corner of my eye.

Thought nothing of it and went about my business. The second time, a month or two later in Zeldine's Region, I saw him with a little boy. The next night he was devouring a girl, slightly older, but she resembled the boy, nonetheless."

A sound close to a gasp reverberated a bit, followed by incomprehensible mumbles. Someone further down muttered *disgusting* as whispers grew louder by the minute.

Gareth shifted in his seat and looked at the informant, who seemed even more uncomfortable than him. "And you did nothing? You did not stop him, kill him, turn him in?"

"It was beyond my reach. The law binds me. Even if it didn't, Charles and his personal matters don't concern me."

"A cold-blooded killer following the law, how admirable," Gareth said sarcastically, his nostrils creasing his cheeks.

Malice smirked. "I try." His eyes fixed on the knight for a split second. He enjoyed watching Gareth grow increasingly uncomfortable and irritable.

Gareth rubbed his face down. "Have you no shame, remorse, conscience?"

Malice said nothing as he stared at a vein throbbing on Gareth's forehead, ready to burst. *No.*

"Using a dead man's name, killing a child, letting that monster," Gareth gestured to Charles' cell, "run around despite knowing what he has done. What else has impeded your judgment, forcing you to do the things you have done? What other absurdity will you claim?" Gareth slammed his fists onto his thighs, his hands so tightly clenched that his knuckles turned stark white.

"If I am using a dead man's name." Malice got up and walked toward the metal bars. "Why wasn't there a single body found in Hordes Kingdom?" He leaned against the cold rods, one arm above his head while the other slung through the gaps. Once more, breaths drawled. *Well… there might have been one, but it was probably picked apart by scavengers before anyone could see it.*

Surprised, Gareth's eyes widened. His Adam's apple slid down and jerked up. "Let's say you are Malice Reap. What happened? Why vanish only to reappear a couple of years later?"

Malice tilted his head, pondered his answer, then spoke, "I have no obligation to tell you." He grinned deviously.

Gareth stood, knocking the stool into the cell bars behind him. The inmate screeched and scuttled to the darkest corner of their cell.

"Fine. I got what I needed." About to walk away, Gareth shot a final glare at Malice. "The king will deliver your verdict tomorrow. Be prepared."

"Tell him it was nice to see him again."

"Not even in your best dreams would I tell the king that." Gareth scoffed, his eyebrows knotted together, and stormed down the hall, the informant on his heels like a lost pup.

Malice fell onto his back when Charles started rambling in his cell and chatter began in others. He closed his eyes with a smile. After seven years, Gareth hadn't changed much. Though it was amusing that he didn't recognize Malice.

On the other hand, Magnus had. Malice was sure of that, if nothing else.

"Magnus"

The clock ticking on the mantle of the hearth read nine forty-two. There were two lounging chairs in front of it, rarely used, the leather pristine. The wall of shelves to his right contained a multitude of books, papers, trinkets, and decorative items. Magnus leaned against his chair engulfed in tree roots, stretching his arms as high as he could. Moving his head to the right, then the left, he cracked his neck, each time popping. He placed both hands on the little surface clear on his desk, his mind wandering to that evening.

Joseph was a young boy. He had so much life left to live. It was a shame he was killed. If he remembered correctly, Joseph was Lucas Knightridge's younger brother. Hopefully, Gareth could break the news softly to him when he returned.

Malice, Magnus thought. There was a familiar air about the cloaked man. Seven years changed someone more than he had imagined. Although he had never dreamed he would see Malice again under those circumstances. He sighed into his hands before running them through his hair.

Gareth would surely come any minute to inform him about the interrogation. If it could even be called that.

Five knocks came to the door.

"Come in," Magnus announced, followed shortly by the door creaking and footsteps. Gareth closed it behind him, crossed the room, and took a seat in one of the two chairs facing the cherry oak desk. "So, how did it go?"

Gareth sighed, reached for his pocket, and pulled out a folded piece of paper, handing it to Magnus. "He claims his name is Malice Reap. He killed Joseph out of self-defense," he said, his voice full of skepticism. "They did not know each other. Malice had warned Joseph of Charles. That was their first and last encounter for a while."

Magnus unfolded the paper and skimmed over it. "Was he tracking Charles?" he asked.

"No. He had noticed Charles as he was carrying out his desires." Gareth shuddered. "It happened three times, and all three times were happenstance."

"It seems Malice was tracking someone related to Charles." Magnus contemplated. A moment or two passed. "My guess would be the ones helping Charles escape from region to region."

Gareth shrugged. "It is plausible."

His fingers tapped on the desk when he glanced toward the clock, then back to Gareth. "Did you ask why he warned Joseph instead of leaving it be like the others?"

As if he finally remembered what he forgot to do, Gareth closed his eyes, exhaling. "No. I apologize for not thinking about such a basic question. My mind was elsewhere."

"It's fine. What else did he say? Anything to note?"

Gareth re-situated himself. "He spoke of a binding law restricting him from acting in other regions. The only law I know of that does this is the *Minding The Peace* law for the rulers created by the founding rulers." He scowled. "It was the excuse he used for doing nothing to stop Charles."

Magnus took a moment to study Gareth, recalling how he had talked about Malice until it clicked. "Do you not recognize Malice?" Sure, Malice was a boy the last Gareth saw him, but to not see the similarities—there was no way it could be true.

Gareth raised an eyebrow. "You believe that man *is* Malice?"

"He is, Gareth. I'm more surprised that you think otherwise." Gareth swallowed and shifted his gaze, the desaturated purple of his cheeks darkening.

To Magnus, it wasn't so much about appearance as the sense of being right next to him. The aura of his cold, detached personality infected him, sending shivers through his body like it was winter. Then his eyes. Those bright serpent-green eyes and how they could look beyond someone as if they were glass. There was no mistaking it. That man was the King of Hordes Region, Malice Reap.

"With that being said," Magnus said abruptly, startling Gareth. "I want two guards stationed outside his cell at all times. Have however many people it took to drain his magical energy sent out every day." Gareth listened, but had a dumbfounded expression. "He was put in section C, right?"

He nodded.

"Good, he'll be participating in the Games."

"You want his magic drained on the day of the Games?"

"Yes. It's the only way to give someone a chance to put a scratch on him." Malice proclaimed himself a criminal, and therefore, was going to be treated like one. *There has to be a different reason as to why he's here.*

Gareth massaged the bridge of his hooked nose. "You do not seem surprised, your majesty. You act as if you knew all this would... did you know all this would happen?"

"Do you think I planned all this? For a boy to be murdered in my streets, or that Malice would suddenly show up as if he told me his plans years ago?" He cocked his head a bit, eyebrows furrowed while his hands rested on one another in front of him.

"That—" Gareth looked away. "That is not what I meant. I am just not yet convinced that is Malice Reap. The child we saw seven years ago differs greatly from the man we saw today. I am concerned more than I doubt you."

Magnus sighed, a tension in his spine that refused to let up. "Has my gut ever been wrong?"

"No, your majesty."

"Do you trust me?"

"With my life."

"Then trust me when I tell you that is Malice Reap and prepare everything I mentioned earlier. Change is coming and I believe that Malice is at the center of it. No matter what, I want to be prepared the best we can for whatever might come."

Gareth considered Magnus, his silver eyes thoughtful, rose, and bowed. "I understand. I apologize for my thoughtlessness."

"All is forgiven. We've had a long day. You're dismissed. Go and get some rest, Gareth. We have even busier days ahead of us." Magnus smiled jadedly.

"Thank you." At the door, Gareth placed his hand on the knob, but stopped and turned his head. "Magnus, I may not know your past with Malice, but do not throw caution to the wind just yet."

"Of course not."

"... See you tomorrow," Gareth said as he opened the door.

Magnus listened to Gareth's footsteps fade to nothing after he closed the door and stood. *Don't throw caution to the wind, huh? I should have said that to you.* He couldn't entirely blame Gareth. He hadn't spent nearly as much time with Malice as Magnus had.

He crossed the floor, and a swipe of his hand quelled the candles around the room. As hard as it may be to sleep with racing thoughts, Magnus wouldn't be able to work, either. He would rather force himself to sleep than stay up all night rereading the same passage because he could not focus on it.

*

The next morning, the same six guards, including the seer, paid Malice a visit before breakfast was served. Two guards now stood outside his cell, the new one peeking in often. Bread, cheese, water, nuts, and dried meat were given three times a day every day. One inmate talked about porridge and how it was a treat from time to time. A bowl of milky white slop that you would hesitate feeding pigs, another voice hawked and spat. The two of them proceeded to argue for a while.

An older man came to Malice's cell. "It would be in your best interest to confess all of your crimes now." The human, fine lines around his eyes and mouth, stared at Malice through the bars. He wore a few layers of thin robes, the bottom was black, then dark blue, and the top layer white, seams and edges gold. On his chest was the insignia of Alucard's Kingdom, three sets of wings spreading behind a one-eyed, golden sun.

Malice pondered briefly, regarding the man with false cheerfulness. "I have done nothing else." *At least not here.*

The man eyed Malice suspiciously, grunted and promptly took his leave, his footsteps echoing down the corridor. *What a purposeless visit.*

It had been quite some time since he was able to relax, but it wasn't in his blood to do so. Being inept to sleep didn't help. If there was nothing to stimulate his mind, his body would have to suffice.

Malice rose from his bed of hay, cracking his neck, and got down on his hands and knees. He placed his forearms flat against the ground and tucked his head down, so it was touching the cool earth. With a deep breath, he brought one leg up, then the other until they were straight in the air. After staying in that pose for a few minutes, Malice pushed himself into a handstand and let go of his breath.

"You putting on a show for me darling?" the inmate from the cell in front of Malice asked. "Why don't you shake that pretty ass of yours so I can get off, yeah?" His voice was higher pitched, but hoarse.

Leisurely, Malice brought his legs down, setting the balls of his feet on the ground as he changed position a bit. One arm tucked underneath his chest, he balanced his weight on his hand while placing the other behind his back. Minutes went by, his breath steady, before he switched hands.

The inmate groaned, "Come on, help a guy out, would ya?" His bare foot tapped impatiently.

"Silence!" one guard hissed and spat at the inmate, muttering something underneath their breath.

The man groused and headed for his bed while Malice went to sit against the wall. It was an old habit of his to exercise complete control over his body if he had nothing better to do. It helped clear his mind for the most part.

Malice's hand moved to fiddle with the blue teardrop earring in his right earlobe, the same one Magnus had in his left. For a moment, he wondered if he would be sentenced to the

Games of Retribution—most likely—but if he weren't, how mad would Magnus be if Malice were to disappear from his cell? How upset would he be if he found Malice sitting in his study?

The Games of Retribution
"The Grand Entrance"

Lit by moving torches, the prisoners climbed up the stairwell into a closed-off room of the coliseum. Two sandstone columns held the ceiling, each had a dark metal holster holding a torch. Wooden crates were stacked alongside the outside wall, but the room was empty otherwise. The sounds of a roaring crowd and feet stomping to their seats thundered overhead. When the last inmate reluctantly came into the room, a guard slid their foot and thrust their fists to the side, closing the wall with a rumble.

That morning, Malice was drained of magical energy again before the same guard that put him in the cell cuffed him and forced him into the flowing river of inmates.

As guards freed everyone's restraints, Malice guessed there to be about eighty prisoners. He expected more. Then the guards stood alongside the inner wall. He turned himself toward the crates. The one by itself was the one he sat down on.

A fishman with bright yellow scales and orange hair taunted a guard, moving around them, pointing her spiny, webbed fingers in their face, and probably spouting nonsense and insults. The guard looked ahead of them, ignoring her.

Charles drooled over a younger person, perhaps younger than Malice. Disgusted, they kicked him in the groin and paraded off. Malice smirked as he watched Charles writhe in pain on the floor and he almost wanted to laugh when no one came to help the bastard.

Closer to him, he heard a group of four chatting about whose deed was most evil. One attempted to burn a stronghold to the ground. The stump of a man proudly told the tale of how he slayed one hundred men by himself. The elf laughed and told their story of assassination. Finally, the demon, using aggressive hand movements and gestures, explained how she got caught stealing from the noble family of Cytor, west of Alucard's Kingdom.

Someone came to sit beside Malice. They smelled of mildew and sweat. The person was thin and lanky, their black hair long and silky as if they had not washed their hair in months—perhaps they hadn't. Their clothes were layers of robes tied at the waist with a white cloth. The smell wafting from them burned his nostrils, so Malice went to stand when their cold, bony hand clamped around his wrist.

"Wait just a moment." Their voice was quiet, each word slipping into the next. "How about a quick chat before the Games start? You seem like someone worth talking to." They smiled, their teeth yellow, and brown at the gums.

Malice sat down again, yanking his hand away. "Really. Then by all means talk." He leaned to the side, using his grip on the edge of the crate to support himself.

"I heard all you did was sleep, is that true?" They closed the gap Malice put between them.

"No." Malice's lip twitched.

"Oh." They brushed a loose strand of hair behind their ear as they moved back. "And are you as beautiful as those pigs say you are? I feel they would call anything beautiful at this point." They peered in Malice's direction, burn scars encased their glazed, hazy eyes.

"I would say look for yourself, but it seems all you can see is magical energy."

A thin, delirious grin spread on their face. It was quite atrocious. "I like that sense of humor of yours. I was burned some time ago." They touched the start of the fleshy scar below their eye. "But I was given the gift of sight once more from god."

"God?" Malice felt a pair of eyes staring, burning holes into his skin. "You believe *god* gave you the ability to see magic?" It was Charles, recovered from his kick to the groin, who was now eyeing Malice like he was a piece of meat.

What luck to be surrounded by such disgusting cretins.

"Who else would have given me the ability to see someone's true nature?" They raised their voice as they slightly turned their body toward Malice. "To see someone's soul? Like yours. It is red, green, blue, and grey but very dark, muddled."

They squinted before their eyes went wide like a full moon, and a hand went over their mouth as if to stop a gasp that never came. "You have sinned a great deal for your soul to become so dark, haven't you?"

Malice paused momentarily, examining their twisted expression. "Yes, I suppose I have." A part of him wanted to see how far this person would go if he fanned the flames.

They slipped from the crate, spun, and swung their arms out. "A sinner like you needs to be purged from this world!" they preached, catching the attention of everyone in the room, including the guards. "Your evil doings will come to an end today! As will everyone else's here. You, with the power bestowed upon me by god, will die by my hand. I will save you from your wretchedness!"

They were pacing from side to side, and the entire room fell silent listening to their rants. A few guards whispered to one another. One stepped from the wall, their hand hovering next to the spear on their back.

"Is that what you did?" In slow circular movements, Malice moved his arm to rid the knot that had formed in his shoulder from leaning on it the way he had. "Judge people then deem them sinners so you could kill them?" Malice guessed.

The crowd above hushed, and a single muffled voice spoke to the crowd. *Magnus...*

Excitedly, the person swept in closer, so they were face to face with Malice. "Precisely!" They lowered their voice to a whisper, making their horrid breath spread like fog over land in the morning. "Which is why after I kill all of you, I'm going to kill the king!" They bit their lip as they righted their posture. Giddy as they were, Malice wouldn't have been surprised if they had started to prance around singing a song about joy and god.

"I'd like to know the name of my killer," he asked nonchalantly.

They stopped, brushed their clothes off, took a deep breath, and answered, "Kuro. Kuro Mantis."

A fitting name for someone so gangly.

"Kuro." Malice stood and the surrounding people returned to their earlier business, realizing Kuro was spouting drivel.

Placing a hand on their shoulder, Malice pushed them to their knees—the pressure he applied the same he would use to pet a kitten.

"You are no match for the king," he said, caressing the side of Kuro's head while holding their gaze. "And Gareth would hardly allow you to blink let alone give you the chance to harm his majesty." *That man has always been protective over Magnus. I believe that is one of many things that hasn't changed.*

Kuro choked on nothing, their body spasming, eyes bulging. After a moment, Malice walked away at the call of the guards. He glanced behind him to see Kuro stumble to their feet from a puddle, their face red.

The wind rushed through the arena and dark clouds obscured the sky. The heavy scent of rain and salt filled Malice's lungs as he inhaled. He stopped a few meters from the hole they walked out of, observing the faceless crowd. To his left, standing at the edge of a balcony, was Magnus looking down at them and waiting. Gareth stood beside him, scorn darkening his features.

Across the dirt and gravel, Charles watched Malice while Kuro tucked tail and ran to the opposite side of the arena. Excitement and bloodlust thrummed through the arena, the air vibrating with it. Bodies anxiously stood around, heads spinning, feet constantly in motion. Participants searched for their target or didn't care, they simply wanted to kill whoever stood in their path. Unlike the prisoners, the other side—the good side—had been armed with weapons and a handful wore armor. Cheers and screams settled as thunder rumbled in the distance.

The king said, his voice carrying, "The heavens cannot hold their excitement, and neither can you, I'm sure. Now that our fighters are ready, the wait is over." He raised his hand deliberately above his head, "Let the battle royale," and swung it down, "begin!"

The people in the stands burst into cheers as the arena erupted into battle cries, weapons clashing. The use of magic against one another caused the ground to tremble.

Charles lunged toward Malice. For his age, he was quick on his feet. Someone else charged Malice from the left. Charles changed direction, jumped, and landed on the person's shoulder. They stopped, screaming, trying to pull him off. Charles climbed to their back, wrapped his arm around their neck then squeezed and pulled at the same time. They fiercely clawed at his arm, their face turning bright red.

After a time, face an unnatural shade of purple, they stopped clawing and collapsed to the ground. Their body twitched and spasmed before they went still. Charles got to his feet. Sweat dripped from every pore, blood welling from the gashes on his arms, his face contorted with anger and thrill.

"Yer mine to kill!" he declared, closing in on Malice with great strides.

Malice peeked up at Magnus when Charles came to a stop a few meters in front of him. The king was a beautiful sight, radiant as the wind blew his red hair out of place.

"Answer me this," Malice said only to be interrupted by Charles taking a step forward. Malice shifted his foot, creating a rift in the ground. Charles tripped, grunted as he hit the ground with a thud. He spat out the dirt and pebbles that got into his mouth. Charles pushed himself up when Malice used his foot to press his head further into the earth.

"Who helped you move throughout the continent?" He looked down at Charles. As old yet speedy as he was, he had help.

Struggling, Charles moved his face away from the gravel. "I ain't telling ya!" he bellowed.

"You made a deal, didn't you? What could *they* ever want from an old man like you?"

"If ya knew, why d'ya ask?"

"Confirmation. Now—" Malice added force to Charles' skull, glancing up. Two more people, one in a full suit of armor and the other a panther beastman, were charging toward him. "Answer my question."

With a flick of his hand, their heads slipped from the bases of their necks. Their bodies soon followed, and their heads hit the ground, a wet thump, rolling to a stop.

Charles stiffened under Malice's foot. "They would transport me from place to place as long as I killed people."

"That was it?"

The old man wiggled his ass up while pushing against the ground and grunted, "I swear! That was it. As simple as it is, that's all they wanted."

Malice's hold didn't budge. Eventually, Charles was out of breath and finally stopped struggling.

"All right." Malice lifted his foot and Charles sent himself flying. The old man, sighing, got to his feet and rubbed his rear.

It sounded as if *they* didn't know how to bargain, that, or *they* didn't care enough to make the deal a bit more worthwhile. The perfect opportunity to gather forces that knew the regions like the back of their hands wasted.

"Now lemme ask ya something."

Malice perked an eyebrow but said nothing.

"How would ya like to die?" Charles' fingers twitched at his sides, a deep sinister grin creased his face with even more wrinkles.

"In the arms of my king."

Charles gave a puzzling look then a high-pitched cackle pierced the sounds of battle.

The air became dry as claws of water formed on Charles' hands. Malice didn't move a muscle until Charles leaped forth, his arms extended behind him. Malice put his hand out to meet

Charles' face. A black smoke-like substance poured from his palm. Terror flashed across Charles' face, his skin paling. But it was too late. The darkness swallowed him whole.

The black mass twisted and swirled into itself at the closing of Malice's fist until it was nothing. Charles was gone.

A raindrop fell and another, lightning flashed, and thunder boomed. Individual battles continued around Malice, blood stained the arena, and glory-filled screams resounded. He peeked toward the balcony where the king stared at him. At his side, Gareth's mouth gaped open. Someone finally caught on.

AHHH! Malice turned and sidestepped simultaneously. A fairy brought their bardiche down, the axe-like blade embedding itself in the dirt. They scowled up at Malice when he lifted his leg and stomped on the wooden shaft, breaking it in two with his bare foot. The fairy leaped, arms out wide, aiming to tackle Malice or wrap their arms around his legs and bring him down.

Their hands were close, inches away from grabbing his pants.

Bending at the knee, Malice grabbed the fairy's head, his fingers digging into their scalp. They yelped. He smashed their face in using the opposite knee. It crunched like he had stepped on multiple twigs—blood gushed and saturated his knee.

Heavy thuds bounded toward Malice. With a fist full of hair, he lowered his leg and flung the fairy into the person behind him. Fairy and armor collided, toppled to the ground, but only the guard got back on his feet. He brushed off his silver armor—the Alucard's Kingdom sigil on his chest plate—and removed a wooden sword from the sheath on his hip. *I don't think Magnus will be too upset with me for killing one of his men. It's the name of the game after all.*

In the blink of an eye, the guard rushed Malice, arm raised above his head, sword in hand. *Should've used two hands, gives you more power and control.* Malice dodged to the left, the guard followed with a flurry of slashes. His footwork was sloppy; Malice counted the guard almost losing his balance five times. He was young and inexperienced, or old and inexperienced.

Malice reeled from a diagonal attack, slid to the guard's side, and kicked his legs out from underneath him. He fell, his armor clunking to the earth as the guard let out a cry of pain. One hand went around the guard's neck, while the other went to the guard's face, Malice's fingers wrapping around them tightly. He yanked his hands in opposite directions before the guard could react. The sound of bones snapping, and flesh tearing was reminiscent of a hungry bear devouring its prey using teeth and claws. Malice gently nudged the guard's body, it fell forward and hit the dirt, his head dripping from the helmet in Malice's hand. After a second, he dropped his head too.

The rain came down heavier, cooling the air. Malice closed his eyes and took a deep breath, enjoying the cold droplets hitting his skin. He had gotten what he wanted, and barely half of the criminals remained. So, when boredom struck, he figured the Games had gone on long enough for the people to get their fill of enjoyment.

Palms facing the sky, Malice lifted his arms, the black from his long nails traveled up his fingers, stopping at his knuckles. He jerked his hands up and darkness surged from the earth. Royals, guards, convicts, and mercenaries screeched or cursed and struggled as darkness climbed their legs, unwilling to let them go.

The ground absorbed every bit of light and refused to give it back. Fear twisted the meaningless faces throughout the audience. Darkness swallowed everyone whole in mere seconds, the coliseum now silent. Malice swung his arms down and out, commanding his magic to settle into the ground. It did, like water splashing down in all directions. Blood splattered the dirt like paint flung onto a canvas. Nothing else was left in the darkness's wake.

When Malice walked to the center of the arena, lightning broke past the clouds and thunder boomed, the ground quaking. From the balcony, cushioning his fall with layers of static, Gareth crashed to the earth. A cloud of dust veiled him, the wind blowing it away. After unclipping it from his belt, his chain cracked against the gravel, pale blue lightning hungrily engulfed it.

"How dare you!" Gareth shouted as he sped toward Malice. "Who do you think you are to come here and ruin the Games like this?"

Gareth, skidding forward, hurled his chains. They wrapped around Malice three times, singeing his clothes. Then he yanked full force, stopping Malice with a hand to his chest. Breath hissed through Malice's lips from the impact.

"I have every reason to kill you right here and right now, Malice!" he snarled, his entire face screwed from anger.

"Do you?" Malice asked with a smirk.

Before Gareth could respond, his body went rigid. His grip loosened on the chains, the lightning disappeared, and in turn they slipped from his hands and off Malice. He staggered, grasping at his chest, trying to breathe. Then he stopped. Relief seemed to wash over him, relaxing his stiff demeanor, but it was fleeting.

Pacify burns like a bitch, Malice thought, the hairs on his arms standing on edge.

Gareth whipped around. Startled, he stumbled over himself and into Malice, who steadied the knight. The king stood behind him, wings like a hawk flapping and folding against his back.

Fists clenched at his sides, the king approached, his scowl fixing on Gareth. "How dare you act without orders!"

He slapped Gareth. The knight staggered sideways, almost falling over, but caught himself. A handprint formed on his cheek.

"You are relieved of duty for the rest of the day and tomorrow. Get your head out of your ass!" Magnus growled in a low tone.

Gareth's eyes went wide, and he stuttered over his words when Magnus glared. "You. are. dismissed."

A muscle tensed in Gareth's jaw. He bowed and left through the gate the fighters came from.

Malice patted out the smoking patches on his shirt while the king watched Gareth disappear into the coliseum. His lilac eyes shifted, looking Malice's body up and down. He sighed.

"Come. Let's get you cleaned and changed out of those clothes." Magnus nodded toward the gate, his feet following. Disappointment was heavy in his tone, but he kept his head held high and his shoulders stiff.

Malice dipped his head. "Thank you."

Magnus didn't respond. Two holes revealed his freckled back where his wings grew from, it made Malice smile as he stayed a few steps behind. Up above, guards guided and ushered the people toward the exit. A little over half of the people were already gone when Malice left the arena, and the rain thickened.

The Truth
IX

"You made quite the entrance today." Magnus paced from one end of the meeting room to the other.

The space was longer than it was wide, with a rectangular, dark-stained wood table at the center. To one side of the table was a wall of high arched windows, grape vines carved into the molding. Behind Magnus was a painting of the castle's garden in full bloom. In each corner and in between the windows, a small round table held something—a vase, candles, a pitcher of water, and cups. The floor of blues, whites, and gold highlighted the trading routes of the region, and a chandelier of glass, creating patches of rainbows, hung from the ceiling.

"You killed a child in my streets. You disappeared, seemingly, off the face of the continent for years. Why?" Magnus stopped at the head of the table beside his chair. "Who were you after? It's clear you weren't following Charles, but you were following someone attached to him. Who was it?"

The castle servants had drawn Malice a bath, then provided clean clothes that were slightly big on him, the wide neckline drooping to show his prominent collarbone.

"Charles moved far too quickly for his age. It said so in a report I stole from Raelle's Region. He disappeared without a trace." Malice leaned onto the table, allowing the edge to dig into his hip. "It was peculiar, so I looked into it and discovered who was helping him."

The more Malice talked, the more Joseph's death shrunk from Magnus's thoughts. "Who?"

"Voidents."

Confusion furrowed Magnus's brows, his head cocked to the side.

"Creatures of darkness," Malice elaborated.

Magnus gave a slow nod and rested his elbows on the back of the chair.

"Voidents have one goal and that is to kill by any means necessary."

"Even recruiting people to do their dirty work." Magnus caught on quickly. "Find the ones who enjoy killing and offer them a deal they can't resist; keep killing and you'll never be caught." He frowned as Malice inclined his head. "But why are you after them?"

"It's the other way around."

"You've encountered them in the past?" Magnus's eyebrow peaked. "What did you do to make them so concerned about you?"

"Few know the existence of voidents to be real. Most believe they are creatures created by minds null of sanity," he said in a roundabout way, then shrugged after seeing Magnus's unamused demeanor. "I killed thousands of them. I think that would piss just about anyone off."

So, it was more than just knowing about their existence. Magnus sighed and pulled the chair out before sitting down. The subject at hand was growing to be a headache. Besides, he had other questions he would have answered today.

"You vanished after the first Kings Summit you had attended as a ruler. Why?" Magnus had a feeling the issue on the voidents wouldn't be going anywhere, anytime soon. They could talk about them later. Malice was being cooperative right now, but that could change at any moment.

"I didn't find my presence necessary," Malice answered instantly in a level tone. Bumping off the table, he walked to the windows, Magnus's eyes following him closely.

"I stayed within my region, doing whatever I needed to cleanse it of the filth my predecessors left behind."

Magnus had heard rumors about the previous rulers of Hordes Region and how they were corrupt. Even Malice had concerns, but to think they were true after all.

"The poison they injected into the kingdom, into the land, ran thick and deep. I tried for many years to purge it the best I could, but it only did so much." Malice watched the storm outside as it waged on, the trees whipping and the wind howling.

"So, you destroyed the kingdom," Magnus said, "the heart of the issue?"

Malice nodded when he turned away from the windows and came back to the table. "It worked. Hordes Region is flourishing more than ever."

"Starting anew... Did you kill everyone?"

He chuckled dryly, "No, I didn't," and gave a small smile. "I made arrangements with the other kingdoms and cities in the region to allow my people refuge. All were welcomed with open arms."

Magnus felt himself relax, but quickly stiffened his posture. Now was not the time to let his guard down. "The ruins of the kingdom had no sign of remains and that would explain why." Although he never went in person, Gareth and his Unit and many others from all over the continent had. It was a great kingdom, larger than Alucard's, reduced to ash and rubble overnight. The rulers thought everyone had perished when it was destroyed, himself included. The memory still felt like a fresh scar in his mind.

"A king is nothing without their people. Isn't that what you once told me?" Malice asked, a smile on his lips.

Magnus's eyebrows jumped up, the corners of his mouth curved into a smirk. "Indeed, I did. I'm a bit surprised you remembered." He had told Malice what his mother told him. He was a child at the time, and didn't understand what it meant, but it sounded remarkable, especially coming from his mother. At the Kings Summit, Magnus declared the phrase in earnest.

Silence descended, and Magnus took the opportunity to study Malice. He understood why Gareth couldn't fully recognize the ruler before them. They were the same height now, whereas Malice had always been shorter than Magnus—that mostly had to do with their age. His voice was much deeper than Magnus's now, as well. His figure was leaner, his shoulders broader, muscles defined like a statue's. The curls he once had were gone, white flares and waves replaced them.

Appearance aside, what changed the most was him. Malice had become colder, crueler. The dead, miserable look in his eyes changed to something more, something that sent shivers down Magnus's spine the first time they locked eyes in front of the coliseum.

From the edge of the table, Malice stepped closer to Magnus. As he did, the royal blue teardrop earring sparkled in the light.

Magnus's lips parted, his mind gone blank. "You kept it?" The words left his mouth before he could think about withholding them. "I was sure you had thrown it away."

Magnus was nine and Malice was four. Their fathers had brought them to the King's Summit and for Malice, it was his first time. Intending to make a friend, Magnus had given one of his earrings to him. He could tell Malice was uncomfortable, so it was partially to ease his worries. Malice accepted yet examined the earring as if he had never received something and didn't know how to handle it. Ultimately, he shoved it in his pocket. However, every year afterward, the bright blue gem dangled from Malice's ear.

Magnus smiled, a part of him wishing they could return to such times.

Malice stopped beside him. "Why would I do that?"

"We had lost touch and grown distant. I wouldn't be surprised if you had thrown it out to curse me without cursing me." Something flashed on Malice's face. Was it anger? Or pain? Maybe both.

"I have more self-control than that," Malice said while sitting down, leaving a chair of space between them—a careful proximity. "I may have been upset, but I would never have thrown it out."

"I see." Magnus readjusted his collar. "I'm glad you have been accommodating thus far. I hope you will continue to be, as I have many things to ask you," he said in a matter-of-fact tone. *I'm getting too wrapped up in my memories.*

"Anything you want to know, I shall tell you." Malice placed his elbow on the table and rested his chin on his thin hand, the bones and veins of his wrist creating ridges.

Magnus pitched him a suspicious look. "Why are you being so cooperative?"

"I didn't realize that was a problem," he retorted with a smirk.

"It's not… I just didn't expect it."

"Understandable." His expression eased, his sharp eyes softening. "I guess you could say I'm trying to get back in your good graces."

Magnus pushed his chair out so he could swing one leg over the other. Not taking this opportunity to learn the truth would be a fool's mistake. Conversation poured from his mouth alongside questions, and Malice answered. While he talked, Magnus tried to discern truth from lie but he couldn't. Ever since he was a kid, Magnus recalled, Malice hadn't lied. Almost as if he couldn't or didn't know how, which made things easier for Magnus.

*

Luckily, the baths were empty, allowing Gareth to soak in peace. Tiles of green and brown twisted to form a tree on the floor. Gold lined the pools of steaming water while the inside was sapphire. The white walls were bare save for the golden heads of lions spewing water into the baths and hooks to hang towels and robes. Against the wall were stools and buckets. Some had soap in them, but most were empty.

Gareth slowly tilted his head, then jerked his shoulder down, forcing his neck to pop before he did the other side. He placed his arms on the edge of the pool, his eyes tracing the lightning scar on his left arm up to his shoulder. As he remembered the day he got it, he snickered at his kid self for thinking he could pull off such a large-scale attack and not suffer the consequences afterward. The confidence he projected had come to bite him in the ass, that was for sure.

He closed his eyes and took a deep breath, hoping the bath would remedy his headache.

As frustrating as it was, Gareth knew what he had done was wrong. Malice won fairly. Even with his magical energy drained to nearly nothing, he overwhelmed his opponents. The point of a game was to have a victor, the Games of Retribution were no exception.

Thinking back, he could not recall everything clearly. A lot of it was a blur of emotions. When Malice used dark magic to kill Charles, he knew Magnus was right, and then rage started a blaze in his stomach. After that, it was blank until Magnus's slap woke him up.

Unconsciously, Gareth lifted his hand and caressed his cheek. The mark was gone, disappeared before he even left the arena. He pushed himself to his feet, stepping toward the center of the bath where it was the deepest, and plunged his body in. The water rushed over every inch of his skin, a warm, soothing embrace.

To harbor such intense feelings of contempt for Malice bewildered him—they were unwarranted, yet he could not shake it off.

He came up for a breath, fingers pushing through his hair, and ran a hand over his face. Gareth admitted he had never been particularly fond of Malice, but he had never wanted to hurt him. Now, however, something was different. Every time he found his thoughts focused on Malice again, his stomach would churn. When he was a child, Gareth felt pity for Malice in the way one would see an abandoned, scruffy kitten in an alley and feel sorry for it. Then he changed. His attitude grew cocky, and the look in his eyes told everyone they were below him. Gareth clicked his tongue at the thought.

He rose and sloshed out of the water after a time. From one of the many hooks, he grabbed a towel, ruffled his hair somewhat dry, and wrapped it around his waist. Directly connected to the baths, on the left, was a changing room with benches and shelves lining two walls. Fully drying his body, Gareth dressed in clean, simple clothes, and headed to his room on the third floor of the castle, across from the king's bedchamber. The many stacks of reports and statements seemed to, unfortunately, be calling his name. He doubted his mind would settle down enough to get things done anytime soon.

*

In the evening, the storm clouds were gone, leaving everything soaked and dripping. The moon shone in a sliver between the ever-moving haze. Despite the warmth of spring, there was a deep chill in the air, even with the sputtering, crackling fire in the hearth.

Once he exchanged his shoes for slippers, Magnus moseyed from the bedside to the wall, running his fingers along the edge of the bookshelves, his eyes glued to Malice. He lay sprawled across the couch Magnus had placed in his room during dinner, a chalice of red wine in his hand.

The king's bedchamber was bigger than a small cottage. An enormous bed was centered against the right wall, a nightstand, and an armchair on either side. Beside the couch, two more chairs sat, a table stacked full of papers in between them. Bookcases, crammed with books and files, wrapped around the doors. On the opposite side was the balcony, the glass doors looking out onto the garden. Blotches of white and dark grey marbled the floor of lapis lazuli while the walls were plain white.

Grape vines carved the crown molding, matching the rest of the castle, and a grand chandelier with gold accents hung from the center of the ceiling.

If Malice were trying to get on Magnus's good side again, he wouldn't be stupid enough to do anything rash. Unless he was blowing smoke up Magnus's ass, of course. Still, it was hard to believe Malice could be reckless enough to harm Magnus. It would start a war. The entire continent would be against Hordes Region. *Malice is powerful, but is he powerful enough to take on an entire continent?* Nearing the door, Magnus checked his fingers—no dust—and let his hand drop to his side before he walked to his desk.

Malice drank as if he had not tasted a drop of wine in years, both guzzling it down and savoring it at the same time. Magnus turned to search for some papers on his mess of a desk— like the one in his study, it seemed he couldn't escape it—and eventually found what he was looking for.

He tossed a stack of papers in front of Malice, sitting in the armchair.

"Read them," Magnus said as he leaned forward and grabbed the chalice of wine, swirled it, took a draught. Malice sat up, put his cup down, and started flipping through the pages. Somewhere in the middle of the stack, Malice plucked out a crinkled piece of paper. When he pulled the document thin, recognition shimmered in his eyes.

"Are you asking if I wrote them?" Malice passed the letter to Magnus.

"It's your handwriting, is it not?"

Malice nodded and continued to scan the parchment. "It is. I scribbled them down and tossed them aside. I wasn't entirely sure if your royals would even pick them up."

"Thanks to those, we were able to capture Charles before he escaped." His expression went sour, and he put the chalice down. "You should have killed him, so he wouldn't have had the chance to kill anyone else. I was disappointed, to say the least, when I learned you had not." The *Minding The Peace* law could be excused by the region's ruler. Malice knew this. He also should have known that Magnus would have pardoned him for killing Charles. Any of the rulers would have.

"He was caught in the end," Malice said coldly. "Besides, as I said to Gareth, it had nothing to do with me."

Magnus frowned. "Why involve yourself by warning Joseph only to kill him, then?" Malice's motives remained as clear as obsidian.

He reclined, throwing an arm over the back of the couch. "I warned him for the hell of it. I knew he wasn't going to listen to me. And I killed him out of convenience. It was better that I took his life rather than Charles, anyway."

"What makes you say that?"

"He was in the cell next to mine. He rambled on and on about how he would torture Joseph with stories of what he did to his sister as he slaughtered him." Malice's green eyes glinted orange as the flames danced. "I showed him mercy compared to what Charles would have done if he got his hands on Joseph. Not that it matters now that both are dead."

"By your hand," he reminded.

Disgusted, Magnus shifted in his seat, unable to get comfortable as he tried to shove Charles out of his mind. The other regions had sent letters to Magnus, both warning him and offering their help to find him. His appearance was as common as a bronze coin. A few reports throughout the continent stated that someone had seen Charles. However, it was never the old blacksmith. The monster had been all over Vinyamar long before he came to Alucard's Region. The details of the letters made him lose any appetite he had, even if he didn't have one, to begin with.

"But I suppose you're right." Magnus sighed, reached for the chalice, and chugged what remained of the wine. "Even still, it doesn't sit well with me, what you or Charles have done." Magnus rubbed his eyes.

"Don't worry, I will eventually meet the justice death provides, just like Charles," Malice said, his tone void of emotion.

Magnus frowned. "That is not what I meant." Hearing him talk so low of himself hurt more than he would have guessed. It reminded him of the little boy who would sit across from him, eyes glued to the ground as he spoke in almost a whisper.

Malice briefly observed Magnus. "You look to have another question on your mind. Ask it."

Even more uncomfortable, Magnus grabbed the pitcher of burgundy liquid and poured himself another cup. "Why did you come back?" he asked, setting the pitcher down, the wine warming his chest and gut faster than the fire. "You said earlier that you've been traveling, so why come back now?"

Malice raised an eyebrow. "I always return for the Games."

Magnus sat up straighter, his eyes growing bigger.

"I rarely come as early as I did, but I plan to stay for a while. It's the time I get to rest and relax while taking the opportunity to see you."

Magnus glanced at the clock ticking on the mantle. "How silly." Abruptly, he stood and marched to the closet behind him, near the desk. "To travel to Alucard's Region every year for a few days just to watch the Games? Am I supposed to believe you haven't come for another reason?"

He picked out a set of nightclothes for Malice and himself, then, undoing the buttons of his shirt, undressed.

"There has to be another reason to make coming all the way here worth your while. What is it?" Once he had changed, he tossed Malice's garments out to him.

When Malice finished, Magnus came out of the closet with a pillow and blanket in hand. Malice's chest was bare, the red silk shirt on the arm of the couch.

If Malice were to stay anywhere in the castle, it would be here in the king's bedchamber, where he could keep an eye on him. Malice had been docile, but if he acted out, Magnus was confident he could stop Malice. Kill him if need be. That was a task his royals were unfit to complete.

After handing the pillow and blanket to Malice, he walked toward his bed and stopped beside it. "How long do you plan to stay?" Magnus finally asked when he turned to face Malice.

Swiftly making his bed on the couch, Malice looked up. "About a year, maybe less, maybe more. Depends on what I can accomplish."

"You *are* here for another reason."

"This time, yes."

Magnus stared without a word, being exchanged for a fleeting time. Malice had filled in many holes earlier, but not everything. His end goal was unclear, and Magnus didn't know if he should be cautious or trust him. The voidents, creatures born of darkness, played a crucial role. He knew that much. So would he and his people at some point. If it came down to it, Magnus would have to choose his home, his people, his land over Malice. Malice knew that too, or at least he should.

"Goodnight, Malice." Magnus drew the sheets back and crawled into bed.

"Goodnight." Malice did the same before spinning his hand around and closing his fist to put the blaze out. The smell of timber and smoke filled the room.

Magnus's mind raced with the events of the past few days. It was more hectic than it had been in years, and he had a gut-wrenching feeling that it would not calm down for quite some time.

For however long, Magnus tossed and turned, finally deciding to roll out of bed. He felt groggy, more so than usual. As his feet swung over the edge and hit the cold floor, a shiver raked his body. He stretched and cringed at the sudden kink in his neck from sleeping wrong. Golden specks danced in the air. Outside, a bird flew past the balcony while the breeze swayed the trees in the garden.

It was time to start the day—the clock confirmed as much—when Magnus shuffled to the closet. He paused at the side of the couch. Malice slept soundly on his back, his arm tucked under his head. The darkness beneath his eyes led Magnus to believe that Malice didn't know how to sleep. He stood there, watching the rise and fall of Malice's chest. His focus shifted to his face. Soft, almost pudgy features had faded with maturity, but he still had those two beauty marks under his right eye.

Malice's eyes sprang open, darting around the room and landing on Magnus, which startled him. Dazed by his surroundings, Malice took a breath and calmed down.

"Are… you all right?" Magnus wasn't sure if Malice was awake enough to comprehend what he said and give a straight answer, but he had never seen Malice react like that. Toward anything.

Malice gave a sluggish nod as he sat up. "… Good morning." His white, fluffy hair was a mess. He appeared lost rather than confused.

"Good morning."

Leaving Malice to wake up, Magnus returned to his earlier task and went to the closet to pick out an outfit for Malice. Their builds were different. Magnus was bulkier and wider, so he threw a belt on top of the folded garments and brought them out to Malice. In the closet, clothes rustled, and the belt clicked. He hated servants tending to him outside of tiding his bedchamber; it reminded him too much of his father.

Magnus chose a simple maroon shirt, black trousers, and an overcoat to match the blouse. Magnus had chosen an all-black outfit for Malice. It had an open back comparable to the one he wore yesterday while the pants were loose. When Magnus emerged from the wardrobe, Malice was already dressed and waited on the edge of the couch, outwardly recovered from his earlier discombobulation. He stood when Magnus crossed the room and joined him by the door.

"Am I to stay with you? Or would you like it if I left?" Malice asked.

"We will be sticking together," Magnus said, his eyes momentarily meeting Malice's. "I don't trust you yet."

Malice arched his brow. "Usually if someone doesn't trust another, a servant or a royal watches after them."

"You won't hurt me, nor would you start anything with me. If you did, I would be the only one able to stop you." Light conquered the dark, always had. Malice and Magnus proved that as children, while playing with their magic. Physically, Magnus was confident he was stronger than Malice. Speed, magic, and experience, however, were not on his side. Not anymore. Magnus would feign otherwise, though.

Malice considered Magnus for a heartbeat and nodded. "You probably could." Smirking, he gestured to the door. "After you."

Soon after a silent breakfast in the dining hall, Magnus started his day in his study, reading letters, reports, requests, and so on, just like any other. Meanwhile, Malice lounged on the furniture nearby. Every now and again, he would get up and grab a book, flip through the pages, then return it to the empty slot. His inability to relax for more than a few minutes was proving difficult to ignore.

Magnus sighed as he set his papers down. "If you are that antsy, you should explore the castle. Especially if you intend on staying here as long as you say." He knew how contradictory he was, but Magnus needed to concentrate on his kingdom, and he could always have someone track Malice. As long as he stayed in the castle, Magnus could reach him before anything got out of hand.

Malice grunted in a contemplating way and turned toward Magnus. "I apologize for distracting you. I'm not quite sure what to do now that I can truly relax a bit."

A twinge of pity rose within Magnus, but only for a second. When Joseph and the Games resurfaced, he frowned, "You can take your indecision elsewhere," and picked up a piece of paper from a shorter stack to his right. "I'm busy."

Malice's expression hardened the longer he stared at Magnus. He caught Malice's questioning gaze, held it, and recalled everything Malice told him yesterday, clearing his memories of Joseph like smoke in the wind.

"That mask you're wearing," Malice said as he moved toward the door, "must work well with others if you can wear it in front of me." The door opened, and Malice glanced over his shoulder. He left while Magnus remained bewildered at his desk.

"We have reports of eight more disappearances, your majesty," a royal informed, his armor shimmering in the afternoon light from the windows. His name was Corgan, a Royal Knight rank S, his subordinate beside him.

"Where?" Magnus asked, his brows creasing the bridge of his nose

"Everywhere."

Magnus clicked his tongue. Someone tapped his shoulder. He turned to see a maid shyly standing behind him. Her eyes darted to the floor, then to the wall and to Magnus, subsequently falling back to the ground.

"Your majesty… we can't find Sir Malice," she said with a bit of panic in her voice.

Snapping his head up, Magnus looked from the maid to his royals. "Excuse me," he said to the knights and rushed around them.

When Malice left after lunch, Magnus had relayed a message to his servants; monitor Malice, make sure his whereabouts are known at all times. *This was a bad idea after all… but would he do anything in another ruler's home?*

The first place Magnus thought to search was in the library on the second floor. Malice had enjoyed books ever since he was young. It made sense to search there when he used to bury himself in stories for hours, days even.

Up the staircase covered in dark royal blue carpet, he raced to the eastern wing. Upon spotting him, servants and royals avoided their king like he was a disease.

The double doors leading into the library were huge, a tree carved in the wood. They opened with a heavy drawn-out creak, exposing a high-ceilinged room, rows of shelves on both sides of the library. Tables and desks had lamps and writing materials at the center of the space. The rear wall overlooked the garden and let in plenty of natural light for plants to grow and wrap around the windowsills. Down each section of books and climbing up to the balcony where books filled the walls, Magnus found no trace of Malice.

As Magnus walked past the windows, he massaged his temples when something moved out of his periphery. He froze and glanced down at the garden to see a head of white sitting on the edge of the fountain. With a sigh, he made his way down to the garden.

The scent of the sea, grass, and flowers carried on the warm breeze. It was peaceful outside. Bird song and rustling leaves were enough to put Magnus at ease. He walked along a stone path, ducking below the branches of small, low-hanging trees and limbs of wild plants. At the center of the garden was a fountain of marble and a statue of a woman, her body soft and curvy, water surrounding her feet and flowing into the pool.

Magnus stopped at the edge of the plants. Malice sat on the fountain's ledge, enjoying the fresh air, Magnus guessed. He was stunning, emptying Magnus's mind until Malice swung his gaze to Magnus.

"I've been looking for you," Magnus said as he approached. "How long have you been here?"

"Not long," Malice answered softly. He shifted his attention to the violet, white, and bright red pansies in front of him once more.

"They're one of the few blooms in the garden that can survive through winter." Magnus stood next to Malice.

"This mask you speak of," Magnus glared down at Malice and resisted the urge to turn his head toward him, so they were face to face, "what makes you think I'm wearing one?"

"I saw how you acted when Joseph was in front of the coliseum. When I killed him," he said, "you—"

"Look at me when you speak," Magnus said as he reached for Malice's chin, but stopped himself and let his arm fall to his side. It didn't matter if he was sitting or standing, the least he could do was look at Magnus during their conversation. It was basic mannerisms.

Caught off guard, Malice stared for a heartbeat, then stood, dipping his head with a grin. "My apologies." His tone and expression lacked sincerity.

"You felt nothing for Joseph's pitiful situation, nor did you feel anything when I killed him," Malice stated as if it was not conjecture but fact.

Magnus slid one foot behind him, his eyes darting to the fountain. "Of course, I was upset. Why wouldn't I be?"

"Why *should* you have been upset?" Malice retorted. "You did not know the boy."

"It is my job to care for my people." Magnus's eyebrows furrowed as he attempted to sound irritated.

"It is," Malice agreed. "However, it is not your job to take things personally. The crime has been paid for. The people who caused his death are either dead or under your thumb."

Magnus half snorted and half grunted when he turned away briefly, then met Malice's green eyes. Unlike the day Joseph died, it felt as though he was looking at Magnus rather than through him. He had almost forgotten that Malice was a king; he had a similar habit when they were kids. More often than not, Magnus had forgotten Malice was a prince.

"For the sake of my people, I will fake whatever I need to."

A flash of anger washed over Malice's face. "You can do whatever you want in front of your people, even your royals, but in front of me, is there a need to?" He almost sounded hurt.

Magnus didn't have a comeback for that. They stared at each other for a while, the wind whistling and the bugs humming, the birds chirping, while the salty draft caressed their faces.

Taking a deep breath, Malice put distance between them. "If you'll excuse me," He bowed his head, "I have much of the castle left to explore. I'll see you for dinner."

In his study, Magnus's legs bounced furiously under the desk and the words on the paper scrambled to where he couldn't decipher the letters. He tossed them down, letting out a long sigh when his shoulder blades and spine pressed into the wood of his chair.

Even if Malice was right, the king had a duty and an image to uphold. The people of this region deserved a king who showed them kindness and compassion, as opposed to disdain and annoyance. His father appeared before him, just for an instant. Abhorrence, for himself and his father, spoiled his blood like milk.

Magnus had plenty of time to gather himself before dinner. The dining hall on the first floor was lively with knights chatting over food and drink, friends and comrades surrounding them. As he walked past, a few friendly smiles and a dip of the head greeted him, to which he returned.

Malice was at the table closest to the windows at the far end of the hall, sipping on a gold goblet of alcohol, most likely wine. The evening sun painted the clouds' soft hues of pink, ginger, and lavender, while the sky faded from a pale blue to a dark, rich azure. Without a word, Malice grabbed the pitcher to his left and inclined it toward Magnus. He lifted his cup and Malice filled the goblet. As he set the pitcher down, a butler rushed to the side of the table.

"Your plates will be out shortly, your majesty," they said. Just as quickly as they came, they left.

By now, the fat chef Terkin would have come out, declared what had been made, and then paraded back to the kitchen. The chef must be Jargus today, an aloof fairy with wings like a beetle's.

Swirling it around, Magnus took a sip, savoring the citrus tang of the wine. The alcohol went down smoothly, warming him up.

The silence had become uncomfortable, but what could he say? The matter of the Games and Joseph no longer bothered him. What Malice said in the garden, however, did. Malice had a point. He saw through his mask easily, so there was no reason to keep up the facade, but there was something about the way he approached the subject that irked Magnus.

"I remember," Malice said abruptly, startling Magnus out of his thoughts, "when we were kids." A small smile tugged at the corners of his mouth. "I told you I wanted to count all the freckles I could see. You laughed and said that it was impossible, that you had too many to count."

Magnus remembered it, too. In one of the abandoned rooms during the King's Summit, they hid from their parents and the other rulers. Magnus ran away first, but Malice followed, despite knowing they would both get in trouble. Gareth located them soon after and gave them two hours before they had to return to the summit. They talked, showed each other their magic, then talked some more.

Malice glanced from his goblet up to Magnus, eyes gleaming. "I would like to try, anyway."

The smile on Magnus's face vanished.

A plate of steaming food was placed in front of Magnus and Malice, the chance to respond gone. "Dinner is served," the same butler from earlier said and scurried into the kitchen.

Malice was good at getting a rise out of people, always had been.

During and after dinner, Magnus found himself seeking a reason to stay mad at Malice and kept coming up short. He spent a few more hours in his study trying to finish what he was too distracted to do earlier. The ticking clock on the mantle caught his attention one too many times and reminded him of all the questions that still lingered in his mind.

Finally, calling it a night, Magnus headed to his bedchamber, passing a few servants in the hallway. When he entered, Malice sat in an armchair with a book in his hands—Alucard's journal—while the hearth's fire popped and snapped. The shadows dancing on Malice's face and person, his position, everything about him emulated a painting, disrupting Magnus's thoughts. He forced himself from his mind, crossed the room, and quickly stripped, changing into his nightclothes. He got a pair of silk forest green trousers for Malice. After tossing the pair of pants to Malice, Magnus went to bed, the mattress supple and chilly. A moment later, the couch creaked under Malice's weight.

"It'll be a hard habit to break," Magnus broke the silence. Malice's curious eyes peeked over the top of the couch. "But I will try my best not to hide from you." He paused. "I am not sorry for how I acted. We are not kids anymore, we are adults, kings. I know that if you wanted to harm me or my royals, you had ample opportunity to do so and didn't. That doesn't mean I fully trust you. It's enough to give you a choice for tomorrow."

"A choice about what?" Malice inquired.

"Whether you'd like your own room in the castle and if you want to spend the day with me."

Malice contemplated for a moment while Magnus pulled the covers over his legs, sitting against the headboard.

"First," Malice said, "I'm sorry for the trouble I have caused. Second, I do not wish to have a room. I've not slept this soundly in years. And third, I would like to observe your royals training tomorrow."

Magnus stared at Malice wide-eyed and a bit flabbergasted. "Of all things, why is that something you want to do?"

"After witnessing a few of your royals at the Games and how Gareth reacted to your pacify, I'm curious," he said. "Perhaps I could help strengthen your royals once I see them up close."

Magnus's eyes narrowed on Malice… but it was a tempting offer. "… Is this related to what you told me yesterday or because you want to rub my inadequacy in my face?"

"Voidents are not something to play around with, Magnus. They are here now whether I am or not. Eventually, they will stop pussyfooting around and start attacking you and your people directly."

"Personal experience?"

Malice nodded. "Better to be prepared. Know your weaknesses now and nip them in the bud before they become your downfall."

How can I argue with that? "Fine, under one condition. You will listen to Gareth, his word is law in the coliseum, understood?"

"Understood."

If there was anyone to learn from, it was Malice, Basia, or Thorn, the three most reputable fighters amongst the rulers. No one Magnus knew could hold a candle to those three, most of all Malice, who had once killed thousands of men in the span of an hour without so much as a scratch. That was hearsay, though. One of these days, Magnus would ask for the details.

To Learn

X

After a day of absence, Gareth waited for his group of royals to arrive, hands at his backside. He'd spent yesterday cooped up in his room working on reports and statements, and now his muscles were stiff. He rolled his shoulders and flexed his back in hopes of relieving some of the discomfort.

Training started at dawn and went on for five hours, just in time for lunch, before patrol began. Each hour was spent with an instructor, a royal knight, who taught their specialty. Close combat, hand-to-hand combat, long-distance, healing, regeneration, magic, mid-range combat, teamwork, defense, and assassination—Gareth taught mid-range. Royals were split between cycles of the day, morning, afternoon, evening, and night for training and patrol around the kingdom.

Royals were made to run the edge of the arena for twenty minutes, longer if a punishment was in order. When finished, they split and lined themselves in front of the knight they were assigned to when they became a royal.

Gareth would be eager, excited if it were not for someone inviting himself and floating next to him humming an annoying melody.

The king and Malice joined Gareth in the foyer that morning. Malice stated his wish to observe training, perhaps to be of some assistance. Gareth did not have the chance to reject the offer before the king said, "As long as you two behave, there shouldn't be any problems." And that was the end of it. It seemed a decision had been reached prior to him waking up. On the way to the coliseum, Gareth told Malice what to expect and to keep himself in line. Strangely, he had agreed, which seemed far too easy.

Sweat bubbled on the royals' skin as they caught their breath and formed four rows of ten in front of Gareth. Royals flocked to their instructors all over the arena, loud stomps echoing through the coliseum.

Minutes passed and everyone had settled into their places. With only one stipulation—you had to be over fifteen to become a royal or guard—his group was diverse.

"Today," Gareth announced as he glanced over the many faces, "you will spar. The person standing next to you will be your partner. Once you acknowledge them—" Royals looked from one side to the next, nodding in silent confirmation to their partner, some happier than others—"You will pick a weapon, then come, and form a circle around me. Go!"

Gareth walked forward as royals rushed past him. Weapons from close to long range were displayed on racks against the coliseum walls. Armor, rags, targets and wooden or straw dummies were as well.

Malice hummed like an unrelenting fly buzzing in Gareth's ears.

"Get down here," Gareth demanded. Malice dropped his legs and gingerly placed himself on the ground a meter from Gareth.

The royals, weapons in hand, circled them.

"Why is the champion of the Games here, sir? And who is he?" someone shouted.

Gareth sighed, expecting someone to ask that sooner or later. "This," he gestured to Malice, "is Malice Reap."

"King Malice Reap?" a royal questioned with surprise.

"A king is not a criminal," a voice behind Malice broke through the murmurs. He smiled.

"You may be Malice Reap, but I doubt you qualify as a ruler." The same royal guard who had hauled Malice to the prison stepped forth, wearing leather armor over her chest, arms, and legs. Ida scowled, her thick eyebrows creasing her forehead. "Besides, news had spread of your death two years ago. Are you saying that it was all a fib?"

"You shouldn't believe every rumor you hear if it is not supported by evidence," Malice said in a smug tone.

Gareth stepped in, a hand out to stop Ida from entering the circle any further. "He is, as you can see, alive. As unfortunate as that is." He shot a glare in Malice's direction.

Ida scoffed, rolled her eyes, and stopped amidst the front row of people.

Gareth looked Malice up and down. *To observe and perhaps be of some assistance,* the demon had said.

"Everyone," Gareth turned his attention toward the circle, "take ten steps back." After a very brief moment of stillness, the royals followed their orders, opening the space around Malice and Gareth considerably.

"You up for a quick spar?" *Might as well put him to use since he offered himself so generously in front of the king.*

Malice spoke, his tone sly. "Looking for a chance to flaunt your stones to your students?"

Gareth's smirk vanished, and a vein throbbed on his forehead as his jaw clenched.

"Tell me the rules of your little dance."

The king must have told Malice something before they met in the foyer to make him so docile. Not that Gareth minded, he was easier to deal with. Not any less annoying, but the king could only do so much to tame him.

"We will not be using any specialty. Fight however you'd like." He added, "To make things a bit more even between us, you can choose one element, excluding darkness."

"Your wish is my command." Malice walked backward a bit while Gareth unclipped his chains from his belt, assuming Malice would use earth to combat his lightning.

"I'll be using earth."

I was right. Wrapping one end of the chain around his hand, Gareth cracked it against the ground as lightning engulfed it. "We spar until one of us is on their ass."

Against Malice, Gareth glanced over his shoulder, regretting the fact that he did not bring his dual blades today. He did not think he would end up sparring until the offer left his mouth.

Malice folded the sleeves of his grey-blue frilled shirt—one that was awfully familiar—up to his elbows. Then, holding his hand out, he stomped his foot, conjuring a curved dagger. He caught it, split it in two, and created dual blades. Even at a distance, Gareth could see the blades were blunt and rounded at the tips. That must be a stab at him for not bringing his secondary weapons. He clicked his tongue.

The anticipation of the royals surrounding them was visceral as activity slowed to a halt around the field and the crowd grew bigger.

It was quiet, motionless in the coliseum, everyone waiting for the first attack. Gareth was confident… to an extent. Rumors only held so much truth, if any, and that was all he had to gauge the demon before him. Physically, he had Malice checked. Over fifty years older, Gareth had the edge on experience as well. But would strength and experience give him the win against the cunning of Malice's mind?

Time to find out.

Gareth whipped his chain at Malice. The end caught the crook of his knees, they buckled, and he fell to the ground. Wrenching his arm, the chains nipped Malice's shoulder, causing his hand to go numb and the dagger to tumble down. Gareth aimed his next attack at the neck.

Malice seized it within an inch of his throat and yanked. *How did he catch that?*

Thrown off balance, Gareth teetered as Malice grabbed his daggers after releasing the chain. Malice threw one at his ankles. The dagger landed in front of Gareth. He stopped himself from tripping, but Malice had already thrown the other blade. Jerking, Gareth fell backward, used the motion, and flipped to stay on his feet. Barely outside of his field of vision, something flew toward Gareth. He dodged just in time as one of Malice's daggers soared past. He stomped again and conjured another. A step back, Gareth whipped his chains from the side. They wrapped around Malice's body. He tugged, and they tightened. Strapped to his sides, Malice flexed his arms but could not break free of their grasp.

Gareth kept his hold on the chains. "I'd say with you captured, this is my victory," he said in a matter-of-fact tone. There was no need to overdo it. This was meant to be an example for his royals more than it was to satisfy his own desire.

"The match ends when one of us is on his ass," Malice reminded.

He crouched and launched forward. Gareth startled, rocking. Malice swept his leg and knocked Gareth off his feet. The chains went loose, and Malice broke free, circling him. Like a snake catching a rabbit, Malice subdued Gareth, his arm enveloping his neck.

"Now that you're on your ass," Malice taunted, his voice a deep rasp, his knee digging into Gareth's spine, "I'd say this is my victory."

Feeding me my own words... Gareth clicked his tongue.

A second or two had passed before Malice let go and withdrew, allowing Gareth to get up. He grimaced at the sudden pain in his back where Malice's knee had dug in. Although, his pride might hurt more. As Gareth gathered his chains and Malice strutted around him, he glimpsed Ida, her furious expression and her bunched-up fists. To make it worse, Malice smirked at her, and her face reddened.

Whispers and gasps spread throughout the coliseum while everyone returned to their sections. Some lingered, as if they couldn't comprehend what had happened. A good handful, however, walked away laughing or smiling.

Gareth admitted, "Today was my loss." He glanced at his group of speechless royals. "Take this spar as a lesson, as an example of what I should see today."

Once his chain was re-clipped to his belt, he dusted the dirt off his pants. "Now, with your partner, spread out and start sparring." There was no need to be a sore loser, he told himself. That was a good learning opportunity.

Royals scattered and got into their stances, weapons poised. Except for one. Ida remained dazed, standing in the same spot Gareth had told all the royals to move to. She walked toward them, her expression hardening.

"Teach me to fight," she demanded, her sights locked on Malice. Her voice was steady and her shoulders proud. Cracks and clangs from weapons clashing and grunts sounded around them.

Gareth frowned. "What makes you want to learn from him?" Ida was promising, with a strong sense of justice. It was concerning to hear she wanted to learn from someone like Malice.

"He took you down and didn't break a sweat." Ida kept her focus on Malice's stoic face. "Anyone with half a brain could tell he was holding back whether they saw him in the Games or not."

As right as she may be, Gareth did not like the idea. Over the last few months, he had noticed Ida's behavior changing. The training had gotten too easy, yet she tried her best to stay engaged. He could understand her longing for strength. Nonetheless, he worried about what Malice's influence might be on her.

Heartbeats passed, and he grunted. "Fine. From here on, Malice will be your instructor during the hour you would usually be with me."

If anything, Malice surely did not want to take on a disciple. He would tell her to focus on the basics or something simple. By tomorrow she would have caught on and returned to training as usual, hopefully.

"So," Malice swung his head to Gareth, "I don't get a choice?"

"No."

"Is this you being a sore loser or—" Gareth glared, his lips curled with annoyance as he crossed his arms.

"Oh!" Malice winced away dramatically. "If looks could kill, I'd be dead ten times over." His sentence ended with a devious grin.

"Ida"

Gareth huffed and walked to the partner Ida left aimlessly looking around with their hands behind them. He said something that surprised the royal, but they did not refuse, stiffly got into their stance, and they started sparring.

Cold eyes inspected her, judged her harshly. Ida went frigid. Malice stalked around her, deliberately, like a wolf evaluating its prey. He stopped and faced Ida, matching her gaze.

"What is your goal? You wouldn't have wanted me to teach you if you didn't have a specific reason in mind."

"I want to stand by the king's side!" she stated with absolute certainty, but Malice's dead eyes made her resolve waver. Her nose scrunched. It was like Ida's answer disappointed him.

"That's all?" It had disappointed him. "Aiming so low when you can have it all..." he trailed off.

Malice turned, walked a few, bent down, and placed his palm on the dirt. It stayed there for a second before he flung his hand into the air. Chunks of earth rose from the ground and assembled into a figure like a poorly carved statue. Suddenly, compelling Ida to back up, the thing moved and stared at her.

Malice sat on thin air, his legs crossed. "You will spar against my golem. Defeat it however you want." He waved his hand dismissively. "This is an assessment for me to see where you are and where I need to begin, so do your best." A thin smile curved the corners of his mouth, making heat swell in Ida's chest as she scrunched her nose.

In response to the jerks and wiggles of Malice's fingers, the golem moved, stretching. Ida had grabbed a spear from the weapons rack earlier, but after glancing at it, tossed it aside. With a roll of her shoulders, she bounced twice on each foot and shook her hands out, putting them up in front of her face. Sure to keep her heels just barely above the ground as she had seen many fighters on the outskirts of the kingdom do, Ida was ready.

Malice had only agreed to train her because Sir Gareth told him to. The look of disinterest was as annoying as his relaxed disposition. Golems were big and slow, easy to avoid and outrun. *When I get around it, aim for Malice and knock him off his seat of air.* If he wasn't going to take this seriously, then he should be prepared for the consequences. Although she knew there would only be one opportunity to land a hit on him.

The golem charged. It was fast, light on its feet despite its size. Startled, Ida stumbled backward, narrowly dodging its club of a hand. She gritted her teeth, realizing her earlier assessment was wrong, and discarded the plan. The best thing she could do was focus on defense while searching for the golems weak point.

The golem swung its leg. Ida brought her arms to her side; she wouldn't be able to move out of the way quickly enough. It connected and sent her flying. She tumbled to the ground, cracks resonating within her body. Swearing, Ida got up, her arms throbbing. Thud after thud bounded toward her. Seemed like Malice didn't plan to give her a chance to breathe or think.

Ida swerved to the side and punched the golem's ribs, but all that did was make her knuckles pulse with a burning pain. Elbow snapping toward her, she reeled. Ida ran and jumped on the golem's back, wrapping her arms around its head to pull it off. It grabbed her shirt and threw her to the ground before she was able to.

As she bit back a yelp of pain, Ida rolled to her side, trying to catch the breath she had just lost. A shadow appeared above her, and she rolled again. A round foot slammed into the dirt next to her head with a loud boom. *Where is its weak spot? Does it have one?* Her ears rang, her arms throbbed, and now her back and lungs, pain lancing through them, kept her short of breath.

Malice listlessly waved his hands around. Ida clenched her fists, anger burning a pit in her stomach.

She focused on the golem.

"Has no one ever taught you how to fight a golem?" Malice called out, surprising Ida into a bewildered stare.

What?

The golem vanished from her sight like the sun during a storm. Ida's eyes flitted to where it once was and the immediate area, but it was too late. Its fist slammed into her gut. She felt every fluid in her stomach rush to her throat. Landing on her back, kicking her legs up, she flipped onto her hands and knees and retched, viciously. The golem stopped.

Sweat dripped into her eyes, stinging them. Ida wiped her face, thinking of what Malice asked. Was it to mess with her, or did it have some merit? Ida spat, then rose, a bit wobbly like a newborn fawn. Malice smiled and swiped his hand to the side. The golem rushed forward, arm and fist cocked. She didn't move a muscle until it was right on top of her.

It attacked. She caught its arm, twisted, let its body crash into her back, and flung it up and over. She retreated once it crashed into the ground. The golem swiftly got to its feet and advanced once more. This time, Ida did too. She leaped into a high kick, aiming for the golem's head. It caught her ankle, and the world spun. Then she was dangling above the dirt.

When shaking its hand off proved inefficient, Ida tried smashing its fist with both hands clamped together. Frustrated, she brought her other leg up and stomped her foot against its pectoral.

She used all her strength and pulled until the golem's arm broke off from the shoulder. She tumbled to the ground, tossing the limb of earth to the side as she got her bearings. The pride that swelled from her toes to the top of her head died fast when the golem sprouted a new arm.

She was at square one again.

Anger getting the better of her, Ida charged, fists up and ready. Unsurprisingly, the golem was prepared as well. She slid in between its legs and turned, but its foot met the side of her head. Everything doubled, tripled, then quadrupled, her brain pounding violently against her skull. Ida dragged herself from the gravel, only to collapse onto one knee.

Something warm dripped from her ear. She went to touch it and grunted at the sight of blood.

"No, I never learned to fight a golem," she yelled, wiping the red stream off her ear and jaw. Admitting she needed help hurt almost as much as the rest of her body.

"There are many who inadvertently want to keep blood off their hands," Malice said in a serious tone, but only if it weren't a riddle it would have been helpful.

Ida stood, gasping at the pain that radiated throughout her body. The golem took one step and another before rushing in full force. *Defeat it however you wish.* Malice's words flooded into her ears.

This wasn't the training she was used to.

The golem closed the distance between them in a heartbeat. She darted to the side of it, closed her fists around her mouth, took a deep breath, and blew into her hands. Grey smoke, like rain clouds, surrounded her and the golem, obscuring Malice's view.

The golem stopped moving for whatever reason. *Good, stay put for a while.* Ida kicked its kneecaps, breaking them. It fell with a thud. She started dissembling the golem limb by limb, then smashing its body to bits.

Heaving, exhaustion heavy on her chest, limbs and head throbbing, Ida sat on the mangled corpse of the golem. Sweat and blood dripped from her head, staining her clothes. When a time had passed and the smoke cleared, she hopped down, still out of breath. She had enough energy to glare holes into Malice as she lumbered toward him. *Cheeky bastard.*

He clapped sluggishly, an amused smile on his face. "Golems are puppets controlled by their masters in the shadows." Malice set one foot down and the other, toes almost meeting Ida's. "You take their vision; you take their weapon."

"What if…" Ida said in between pants. "They are… a seer?" Seers were blind, so taking their vision would be a waste of energy.

"Find them quickly or destroy every golem they throw at you until their magic is gone."

Her glare softened. "Do I run or kill?"

"Depends on your mission and your target," he said, the volume of his voice low, but not quite a whisper. "If you are to do either, do it before the smoke clears or before they have the chance to escape."

She nodded. "Don't let them see you coming, don't let them see you leave."

"Precisely." He patted her shoulder, making her wince. "We are done for the day."

He smelled of sun-kissed clothes and minty soap as he strode toward Gareth, who continued sparring with her partner.

Baffled, Ida spun around, but Malice was already gone without a trace. Gareth looked at her, his eyes gone wide, then they closed, and a heavy sigh escaped from his lungs—his shoulders drooped as his chest deflated. Ida gimped to Gareth, glad she had some armor on, or things could have been much worse. Perhaps it would be a good idea to focus more while Sir Barren was talking or to wear more armor while training with Malice. About to offer to retake her place as the royal's partner, a high-pitched whistle cut through all the noise, signaling the end of the hour. Ida hurried to the next instructor. *Four more hours,* she sighed.

Food was always prepared and served on wooden trays by the time Ida and her group of royals got to the mess hall. A building of stone, concrete, and wood, south of the barracks and north of the coliseum, was plain inside and out. Long tables with benches filled the floor. Three candle chandeliers hung from the rafters. On the back wall, the kitchen closed off, was a counter half as long as the building where meals were put out almost constantly.

Tray in hand, Ida quickly located an empty spot away from the rowdy tables near the entrance. Usually, she didn't mind the loudness, the drunks babbling and slurring their words despite how early in the day it was, and those who proclaimed their triumphs or whined about how unfair something or another was. Today, however, she wanted the mess hall to be quiet so she could process that morning.

Cinnamon and berries sat on the surface of oatmeal, slabs of roasted ham, chunks of cheese, and toast smeared with oil and garlic with halved green olives on top spread across multiple plates. There was a cup of orange juice at the corner of her tray, most likely unsweetened and plenty of pulp floated on the surface. Ida poked at the oatmeal, submerging the berries, which made it appear more like vomit than something edible.

Footsteps marched closer, a metal tray clanking on the wooden table when Laci sat on the bench. She groaned theatrically. Her caramel brown hair was drawn tight into a ponytail, accentuating her square face.

Laci scooped and shoved a spoonful of oats into her mouth. "What's the matter with you?" she asked gruffly between bites. "Why so lethargic?"

Ida, stirring her gruel-like oatmeal, glanced at the black diamond tattoo on Laci's chin that split in two, the ends curving into itself. Laci said, a little after they had met, that it was her warrior tattoo. *It hurt like a bitch*, Laci had told her.

"… Nothing," Ida mumbled. Malice handed her ass to her on a silver platter, so she'd rather not talk about him. "What's wrong with you?" If anything, Laci seemed more irritated than Ida was.

She groaned, her amber eyes rolling. "Sir Lucas."

"What about him? He's not even here." Sir Lucas of Sir Gareth's Unit had been sent out on a mission weeks ago. Same went for everyone else in Unit One.

"I miss him," Laci sighed. "I'm tired of staring at Sir Arthur's ugly mug."

Ida thought he was attractive for a man—tall, lean, jet-black hair, arrogant, sure, but strong. He was one of six royal knights at the rank of S.

"You're too driven by your desire—sexual desire. Can't you learn to keep your pants on?"

"Excuse me for trying to live while I'm young, unlike somebody." She eyed Ida, her tone dripping with sarcasm. "Enough about me. What really has you upset?"

Ida grunted. *Am I that easy to read?* "Got my ass handed to me after I asked for it, that's all."

Laci paused mid bite, head tilting up to look Ida in the eyes. "That was you getting thrown about like a rag doll by the golem?"

Ida half snorted, half grunted. "That was me, the rag doll."

"Who were you fighting against? Couldn't have been Sir Gareth, he has lightning magic."

"… Malice Reap, Champion of the Games." His name left a sour taste on Ida's tongue. She cringed and downed her pulpy orange juice.

Laci contemplated, her expression temporarily screwing with concentration. "What's the big deal? You asked for it, quite literally. So long as you learned something, no harm done, right?"

"I guess." If only she knew that Malice was a criminal, someone who killed a boy in the middle of the street for no good reason. And if only she knew about the bruises all over her body, throbbing with every other movement.

"Anyway," Laci smirked, "was he as handsome as they say?"

Ida—not surprised—sighed, and shrugged, frowning. "How am I supposed to know?"

"You're right, my bad. I should ask someone who is interested in… you know… men," Laci said mockingly and finished the last of her toast.

"He's gorgeous. Happy?" *Always lusting after men. I don't get it.*

"Not if you're saying it to spite me."

Ida shoved more food in her mouth, choosing not to answer.

Laci finished her meal, and after gulping the rest of her orange juice, stood. "I'll be off first. Good luck today and see you this evening."

Laci's patrol shift ended at the same time as Ida's. They lived in the same house, so the two of them would run into each other no matter what time either of them returned to the barracks.

Ida nodded. "See you this evening and uh—" Laci had turned but stopped and peeked over her shoulder. "Don't piss anyone off today."

"HA! In what world are you living in?" she blurted with a big grin and took off.

Ida chuckled to herself, ate the rest of her food, and returned her tray to the counter. Although the talk with Laci had calmed her down some, the burning pit of annoyance, anger, and shame still flickered in her stomach and chest as she marched outside.

The afternoon went smoothly. Ida and the guard she was posted with only had to break up two petty squabbles. The first was between a store owner and a customer. The second, early in the evening, was between two drunks. One of which had retched on the guards' shoes before they passed out. The other drunk, wobbling like a newborn calf, could walk by themself. Ida's partner told her to head home while he walked the heavy, limp drunk back to the tavern. She didn't argue and left.

If it weren't for him taking his sweet time after lunch, they might have made it in time to stop that boy from getting killed the other day. Ida felt bad for him. Her partner said his name was Joseph. The fact that it happened because they were late, because of him, made her bitter.

Ida trudged up the stairwell in one of the barracks after eating dinner at the mess hall. Roasted duck with mashed potatoes, carrots, peas, cheese, and bread. All of it was overcooked, the duck was tough and dry while the vegetables were mush. The only good thing was the potatoes—those were hard to screw up. It was enough to fill her gut, and that was all she needed, but at times, she missed her grandmother's cooking.

Ida's room was on the third floor at the end of the hall. As she opened the door, she groaned at the thought of going for a bath. Out from under her bed, she dragged and opened a trunk, digging for some nightclothes. Whenever she moved wrong, her stomach cramped and her head throbbed. *I have to work on my regeneration.* If anything, she wanted to return that hit ten times harder. Maybe then Malice would feel it, too.

The bathhouse was huge, with four steaming shallow pools inside and two closed-off rooms for people to change. The walls were painted a pinkish cream and light blue square tiles made up the floor. A few others were washing the day off them as well, reclined against the edge of the pools, talking, or enjoying the peace and quiet of the bathhouse. As she undressed herself, bruises of black and blue, purple and red, some yellowish, bloomed all over her body. The places she wasn't to fully defend were the spots most tender. Tomorrow they would be gone. Mostly.

The sky was a blanket of dark blue when Ida returned to her room and threw herself onto her bed. Crickets croaked outside alongside bursts of laughter from neighboring houses.

Motionless for a moment, Ida flailed her arms about and kicked the bed until she was out of breath. Then she turned over to her back, scowling at the ceiling. Malice's face continuously popped up in her head and his words echoed in her ear, her blood boiling. *Prick.*

Ida's tantrum sucked the little energy she had left out of her. She wrapped herself in the covers and turned onto her side, thankful the bath soothed her aching muscles and injuries. Except for her pride, of course. Underestimating that golem resulted in one hell of a beating. Even when she had first joined the royals a year ago, she'd never got her ass handed to her the way Malice did today.

For as long as she could remember, she had wanted to become a royal, a knight. There was an oak behind the inn her grandmother ran, and Ida beat on that poor tree day in and day out. Still, she wanted to help her grandmother run the inn on the southeastern skirts of the kingdom. Business was slow, but it was enough to keep a roof over their heads and food in their guts. After her grandmother passed in her sleep due to old age, Ida left the inn with a sack of her belongings and started training the next day. She was just barely old enough to join too. She had been promoted from Rank E to Rank A within her first year, and soon enough, she would start going on missions.

Aiming so low when you could have it all. Ida scowled, shut her eyes, and willed herself to sleep. She'd be damned if she had to listen to Malice's vile voice whispering in her ear all night.

To Learn
"Unit One"

The tale of gods Malice told Magnus had been swirling in his mind for days, festering, corrupting his thoughts like a plague. It reminded him of a journal he read a long time ago, written by his great grandfather Alucard Castine. Magnus thought it was delusional, perhaps a warning of ill deeds and their consequences rather than a story of truth. Coatliris was the god his grandfather wrote about. The passage was short and sweet, but it matched what Malice had told him.

Space was abundant in this enormous castle, occasionally overwhelming, but otherwise perfect, as Magnus could escape the usual box that was his study. Before the start of the servants' barracks in the eastern wing, there were many rooms, some used for storage, lounges, and studies. The floor of marble and walls of stone painted white and trimmed with blue echoed the clacks of his shoes. Windows to his left cast his shadow long against the wall and floor, the warm morning sun bathing his body in gold.

Malice was at the training grounds, as was Gareth. He wished to be completely alone, but he knew he wouldn't get that lucky. When Gareth wasn't beside him, another knight was. Trailing a few meters down the corridor, glancing at the interior, was Corgan, a knight second to Gareth in terms of skill. His mind, however, was usually jumbled with alcohol.

Magnus continued to the servants' barracks through the doubled-arched wooden doors. The walls to his left changed from white to periwinkle while the right opened to the garden, the smell of perfume and soil enveloping Magnus.

Alucard's Region had flourished for centuries. It continued to do so, but two things threatened its prosperity. Voidents and slave traders. The voidents issue was being handled now that Malice was here. Magnus also sent Unit One, the Unit with the highest success rate amongst his royals, to the kingdoms, hoping to find more information on them. That wasn't the only reason he sent them on the mission.

The Kingdom of Phoenix, the youngest and smallest city in Alucard's Region, had been tangled up with slaves for at least two years. When he brought the matter to Malice, it certainly caught his attention. Magnus had forgotten that the prior monarch of Hordes Region, Queen Vendetta Reap, was the biggest slave trader on the continent and that Malice was the one who put an end to her reign. *It might be the last few residuals of Vendetta's followers trying to rebuild what they had,* Malice had suggested. It was plausible, and that made Magnus's stomach churn. Malice wasn't too pleased based on the disgust that washed over his face when he pitched the idea.

Servants greeted Magnus as he rounded the corner, Corgan's boots sounding behind him, and into the southern sect of the castle, which was an open corridor looking out to the coast. The ocean was a shimmering blue mass in the distance, the cry of gulls faint, while plains of swaying grass and wheat stalks filled the space between. Gentle salty mist hit Magnus's nose, mixing with the flowers of the garden, calming the queasiness of his stomach.

Lycn Grove, a member of Gareth's Unit, was sent to the Kingdom of Phoenix soon after Charles Bilgen's arrest. He was born just outside the kingdom, raised in the streets of Phoenix, and that was why he was dispatched there. Without evidence, Magnus felt he couldn't remove the Priek family from their position as nobles. Lycn should be able to bring Magnus what he needs. *If he's not blinded by his nostalgia, that is.* Lucas Knightridge, another member of Gareth's Unit, posed a similar problem, but he knew the streets of Ivory's Kingdom better than most. Once his father died, Magnus believed all of Lucas's attachment to that kingdom died as well. *It's a shame. Cesar was an excellent knight, and so was Elena.*

The western wing housed the royal knights belonging to Units, each apartment's door marked with the corresponding Unit's number. The walls once again shifted in color, changing from periwinkle to a robin's egg blue. Magnus strutted down the long, mostly empty corridor, only a few stray royals chatting down the way. They bowed and greeted Magnus when he approached, and he returned the pleasantries. They did the same for Corgan.

When he was eventually out of earshot, he sighed. Stacks of paperwork sat on his desk, a menacing white mountain, words tumbling down the sides like boulders. He was in constant communication with his kingdoms. Magnus felt it was important to both prevent them from doing whatever they pleased, but to also make them feel heard and seen. Something his father neglected to do in the last few years of his reign. Alcohol was much more important to him. Magnus scowled, his skin crawling at the thought of his father. He brushed them away like dust off his shoulder. He needed to keep his mind clear and focused, especially with Unit One expected to return any day now.

"Ida"

As always, the instructors were already in the coliseum's arena waiting for the royals. Malice was too, but he sat on top of a barrel, which Ida found peculiar. He had brought one leg up to his chest and the other dangled over the edge. She ran laps around the field alongside the others. She was at the front, leading the pack per se, while Laci was usually at the rear.

The crisp morning air created a puff of white with every breath, yet it wasn't enough to cool them down after running so hard. Hastily, everyone gathered by their instructor. Instead of starting with Gareth like yesterday, Ida's group would begin with Sir Barren, a lion beastman. He was a Royal Knight rank B specializing in defense. Ida, on the other hand, reluctantly went to Malice near the center of the arena.

"Comfortable?" she asked in a sarcastic tone as she approached. "Didn't have a good enough view yesterday?"

"Matter of fact, I did." Malice wore a tight black dress that went past his knees but split at the sides. He was never suited for battle or training, his choice of clothing strange and inappropriate.

"You learned what I wanted to teach, so now we're moving on." Ida looked at him a bit perplexed but remained silent. "Go arm yourself. Any weapon is fine before you ask."

Ida scowled, scrunching her nose, and paced to the weapons racks. Two racks side by side had swords. The first was wooden, old, and scratched. The second was metal, but the blades were padded with thick stained cloth. She grabbed the practice sword first, twisted it around in her hand. Something was off; the weight wasn't right. It wasn't heavy enough. She leaned the wood into its place and grabbed a padded sword instead, swung it around. The weight of solid steel in her hands was nice. She nodded to herself and turned.

At the inn, the most she had to work with was a knife or a stick. Shops and forges throughout the kingdom sold practice swords and common swords, but they were pricey for someone barely keeping her head above water.

Malice had slipped off the barrel and kicked it over, spilling the contents. Water splashed out and rushed over the dirt and gravel. He shoved the barrel out of the way, bringing his hands up. The water followed and collected. Hands rising still, coming closer together, the water configured. Ida watched, forgetting about how light and dark magic entailed the use of the four main elements as well. Then, once his hands were centered, he flipped his right hand skyward, his left down. The water formed into a golem. It moved when he jerked his wrist and wiggled his fingers, the golem cracking its neck, stretching, just like the earth golem had.

Malice glanced around the water golem. "Take the padding off," he said.

"Why?" Ida pushed the stained cover from the hilt upward and tossed it aside.

"It'll get wet, making it harder for you to control." Now that it was out there, the answer was obvious, and Ida averted her gaze, cheeks burning.

"You will fight however you want."

The water golem moved into a different stance. While the golem from yesterday had a wide bulky posture, its fists up and ready, the water golem was graceful. Its body was parallel to Ida's and its hands were open, relaxed, one further out than the other. She wondered if this was Malice's way of showing off the different techniques he knew.

In any case, Ida readied herself, shaking her shoulders and bouncing twice on each foot. Both hands had an iron grip on the handle just below the guard, knees bent slightly, eyes locked on her enemy.

Ida attacked first, swinging her sword up diagonally. The golem tilted to the side, dodging it. She circled the sword around to strike it from the right. It stepped back, and with a flat palm, slammed its hand into Ida's chest. This golem was even faster than the earth one but gentler. That blow should have knocked the wind out of her, yet it didn't. Was he being considerate?

"Dead," Malice called out. The water golem halted, and Ida whipped her head around. "Lethal blow to the chest. Start the fight over."

Ida's lips flared with annoyance and disgust. She moved to her starting point, as did the golem, and spat at the ground, her eyebrows furrowed. Going into a deeper squat, they both retook their stance.

Inhaling and exhaling, Ida ran forward, brought her sword above her head, snapped it left and right, dancing around the golem as it deflected every one of her attacks. Even with a chain of strikes, the golem dodged everyone. Suddenly on the offense, it spun on the balls of a foot, swung its leg, its heel biting Ida's jaw. She hit the earth but never lost her grip on the sword. A tear, however, stung her eye as blood and pain filled her mouth—she'd bitten her tongue and spat red.

"Dead. That hit would have snapped your neck. Restart," Malice said while examining his long black nails.

Ida grunted and got to her feet, returning to her original position. What was the point of calling out every lethal blow? It made no sense to her.

As Ida bent her knees, grip tightening on her sword, sweat bubbled on her skin, and the golem rushed forward. She took the defensive, holding her blade in front of her torso. The golem struck, fast and heavy. She was losing ground, her heels digging into the dirt. The golem shifted to the side, most of its weight on one leg. Ida rushed forward, startling the golem—or Malice. She couldn't tell most of the time. It really seemed as if the golem had a mind of its own. Its balance was lost. Forearm to head, Ida's blade sliced the golem. It stumbled backward and went still.

"Dead." Jaw tightening, fists clenched, she whirled around when Malice continued, "You dealt a lethal blow through the chest and head." He nodded as if he was acknowledging her first win. She stopped dead in her tracks, blinking.

"Again."

Ida's shoulders adjusted. They were prouder, and her mood lightened a bit as she strutted to her spot. A euphoria overcame her, and for the split second it did, it was nice.

The triumph was short-lived. The golem struck over and over and over again. By the end of the hour, Ida had landed two more lethal blows, once through the heart and the other she didn't know, and Malice wouldn't say. She lost count of how many times she went down. Malice had explained nothing to her. He stood there, moving his fingers and wrists around as if shooing a bug away. Perhaps she was the bug he was trying to shoo. It was frustrating, yet Malice got a quick laugh out of watching her struggle. *Prick.*

Probably noticing the fierce glare Ida was giving him, he stopped her before she went off to the next instructor.

He said, "You asked for my tutelage—" His voice was unnaturally deep, a rumble of thunder in the distance—"and now you're receiving it. If you wanted something easier, you should have stayed with Gareth."

Malice turned and left. Ida stared at his back as he walked away, bunching her fists so tight her nails drew blood. There was no time to dawdle on Malice, not when she had four more hours of training.

Sir Isaac, Royal Knight rank C, taught the ins and outs and benefits of teamwork. Her opinion on it was neither here nor there. She knew she would have to work with a Unit at some point.

Hour three was spent with Lady Taryn, Royal Knight rank A, a healer teaching a mix of the basics and more advanced techniques to those who chose healing over regeneration. There weren't many. Next were instructors Sir Howard and Sir Amos, Royal Knights rank A. Since magic and regeneration were intertwined, they had combined their time. Although the smitten atmosphere between them suggested there was an ulterior motive behind it. Finally, Lady Edith, Royal Knight rank B, her mastery in long-distance combat was one to behold. Ida still preferred hand-to-hand combat, though.

After training, it was lunch, then patrol, then a bath, and then sleep. A never-ending cycle.

Ida, an arm under her head, lay on her bed while tossing up and catching a rice-filled sack. Light from the half-moon outside bled through her window, painting everything in a pale blueish color. She sighed, thinking of her time with Malice and his teaching methods. He wanted her to figure things out on her own. That much was obvious, but what was it this time? She learned to move quicker, strike harder, defend better, but there was nothing else she could think of that made this form of training make sense.

Perhaps it would be better to let things go back to normal. Train with Sir Gareth again.

She frowned, caught the sack, and held her arm out for a while. It had only been two days and already she was thinking of giving up. Grandmother had never given up when her inn lost its popularity, nor had she given up on Ida when her own parents had. *Grandmother would scold me right now if she knew what I was thinking.* Ida sat up, throwing the sack to the floor beside her bed. What kind of knight would give up so easily because things got tough? Not a good one.

She analyzed Sir Gareth's fight with Malice and the Games of Retribution, thinking his way of fighting would provide some sort of clue. Nothing came to mind the way she had hoped. He was fast, powerful, and deadly. Flopping down once more, Ida's sandy locks flew out of her face.

That's all? Malice's words, unwelcomed, rang in her ears. *Aiming so low when you can have it all.* That, too, was frustrating. So far, everything about that man was frustrating, but he was useful and patient. Which annoyed her even more now that she was thinking about it. On her side, she forced her eyes shut. Tomorrow was another day. Speed, precision, and lethality. That was what she needed, so that was what he was going to get.

After a good night's rest, Ida was excited to wipe that bored look off Malice's face and rushed to the coliseum, only to find that neither Sir Gareth nor Malice were there. Instead, Sir Corgan, another royal knight, stood in Sir Gareth's place, scratching his gut as he yawned. With a quick glance around—not knowing what else to do—she started stretching. When she finished, she waited for the rest of the royals, so training could begin.

A group of royals strode past. "Did you hear?" one asked.

"Hear what?"

"Unit One has returned from their mission!" the first voice exclaimed, and the rest of the group gasped.

The rest of the conversation was inaudible as they walked out of earshot. When a high-ranking Unit returned from a mission or went on one, it was always the big talk amongst royals. Ida headed toward the small group of people at the edge of the arena, a little disappointed. *So much for that.*

"Magnus"

Magnus had been tracking the strange disappearances around the region. When Charles was arrested earlier that spring, Magnus had sent Unit One, excluding Gareth, on lone missions to each kingdom. All four had returned late last night and this morning. Now, Magnus waited for them in the throne room on the first floor of the castle.

It was truly a beautiful, wide-open space. White and gold lines illustrated the map of Alucard's Region on the rich blue floor. Four portraits hung from the pale walls, each of a ruler, including Magnus. It always felt strange to look at his painting, like staring in a still mirror. To the left of the raised dais the throne sat upon was a wall of windows overseeing the eastern courtyard and kingdom, the old chapel taller than the other buildings. It was no longer in use, abandoned centuries ago, but it was a magnificent piece of architecture that Magnus didn't want to tear down.

Magnus eyed the marble angel hovering over him as if it were shielding him from any danger with its arms and wings. He remembered being mesmerized by the throne his father had once sat on; the same sense of awe he had as a child bubbled to the surface. Shifting his mahogany fur cloak on his shoulders, Magnus turned his attention to the dark pine doors. They opened, squeaking sharply. A butler tailored in white and blue strode in, stopped at the edge of the door, and bowed.

One by one, Gareth's Unit walked into the throne room. Ahenobarbus Narine, a wingless angel. His skin was almost as dark as Magnus's, his long hair and beard a rusty orange. Barbus—as he liked to be called—was a fan of ale, his round gut a testament to his favored pastime. It was a wonder how the man's shirt stayed tucked below his stomach.

Next was Lucas, a prideful elf, son of Cesar and Elena Knightridge, excellent knights who served Magnus's father. He wasn't as tall as Barbus, nor as wide, but he was lean, his ruffled shirt and trousers made of fine materials. He wore rings of silver on his hands, catching the sunlight, a long sword resting on his hip, swinging with every step.

Then Lycn, the half-blooded coyote beastman, a sturdy man. He was more muscular than Lucas, his skin tan, his close-cropped hair a light blonde, almost sandy. Lycn wore a simple blue tunic and black trousers. Finally, Pich, a fairy who had wings like a dragonfly's and big round glasses. They were the shortest in the room, save for the butler they walked past. With round features, thin limbs, and messy, dark brown hair, they resembled a child.

Once they reached the middle of the floor, each knight bowed, dropping to one knee, their heads lowered.

"Rise," Magnus ordered, his voice echoing off the walls. They did, hands tucked behind them.

"Your majesty," Barbus said as he stepped forth and dipped his head. "Our findings are similar, if I may be the one to report them."

Magnus frowned. *Are they now...* "That is fine." Gareth stirred to Magnus's right, readjusted his shirt's collar, and clasped his hands at his backside. He never did like dressing up.

"Thank you." Barbus took a deep breath. "People reported the victims' shadows—they moved strangely for days on end before the victim vanished. It was like they had a mind of their own."

Magnus nodded, a flicker of movement catching his eye. Barbus's shadow had lightened. Or was that his imagination?

"We saw it too. I followed a victim, hoping to warn'em," the angel said, his accent from Zeldine's Region coming through thicker. "I watched as their shadow grew and consumed'em, leavin' nothin' in their wake." He scowled at the memory. "I don't think they're alive, your majesty."

"They're dead." Malice's voice disrupted the calm, a deep rasp that seemed to hang in the air and make everyone in the room jolt. Magnus glanced toward Malice as his green eyes darted from knight to knight. *No, not them. He's looking at their shadows. Damnit.*

Gareth's royals regarded one another, surprised, eyebrows raised, a shrug, and a shake of a head.

"Who is that, your majesty?" Lycn asked, his honey-yellow eyes narrowing on Malice as he stepped closer to Pich.

"Malice Reap, King of Hordes Region." Magnus wasn't concerned about their reactions as much as he was about Malice's. *Don't speak,* he had told Malice on the way to the throne room, *unless you know*, and he had agreed to that. "He speaks the truth, but will remain silent."

Malice eventually glanced at Magnus, smiled, nodded, and propped himself on the edge of the throne with his elbow.

"Before we move on," Magnus said. "Do you have anything more to add from your missions?" He looked pointedly at each of them, lingering on Lycn and Lucas.

"I don't think so, your majesty." Barbus, dipping his head once more, slid back to his original spot.

Magnus sighed. "The person you saw consumed by their shadow fell victim to a voident. A creature created by darkness, born from the god Coatliris. The ones terrorizing my people are puppets, footmen, obedient dogs." Malice called them the mindless.

"Are you implying there are voidents of higher intelligence, your majesty?" Lucas asked politely.

"They also have a sense of reason, a personality. Some have but a shred of humanity, though not many. The founding rulers encountered the voidents and their creator five hundred years ago after the war." Magnus, regarding his knights, went on after a moment. "They subdued them at the cost of their own lives, but now they have returned."

"What would you have us do, your majesty?" Pich pushed up their glasses, their big eyes fixed on Magnus. Lycn's hand extended until it found Pich's, and their hands clasped together.

"I would send you on another mission in one month's time, back to the kingdoms. A life-changing mission, I'll admit." *Perhaps if they were not marked, it wouldn't have to be this way.* "But you'll go to the Kingdom of Phoenix first and Malice will join you."

Shock rippled over the knights, but no one dared say anything. "A week before you leave, we'll go over the details of the mission. Until then, rest up. You will need it."

Barbus, Lucas, Lycn, and Pich bowed. "Thank you, your majesty," they said in unison.

As they made their way to the doors, Gareth nodded toward Magnus and pursued them, his shoes clacking loudly on the marble floor.

"Gareth"

"How were your travels?"

Across and next to his unit in the dining hall, Gareth sipped on a goblet of ale. Barbus sat beside him, a thin line of white on his mustache from the beer in his cup. Lucas was on his right, swirling a chalice of red wine before taking a long draught. In front of him, close together, were Pich and Lycn, both with a cup of mead. All of them, except for Barbus, had changed into more casual clothes.

"They were fine and all but," Barbus set his goblet down and rocked his chair on its hind legs, "let me tell you!" He waved his finger all around. "It would have been much better if I had wings, faster too!" Despite his accent fading over time, it was without a doubt from Zeldine's Region, the land of orcs and swamps, west of Alucard's Region neighbor to Hordes and Raelle's.

Lucas snickered into his chalice. "Even if you had wings, they wouldn't be able to carry your fat ass."

Lycn cracked a smile as Gareth tried to hold back his laughter.

"Wha?" Barbus stared, dumbfounded, at Lucas and looked down at his protruding gut. "I haven't got that big, ya wee shit!"

"You could lose some weight," Lycn chimed in with a smirk. Pich elbowed his side.

The fairy smiled at Barbus. "I think you look fine, Sir Barbus."

"Aye," he said and bobbed his head. "I'm glad someone here thinks so!" He grunted, scooped up his cup, and downed almost a full thing of beer, waving down one of the servants in the dining hall. Instantly acknowledging Barbus, the servant scampered to the kitchen. In no time, they brought out another pint and placed it in front of the knight. "My thanks."

Gareth watched his Unit, a fondness relaxing his posture, and changed the subject. "Pich." They perked their head toward him, eyes round and curious. "How was your first mission alone?"

A nervous grin spread across their lips, their gaze dropping. "It was fine, better than expected." They peeked up at Gareth for a split second, then down to the table again.

"Did you even go alone?" Gareth glanced at Lycn, who set his goblet on the table.

"No."

"Yes," Pich and Lycn said in unison.

"I thought we weren't going to say anything." Pich pouted, grabbed his arm, and shook it a bit.

"They would've realized eventually. You're a terrible liar, you know." Pich crossed their arms, grunting.

Gareth had grown used to the dramatics those two put on. Often.

Any moment now, Lycn would turn to Pich and apologize because he couldn't stand it when they were upset with him. Gareth's eyes darted between the two, counting the seconds, watching as Lycn became antsy and his expression grew worrisome.

Lycn gently spun Pich so they were facing him. With a flutter of his eyes, he said, "I'm sorry."

Pich stared at him for a moment, sighed, and ruffled his short hair. "Fine." They always caved to his puppy dog eyes. "You're forgiven."

He leaned forward and gave Pich a peck on the cheek. "Thank you."

Lucas groaned and rolled his eyes. "Were you that concerned about your beloved? I think we were all a little worried, but who would do anything to such a cute fairy?" he asked tauntingly, his eyes narrowing on Lycn, a grin twisting the corners of his mouth.

Lycn's expression soured.

"Or were you too scared to be on your own?"

Lycn threw his head back, laughing humorlessly, then met Lucas's devious gaze. "If I had my staff, I'd shove it up your ass right now."

Lucas reclined into his chair, swinging his cup as he talked. "I'm sure you want to, but I doubt you could. You can't even beat me in a bout." He brought the chalice up to his lips and took a swig.

Lycn's jaw twitched, his face reddening. "It's been a while since the last we fought. Care to test your theory?" he said through clenched teeth.

Barbus and Gareth burst out laughing, unable to hold back any longer. Gareth subdued his laughter for the most part. Meanwhile, Barbus had both of his hands on his jiggling gut as he cackled, drawing the attention of the other tables.

"You sure it was a good idea to put these two in the same Unit, sir?" Still chuckling, Barbus wiped the tears from his eyes.

"They bicker but this Unit is like family" Gareth's smile faded, and his sentence trailed. Suddenly, his mouth became dry, the word *family* sticking to his tongue. Joseph, Maryjane, and Cadmus flooded his head like high tide. The necklace he had placed on the desk in his bedchamber flashed behind his eyes. *Give this to his brother, Lucas Knightridge.*

"Sir Gareth." Lucas raised an eyebrow. "Are you all right?"

Head jerking up, Gareth looked at Lucas. He averted his eyes, now meeting the curious stares of Lycn and Pich. He nodded. "Yes, I'm fine," he said, plastering on a smile. "It feels good to have everyone home." Goblet in hand, Gareth raised his cup and leaned forward. "To coming home safely."

Everyone grabbed their drinks and thrusted them toward Gareth's, a loud clunk, and a splash. "Cheers!" The Unit exclaimed, chugging their alcohol and slamming the cups on the soaked table.

Gareth waved down another servant with a twirl of his hand. They disappeared into the kitchen. He was too sober if he was thinking about Joseph and the necklace. In spite of that, it was nice drinking with his Unit again. Even before they went off on their missions, it had been too long since they shot the breeze together, enjoying some good alcohol as they did. After the hell of a week, Gareth's had, this was just the thing he needed to unwind a bit.

"Ah!" Barbus grunted.

Two servants returned to the table, one with two glasses and the other with three. They passed them along to their rightful drinkers, then bowed and left wordlessly.

"How did the Games go?" He used his elbow to nudge Gareth's arm, making Gareth rock in his seat.

Pich sniffed the mead, their nose crinkling. Lycn instantly switched their goblets. "We heard the king was planning to change things up a bit to celebrate the tenth year of his reign." This time they didn't sniff the alcohol and took a long savoring draught, which ended with a refreshing *ahh*. Lycn smiled into his cup as he slid his arm to the back of Pich's chair, shifting closer.

"I heard his majesty wanted over three hundred participants this year," Lucas added.

"That many?" Pich's jaw dropped, and their eyes went wide. "How could he do that?"

Lucas shrugged. "Probably gave a lot of lifetime prisoners a choice; stay and rot or take part in the Games. I would assume most accepted the offer."

"So," Barbus pressed, "what happened? I'm honestly a little disappointed I didn't get to see it myself but—"

"None of it happened," Gareth interrupted with a solemn expression and a bitter tone. The sudden change in his mood startled Barbus into leaning away from Gareth, baffled. Lucas, Lycn, and Pich exchanged glances.

"Why?" Lycn broke the silence, re-situating himself so one leg rested over the other, his arm still around Pich's shoulders.

His teeth ground. "You are right. The king wanted to turn the tournament into a battle royale with hundreds of participants, both fighters and prisoners alike." His eyebrows furrowed at the memories clawing their way to the surface of his mind.

"His majesty wanted to end the Games when about fifty participants were left, so it would not be a complete massacre."

Forward, Gareth rested his elbow on the table and massaged the bridge of his nose.

"That is, until Malice showed up and killed a boy in front of the king and I."

"What? Why hadn't he stayed in prison?" Lycn growled.

"Because of the technicalities." Gareth sighed, crossed his arms, and reclined fully into his chair.

"Which are?"

"He defended himself. The boy attacked first, aiming to cleave his head in half." He took a swig of ale, glancing at Lucas but just as quickly looking elsewhere and setting his cup down, guilt a dull pang in his chest.

"The king sentenced him to the Games and reduced the number of participants to a third of the planned participant count. We received many complaints." Gareth stared at the edge of the table, focusing on the details of the royal blue tablecloth. "Despite having his magic drained every morning, including the morning of the Games, Malice killed half of the survivors."

Slowly, he brought his palm to the sky, jerking his wrist upward, flipping his hand, and bringing it down and out, mimicking Malice's hand movements. "Just like that."

The Unit went silent, tension settling on the table.

Pich shook their head. "How is that possible? If his magic was drained once, he shouldn't have had the power, energy, or strength to kill that many." Being a healer, Pich knew most everything there was to know about magical energy. From a logical standpoint, it was impossible, Gareth knew that.

"Aye." Barbus addressed Pich with a serious expression. "But what's done is done, no point dwelling on it."

"That's the thing." Lucas glanced from Barbus to Gareth. "He wouldn't be so upset if there wasn't something else you wanted to tell us, right?" Lucas had always been quick to grasp situations, good at reading people.

Gareth took a deep breath in and let it go. "With Malice joining our mission, I am sure the king will tell him to make nice."

"… That's your problem? So what?" Lucas grunted.

Gareth's head shot up when he realized his royals hadn't had the displeasure of interacting with Malice as much as he had.

"Sir Gareth." Barbus gripped his shoulder, gave it a light shake. "I'm sure I speak for all of us when I say that none of us trust a man with so many rotten rumors tailin' behind him like Malice does. We knew for the mission the moment the king informed us about him tagging along, that we'd have to look past it for now."

"He's right," Pich said, nodding enthusiastically.

"That's why we didn't question things. We know how important this mission is and if we must work beside our greatest enemy for the sake of the region, then that's what we'll do. It's what we all swore to do."

Sometimes, Gareth wished he hadn't taken that same oath all those years ago. Because of it, he'd had to watch comrades charge to their deaths for the people of this region, *his* people. Their faces remained fresh in his mind, their dead eyes staring into the abyss as the earth claimed their decomposing bodies.

"We have to make friends, so that's what we'll do," Lucas said.

Gareth's heart stung. If he knew what Malice had done, would he still be saying that?

Lycn sniffled. "I will make no such promises. I don't like him, and I doubt I'll like him in the future." He messed with his chalice, his finger circling the rim, swaying the body, the mead tempting the edges. Pich gazed up at him, expressionless, but said nothing before they shifted, eyes slipping to the table.

"That is fair," Gareth chuckled dryly. *What a way to ruin the mood.* He sighed. "If he approaches any of you—"

"Yeah, yeah, be kind and all," Lycn grumbled.

"No." Gareth gathered himself with a crack of his neck and regarded his unit. "Watch him like a hawk. Remain cautious until the end of the mission."

Stunned, Barbus stared at Gareth, his brows creasing his forehead.

"The king may have him wrapped around his finger, but who knows how long that will last. Malice is not to be trusted," he said bluntly, cold eyes passing over each member of his Unit. It may seem overly prudent to them, but he had known Malice a lot longer than they had—not that it amounted to much. Every instinct in his body was telling him to stay vigilant, that Malice was a danger. He had been alive long enough to know better than to ignore such feelings.

Gareth heard the edge in his tone, hinting at fear and anger. He tried to swallow it down with another swill of ale.

"All right." Barbus gave Gareth's shoulder another squeeze. "If it's what you want, that's what we'll do."

Of course, he did not want that. To have Malice come on a mission or to have him here in Alucard's Region at all. He did not want the constant worry clawing at the back of his head, but it did not feel like he had much of a choice.

"Good."

The king made his decision, so the time to prepare was running out. One month, he reminded himself. *One month.*

To Learn
"Bolorsetseg's Tavern"

Drinking with the Unit yesterday was nice and all, but Lucas had been looking forward to drinking lukewarm wine surrounded by chatty patrons as he sat at a table winning a couple of handfuls of coin. Besides, the king's announcement didn't sit right with him, and he wanted to get his mind off it.

There was a tavern in the eastern district of Alucard's Kingdom, Bolorsetseg's Tavern, run by a giant. Lucas didn't know her name or face and didn't care to learn, so long as wine kept filling his cup.

The streets were lively as always, people nattering, rushing, or taking their sweet time getting to their destination. Carriages and wagons stayed in the middle of the road, hooves clattering against the stone. Lucas was thankful it didn't smell of dung. The scent of bread, grass, and salty water sat in the air instead.

He glanced toward the cloudy sky, noticing he was close enough to see the abandoned chapel towering over the local houses and stores. He heard it was used during the founding ruler's time and had since lost its appeal. People had worshipped the god of life and death, whatever its name was. Now it simply stood as a beautiful building, gradually succumbing to moss and vines as the years went by.

From the flagstone streets, Lucas entered the white brick building, the dark-stained oak doors screeching. He was hit by a wall of alcohol, sweat, and cheap perfume. The door slammed shut behind him, but the bustling tavern didn't notice. Two pillars of wood with stone bases stretched to the cathedral style ceiling, vaulted with the same dark oak beams as the door. Round tables filled most of the floor, booths hugged the corners and cream-colored walls on the right side, while a bar occupied the length of the left wall. Metal holsters, lambent torches inside, were spaced at even intervals throughout the room, giving the tavern a nice orange hue.

Lucas made his way to the bar's edge, weaving around tables and dodging drunkards, who were flailing their arms around as they spoke. The sounds of dice and goblets hitting tables, cards being thrown down, and boisterous talk would have been deafening if he weren't used to it.

"Well, if it ain't Lucas," a barmaid said as Lucas finally got to the waxed bar top. Tali, a rabbit beastman—energetic for someone her age—smiled at him, her buck teeth poking out from her top lip. Then her attention went back to the person a seat down. Tali tapped the bar with her finger, an eyebrow raised, her flat nose twitching before the person slapped a few bronze coins on the bar. She happily relented the drink, white foam spilling off the edges of the wooden stein, as she gathered up her coin.

"So, where you've been?"

"On a mission," Lucas almost had to shout before Tali moved to stand in front of him. "When have I ever not come for longer than a week otherwise?"

Tali's long, fuzzy ears twitched away as someone called for her. Another barmaid took her place, though. Irena was her name, an older woman with black tattoos on her chin. "True enough. So, ya want'cher usual?" Tali asked and leaned her forearm against the edge of the bar top, strands of her long, brown hair slipping from her ponytail.

"What else would I have?"

"Ya could try ale every now and again. Don't most you men love the stuff?"

Lucas scoffed, a bit offended Tali would lump him in with every other man she saw. "Drinking piss isn't something I like to do, Tali. Red wine will do me just fine."

She shrugged, a smile tugging at her lips. "Suit yer'self."

When she paraded off, Lucas took in the collection of alcohol behind the bar; barrels of ale, beer, mead, wine, and even chicha from the south of Vinyamar, a strange drink derived from maize that was yeasty and sweet. Certainly not a drink Lucas would sip on again. Tali returned quickly, a stein of wine in hand, and set it down a few inches away from his hands. While he dug around in his pocket, grabbing four bronze coins, Tali clicked her tongue, stopping him.

"No need. Keep yer coins, mister knight," she said with a wink.

"I always pay."

"Keep yer money this time. It's not like we ain't got enough to cover a drink or two fer ya."

Lucas looked into her eyes, the pinkish color a few shades too light to be blood red, then put his hands up. "Fine, you win today. Once I get to my third drink, you will take my coin. Got it?"

Backing away, Tali shrugged again, a smugness taking over her face. "Ain't making no promises, Knightridge."

Lucas shook his head, grabbed his drink, and turned. That little rabbit was stubborn, especially when it came to royals. The Bolorsetseg's owner used to be a royal and had a soft spot for them, but that was idle talk.

Lucas scanned the room, searching for a table to join, so he could leave with heavier pockets. In one of the corner booths, a table of three was passing out cards, the table's surface crowded by steins, probably empty. He crossed the floor, avoiding rogue hands, tipping chairs, and barmaids.

Two women and a man. The women were sisters; they were too alike not to be. They both had dark green hair, their eyes black in the low light, even the scales on their bare arms, face, and neck were a pale green-blue. The only difference was the one on the left had short, shaggy hair and down-turned eyes. While the one on the right had sharp eyes and long, wavy hair that reminded Lucas of kelp. Finally, the man in the middle, he bore some resemblance to someone Lucas had met yesterday. His eyes were amber, had high cheekbones, white hair, and broad shoulders. He was missing the cold beauty Malice had, though.

"Mind if I join you?" Lucas asked, coming to stand beside the booth, a friendly smile on his face.

All three looked up at him, confusion as clear as day written on their drunk faces, then amusement as the ladies turned toward the man for an answer.

"Sure." He belched, which made Lucas cringe. "Why not, more the merrier… elf."

Elf? The smile vanished instantaneously. He glared, the man holding his gaze when a snicker escaped his foul mouth. Anger sparking in his veins, Lucas spun and headed to the bar, taking up a stool when he got there. Higher-pitched voices called after him and he ignored them, his mood now in the gutter. Downing his wine in one go, Lucas slammed the stein on the bar top and asked for a refill. It wasn't often he ran across bastards with race prejudice, but by the gods did it grate on his nerves whenever he did.

Tali had walked past him, taking his stein with her. Heartbeats went by and his cup, filled to the brim, was set before him, Tali racing to the next patron.

The wine reflected his furrowed brow when he brought it to his lips, savoring its rich, bittersweet taste, unlike the first time. He had wanted to get his mind off the upcoming mission. It'd been badgering his thoughts since he left the dining hall yesterday. Of course, he also wanted to have a good time, share a few drinks and a few laughs. As if that was going to happen anymore.

Gareth was odd, constantly averting his eyes from Lucas's. He was hiding something. For someone in his seventies, Gareth wasn't the best at keeping secrets. Lucas snickered at that. *He's too honest for his own good.*

Malice was a surprise, an even bigger surprise when the king said he was joining them on such a dangerous mission—*life-changing*, as the king stated. He didn't think kings could go on missions, yet again, they were rulers, they could do as they pleased. His majesty may have been the one sitting on the throne, but Malice had the biggest presence in the room. Whatever he did had Gareth paranoid, too. Gareth was always cautious, telling his royals to stay alert, but not like that.

After a time, Lucas finished his second cup of wine, waving down Tali for his third. It was no fun drinking by himself, but the alcohol was too good to pass up. His father liked wine as well and tried to make it once when Lucas was a boy.

They had waited until his mother was out for a while. Then Cesar went to his underground forge and brought up a barrel of wine. It had been fermenting for a few months. He also told Lucas not to tell his mother what they were doing. Lucas had sworn to secrecy before breaking it open. The sour smell was so pungent that Lucas's eyes watered, but Cesar, his own eyes watering, reassured him it was supposed to be that way. They had a glass of it and both of them nearly retched the moment the supposed *wine* hit their tongues. To this day, Lucas couldn't understand how his father had fucked up wine that badly.

"What'cha chuckling about?" Tali asked as she refilled Lucas's stein.

Was I chuckling? "Just remembered something about my father." There was a tug in his chest, and he winced.

Concentration drew Tali's expression taut for a moment. She gasped and shook a finger in Lucas's face. "Cesar Knightridge? That ole knight used to come here for the longest time back when I was a lil' crotch goblin!"

"You… knew my father?" *How long has it been since I've heard my father's name?*

"Sure did!" she beamed. "Used to bring me a handful of sweets every time he visited. Kind man, lemme tell you, handsome too. Heard he retired about thirty years ago, though. Say, what's he doing now?"

Air caught in Lucas's throat—more like a lump of sludge he barely swallowed. "Dead," he eventually spat, the word feeling like a stab to the heart. "He was killed… seven years ago, when I was eighteen." Seven years, yet the memory of finding him on the streets, blood soaking into the ground, all the warmth gone from his body, was still vivid, a throbbing wound.

Tali made a sound half between a sigh and a gasp. She leaned over the bar top and rested a hand on Lucas's arm. "I'm sorry, sweetheart." She offered a warm, gentle smile, one he didn't return. Irena called Tali away. She left, but not without a hesitant glance over her shoulder.

He sighed, fished some silver coins from his pocket, and stood, leaving his third helping of wine on the bar alongside his money. *Not my day, is it?*

Lessons From The Wise
XI

Again, Ida couldn't figure out Malice's lesson, and she got a black eye for it too. At the mess hall, she sat at an empty table near the back wall. On her tray was lamb, broccoli, peas, cut carrots, and a steaming baked potato. A small bowl of red grapes and apple slices was next to an even smaller bowl of nuts and cheese with water to drink. Laci sat beside her, a third of her plate gone. She went on and on about training as Ida listened. She would throw her opinion in every now and again just to keep Laci going. It worked every time.

The room dwindled to whispers while Ida focused on eating, her mind running over the morning training. *Can't he tell me what he wants me to do?*

Laci nudged her arm. She looked up first at Laci, who had paled, then turned her head. Chin resting on the back of his hands, Malice sat across from Ida. She choked on her food and started coughing. Grabbing her drink, she guzzled, water spilling from the corners of her mouth, and slammed it on the table.

Breathing heavily, Ida wiped her mouth with the inside of her shirt's collar. "What are you doing here?" she asked bitterly, her eye throbbing.

"Who is this? You know him?" Laci leaned into Ida, cupping her hand over her mouth to whisper in her ear.

"Stay quiet, Laci Holigan," Malice said without so much as glancing in her direction. Laci nodded instantly and poked at her food.

Ida glared. *How did he know her name?*

"It seems you're struggling with my lesson this time." Ida's nose scrunched up. "Shall I give you a piece of advice?"

She swallowed her mouthful. "If you came here to rub my struggles in my face, beat it."

"As fun as that would be, I'll spare your feelings." His eyes narrowed on Ida. She shivered.

"… Fine, then tell me your advice." Ida waved her fork in the air, stabbing it into the lamb and cutting a bite-sized chunk out of it.

"Do you know the difference between a spar and a fight?" he asked.

"Didn't realize there was one."

Malice readjusted himself by lifting his head and interlocking his fingers on the edge of the table. "A spar is a learning opportunity, a chance to try something new, show off a bit. You would be a fool not to make it last as long as possible."

"A fight is something you never want to drag on unless you know for certain you can win. At the end of a fight, one will walk away, and the other will be dead." The subtle difference in his tone toward the end of his sentence made goosebumps race up her arms.

Ida stopped, peeked at Malice and Laci. Suddenly her clothes felt uncomfortable, and the air was thick, hard to breathe. Then he stood.

Ida held her hand out. "Wait." Malice glanced over his shoulder. "Why help me? I thought you were going to let me figure things out on my own." *Not that your riddles actually help.*

"Aren't I still doing so? You don't know what I want from you, right?"

She looked elsewhere.

"Right. I hope you figure it out tomorrow." Ida watched as Malice left the mess hall. The entire room erupted into chatter once more. Beside her, Laci took a breath of relief.

She placed a hand on Ida's shoulder. "How can you stand his presence like that? It felt like I was suffocating," Laci said in a slightly panicky voice, sweat glistening on her pale skin.

"Probably because he's the one who trains me. I've gotten used to the proximity." She shrugged and dug into her meal again.

Laci's eyes darted between Ida and the door. "That was Malice Reap?" She grunted as if answering her own question.

Ida nodded and picked up a grape, tossing it in her mouth.

"Damn!" Laci slammed her fists onto the table. "How can someone so beautiful be so dangerous?"

With a disappointed groan, Laci gobbled her food as Ida rolled her eyes. She didn't understand what the fuss was about, nor did she want to.

Laci headed west after she and Ida cleared their trays while Ida didn't have to go far, patrolling in the kingdom's heart.

If there was such a difference between a fight and a spar, then Ida had never fought. Never had to think of whether her life was in danger or not because she knew there was a line whilst training. A knight would intervene if the line were to be crossed. She had scarcely seen it happen. Although she'd heard about it often.

Perhaps she needed to act as if her life *were* in danger. One false move and she'd die.

*

Rain and dew were heavy in the air as murky clouds rumbled overhead. It was surprisingly dark when there should have been some light spilling into the sky. Torches had been placed around the walls of the coliseum, two lampposts in the center of the arena.

Ida went to the weapons rack and grabbed a padded sword. Sweat trickled down her spine as her heart pounded—she'd just finished running. Absently, she touched her under-eye, which was tender from the day prior.

As she walked toward Malice, Ida tore the padding off the blade, adjusted her shoulders, and bounced on her feet, then finally took her stance. Malice smiled and held his hands to either side of him. Flames shot from his palms. A twist of his wrists made the fire into a golem. Embers shot off its body while steam swirled into the air. Ida's eyebrow jumped. What was the point of creating an inferno when it looked like it was about to rain any second? Probably another show of skill, Ida assumed. No matter, today she was confident, ready for what he had to throw at her.

Around them, training began. Weapons clashed, magic soared, commands echoed, and grunts and cries of pain sounded between thunder. For some reason, the training seemed harder.

Royals were tiring out faster and knights were putting in more effort.

Ida sucked a breath in and held it, focusing on the golem when it lumbered forth. It brought its arm over its head, slicing down. Ida parried and released her breath, a wave of heat prickling her skin. The limbs she cut off vanished. Quickly, Ida found an opening and took it. With a single movement, she cut its head off.

At least, she thought she did. The golem ducked and whirled back, its extremities fully regenerated. It swept Ida's legs out from under her. Faster than Ida could keep track of, the golem got to its feet and slammed its foot into Ida's head. A burning sensation traveled into her lungs. She winced and shut her eyes, the pressure that followed bringing her to her knees.

"Dead," Malice said. "Lethal blow to the head. Start the fight over."

The golem retreated. She stood, head throbbing. At least the rain cooled her overheated skin.

Dead. Dead. Dead. And Dead again.

Ida was out of breath. Her head, chest, arms, and legs all burned and ached beyond belief. The hour was almost up and the confidence she had in the beginning was gone. She was no closer to discovering Malice's lesson than she was four days ago. Thunder boomed overhead and rain started coming down in big, heavy drops. After being thrown to the ground like a sack of potatoes, Ida got to her feet, groaning. She picked her sword up, twirled it, and gripped it double-handed.

She rushed in, aiming for the left side, feigned to the right. The blow chipped off some of its shoulder. She spat and ran around to its rear, where she stabbed just below the ribcage, but Malice said nothing. It must not have been enough.

She withdrew, turned on her heel, and swung her leg into its side, the fire burning her pants. The golem hunkered down, sliding across the dirt. It shifted past the thrust of Ida's sword. The golem caught her wrist, jerked her forward, and grabbed her other wrist. As it wrenched her arms back, there was a sudden tension between her shoulder blades. Her skin sizzled in its grip. It was pulling her arms and pushing her forward with its foot.

Her shoulders popped before a searing pain had burst. She repressed the agony by biting her lip and struggled to get out of its hold. If this continued, her shoulders would be yanked out of their sockets if not completely ripped off, and her wrists would be charred black. Panic sent a wave of nausea through Ida. She couldn't collect her thoughts. Everything was happening too fast. Her heart thundered louder than the storm.

Across the field, someone threw their opponent over their head. Her eyes twitched. Gritting her teeth, Ida grabbed hold of the golem's wrists and flung it over her head into the ground. Its back crashed in a flurry of embers, steam pouring out from under it. Ida leaped away and fell to her knees.

Her shoulders felt broken, but she could move them. Her wrists throbbed, skin blackened, bones peeking out of the glob of melted flesh, the smell piquant. Tears blurred her vision, the pain almost unbearable. Sucking in haggard breaths, Ida concentrated her magic on her wrists, life slowly returning to the skin and mending over bone, though her fingers still jolted randomly.

The golem propped itself up and anger rose from the depths of her stomach. She mustered as much energy as she could and ran for the sword, scooped it up, cleaved the golem in half from its head to the ground.

Upright, Ida stumbled, chest heaving, her clothes soaked from sweat and rain. Everything was cold and hot at the same time, her vision hazy. She was amazed she had been able to pick up the sword, let alone wield it. *Guess my regeneration isn't all that bad.*

"Dead. You cut the golem in half. What more is there to say? Restart the fight," Malice said with a straight face.

Ida's nose scrunched as she mocked Malice in her head. Restart *the fight,* he said. Restart the fight. Ida looked down at the sword, the steel blackened from the golem's flames. She snorted and busted out laughing. She must be a fool. It was simple, as plain as day, yet she couldn't see it until now. Soaked, she used her sleeve to wipe her face, then turned to the golem, smirking.

The golem jumped, its leg high, and slammed into the field. Ida had barely moved out of the way, her legs practically numb. It forced its leg back and up, its foot coming within a splinter's length of her face, heat following like thousands of needles caressing her skin. Twisting and swaying forward, its fist closed in. Ida used her sword to take the blow and push it off. For sturdy footing, she spread her legs and slashed the golem diagonally from the belly to the head in one fell swoop.

It disappeared completely in a plume of steam.

Ida stabbed her sword into the earth, kept her hands on the grip, got down to her knees and rested her forehead on her knuckles. The cold mud soaked through her pants. Each breath and muscle stung, a sharp pain radiating from her core. She used too much magic to regenerate her injuries. Despite the pain, she was glad they were finished.

Malice walked over to her. She only realized it when she saw his boots. She peeked up and took the hand he offered to help her to her feet—his hand was… rougher than she thought it would be, based on how pristine his skin appeared.

"Never," he said in a low voice, "drag on a fight. Always go for the kill." Serpent-green eyes raked her body as Malice pulled the sword out of the ground.

Ida panted, "How did you keep… the golem… from being extinguished?" The sword was strange in Malice's hand. He looked better without a weapon.

"A fire that is strong enough and big enough will not be extinguished by rain."

Malice put the sword against the rack, picking up the padding and sliding it over the blade on the way. Then he walked over to Gareth, who glanced at Ida after a few seconds, and nodded with a wave of his hand. Once he had found who he was searching for, Malice strutted to a group and removed one of the royals. The person he plucked suddenly bolted around him, dashing toward her. Laci. Her expression was dour as she approached. Laci grabbed Ida's arm and draped it around her shoulders, bracing Ida's weight against her body.

"Let's get you home," she said determinedly. "And before you ask, Sir Gareth gave you permission to recuperate for the rest of the day."

Laci regarded Ida, brows knitted together, and started toward the closest exit. Ida smiled, too tired to argue. It was surprising to see that Malice, of all people, could be nice or at least have mercy on someone. Honestly, her small warm bed that squeaked when she moved too much sounded good, even better than a meal or a bath. Although, those sounded good too now that she was thinking about them.

"Magnus"

The rain stopped, but the sky was still a dark, menacing mass of grey rumbles and white flashes. It was too late for the sun to shine; the clock ticking past the evening hours.

Magnus ate lunch and dinner in his study, reading letters from the rulers and responding to them. Four rulers kept in constant touch, sending letter after letter at a rate Magnus found difficult to keep up with. The rulers from Jared's, Raelle's, Braxton's, and Wolfgang's Regions were growing upset about Magnus's lack of details. They had wanted to know how the Games went, what happened to Charles, had he heard of the recent string of disappearances throughout Vinyamar, amongst other things. The other rulers didn't seem to mind or care. As of two days ago, Magnus stopped replying to the four hounding rulers and had only been reading their mountain of complaints or worries before putting their letters in one of the drawers of his desk.

After training, Malice didn't come to the study. When Magnus asked the maid who brought his dinner where he was, they said Malice was in the library and that he also requested his food to be sent there. It reminded him of when they were kids at the Kings Summit, and he chuckled.

Malice had no interest in what was happening around him, so he made a break for it. The second or third time he had done this, Magnus followed him. There was a trapdoor in the library that led into a deep underground archive. He sat across from Malice and read a book about extinct races, enjoying Malice's presence, until the summit was over.

A knock came to the door, breaking Magnus from his thoughts. "Come in," he said, and the door opened. *Speak of the devil*. Malice entered, walking toward the desk. "Spent quite a bit of time in the library, didn't you?"

He nodded. "Alucard liked to record his knowledge. It's interesting comparing it to other sources."

"Other sources?" Magnus questioned.

"Hordes liked to do something similar, but his journals were always biased whereas Alucard's are not," he said as he sat down.

I forget how close Hordes and my great-grandfather were. Magnus gathered the papers in front of him, stacked them against the desk, a loud clack, and set them aside. "Tell me of your day."

"Ida finally grasped the concept of a spar and a fight."

"I'm glad to hear it." Ida was young, not even seventeen, yet she was a Royal Guard at the rank of A. Her potential was higher than Gareth's at her age, perhaps greater. With Malice's guidance, Magnus felt she could become a pillar for the royals one day.

"Gareth allowed her to rest for the day, so she's probably sleeping."

Magnus raised his eyebrows. "I'm a bit shocked he allowed that." Lenient as he was, Gareth was a stickler for routine and duty.

Malice shrugged. "I've run her ragged for three days. She is no good to him if she drops dead and he knows that."

"… You said that to him?" Magnus guessed.

"More or less." Malice looked at him as if that were to be expected. "The body and mind need rest every now and again."

"That they do."

Malice's long black nails tapped against the arm of the chair. Outwardly, he was so *human* that Magnus often forgot Malice was a demon. Once, he had mentioned his true form, saying that it was difficult to control and horrendously ugly. Magnus's eyes shifted to Malice's, to his slit pupils. Just how ugly could his true form be when he himself was so handsome?

"By the way." Magnus pushed himself out of his seat. "I know for your wings why you wear open-back shirts, but why so low?" He moved around his desk then sat on the corner, recalling the time they had shown each other their wings as children. His own were feathered, rich cream, tan, and brown. Malice's mirrored a dragon's, scaly and black.

Emerald eyes sliced up to Magnus's. "It's comfortable foremost, but mostly out of habit from when I was young, still trying to control my appearance."

Magnus's eyebrows rose and Malice continued, "My tail would rip my clothes. Besides, when I fly, it stabilizes me a bit, so I bring it out from time to time."

"Wait." Magnus blinked. "You have a tail? Like an actual tail?" A smirk crept onto his lips. He didn't know whether Malice was jesting or if it was true.

Malice chuckled, "Yes, an actual tail." His expression changed, it became mischievous. "Would you like to see?"

"Yes!" His face flushed with heat when he realized how fast he answered.

Malice's eyes jolted. "Is a tail that interesting?"

"A fluffy tail wagging side to side on you? Absolutely," Magnus said.

Shaking his head, a lighthearted smile blessing his mouth, Malice stood and stepped around the chair.

Magnus tracked Malice's long fingers as he undid his corset, dragging the silky string through every eyelet. Once completely out, he took the corset off and set it on the chair's rest. Then, pulling it from his pants, Malice drew his shirt over his head in a fluid motion. He uncuffed his pants, pulling them down a little.

His chiseled muscles were just as pale as his face and arms, his torso free of past injuries. As Malice turned, from the bottom of his spine, a tail grew, pushing his pants down even further. It was long and thick at the base—reddish grey—and tapered toward the black, barbed tip. It waved and flicked back and forth like a cat's, a few spots shimmering. Magnus reached for it, but withdrew.

"Can I touch it?" Magnus asked, fixated on the moving tail.

Malice glanced over his shoulder. "Sure."

Delicately, Magnus caught his tail and pet it down till it slipped from his hand—it was warm. The smooth scaly texture was like petting a snake, following the flow of its scales. It was strange petting someone's tail, despite how Malice didn't seem to mind. Magnus wondered if it was sensitive. If it was, he gave no indication. He stopped after a minute or so, still surprised Malice even had a tail and that it wasn't hairy or thin like most of the tails he had seen, animal or otherwise. Malice pulled up and buttoned his pants, then put his shirt on, but left the corset off as Magnus laughed.

"What's so funny?" Malice sat beside him.

"I just," Magnus faced him, "can't believe I was amazed by something so simple." He chuckled in between words. "I've seen plenty of demons, fairies, beastmen, even fishmen with tails, but it didn't cross my mind for a second that you had one."

Malice turned away as a soft laugh escaped his mouth, his shoulders shaking. Embarrassed, Magnus laughed at himself until his stomach hurt and tears stung his eyes.

The sensation of Malice's stare suddenly penetrated Magnus's skin, the room growing silent. Malice was smiling when Magnus glanced at him. It was faint, but there, nonetheless. Malice had the type of beauty only winter could provide—cold, merciless yet bewitching, awe-striking—and those bright green eyes were something Magnus could lose himself in, would gladly do so too. His gaze slipped down to Malice's lips. They were plump in their rosy color and most likely soft.

Magnus's head was floating for an instant.

Then Malice's hand moved to Magnus's ear, his chilled fingertips following the curve of it. Soon, his hand slipped into his hair. His snow white eyelashes were long, his pupils cutting through them like a blade. *Just this once,* Magnus told himself. *What's the harm in one kiss?*

The warmth of Malice's lips gently pressed into Magnus's. He expected something fiercer and more impatient than a peck when he angled away. The lingering sparks on Magnus's lips left him wanting more and wondering why Malice held back. There was seldom anything else the demon held back on.

Magnus grabbed Malice's nape, his hair brushing against Magnus's fingers. Their lips locked before they parted over and over again, a litany of touches Magnus knew he'd never be able to forget. His tongue glided into Magnus's mouth. He gasped, heat rising in his chest. He kissed Malice harder and deeper. Malice's hand ran through his hair while the other leisurely caressed his thigh. Lightning pulsed at Malice's tenderness, the sharpness of his nails a soft graze.

Magnus felt every knot of muscle in Malice's torso. Underneath him, Malice shivered and moaned. Their tongues mingled, their breath harder to catch. Magnus's mind slowly went blank, lost in the sensations of Malice's touch.

Malice moved, his lips leaving Magnus's, when he shifted to stand between Magnus's legs. Magnus tilted his head up to look at him, gulping. *He's blushing.* A redness tinted Malice's cheeks and ears as if he had been standing in the freezing cold for too long. Malice leaned down and forward, his hands gripping the edges of the desk, eyes focusing on Magnus's.

Once, twice, Malice kissed him, his reason melting from the heat they shared. As their mouths parted, Magnus shuddered, the sound of Malice's low, soft moans and gasps having an intoxicating effect.

So, this is the harm.

Magnus pushed his hand up Malice's shirt, and they briefly separated to take it off. Again, they crashed together. *I should stop.* His body and mouth refused to listen to his muddled head. Malice pushed the papers out from behind Magnus. Things rustled and fluttered to the ground. They both fell back onto the desk's surface, Malice's body on top of Magnus, yet his weight was suspended. *Good.* Magnus knew where this was heading. Doubt cleared the fog even if it was for a split second. Just because something didn't feel wrong didn't mean it was right.

"Magnus," Malice groaned.

Magnus wrapped his legs around Malice's hips, pushing their bodies together. The desk squeaked in protest at the movement. Malice unclipped the cloak on Magnus's shoulder. Then he undid the top button of his shirt, and the second, and the third.

Five knocks.

"Your majesty." Gareth. "The knights and I would like you to join us for a drink."

Malice and Magnus broke from each other, panting and hot. Malice wiped the wetness from the corner of his mouth with a look on his face that could kill. Whirling, he stepped away from the desk, bent down to grab his shirt off the floor and put it on. After a second, Magnus buttoned his shirt.

"That's fine," he called out. "I'll be down in a moment."

"See you soon." Gareth's footsteps echoed down the hall until they were gone.

Relieved and disappointed that someone had interrupted, Magnus sighed. He couldn't believe himself getting wrapped up in a kiss while there was still work to be done. Magnus pushed himself off the desk, grabbed his cloak that had barely stayed on the edge, and clipped it on his shoulder. Malice had finished restringing his corset, pulling it tight. He quickly tied it off as Magnus walked toward the door.

"Would you like to join us?" he asked, trying to lighten the mood and lessen the awkwardness. A part of him hoped Malice would decline the offer so he could process what had just happened.

"I'm not in the mood for drinks at the moment," he said bitterly, which stung, considering the moment they just shared. Simultaneously, Magnus was glad.

"Good night, Malice." Magnus turned the doorknob and began to open it when Malice slammed it shut from behind.

"The next time, we won't stop," he whispered in Magnus's ear, placing his hand on top of Magnus's and pulling it open. Magnus stood motionless, his heartbeat counting the seconds.

"The next time, we won't be interrupted." He stepped out, his cape flaring behind him as he strutted down the hall. *Next time? What the hell am I saying?*

Lessons From The Wise
"Display of Power"

By the time Magnus had arrived at the dining hall, most of the knights were drunk, slurring their words, their faces alcohol-tainted, and Gareth was tipsy, the smell of ale strong in his breath. After a few glasses of wine, Magnus called it quits and went off to bed, leaving the knights to drink the rest of the night away.

The wine was just enough to take the edge off the humiliation he had felt since leaving his study. At his bedchamber, Magnus hesitantly opened the doors. It was dim, only a few candles lit the room. He stepped in and closed the door, looked around. Malice wasn't there. His mixed emotions today were getting the better of him, as he was both upset and pleased with Malice's absence.

After hanging his cloak on the black iron coat rack to the left of the door, Magnus walked to the hearth, threw a ball of fire into it, and cast small flames to the chandelier. His bedchamber bright, he noticed a folded note on his pillow. Magnus flipped it open with one hand and untied his shoes with the other when he sat on the edge of his bed.

I'll be staying in the library tonight,

See you tomorrow.

Magnus crumbled the note and tossed it at the door, slipped out of his shoes, and walked to the closet. *Why did I let him kiss me? Why did I kiss him back?*

There was something Magnus felt toward Malice when they were kids, something he put an end to when he entered adulthood and Malice did not. Magnus undressed himself, thinking that something was affection, kinship… sympathy. It was curiosity at first; Why would a prince act like a peasant unused to living in luxury? Magnus got his answer eventually. When he did, he felt pity and understanding. *What changed? When did I stop thinking of Malice as a friend?* The question eluded Magnus as he fell onto the couch, the blaze's warmth kissing his bare feet, hands, and face. He sighed.

As Gareth held Joseph in his arms three days before the Games, Magnus stood there. He knew the effects of intimidation. His skin had bristled from it. Yet the only one truly affected by the formless magic was Joseph, undoubtedly an ability few possess. Joseph died in Gareth's embrace, the magic from the cloaked man waning. The man's travel-stained cloak, torn and frayed at the edges, the fabric brown from the sun, concealed his face perfectly—unnaturally. It was then Magnus knew who they faced. His heart pounded violently against his ribcage, as if it wanted to escape. *I need to be sure it's him,* Magnus had reminded himself.

Lifting the man's hood, the crowd surrounding them came to a halt. Green eyes stared back at Magnus. Stared beyond Magnus. Malice. No longer a boy who wore a crown that shouldn't have been laid atop his brow. He was a dead man walking, and that was who stared through Magnus that day.

Tonight, however, Malice had *looked* at him. Seen him. Kissed him. He shivered as he recalled how Malice pressed his lips against Magnus's, the sounds that filled the space between them. Magnus swallowed the dryness in his throat and watched the wavering fire.

Malice was a king who had the world in the palm of his hand. Hell, Magnus believed Malice had the entire continent in his pocket, too.

What did that change? Malice had his goals, Magnus his. They gained middle ground, but that didn't mean Magnus agreed with Malice's approach. Choices were always harder to make when hundreds of thousands of lives were at the forefront of one's mind. The question he had to ask himself was how much he was willing to sacrifice for the bigger picture. *You've made your bed, Magnus, lie in it.*

Standing, Magnus closed his hand into a fist like he was catching a bug, extinguishing the fire, before he shuffled to the bed. His bed was always much bigger than a single person needed. Onto the mattress, feeling it give to his weight, Magnus pulled the sheets up to his forearm. He lay on his side, so he could gaze out of the windows. The moon was bright, shining amongst the passing clouds. Crickets chirped in the garden and owls hooted. *Beautiful night...*

"Ida"

Ida stood front and center, hands behind her back and chin held high, refreshed and excited. Her locks were half up, tied with thick string. With leather armor worn to hell, stained but clean clothes, and boots that could fall off her feet, Ida was ready. Malice raised an eyebrow, scanned her up and down as if he were noting her appearance, then smiled.

"Today I'll teach you to fight using your magic," he said. "I noticed you don't know how to use or control your magic effectively in battle."

Ida's head lowered. "Not many have smoke magic. It's not easy learning to use it without an example," she said bleakly.

"Dark magic is similar. I can teach you to use it, how to strengthen your fists and sharpen your blade."

She didn't quite understand how darkness was like smoke, even after watching him in the Games. She nodded. Excitement bubbled to the surface, and she quickly put a cap on it.

"Right now," Malice took his hands out of his pockets and held them out, "you only know how to create a smoke screen, correct?"

Ida nodded again when a black smoke-like substance flowed from the palms of his hands. It quickly surrounded them. The light of day darkened before it dissipated. *He's good at reading expressions... I'll have to work on that.*

First, Ida must imagine her magic as an extension of her body, starting with something small and something that needed to stay close to the body. Malice created a dagger no bigger than the length of his forearm and had Ida touch it. The dagger was hard like steel and just as sharp as an actual blade. His fingers wrapping around it, Malice's dagger dissolved.

Ida thought it wouldn't be too hard to replicate a knife, had seen one enough to know what it looked like, felt like. Palm side up, she held out her hand and closed her eyes, focused on the straight edge of a knife. The curved metal sharpened to cut anything, the sturdy handle somewhat rounded for a better grip. After a breath, Ida opened her eyes and there was a knife of smoke in her hand. She smirked, tried to flip it around to grab it properly when it puffed and floated away in a cloud. Her smile vanished.

Malice watched for minutes on end, silent in his observation. Over half an hour later, Ida's knife would hold its form for just a moment.

"Tomorrow," Malice broke Ida's concentration, "I want you to be able to conjure a knife for a few minutes."

"What?" She squinted and scrunched her nose, the knife in her hand spilling off the sides of her palm. "Isn't that too soon?"

"Not when you've never done this, yet you can materialize a knife for three seconds. By tomorrow, three minutes shouldn't be a problem."

"What happens if I don't?" Ida crossed her arms and glared up at Malice. As much as she enjoyed getting under his skin, the twinge in her core concerned her.

"Then you'll become a pincushion." Malice's stony gaze cut through her, sending a chill down her spine. A lump caught in the back of her throat as she watched his pupils dilate.

The coliseum became stationary, all sound going dead. Until she heard the gasps. Ida spun on her heels. Around her, royals clutched their chests or throats and started dropping like flies. Even the knights were gasping for breath as they fell to the ground. The air was rigid, each gust of wind like a wave of needles crashing into Ida. When she returned to Malice, she realized what was going on.

"Intimidation," she muttered in disbelief at the scale of his magic. "Why show me this?" The control he'd had over the golems was more than enough to convince her of his power. The Games and his spar with Sir Gareth were fresh in her memory as well.

"A lesson you should take to heart," Malice finally said.

His pupils dilated, the slits thinning again. Great inhales sounded throughout the coliseum like wildfire. Royals sprang from the dead, coughing and heaving, hands on their chest, horror pinching their faces. A few remained on the ground. Ida couldn't tell if they were dead, unconscious, or trying to collect their thoughts.

"You can have all the power in the world." Ida snapped toward Malice, her face twisted with anger and fear. "But if you can't control it, what use does it have?"

Control?! Ida gawked at Malice, at the surrounding royals recovering from his attack, and the knights who were either furious or confused. Spreading magic without an element was the most difficult to control; it was unpredictable. Most used it in a situation where they were outnumbered, or they could afford to let loose. It didn't matter if a royal could focus their magic on a single person, the surrounding people would still be affected. To do the exact opposite and let it affect all but one person… was unheard of. Ida would have thought it to be an impossibility if she hadn't witnessed it firsthand.

She glanced at her trembling hands. What *kind of person did I ask to train me?* She laughed dryly to herself as Malice walked toward the western gate.

"Gareth"

"Your majesty," Gareth fumed, his fists bunching at his sides, "this cannot go unpunished. He attacked the entire coliseum!" He flung his hands toward Malice, who was beside him.

He recognized that feeling of suffocation as an incredible weight forced him to his knees, his blood running cold. Gareth had had to use his intimidation only a handful of times, even less had it been used against him, but the sensation never changed. Hatred threatened to burn a hole in Gareth's stomach.

The king, tapping his finger against the desk, considered both Malice and Gareth, then sighed. "Why use such a large-scale attack?" he asked, disappointment heavy in his tone.

"To teach my disciple a lesson about control," Malice replied in a controlled manner like he did not care about how he could have killed many royals in the coliseum.

Gareth's jaw tightened. He snarled, "You could have killed over a third of those royals today. Do not play 'the wrong actions for the right reasons' card!" He whipped around to face Malice, breathing heavily as he loomed over him. *Control yourself, Gareth, you are in front of the king.*

As Gareth went to step away, Malice said, "I'm training Ida the way I was trained, but I never claimed to have the right reasons or the right methods, Gareth." Malice turned, the two now toe to toe. "If you nor your royals could handle a low dose of intimidation, you might as well dig their graves alongside yours. I'll even lend you a hand."

"Enough!" the king shouted as he jolted out of his seat. "This will be the only time I give clemency for a deliberate act of subversion against me and my royals, understand?"

After glaring at each other for a moment longer, Gareth took a step back and fell into his seat. Malice remained standing.

"You have my permission to continue to train Ida, but never," he growled, "attack my royals again. If you do, there will be consequences."

"As for you." The king shifted his attention toward Gareth. "Malice is right."

"How?"

"I left you in charge of the training regimen years ago, but it seems my royals have grown weak and so have you."

Gareth recoiled as if shot by an arrow.

"You could barely tolerate my pacify after the Games, so it's no wonder you can't tolerate his intimidation now." The king's hand gestured between the two. "It's about time you regrow a pair, Gareth. Has your age sullied your battle-hardened spirit? Or have your duties become too much for you?"

Gareth's mouth gaped open, his eyes were ready to jump out of his head. In all his years, he had never been doubted. It was like a slap in the face. He had been a royal for over fifty years, had outlived too many to count, and watched just as many retire. The past three rulers had acknowledged his skills. The previous king went as far as making Gareth his right-hand man.

Snapping his mouth shut into a tight line, he looked down at the desk, nails digging into his palms. "Neither... your majesty."

"For your sake, I hope not." Magnus drew his hand over his face, clearly exhausted from the situation, and sat down. "You're dismissed."

*

Gareth swiftly rose and turned around the chair, walked to the door, and closed it. Magnus was impressed he could keep his cool and not slam the door on his way out. Still, that could have gone better.

"Malice," Magnus sighed into his hands, pushing his fingers into his hair. "Your method was extreme, and it was not what we talked about."

"You're right, I apologize," Malice said. "However." Magnus perked his head up. "If I hadn't gone to that extreme, do you think just lecturing Gareth would've made him see the error in his ways?"

He had a point. Gareth was stubborn, sometimes too much for his own good. A dose of harsh reality might have been just what he needed to see the weakness he embedded in the royals. *A weakness that will kill too many if I let swelter any longer.*

"Probably not," Magnus admitted. "I meant what I said earlier, nevertheless. You do this again, whether it be attacking my royals or going against our plans, there will be consequences."

Fixated on Magnus's stern expression, Malice smiled after a moment. "I'll be sure not to make the same mistake again."

He nodded and reclined, feeling the cold of the chair seep through his clothes. Never having broken his word, he thought he could trust Malice and let the incident go.

Magnus closed his eyes. "So," he said and changed the topic a bit, "Ida, how is she doing? I know you've taken a personal interest in training her."

Malice grunted approvingly. "She's quick to pick up on things, but she lacks the ability to think on her feet. She's used to being told what the lesson is and how to do it. Our first training session was substandard at best."

"You're trying to break that habit?" Magnus said when he picked his head up and opened his eyes.

"Amongst teaching her other things, yes."

"I'm glad it's going well. I didn't think you would take this as seriously as you are, nor did I think you would enjoy it so much." Ida taking lessons from Malice now could help provide an example for royals later. Again, Ida could become an invaluable royal for the kingdom.

"Neither did I." Malice chuckled dryly, uncrossed his legs, and stood to head for the door. "See you tonight," he said as he opened the door, then stopped with a gasp and spun. "I almost forgot." Magnus inclined his head. "Where is Pich Conwrath?"

Magnus looked Malice up and down, surprise painting his face. "Why do you want to meet them?"

"I have a few things I wish to learn." He smiled.

Lessons From The Wise
"Healing"

Knocks sounded on the door. Pich stumbled over their own feet before they opened it to find Malice Reap standing there.

"Pich Conwrath?" Malice peered down at Pich with a thin smile, as if he were trying to appear pleasant. He wasn't as tall as Lycn, but tall enough for Pich to tilt their head up to look him in the eyes. They had heard the King of Hordes Region had been born of snow—a common saying that meant someone was born with albinism—which made sense. Malice's hair would be pure white in the sunlight, his lashes as well, and his skin was so pale that Pich could see a few blue veins underneath the skin of his neck.

They nodded and pushed up their glasses. "Did you need something?" They kept what Sir Gareth told them to do in the back of their mind. *Be wary and stay vigilant.*

"I do," he said. "I heard you're the best healer in the region, and I'd like to learn a few things from you." His tone made it difficult to discern any emotion or hidden intent. They scanned him, eyes narrowed.

"Come in." They opened the door and smiled. "We'll get started right away."

Pots of flowers, tapestries of woodlands, and vining plants decorated the inside of Unit One's quarters. Weapons leaned against the walls—swords, bows and arrows, and staffs. There was a single bookshelf on the wall to the left, two shelves had books, one had a hand fan with cranes on it, and the rest were empty. Most of the decorations Pich had placed there themself.

"Follow me," Pich said and rushed around the furniture in front of the hearth. "Here it is." Extending their arm, they gestured to their room.

A small bed was centered on the rightmost wall, a nightstand on either side. One had a lamp and the other a journal. Above their bed hung a bow. It was used well, the bowstring slightly frayed, cracks in the wood of the main body. Sir Gareth gave them that bow when they became a royal.

Beside the door were two armoires. A long desk starting from one wall, bending at the corner, then stopping in the middle of the other, was covered with notes, jars and vials, bandages, needles and thread, and books on medicine and healing. Herbs and plants in sacks, jars, pots, and even more books filled the shelves above. *Books I've read too many times to count. Maybe I should get rid of them.*

"Sorry for the mess." Pich fixed their glasses as they made their way to the chair at the desk. "Come," they put both hands on the back of the chair, smiling, "show me what you know." Despite trying to keep their voice under control, they were excited to share their knowledge with someone. It was unfortunate that someone was Malice.

Malice walked over and sat down. "Not much, if I'm being honest." He looked up at the shelves and pointed. "I do, however, know a little about medicinal care."

"Really?" Pich's eyebrow shot up. They wouldn't have guessed that someone so perilous would know about healing practices.

He nodded. "My brother taught me when I was a boy. He offered to teach me how to heal, but like a fool, I declined." He stopped, glancing at the clutter in front of him. Pich felt their cheeks flush. *I should have cleaned up today.*

"I'm not sure if I can learn much since my regeneration abilities are so extensive but—"

"I'm sure you'll do just fine!" they interrupted and glided to the chair's side, their wings fluttering. "But I would like to know why you want to learn all of a sudden." *Be wary.*

"I feel as though it will be important if I learn. Who knows what the future entails?"

Pich stared inquisitively at the demon, thinking over his answer. As long as they stayed cautious and kept an eye on him, it should be fine. Right?

"Shall we begin?" Pich liked his answer for now, at least. If he did anything suspicious, they would have no choice but to stop. The thought saddened their heart. It was not every day you met someone interested in learning how to heal when regeneration was an option.

Grabbing down a book and placing it in front of Malice, they flipped through the pages. Near the halfway point of the book, they stopped and pointed at the top of the page. Pich traced the sentence they were reading aloud from as Malice followed along.

Medicinal care was usually reserved for witch doctors, though Pich had brushed up on the topic a few times for knowledge's sake. Witchdoctors used plants, potions, rituals, and chants to heal their patients. Healers and doctors used science and modern technology to treat people.

Pich watched Malice's reaction to the information in the book. He knew about both aspects of medicine. He didn't tell them everything then. Pich frowned but pushed the detail to the hindmost of their mind for now. If Malice raised any other suspicion, they would bring it up.

The next chapter was about using one's magic to heal another.

"Healing was as simple as regeneration really, at least to me it is."

Malice nodded in agreement.

One needed to guide their magic into a person's body, let it flow through the canals of energy, forcing their own magic to move, and eventually heal the injury. Pich had trained to expand the amount of magic they could put out while quickening the healing process. They could mend a severed limb in less than thirty seconds. *Eighteen seconds, to be exact.*

Proudly smiling to themselves, Pich noticed how Malice stared at them, a smirk on his face.

"What?" they asked.

"Eighteen seconds is impressive," he said. "Your reputation certainly does you justice."

Pich startled, eyes wide. "Can you read my mind?" *I don't think demons have that ability, but who knows with this one.*

Malice snorted. "If by reading your mind you mean listening to the words spilling out of your mouth, then sure, I can read your mind."

Pich's face reddened, heat spreading from their chest into the rest of their body when they cleared their throat. "Keep reading," they said and pointed to a random paragraph on the page.

Eventually, Malice began reading on his own, his eyes running across the page faster than Pich could keep up with. They sat on the edge of their bed, legs stretched out in front of them, hands twisting and pinching their tunic. Malice was an enigma to Pich, a creature that rarely ventured from its home and a creature too dangerous to approach openly. They looked him up and down, taking in his relaxed poise as questions started entering their mind.

"How old are you?" they asked out of the blue.

Malice's eyes never left the book, but his eyebrow peaked. "Twenty-one," he said.

Pich gasped, "You're younger than me?"

"I'm younger than everyone in Unit One."

They opened their mouth to say something but paused, their eyes narrowing on Malice. "How do you know that?"

"I was told about the members of Unit One before you returned." Malice peeked over at Pich, his green eyes housing no sparkle. "I know quite a bit about all of you."

Pich swallowed. They didn't like his tone, not one bit. It made them uncomfortable, like a hair caught inside their shirt that kept tickling their skin. After a moment of silence, Pich thought to change the subject. "Do you have any siblings?" Pich didn't. They were an only child. A rather common occurrence for immortals.

"They're mostly dead," he said bluntly.

Good going, you idiot. Pich glanced around their room as if they had never seen it, the air awkward now. What were they supposed to say to that?

Outside of Pich's room, the door opened, and voices murmured. *Thank the heavens.* Sighing, Pich excused themselves and hurried to the main living space, leaving Malice to read.

When they came around the corner, Barbus had already plopped on the couch. He seemed as if he were about to fall asleep, his eyes droopy. Lucas was walking to his room when Lycn closed the door behind him and crossed the living space to Pich. He bent down and kissed them on the cheek.

"How has your day been?" he asked with a fond smile.

Pich looked at the floor, contemplating how they should tell everyone about Malice. "Umm..." They tilted their head. "You can't be mad."

Lycn's eyebrow rose as Barbus leaned his head over the back of the couch. "Why would I be?"

They scratched their neck. Pich knew no matter what they said, Lycn was going to be upset, even more so because it was Malice. "Malice is in my room... right now. He's reading about medicine because he wants to learn about healing. He's been here for a whi—"

"What?" he shouted and rushed past Pich.

A hand slammed against the doorframe. Pich dashed after Lycn, his frame blocking the entrance. Pich hit his arm. Lycn tensed and moved aside.

"See?" Pich turned around in a huff. "He's reading. Malice came to me to learn."

Lycn's honey-yellow eyes were glued to Malice until he ultimately grunted and stomped away.

Pich glared at his back, frowned, and shook their head. *So temperamental sometimes!* "I think that should be all for today."

Malice slammed the book shut and set it down on the table. He stood, now face level with the shelves above Pich's desk. A book must've caught his eye. He plucked one down and held it out for Pich to see.

Malice asked, "May I borrow this for the night?"

They squinted at the cover, "Sure," and pushed their glasses up. "But are you sure one night will be enough to read all that?" The book was as thick as a blade was wide.

"It will."

After a moment of consideration, Pich nodded toward the door, smiling. "I'll show you out."

Malice followed not so closely behind Pich, out of their bedroom and through the living room where the Unit watched him leave. Lycn stood against the wall, his arms crossed, scowling. Pich was right. Lycn was taller than Malice, not by much though. Barbus's hair was in a warrior's braid, his massive arms slung over the couch. Scars treaded up his fingers onto his forearms. *That one's a brute.* Lucas had stepped out of his room to lean against the doorframe, arms folded, his bright blue eyes trailing Malice. The long sword attached to his hip gave him a lean, somewhat muscular build.

Pich found everyone's apprehension ridiculous yet understandable, based on what Sir Gareth had said. That didn't necessarily call for the glares. Malice seemed unbothered.

Stopping at the door, Malice peeked over his shoulder. "Thank you. Same time tomorrow?"

Pich brightened with joy, the flutter in their stomach revealed by the flutter of their wings. They wished those darn things didn't have a mind of their own. "Please do!" It had been a long time since someone had gone out of their way to seek Pich's knowledge—not since they left their home village. The few they had taught in Alucard's Kingdom were sent to Pich on their superior's command.

Malice returned the friendly smile, then, glancing at the others, the door clicked shut behind him. The room stayed silent for a time.

"I don't like him," Lycn blurted.

Pich whipped around, pouting. They rolled their eyes and marched across the living space. "You don't even know him." Granted, neither did Pich, but Malice gave no reason for them to suspect him today—save for how much he knew about medicine. Didn't even swear. His reputation made their hands tremble whenever they thought about it, but having the chance to spend a bit of time with him soothed some of their fear.

"I know of him," Lycn said. "Need I know more?"

"I think you do," Barbus said as he hoisted himself up from the couch, groaning. "Setting his reputation aside, all we know is that he wants to learn the basics of healing. Seems innocent enough to me."

Pich nodded in agreement as they crossed their arms.

Lucas bounced off the doorframe, instantly putting his hands in his pockets and looking down at his shoes. Then his eyes darted to each person. "I'm with Lycn. There's something about him that makes the hairs on my arms stand on edge. I don't think he's someone we should trust or go on a mission with, not when we'd be putting our lives in his hands."

Barbus sighed and closed his eyes, shaking his head.

"It's not like we can do anything," Pich said, glancing between Barbus, Lycn, and Lucas. "The king's orders are absolute. I truly think if he wanted to hurt any one of us, he would have done so when he had the chance. Why don't we just try to get along? Make the best out of the situation?"

"Fine." Lucas shrugged and turned into his room before slamming the door.

While rubbing his gut, Barbus waddled to his room. He patted Pich on the shoulder, winked and closed the door behind him. A loud thud sounded inside from Barbus throwing himself onto the bed. Perhaps he should lose some weight. He might break his bed one of these days.

Finally, giving in—or at least calming down—Lycn nodded, walked to Pich, brushed the bangs off their forehead, and kissed it. He caressed Pich's cheek with his thumb, eyes steady on theirs. "If he does something to you—"

"He won't. You worry too much." Pich brought their hand up to cup the side of Lycn's face. His concern was sweet and, as much as it annoyed them, they couldn't stay mad at him. He nuzzled into their palm, his cheeks warm, almost hot, and so was his hand. Grabbing his other hand, Pich led him into their room and closed the door.

"Magnus"

Malice lay on the couch reading the book he borrowed from Pich while Magnus got their nightclothes ready.

He had many things whirling around in his head. Magnus told the rulers of Malice's return, not that he did so joyfully. The rulers were up heaved about the news. Some wanted to push the date of the Kings Summit up, to make it happen sooner. As if that could be done with the snap of his fingers. Thankfully, the Queen of Jared's Region had calmed them down for now. Although, with reports piling in about how someone new had vanished more often than he wished, the thought was tempting. If it weren't more of a hassle than what it was worth, Magnus would have agreed.

As Magnus stepped out of the closet, Pich's book was on the table in front of the hearth and Malice had reclined. It was still silent when he placed Malice's garments on the arm of the couch, returning to the closet after he did. The only sound filling Magnus's bedchamber was the crackling fire and his footsteps on the marble floor.

How could he act as if it didn't happen? They had yet to talk about the kiss they shared a week ago. Was there anything to talk about? What would change if they were to?

Magnus emerged from the closet, Malice dressed in a pair of silk pants, the floral design gleaming. *Why do I keep giving him the shirt if he's not going to wear it?* He padded to his bedside, threw the covers back and climbed into bed, frowning.

"We need to talk," he said after a while, glancing toward the couch.

Malice got up and faced Magnus. "We do."

When Magnus patted the empty space next to him, Malice quickly filled it, the bed squeaking with his movement.

"What am I to you?" Magnus asked.

"… I think you need to ask yourself that question." Malice turned his head toward Magnus, his eyes half open. He sighed. "You are a sanctuary, Magnus," he said. "I wouldn't have kissed you if I didn't feel anything for you and I don't think you would have either."

"So, what do we do? Hide our relationship? Join our kingdoms? Marriage? Or do we stop before…" Magnus scowled at the bed sheets over his legs. He had pushed Malice out of his life once. He wouldn't do it again unless that was what Malice wanted.

"You didn't answer the question."

"What you are to me?"

Malice nodded.

"… I don't know." It was truth, and it was one that Magnus felt horrible in admitting aloud.

"Until you know," Malice said, his voice soft, "we don't have to be anything just yet. I'm fine with waiting. I've always been fine with waiting, so long as you don't push me away again." Something darkened his expression.

Magnus's heart ached. Malice probably thought of the final letter they had sent one another.

Five years older than Malice, Magnus entered adulthood a year before Malice was crowned King of Hordes Region. If Magnus had only felt friendship toward Malice, that letter wouldn't have been the last, but he didn't. It was more than that and it was wrong, so he cut Malice off. In the process of doing so, he made it sound as if it was all Malice's fault. *I'm sorry*, was what Malice wrote back. The guilt was like a sword fresh out of a furnace, sluggishly penetrating his chest.

"I won't. Not again," Magnus muttered, his fists balling up the blankets. A pale, bony hand slid on top of his dark skin, gently squeezing.

"Then we have all the time in the world."

Literally. Magnus smirked, a breath escaping through his lips. "Right now," he said, "we have other matters to discuss."

"Ready to tell me about what's been on your mind?" Malice mused.

"There's a lot. Sure you want to hear about it all?"

"I want to hear everything."

Greed
XII

Royals gathered in the coliseum as usual. The sun blazed overhead as small white wisps moseyed in front of it. A warm breeze from the south carried the smell of freshly baked goods and damp grass around the kingdom.

Ida stood across from Malice, wearing brown trousers rolled to just below her knees and a black shirt. After a good healing session with one of the royals in her barracks, the burns from yesterday were gone. Had she waited any longer to see them, the nerves would've been permanently damaged. Peeking down at her wrists as she rubbed them, the sensation of overwhelming heat returned for a split second. She lifted her eyes.

Malice wore a sleeveless black shirt and thick pants that cuffed around his ankles, his clawed feet bare. There was something off about him today. His presence seemed more intense. Nerves tore up her throat, but she swallowed them down, crouched, and clasped her knife of smoke. She waited. Malice did nothing.

After a few minutes had passed, Ida yelled, "What are you waiting for?"

"What do you mean?" he said. "You strike first."

Ida straightened herself. "Strike against what?" she asked, gesturing to the space in front of and around her, left generously by the other royals and knights.

Malice stepped forward, bent down to scoop up a handful of dirt, then threw it. The dirt collided with a wall of air, the dust forming around the side of a golem, disappearing. Ida's jaw dropped.

"How am I supposed to fight something I can't see?" She stomped and whirled away, the knife vanishing. She rubbed her face down with her hands. Air was invisible. Sure, one could feel it, smell it, and hear it if the wind was strong enough, but there was no way to see it. None. Ida's nose scrunched as she turned back to Malice.

"Are you trying to make a fool out of me?" she barked, her eyebrows furrowed, a vein throbbing on her forehead.

"You're already the fool."

Ida groaned, even more frustrated than a second ago.

Wind caressed her skin, loose dirt and gravel gradually creating a circle around her feet. Then, she was a few meters in the air. It felt like a tree trunk had abruptly smashed into her gut, slamming her to the ground. She gasped, all the oxygen leaving her lungs. Rolling over, the contents of her stomach poured onto the dirt. She coughed and gagged, both trying to breathe and trying not to vomit again. Her throat burned and her eyes stung, her back now riddled with pain.

That was the second time that bastard made her retch.

Ida pushed herself up, arms trembling. The golem made no sound, it had no smell, and she couldn't see it.

In her right hand, she conjured a knife, crossed her arms in front of her face and chest. Each foot shuffled when she found solid footing. The golem. Ida's eyes darted toward Malice, looking for his hands, but they were tucked behind him. She gritted her teeth. Searing pain sliced her thigh. She glanced at it. Thick red gashes like claw marks appeared from her knee up, blood soaking and turning her pant leg black. She winced and focused on regenerating her leg. The bleeding slowed, but her knife disappeared again. Pain bloomed in her shoulder. Another slash, and she clutched onto it, sweat dripping from her pores.

Fuck.

*

"Is this not a little much?" Gareth heard the crash from Ida slamming into the earth. He stood at Malice's side, concern twisting his gut and face. "I think you are being too harsh," he insisted.

"I think you've been too soft."

Gareth frowned. "What is the point of this?" Pounding her down made little sense to him, but above all else, he hated watching someone so young get beaten like that. As if she were another target at the edge of the arena. "Are you just going to let her drown?"

"Right here," Malice kept his eyes on Ida, observing her struggle, "right now, Ida needs to learn something. She needs to sink or swim within one hour."

"If she does not?

"Then today will be the last I train her."

Gareth's eyes moved from Malice to Ida. Fatigue was what he saw in her as blood seeped through her clothes and dripped to the dirt. She guarded herself well, but that meant next to nothing when the enemy was unknown. Ida might as well spread her arms out, close her eyes, and stand still. He glanced to his left, hoping Pich was looking at him, and they were. For a split second, relief washed over him as he waved, beckoning them to him. He was glad his Unit took over for some of the other instructors today.

Pich smiled, said something to the royals, and ran to Gareth. He held a hand up as they arrived and pointed at Ida. Pich caught a glimpse of her, their expression suddenly serious. Nodding, they took their place a little behind him on standby.

*

Ida panted and wiped the sweat building on her brow. Her shoulder seared with pain, her thigh throbbed, but at this point, her entire body hurt. She peeked at Malice. Sir Gareth and Pich stood beside him now. She smirked, thinking they were called to watch her fail.

A gust of wind from the west. She stepped diagonally back and to the east. Her locks swayed from the draft. She managed to dodge for the first time but doubted she would get that lucky again. The golem didn't always leave bursts of air and even if it did, she couldn't predict where it would strike from. So far, the stupid thing was tossing her around like a rag doll or giving her nonlethal injuries. Was it trying to bleed her dry and tenderize her?

It was hard to think, but Ida forced herself anyway. Another gust of wind came from the side. She backed up right into its foot from the feel of it. It launched her forward. She hunkered herself down and tumbled to a stop. Crouched, Ida closed her fist, realized nothing was there, and created another knife.

The world went black, and her face was in the dirt. Pebbles embedded themselves in her skin. Rising to her elbows, she shook her head and brushed the small pieces of gravel off her face. Blood gushed from her nose like a waterfall until it reduced to a steady drip. How long she had stayed on the ground afterward, she didn't know, but she waited.

The hairs on her arms stood.

Ida rolled to her feet, a whoosh going past. Like a drunkard, she stumbled and threw knives of smoke, each one planting itself in the dirt at the edge of the open space. Her erratic footwork seemed to work against surprise attacks, since Malice couldn't predict where she was going.

Then her feet were swept out from under her.

Smoke poured from Ida's palms, bracing her fall just enough so she didn't crash. *That didn't work as well, or as long as I thought it would.* She dared to steal a glimpse of Malice, an amused grin on his face. Grinding her teeth, Ida spat, righted herself, and clapped, the knives surrounding her exploding. Grey clouds surged toward the middle of the arena, hitting an invisible wall encasing the golem to her right.

All she needed was one more minute.

Ida steeled her strength and will and rushed in barehanded. At the last second, a dagger manifested in her clamped hands before she plunged the blade under the golem's ribcage. If it were a person, the dagger would have punctured a lung, hopefully killing them. If it didn't, the snapping of her fingers making the knife burst would.

Gareth and Pich ran to Ida's aid when she staggered. But she caught herself. As she turned, she glowered at Malice, a fire burning in her chest. Malice's grin deepened while Pich placed their hands over Ida's shoulder. Barely a heartbeat had passed when the cut on her shoulder was gone, and they moved on to her next injury. *Damn, they're fast.*

She took a breath, Pich's healing easing the pain. "You wanted me to learn to use my magic more in a fight. Use it strategically above all else," Ida said, though she said it more for herself than for Malice.

Malice walked over, his demeanor calm and collected. "Magic is just as much of an ally as a sword or your fists. You're talented. Why limit yourself?" He gently pressed the tip of his fingernail into her forehead. "You need to use your head before you lose it." Then pulled away. "Being a master of one will most likely lead to your downfall. You'll be bested by someone better, someone who can think on their feet and use everything to their advantage."

Ida's expression soured as Pich's healing session wrapped up. She didn't know why his words hit deep, but they did. Until now, Ida thought she was one of the best, able to think on her feet and prevail. She could not have been more wrong. Looking down at her calloused hands, she recalled the Games of Retribution, how Malice had beaten Sir Gareth, and how he had trained her. He was a master of all, someone who had taken down thousands of men with a swipe of his hand. Or at least that was what the rumors said.

She met the intensity of Malice's eyes. "A master of one is someone too weak and cowardly to grab onto more. I'm no coward and I'm sure as hell am not weak." Ida smirked. "But I am greedy."

Malice held her gaze. Nothing changed to Ida's knowledge, yet something made her shiver, a sliver of ice running up her spine. "So am I."

The hour was up. A high-pitched whistle rang off the coliseum's walls. Malice left as he always did when he finished beating Ida into the earth. She wondered if he planned to put her in an early grave. Though, thanks to Pich, Ida was fine. Her limbs felt light, a newfound energy coursing through her veins. Sir Gareth sighed while the royals moved to their next instructors. He seemed exasperated. *Not surprising when he has to deal with Malice more often than I do.*

Ida followed her peers on to the next knight, a member of Sir Gareth's Unit, Sir Lycn Grove. He was tall, muscular, tan-skinned, had dirty sand-colored cropped hair, and down-turned eyes. Sir Lycn never smiled, save for when he was interacting with Pich. He frowned a lot, though, like right now. His eyes trailed after someone. Ida glanced over her shoulder in the same direction, Malice's white hair disappearing beyond the western gate. *No one's a fan of him, are they? I would feel bad if it were anyone else.*

"You," Sir Lycn said when the royals formed a semi-circle around him, his gaze fixed on Ida.

Ida stepped forward. "Yes, sir?"

"Why is Malice training you?" he asked, his voice slightly adenoidal.

"Sir Gareth and I told him to." Sir Lycn flinched, his brows furrowing. It was truth, as ridiculous as it sounded.

He stared at Ida for a time, seemingly lost in his thoughts, until he said, "Spar with me."

"What?"

"Are you deaf?"

"No, sir."

"Then get ready," Sir Lycn barked, impatience consuming his tone.

So Ida did, lowering herself in a wide stance, conjuring a short sword in her right hand. Pain stabbed at her core. She gasped, and the sword vanished. *I overdid it.* A burning throb quickly replaced the sharp pain. Sir Lycn considered her a moment, a scowl aging his features. He grunted.

"I didn't tell you to use your magic. Go arm yourself with a proper weapon," he said.

Straightening herself, Ida wondered why, but didn't bother asking. Sir Lycn wasn't the type to answer questions like Sir Gareth was. Even Sir Lucas answered questions when he was in a good mood. She plucked a wooden staff from the racks against the wall to match Sir Lycn's weapon, though she hated using it. It was impractical for combat intended to deliver death. This stick delivered nothing but bruises, welts, and goose eggs.

Ida retook the low stance, Sir Lycn eyeing her suspiciously, probably questioning her choice of weapon. She had seen him spar countless times against other royals, once or twice against Sir Lucas. However, the same could be said for her. They knew one another's techniques, which made winning both easy and difficult. Ida suspected experience or the ability to pull something new out of her sleeve would decide the victor.

'You'll be bested by someone better, someone who can think on their feet and use everything to their advantage.' Ah, yes. Thank you for the kind reminder, Malice. Ida rolled her eyes at Malice's voice in her head. *I got it. Try something new, this is a spar after all.*

"Attack when you're ready," Sir Lycn said.

Ida sneered. That would be a mistake she'd make sure he would regret.

*

Malice brushed up on the studies his brother taught him while Pich showed him the basics of healing. It was simpler than he imagined, but strenuous. To heal, he had to inject his magic into the recipient's body, guiding the energy to the core, and forcing their magical energy to flow. That was if the injury was unknown. If it was known, Malice had to coerce his magic into the wound through the body to the core, focusing on that one spot.

Lycn steered clear of the dorm after morning training finished. *Avoiding me like the plague,* Malice thought to himself. The coyote's bitterness, however, seemed to double after Ida bested him in a spar—Malice wouldn't be surprised if she kicked his stones hard enough he'd never produce seed again. Lucas was there some days and gone the others. Magnus had said that Lucas was one to frequent the kingdom's taverns whenever he had the time. Barbus, on the other hand, quite liked to listen in on Pich's lessons, so he was there every day Malice was. A part of Malice believed Barbus was also there to protect Pich in case he decided to do anything.

Less than a week after they started, Malice learned all he could. He could not go beyond healing the equivalent of a bird's broken wing and a shallow stab wound. Malice laughed at himself. His brother Kiran at eight years old could do better than he could at twenty-one.

The last day they had spent together, Pich offered a book. It was thick, the leather worn and scratched. They said they had read it a million times, so Malice accepted. He flipped through it. Nothing inside was familiar, pages upon pages about herbs and medicine, their history, and current knowledge. The book even told of the whereabouts of certain herbs in Vinyamar, and illustrations of the plants were on almost every sheet. Malice was rather grateful to receive a relevant source of information. It would come in handy soon.

"Magnus"

It was late; the sky littered with white dots as the wind blew in from the balcony windows, the candle flames flickering. Magnus, wearing dark blue silk nightclothes, stood on the balcony, star gazing, his elbows against the cold metal of the rail. The mission weighed heavily on his mind. Unit One wasn't the concern. They swore their lives to the region and swore they would do anything for it, even die if they must. The success or failure of this mission would determine the fate of Alucard's Region. Success would lead to survival and a chance to get ahead while failure…

He sighed, letting his head drop and his eyes sweep across the garden. Everything was a muted midnight purple, the foliage a deep-sea blue. Magnus took in the salty floral scent, which relaxed him some.

A cold hand gently crept onto Magnus's shoulder as Malice came to stand beside him. It gave him goosebumps. Then Malice's hand rested on the railing near Magnus's. His footsteps were always silent, no matter the surface he walked on. It was a technique used solely by assassins. The only reason Magnus knew that was because of Vinney, a Royal Knight rank S, the one assassin in his troops. The previous king, Magnus's father, recruited him a couple of decades ago. He had considered letting Vinney go, but he had proven useful outside his specialty.

Magnus sighed again and pushed himself off the rail. Malice glanced at him but said nothing. He studied Malice's features in the moonlight, the nights they had spent talking flooding his mind until Malice's gaze sliced to his.

He cleared his throat. "What do you think about Unit One?" he asked, hearing a crack in his voice, a rush of heat going to his cheeks.

Malice, who didn't seem to mind, said, "Complacent. Irritated by my joining their mission. Divided to an extent."

"They don't appear close?" Magnus questioned.

"They appear no closer than friends." Malice shrugged. "Gareth and Barbus are like brothers in their loyalty. Pich and Lycn have this puppy love. How far it goes, I'm not sure. Then there's Lucas."

"The outlier," Magnus said. "He wants to follow in his parents' footsteps."

"He wants more than that."

"But I don't know what that is for him."

"I doubt he knows either," Malice said, moving away from the rail. "Perhaps the mission will clear that fog. For all of them."

"Perhaps." *Or deepen it. Only time will tell.* Firelight drowned his bedchamber in orange as Magnus padded through the balcony doors. "Do you think you can teach me how to heal?"

Malice followed behind him, closing the glass doors. "I'm surprised you want to learn," Malice said in a curious tone.

Magnus turned to face him. "My mother was a healer, but my father was against me learning the practice, so mother never got the chance." Just for a moment, when he mentioned his mother, his heart ached.

"I've always had an interest in healing, always wanted my regeneration and healing abilities to be as equal as I could get them. The opportunity hasn't necessarily presented itself." He paused, a humorless grin spreading on his lips. "I suppose it sounds like an excuse now that I've said it out loud."

"Excuse or not, if you want to learn, I'll be more than happy to teach you." The corners of Malice's mouth curved upward a bit.

Satisfied, Magnus stretched his arms high. Pich was a good person, chipper, bright, but there was something about them that Magnus wasn't particularly fond of. He couldn't place his finger on why.

"Shall we get started tomorrow?" Magnus never thought he would get an opportunity like this. He partially believed he wasn't allowed to learn as his father's voice would echo whenever the thought popped into his head.

"Whatever you want." Malice scooped up Magnus's hand and kissed the back of it. The warmth of his lips made Magnus's hand tingle, and their kiss surged from his memories. Abruptly, he retracted his hand and held it against his chest. Malice's smile fled.

They stared at one another, Magnus's mind vacant, before Malice spoke. "I apologize," he said simply, then walked past Magnus toward the couch.

"Wait." Magnus spun, whipping Malice around by the shoulder. "I want more than that," he said as he tugged Malice's chin and kissed him.

They parted after a moment, his eyes searching for something within the sea of green that stared back at him. Magnus kissed him again, sliding his hand down Malice's arm and wrapping it around his neck. Malice moved closer as his mouth opened, gasping, his tongue meeting Magnus's.

This was what Magnus had been thinking of any time his mind relaxed. The warmth of Malice's lips against his. The way he glided his tongue into his mouth, the whimpers that made Magnus shudder every time. How Malice let his hands gently explore his body. Malice's kiss had been on Magnus's mind for over a week, but it was different. He was taking his time, feeling every movement and pulse instead of letting impatience take over.

Malice brushed Magnus's hair behind his ears and looked him in the eyes when they finally released each other, both breathing heavier. They were hungry, starving, as if he wanted to devour everything Magnus had to offer and leave no scraps behind. He kissed Magnus again and again, then one last time.

I want more.

"We should go to bed," Malice said, his voice low and raspy.

"Should we?" Magnus tilted his head as he caressed the side of Malice's face, his cheeks flushed—same as Magnus's— the blue teardrop earring swaying. "I could stand here all night simply enjoying the taste of your lips if you'd let me."

Malice's eyes glinted, "I never said we had to sleep," and he smiled.

Greed

"Briefing"

Magnus sat in an armchair, his white shirt halfway buttoned, showing his lower chest, his feather necklace rocking whenever he moved, while Malice stood behind him, silent, his hair glowing a soft orange. The room was warm from the hearth and all the bodies huddled together.

Gareth glanced over his Unit, all staring down at the stout table in front of them, a map spread over its surface. They were in one of the lounges on the second floor, eastern wing just before the servants' barracks. The walls and floors were dark, the furniture and fixtures painted with light colors to contrast it.

Barbus sat next to Gareth on one of two couches, half-ass paying attention and greedily licking his lips as he eyed the chalice of ale at the edge of the map. Pich and Lycn sat on the couch across the table, Lycn's arm around Pich's shoulders as their wings fluttered every now and again. The back of the couch had been lifted for their wings, so they could sit comfortably. All the furniture in the castle had that feature, since many royals and servants alike had wings. Lucas sat opposite of Magnus in another armchair, his demeanor relaxed, uninterested, but his eyes were fixed on either the map or whoever was speaking.

"There are two ways to reach The Kingdom of Phoenix," Magnus said and pointed to the map, leaning forward as he did. "You could go through the kingdom," his finger traced the path he spoke of, "and avoid Howlers Forest."

"That would take quite a bit of time, your majesty," Lycn said, his free hand going to stroke his stubbly chin. Pich nodded.

Gareth was glad to see Lycn had gotten over his need to glare Malice down. It had taken a time to get there though.

"You're right, which is why I suggest option two." Magnus placed his finger on Alucard's Kingdom, dragged it around to the southeastern bridge to the mainland, and, beyond Howlers Forest, he tapped on Phoenix. "Going through Howlers Forest cuts travel time in half, if not more, even if you were to take your time. The dangers of the forest are for you to consider, however, not me."

"They are worth taking," Gareth said. "Traveling with a light source should keep us safe." Howlers were blind and sensitive to the light. "If it does not, I am fairly confident we can handle ourselves or flee, if need be."

"Afterward, you'll head to Ntesal, Liotkin, Anddulia, Ivory's Kingdom, and finally Cytor and return home. No need to zigzag around. Each of you will travel on horseback. No wagons or wains. It'll slow you down too much." Magnus had practically circled the entire map, a single oval movement covering each kingdom before he reclined in his seat. "Since the path is now set, let us discuss what you will be doing."

"You said this mission will be life-changing," Lucas chimed in, shifting weight from his left side to his right, blue eyes gleaming. "I can't imagine how. Most missions are dangerous, your majesty."

"Not like this." Magnus's gaze slid from person to person. "I am not concerned about you losing your life. I'm concerned…" he trailed. "We don't need to talk about that right now."

Gareth studied Magnus, briefly searching for something beyond the veil of calmness. It was strange that he was unwilling to address whatever this change was, but he understood why the topic had moved on. They were here for a briefing on the mission and its details, but they had not gotten very far yet.

"Voidents are most active in the kingdoms because of the abundance of people," Magnus said, "I want you to find them. Just one is fine. Capture it, see if it has information, discover how to kill it. I want you to learn anything we do not already know. The more we know, the more we will be able to deal with them, stop their killings before they decide to get barbaric."

"You think they'll get impatient?" Barbus tilted his head while licking the top of his mustache clean of foam and ale. *Couldn't contain yourself for long, could you?*

"I do." Gesturing toward Malice, Magnus added, "Malice had encountered voidents a long time ago."

Not surprising. Gareth glared up at Malice.

"They were biddable at first, quietly taking lives out of sight, so no one would realize their presence. Until they weren't and voidents started slaughtering people in broad daylight." Magnus scowled at the map, a muscle tensing in his jaw.

Gareth sighed when Malice looked away, a flash of emotion twisting his expression. *So, he has feelings too. Who would have guessed?*

"I'd much rather it not get to that point, and I'd prefer we take care of the voidents as discreetly as possible for as long as possible."

"Don't want the people to get upset," Pich mumbled more to themselves, it seemed, than anyone else.

"Exactly," Magnus said. "Any questions?"

"Is there a time frame?" Lycn asked, his facial features harder than usual because of the shadows from the hearth behind him. Sweat glistened on his skin. It must be getting too hot for him sitting right next to the fire.

"Ideally, three months."

Gareth nodded thoughtfully. "I do not see why we cannot do that." For essentially a reckon mission, three months was plenty. They had been sent out on more tedious missions and completed them in half the time.

"Why is Malice joining us, your majesty?" Lucas slid to the edge of his seat, eyeing Malice behind the king's chair.

"I believe he will be useful, and he agreed to do it." Magnus didn't acknowledge Malice like the rest of the Unit did. Malice smiled, but it did not reach his eyes, making it demented. Gareth cringed.

"Why us?' Barbus leaned forward and set his chalice on the table, his chest inflating as he held in a burp. He blew his breath away from the group. Lucas still shot him a disgusted glower and moved as close as he could to the other side of his seat.

"Because Unit One," Magnus said, "has the highest success rate, and I trust the five of you with my own life. Why wouldn't I trust you with the lives of my people as well? Unless you have a protest to the mission… Do you oppose going, Barbus?" His voice was calm, but there was an edge, something resolute underlying Magnus's tone.

Barbus laughed awkwardly and shook his head. "'Course I don't, just curious is all. You got plenty of fine royals, helped train a good number of them."

"And for that, I am grateful," Magnus inclined his head, "but I need to think about the safety of my people and how the success of this mission will affect them. You understand?"

"Aye."

"Good. Anything else before I call it a night?"

The crackling flames were the only sound in the room, the hush growing uncomfortable.

"I'll take that as a no. You are dismissed."

"Thank you, your majesty," Unit One said collectively and stood—Gareth included—filing into the hallway.

The walk to the main corridor was silent, shoes clicking on the floor. Gareth turned toward the stairwell and said his farewells to his royals. It was late, the star's bright white specs beyond the ever-moving clouds.

Gareth would be lying if he said he was not concerned. His gut told him to march back to Magnus and demand that he tell him what he was hiding. *What if he is not hiding anything?* Magnus was getting his information from Malice. Malice knew a hell of a lot more than he was letting on, and if there were anyone who could get that information, it would be Magnus. If Magnus truly did not know, why hadn't Malice told him more about the voidents? What does he want from this mission? He probably would not answer, even if he were tortured. Stubborn bastard.

Rounding the corner to the third floor, Gareth sighed. At the very least, he was glad to have told his knights to be cautious around Malice. The demon was planning something, of that Gareth was certain.

*

"Tell me again why I'm sending you on this mission?" Magnus was lying under Malice's arm, his warmth seeping into Magnus's back as he stared out of the glass balcony doors across the bedchamber. They didn't always sleep together, just on the nights they would spend hours talking and doze off without realizing it. *Which is rather often now.*

Magnus… didn't mind. It was nice.

Malice stirred behind him, a small movement, when Magnus felt his body press against him, his breath tickling Magnus's nape. "We need whoever is behind this to think that I'm under your control and have been for a while," Malice said, his voice a soft, deep rasp. "Or at least working with you."

The mission would start tomorrow soon after dawn, and Magnus was running over all the details in his head. For the hundredth time that day.

"We need them to think that you know nothing," Magnus said. "That you are just as oblivious as Gareth and the others." Malice nodded, his hair brushing into Magnus's.

The Games started it, training Ida helped, and now going on the mission with Unit One would seal the deal. Malice mentioned three separate entities that could be behind the attacks in Alucard's Region. Lazarus, the most plausible. Zephyrus, though highly unlikely since he was presumed dead quite some time ago. Another highly ranked voident—one of the commanders—who Malice left nameless because there were a total of four. All of them were at the top of the food chain in their social hierarchy. One of them had been watching Malice off and on since the Games as well. Their presence, Malice said, was unmistakable. *He has a habit of collecting enemies like books.*

"You cannot tell them anything until the objective has been reached." Magnus carefully turned to his side, so he was facing Malice. Eyes closed, his white eyelashes kissed his pale cheeks. They opened sluggishly, the slit pupils dilating ever so slightly.

"I promise," he whispered and his eyes fluttered closed.

Malice had been sleeping most of the day, knowing he wouldn't be able to sleep much, if at all, during the mission. Magnus reached over and caressed the side of Malice's head, his soft hair tickling Magnus's fingers. The bareness of his earlobes reminded Magnus of that afternoon. Malice had taken out his earrings and handed them to Magnus for safekeeping while he explained where he got them from.

One deep breath filled his nose with lavender and mint from Malice's shampoo. Staring at Malice's face, Magnus began to drift, his racing mind finally slowing down, his eyelids drooping.

The Price of Decisions
XIII

Part I

Cicadas screeched in the brush and on trees, the sky clear. It was early morning, the sun not yet fully above the horizon. As a breeze carried through the wooden paddock west of the castle, Gareth checked the tightness of the saddle straps across his horse's underside. It was secure. Petting the bridge of the stallion's nose, Gareth looked behind him.

Pich was a few stalls down, their chain mail sparkling every so often when they moved in the sun just right. Then, with a grunt, they hopped onto their horse. The mare was lean, her auburn coat smooth and shiny, and smaller so Pich would not struggle to ride her.

"You know," Barbus said as he placed a faded red rug on his giant horse. It was an Ardennes, a heavy-boned, thick-legged horse bred for transporting big loads across the regions. "I'm getting' excited. My hands are tinglin'. Feel it in my bones." He wiggled his scarred stubs for fingers.

Gareth half snorted with a smile. He enjoyed the high of battle, like most warriors did. Though something in his gut, like maggots wriggling around, told him the battles yet to be fought would not be like anything they had experienced. The exhilaration of going on a mission was dead, replaced by an ever-growing dread.

"So long as that tingling sensation stays in your hands and not your pants, I think everything will go smoothly." Lucas, his grin snide, was already in his saddle, his Lusitano's hooves beating the straw and dirt. He wore a breastplate branded with the region's insignia and greaves, both of which were polished well enough to be used as a mirror.

Barbus huffed and yanked his pants up, slapping his gut. "For your information, I got a lass waitin' for me when I return, and that tinglin' will be saved for her." He smiled, his beard moving with it. "Unlike someone."

Lucas frowned, rolled his eyes, and cantered out of the paddocks.

"Same goes for you, sir," Barbus said as he turned his attention toward Gareth, who simply raised an eyebrow. "You should find yourself a good lass to settle down with, eh?"

"Sure, I will get right on that."

"At least get laid when we get back. It'll loosen you up."

Gareth shot him a glare. His love life was no one else's concern but his own.

Barbus flinched, cleared his throat, and looked away. "Aye, went too far... But my point still stands." He shrugged and continued getting his horse ready. "You're going on eighty. The next thing you know, you'll be a hundred and alone." Eventually, he mounted the stallion, the horse's muscles rippling underneath his deep brown coat as Barbus situated himself.

Kicking the side of his Ardennes, Barbus strode past Gareth. "Just keepin' an eye out for you sir." He winked.

Gareth hadn't thought much about love, did not have the time. He had brought a few into his bed, but even that had been quite some time ago. He frowned to himself. *Now is not the time to think about such things.*

When Gareth swept his gaze toward Lycn, the beastmen wore a scowl as he mumbled several things under his breath. Curses, no doubt. He had put his staff in a leather holster on his horse's side, shoved his foot in the stirrup, and jumped, throwing one leg over, then adjusted the reins in his hands.

Mounting his own horse, Gareth followed his Unit and squinted at the sun's rays. They rode around the western side of the castle, the smell of the ocean filling his lungs, and into the front courtyard.

The king waited patiently, Malice by his side on a Menorquín. A beautiful horse, slender and elegant, its coat as black as night. There was a supply horse before them, a stableboy holding the horse's reins as they waited.

Pride swelled in Gareth's gut when he observed his Unit. His subordinates were some of the best knights in the region, each riding with posture that could rival scholars. To a halt, the Unit passed Gareth, bowing their heads to acknowledge the king.

"Your majesty," Gareth said and dipped his head, a faint smile on his face. They had exchanged goodbyes and concerns earlier that morning.

Magnus returned the smile. "Gareth, I wish you the best of luck on your mission."

"Malice," Gareth said in a less than pleasant tone, his eyes slicing toward the nuisance of a man.

"You could pretend not to hate me so much, you know." Malice smirked, gripped his reins, and tugged them away from

Gareth. His horse followed the direction and stamped to Unit One.

Gareth glared at him for a moment. *You do not make that easy.* With a final nod at Magnus, Gareth made his way to the group. Barbus shushed his horse after it kicked up a cloud of dirt, his hand patting the stallion's snout. He whickered in response.

From behind, passing Pich, Malice, and Lycn, Gareth stopped at the head of the Unit, turning to face everyone. "Danger will be breathing down our necks every second. Stay vigilant. Never let your guard down. It is time to depart." Gareth was never good at composing speeches. He usually left that to Magnus.

The Unit trotted toward the front gate, Barbus came up next to him, Lucas, and Malice were in the rear while Lycn—who had the supply horse's reins tied to his horse—and Pich were at the center.

At noon, just outside Howlers Forest, the Unit stopped and ate a lunch of nuts, berries, cheese, bread, and dried meat, washed it down with water before saddling up again.

Howlers Forest was named for its fearsome residents, howlers, which were more like bears than wolves. Gareth had only encountered a few of them in his life. Light repelled Howlers well enough for them not to be of concern. The problem was the proximity between trees and the thickness of the foliage, making it difficult to travel through the forest at a decent pace. *Slow and steady this time around.*

The positions changed as Barbus and Lucas switched places, so Lucas could light the way. Flat land and a measured speed meant the horses would be fine till nightfall. Although Barbus's stallion might have a problem.

Dark shadows cast down upon the Unit, turning day into night, cooling the early summer air. The trees were thick, not allowing for any sunlight beyond tiny specs. It reminded him of Dun Raik. Moss covered the ground and climbed up the tree trunks. Stray roots jutted through the moss all over the forest floor, but that was close to being consumed as well. Ferns spilled over the tops of tree branches. A stringy moss twisted around hanging vines as bugs zipped past or buzzed close by. The further the Unit traveled into the woods, the more mushrooms and other fungi sprang to life.

The sound of flowing water became louder and soon enough, the Unit trotted beside the stream, their formation changing once again. Now filed into a straight line, Gareth, Lucas, Barbus, Pich, Lycn with the supply horse, and Malice was at the tail end, a fire in his hand. Everyone kept their eyes peeled, watching the shrubs and the trees. *Can never be too careful.*

Gareth held a tight lip and focused on the trail in front of him. He had hoped the others would have done the same, but Pich and Barbus babbled on about medicine, royals, alcohol, their lovers. Lycn would chime in while Lucas would grunt approvingly or disapprovingly, depended on the subject. Malice stayed quiet. The handful of times Gareth had glanced back at him, Malice focused on his surroundings as if he had never been in Howlers Forest.

When night descended, Gareth's breath fogged, his purple-ashen skin goose-bumping. The Unit continued forward a while longer and stopped at an open space not quite big enough to be a glade, setting up camp. After dismounting and tying the reins to trees around them, the Unit unpacked the supply horse. Fur hides and blankets were passed to Barbus from Pich while Lycn scouted the vicinity and Malice and Lucas gathered firewood—usually a role left to just Lucas, but Gareth would be damned if Malice sat around doing nothing. Gareth refilled waterskins, unpacked wood plates, and dished the food.

Lycn returned within thirty minutes. In that time, a bonfire had been started, the beds made, and food filled the plates. It was nothing spectacular: bread, cheese, a few fish from the stream cooking over the fire, and apples. Gareth's eyes followed Lycn until he plopped down hard on the fur skin next to Pich, who was eating a hunk of bread.

"It's clear," Lycn said. "I saw nothing of concern, not even paw prints." Pich passed him a plate, and he ate the small cubes of cheese, barely chewing.

Gareth nodded as he swallowed. "Good, but I want a watch tonight anyhow." Leaning forward, he grabbed a stick with a steaming fish at one tip and waited for it to cool down, biting into its tender flesh when it had. It was bland but juicy.

"Why is the Kingdom of Phoenix called the Kingdom of Phoenix?" Pich asked.

Gareth had wondered when the questions would start pouring out of their mouth.

"It's an old legend, you see," Barbus said and shifted his belt around his gut.

Lucas groaned, "Not this again."

"Would you like to hear it?" Barbus asked, ignoring Lucas's negative attitude.

"Yes!"

Gareth did not bother stopping them, it would wind everyone down for the night. Though Lycn concerned him. The beastman hadn't taken his sights off Malice since he sat down. Gareth could see the thoughts swirling behind those honey-yellow eyes and hoped Lycn had the self-control to keep them at bay. Their little camp was peaceful, and he would like to keep it that way.

Barbus cleared his throat, his fist to his mouth, and began, "The legend tells of a dragon, old and weary, layin' to rest. The dragon soon died and over time its corpse faded to nothin.' Decades went by and people settled on the dragon's deathbed. Eventually, the little town became a mighty kingdom. The kingdom thrived for quite some time." His hands moved and flung around as he talked, his shadow dancing behind him.

"Until," Barbus proclaimed with a finger pointing skyward, "one day the wind was stronger than a hundred men, the earth trembled beneath people's feet, and the sea was stormy… There are two versions of the story."

"The more well-known version," Gareth intervened, as he had heard the tale time and time again. Knew it by heart at this point. "Is where the dragon rises from the ground. When it spread its wings, its body burst into an inferno. The now phoenix commanded the earth to be still, the winds to calm, and the sea to be gentle, thus saving the kingdom. In honor of its heroics, the people named the kingdom after it. The end." Gareth's tone was not as enthusiastic as Barbus's retelling.

Barbus shrugged. "The not-so-kind version goes like this: Awakened from its deep slumber, the dragon saw that its death was trampled upon. The dragon, rage-filled, erupted into flames as it rose from the ground, leavin' nothing in its wake. It roared, forcin' the earth to become unmoving. It commanded the sea to settle and the higher it flew, the calmer the wind became. Then it vanished as if it had never been there. The survivors believed the dragon to be a phoenix and thought it saved them. In honor of the phoenix, the people dedicated a kingdom to its deeds."

"… That was quite the tale," Pich said eventually to humor Barbus. Gareth smiled.

"What?" Barbus scoffed. "You don't believe it to be true?"

Pich said nothing.

"Of course, they do not believe it," Gareth remarked. "It is a children's bedtime story. They heard it a million times as babes, I am sure. Perhaps in different ways, but the tale remains the same."

Barbus hawked and spat into the fire while Pich chuckled. Lucas had a grin on his face while Lycn… was still scowling at Malice. Gareth sighed.

Lycn said, "Who's on watch tonight?" He finally looked away from Malice, his eyes moving toward Gareth.

"I can take the first watch," Malice volunteered himself.

"Why? So, you can let a howler eat us?" Lycn accused, his tone bitter and his face sour with disdain. Gareth frowned, his eyes darting between the two of them.

Malice raised an eyebrow. "What reason would I have to do that?"

That is a good question, Gareth thought.

"What reason would you have to kill ten thousand men?" Pich elbowed Lycn as hard as they could in the ribs. He winced, but did not relent. "What reason could you have to kill your kin?" The hairs on Gareth's arms stood, goosebumps spreading across his skin. He knew where this was going.

"What reason would you have to kill Lucas's—"

"Lycn!" Gareth growled, his fists clenched over his lap and his body stiff. He silently willed Lycn not to utter another word. *Not right now. I will tell him when we return home.* Lucas glanced from Gareth to Lycn to Malice. The camp became quiet, the tension so thick one could cut it with a knife.

"To kill my what?" Lucas asked, disregarding Malice, and instead, was looking at Gareth.

"Now is not the time for that," Gareth said flatly. If he were to say anything, now, of all times, there was no telling what could happen. *Please, drop it.*

"He has the right to know," Lycn snapped.

"Not right now." In that moment, Gareth knew he should not have told Lycn anything.

Who is Joseph Knightridge, sir? Lycn had asked one day. What other choice did he have? If guards were talking about Joseph, it would have only been a matter of time before Lucas and the rest of Unit One learned the truth. He had told Lycn to keep his mouth shut, so Gareth could tell Lucas at the right time. Gareth was surprised Lucas had not gotten wind of his brother. He wanted the matter to cease, nevertheless, for Joseph to disappear until the mission was over.

Lucas's brows furrowed with frustration. "Know what?"

"I killed your brother," Malice said calmly, taking another bite of his apple, the crunch almost deafening.

Lucas froze, then slowly turned his head toward Malice. Immediately, Lycn snapped to him as Pich's mouth fell open. Barbus was shocked into silence. Gareth stared at him too, a single pulse of disgust racing through his veins.

"Joseph, was his name? I killed him just before the Games. It was what got me sentenced to them." Malice tossed the apple core into the fire. It crackled and snapped. "I killed Charles as well, the one who killed your sister, and there was another one… what was their name?"

Lucas was like a statue, his stunned expression and stiff body unchanging.

"Kuro," Malice said at last, "Kuro Mantis, the man who murdered your father, Cesar Knightridge. Alongside everyone else left in the arena."

Lucas had winced at his father's name, then pulled a face, anger and hurt contorting his expression. Gareth remembered the day Lucas returned from throwing Kuro in their cell. Bloodlust and absolute rage radiated from him like storm clouds off the ocean. It took everything in Lucas to stop himself from killing Kuro that day. *But how does Malice know… Magnus.*

"All right," Lucas breathed.

"That's it?" Lycn said, eyebrows jumping up. "He killed your brother, and that's all you have to say?"

"… I knew… about his death."

Gareth's chest tightened, Joseph suddenly in his arms again, the resemblance he had to Lucas flashing in his mind. Lucas sounded small and defeated, looked that way as well.

"When did you find out?" Barbus asked gently.

Lucas's hand pushed his loose curls back, the vulnerability from moments earlier hidden behind a scowl. "It's hard not to know when people can't keep their mouths shut. Besides, I found the one who threw Malice into his cell and asked her about it." His eyes narrowed on a nearby tree. "I also asked the king for confirmation."

Gareth's eyes widened. He had to stop his mouth from gaping. Lucas had as much right as Gareth to waltz up to the king, yet this was the first time he heard of Lucas going to Magnus for anything.

"That doesn't excuse what he did." Lycn glared at Lucas, then Malice, his fists bunched in his lap. "How could you let that go, Lucas? He was your brother, your blood, and yet you're fine—"

"Lycn," Lucas snapped. "If you have any shred of respect for me, drop it." He regarded Lycn with somber eyes, exhaustion pulling his features all of a sudden. "Please."

Lycn opened his mouth, but shut it just as quickly, whipping his head around to see that Pich had put space between them. He grimaced.

Taking a breath, Lucas said, "I didn't ask the king for details but I'm asking now; why did you kill Joseph? Why didn't you leave him or injure him? Had you knocked him out, you would have gotten into the Games all the same." He paused, eyes lifting from the ground to Malice. "Why didn't you stop Charles and prevent Maryjane's death?"

Does her death weigh on him more than I thought? Gareth had questioned Mrs. Knightridge on the day of Maryjane's death, had asked many questions about Maryjane and Joseph as well. She was a sweet, outgoing, and goofy girl, a bundle of energy. Joseph was reserved, intelligent, and, in his own way, protective of his family. The thought of them reminded Gareth of the sunflower necklace Cadmus had wished to be in Lucas's possession.

Looking at Lucas now, he resembled his mother, only his eyes took after his father, the sharpness of them. Joseph mirrored Cesar though, save for the blonde hair.

"He attacked, so I defended. It's as simple as that," Malice said bluntly, forcing Gareth from his thoughts.

"There's more," Lucas said.

Malice went silent, as if contemplating his next move. "I killed Joseph on a whim, and I'm quite glad I did. He's saved me a lot of trouble. As for Charles, by law, I couldn't do anything, although the king would have forgiven me."

Do not put words in Magnus's mouth! A flare of anger rose and consumed Gareth's body, a rush of white-hot heat that died on his command. He exhaled.

"Simply put," Malice went on. "I didn't want to."

Lucas cringed, his jaw clenching and eyebrows furrowing, his mouth drawn in a hard line. "Thank you for avenging my father but know, above all else, that you disgust me," he spat like poison coated the inside of his mouth.

Malice stared blankly at the elf, then laughed. "I'll add you to the long list of names."

Lycn's eye twitched. "What the fuck is wrong with you all?" Pich gasped and punched his shoulder, none too softly from the way he flinched.

A shadow casting over Barbus as he shifted made him appear hard, mean, an unusual appearance for the laid-back angel.

Gareth clicked his tongue. "Enough Lycn. The truth is out there now. Let it rest."

"So, what if it is?" Lycn snarled. "We're going to let Malice stay? After everything he's done when we know nothing more than what the king has told us?" Lycn's voice echoed beyond the trees. "Why does it seem like I'm the only one who doesn't trust that piece of shit?"

Barbus reeled, his head and hand shaking in unison. "Whoa there lad, slow your roll. I trust him as much as I can beat him in a fight. But what's the point in holding things against him, eh? Our lives are in each other's hands and if the king believes he'll be useful, I've decided to let bygones be bygones. That doesn't mean I fully trust him." With satisfaction, he huffed at the end of his speech and sat up a bit straighter, nodding to himself.

"I trust him enough not to kill me, lad, and that's all."

"I agree," Pich said quietly.

Gareth sighed and stretched his legs out from under him, bringing one knee to his chest. "You and the king have an agreement, right?" he asked. No one trusted Malice except Magnus, but their relationship was that of equals, whereas the relationship between Malice and the Unit was that of a wolf and a rabbit. The wolf was letting the rabbit do as it pleased.

"Of course. This isn't my region. I cannot do whatever I want." His gaze stayed on Gareth. "Everything I've done has been cleared by the king, and everything I plan to do has been as well. For now, you should listen to Barbus." Barbus jolted and swallowed.

"Trust that I won't kill you, and I'll trust that you won't ruin the mission." Malice's tone was lighthearted, but the silvery gleam in his eyes sent shivers down Gareth's neck, a spider crawling down his spine. "I'd prefer not to clean up after you because your confidence was incompetence under a guise."

Gareth's teeth ground. *Let it go...* Massaging his temple, he concluded the conversation. "Let us get some sleep. Malice, you are on watch."

Whatever food left on plates was dumped into the flames as Malice got up, brushed his pants off, and walked into the woods. The camp was tense, the air thorny, while the only warmth seeping into Gareth's skin was from the campfire. Barbus stretched his arms high, grunting, and released a heavy exhale.

"I don't mean to start somethin' up again but—"

"Then do not." Gareth had started to crawl under the blanket and situate himself. He was mentally tired and hoped a decent night's rest would make the coming days bearable after what transcribed tonight. *Not if Barbus keeps yapping, though.*

"But," Barbus repeated himself, which made Gareth groan, "why let Malice do the night watch?"

"He offered, and he does not need sleep."

"Neither does—"

"End of conversation," Gareth snarled as he tucked his hand under his head, shifting to get comfortable. Barbus grumbled and did the same. *This is going to be a long few months.*

The Price of Decisions
"The Answer on Spikes"

It was always like this. Excitement kindled in Lycn's stomach. The Kingdom of Phoenix was a day's worth of travel ahead of him. He had often visited the kingdom as a child, running through the streets, causing mischief with a group of his friends. The outskirts of Howlers Forest were something they ventured into, seeing who could go the furthest. He had always won knowing that howlers hated sunlight, so they stayed away from the outer edge. His friends knew that as well, but they were too scared of what the darkness was hiding.

It had been four nights since Malice clarified the details of Joseph's death. Lucas had been silent, trotting beside the trees, his expression solemn, shoulders slumped. Lycn huffed. *Weak-hearted.* Pich wasn't too happy with Lycn either, for his persistence that night and his profanity. They hated curse words. Barbus seemed indifferent, blubbering on about whatever his heart wanted. Sir Gareth, on the other hand, had become edgy, twitching at every noise, constantly glancing over his shoulder. *Is he waiting for a fight to happen?* Malice had stayed in the rearguard on top of his stallion of night. It was good that Lycn didn't have to look at him, but having his back exposed to Malice didn't bring much comfort, either. *Damned if I do, damned if I don't.*

Lycn lifted his head as the breeze rustled the leaves to clear his mind. Taking a deep breath in, the forest was full of dozens of scents—grass, moss, bark, sap, dung. None of those things reached his nose over the stench that hit him instead. He heaved, stopped his horse, and retched over the side. *What the hell is that?* The odor was sweet yet sickening, like rotting food in the corpse of an animal. He'd never smelled anything so volatile in his life. Lycn heaved again.

The entire Unit came to a dead halt.

"Lycn?" Sir Gareth whipped his horse around.

Pich jumped off their mare and helped him down, let him kneel on the ground as they grabbed their waterskin and had him drink. "Breathe through your mouth," they told Lycn.

"You all right, lad?" Barbus quickly swiveled his horse in front of the others, containing Pich's, Lycn's, and the supply horse.

Lycn panted, bile thick in his breath, sweat beading on his face. "Smell," he choked. His throat burned worse than his eyes did. Reaching for Pich's waterskin, he drank and swished the water, spitting his mouthful into the stream. All the while, Pich's hand rubbed his back in circular motions. He continued to drink, the cold water soothing his sore and scratchy throat.

"You smell it too?" Sir Gareth asked someone.

Lycn tilted his head and followed his leader's gaze toward Malice.

Malice acknowledged him with a quick dip of his head. "Rotting flesh."

"Are we too late?" Lucas had moved closer to Lycn and Pich, shedding some light on them, his complexion pale. Malice shrugged and looked at Sir Gareth. Brow set, Sir Gareth's focus was elsewhere as he lost himself to his thoughts.

Lycn didn't want to know how Malice could tolerate that smell without so much as a flare of his nostrils. The stench wafted toward him again, making his stomach twist and lurch. He swallowed the building saliva in his mouth, hoping it was enough to keep from retching. Pich waited a moment before offering the waterskin once again to Lycn, who finished it. By putting their arm under him and pulling him up, they got Lycn to his feet. He thanked Pich, a wry smile on his face, waving them to their mare. After a quick glance, Pich went to their horse as Lycn wiped his mouth and remounted his mare.

Sir Gareth carefully considered Lycn, and he gave a nod of reassurance.

The dark elf spoke. "Our destination is still the Kingdom of Phoenix. Once we confirm the state it is in, Malice, you are the fastest. I want you to fly to the other kingdoms and cities, check their status. Some way or another, give us a sign telling us where to head next."

For a time, his gaze was fixed on Malice, like they were silently conversing with one another. Lycn gritted his teeth. This time, Sir Gareth was right.

"In the meantime, we need to deal with the bodies before sickness spreads, then we move out." A yank of the reins and Sir Gareth spun his horse around. "Oh," he glared over his shoulder, "and we double the pace from here on out."

Kicking the side of his horse, Lucas rushed ahead to light the path. Sir Gareth and the others followed in a tight formation. Hooves pounded the earth in a rhythm Lycn found calming despite how the situation changed. There was no time to dally or laugh. An entire kingdom may be dead. Assuming voidents wouldn't be so daring as to kill thousands of people in one go was bold and a mistake. They should have ridden hard from the beginning, cutting their travel time in half, instead of trotting so leisurely. He was sure Sir Gareth was thinking the same thing.

Lycn had been excited to see the Kingdom of Phoenix again, even though he was there not too long ago. The city was peaceful, a place for the elderly and families to settle down. Someday, he would have asked Pich to marry him, build their own house, and live out the rest of his days in bliss. Then Pich would bury him since fairies were immortal and go on to live their life. That excitement, however, slunk from his body, replaced by a gut-wrenching sense of foreboding.

Light breached the forest's canopy the next morning—Howlers Forest was gradually thinning. Only stopping a few times for half an hour to let their horses breathe, eat, and drink shaved a day or two off their travels. As the horses rested, the Unit stuffed their mouths with food and water. They set off again and rode through the night.

Howlers Forest brightened as they neared the kingdom, that rotten stench growing stronger. Unit One's speed dwindled to a trot when they entered the city. Lamps on either side of each street were burnt out, the glass charred black. The kingdom, which should have been noisy and bustling, was silent and still. Memories of the people roaming the streets filled Lycn's thoughts, a heaviness resting on his chest.

Decay, feces, and blood were thick in the air, causing Lycn's head to spin. Bodies littered the streets, picked apart, but whatever skin that was left on bones was full of blisters. Some bodies were turned upright or were against a building so their faces, distorted with fear, pain, and anguish, could be seen. Blood and gore, now black or dark brown, painted everything: the ground, the walls of buildings and homes, fences, and signs. Lycn had seen nothing like it. A few dead bodies, sure, but this… his stomach flipped again.

Unit One continued to trudge down the streets. The castle at the center of the kingdom, belonging to nobles, stood tall, the banners waving in the wind. Heads on spears lined the stone path leading to the front doors of the castle. They were purplish red, the features sunken in and skeletal. Grey swarms masked the details.

Perhaps if they had arrived a day or two earlier, Lycn would have been able to recognize a few of those faces.

Pich audibly gagged beside Lycn, both hands quickly covering their mouth as if that would help keep everything in. He himself found it difficult to keep the maggots of disgust that writhed underneath his skin, burrowing into his veins, at bay.

"Malice," Sir Gareth said in a low, solemn, yet firm voice.

Lycn glanced over his shoulder to see a smirk on Malice's face. An instant flare of anger surged through him.

Malice hopped down from his horse and passed the reins to Pich, taking several steps back. Black, scaly wings, like a dragon's, spread out when he crouched. They were twice, no, thrice the size of Malice. A single flap launched him into the sky. Within a heartbeat, he was out of sight. *Good.*

Sir Gareth dismounted, walked his horse to a lamppost, avoiding the bodies, and tied the reins to it. Everyone followed suit, quickly coming to stand before Sir Gareth.

"Barbus, make a pit of lava," Sir Gareth ordered. "We need to burn the bodies. We do not have time to bury them." Barbus nodded. As a seer, Barbus wouldn't be of much help. Magic doesn't flow within the dead after all.

"Lucas and Lycn, on the other side of the castle, gather bodies and incinerate them. Pich will quell the fires after they are done checking for survivors while Barbus and I stay on this side. Understood?"

"Yes, sir."

Lycn would have rather worked alone, but now wasn't the time to fuss. As he hurried alongside Lucas down the streets, the ground trembled beneath his feet. Lycn turned just enough to see when Barbus had created a pit of lava, the bright red goop flowing from cracks in the earth. He was glad he wasn't close enough to feel the heat.

Out of the corner of his eye, Lycn glimpsed Pich's chain mail disappear beyond a line of stone-faced houses. He lingered on them for a moment, his heart aching to know that they probably wouldn't find any survivors. If he had known this would happen, Lycn would have insisted that Pich stay behind. Protecting them from the horror they were about to see would have been worth their wrath afterward.

Well ahead of him now, Lucas turned down the brick streets. Lycn eventually caught up. Using a rope of fire, Lucas dragged the bodies into a pile. Lycn, cringing, did the same and gathered the rotting corpses with his magic. Soon, Lucas set the mounds ablaze. Flies buzzed lazily all around. *Fat and happy bastards.* Vultures sat on top of the shingled roofs, heads jerking at Lycn's and Lucas's movement, beady eyes glowering down at them while crows circled above the city, cawing impatiently.

To see the people of Phoenix as anything more than grotesque blobs of flesh and bones was nearly impossible. Lycn watched the flames of several piles dance as it consumed the bodies, wondering if some of the people there were the friends he used to run around with. He scowled at the prospect.

Pich had extinguished every heap of death by late noon, early evening, so now thin, squiggly pillars of smoke rose and drifted in the wind.

The lava pit Barbus created after Lycn and Lucas left was no more, covered by earth as if it had never existed in the first place. Both Barbus and Sir Gareth were waiting beside their horses, downcast and sweaty. The dark elf, however, was covered in ash, unlike the angel.

Lucas returned to his horse, unclipped his waterskin, and took a draught, dumping water over his hands and face. Lycn more or less did the same, unable to get the sensation of filth off his skin. After a while, he stopped trying to clean his hands and kept a lookout for Pich's return.

It wasn't long before the fairy stumbled around the corner of the street, knees, hands, face, and arms covered in dirt and grime. Lycn grimaced, his feet moving toward them thoughtlessly. He met them a little way from the horses, catching them by the arms and pulling them into his embrace. A sob raked their body, a ripple of movement, and then a sniffle when they peeped up from his chest. Pich plastered a weak smile on their exhausted face. With an arm around them, Lycn walked toward the Unit, guiding them to their horse and helping them to the saddle. Words of comfort were nowhere to be found, so he mounted his mare, and the Unit was on the move again.

"Lucas"

Following the edge of the region's border would lead to Ntesal, one of the oldest established kingdoms in Alucard's Region. To the east was a smaller forest, beams of golden light blotching the ground. On the other side was a meadow crossing into Cain's Region. In the southeast, filling the horizon, white snowcapped mountains peaked in the sky.

Lucas allowed himself to focus on the surrounding nature, forcing the chaos in his mind to numb. The air was fresh, warm, bugs and birds chirping. He was riding in the Unit's rear, Lycn, Pich, and the supply horse at the center, Barbus, and Gareth in front. Absent-mindedly, Lucas reached forward to pet his mare, her sand-colored coat soft and damp under his palm and fingers.

The Unit stopped at nightfall near a small, shallow body of water. Frogs croaked on lily pads that floated on the water's surface. One by one, everyone washed off the filth from earlier, the water turning murky from soot and dirt. After starting a fire, the Unit ate, not because they wanted to but because they knew they had to. At least they weren't eating fresh meat. Lucas didn't think he could have stomached it if they did.

Despite constantly tossing and turning, Lucas was able to rest through the night, his dreams nothing more than scrambled images and incomprehensible noises. At times, he envied Barbus and his blindness, but only in times like those. It was a curse as much as it was a blessing.

The Unit rose with the sun and set off with great haste. It would take a few more hours before they arrived in Ntesal. In the distance, a billow of smoke rose above the plains, a village most likely. Closer, however, was a wide and tall silhouette slightly east on top of a hill. Lucas strained to see it. He wasn't the only one who noticed it. Gareth altered the path a bit and slowed the Unit to a canter. Lucas finally realized it was a monolith of earth, dark lines etched into the front of it.

Gareth trotted up to it, stopped, then read the message carved in thin writing. The rest of the Unit stayed at the foot of the hill. Lucas assumed that was a message from Malice. Who else would have left a monolith in the middle of nowhere? When a few seconds had passed, Gareth suddenly jumped down from his horse and smashed the hunk of earth to bits, his kick enforced by lightning, the boom echoing.

Good news is for the fortunate, I suppose.

"We ride to Ivory's Kingdom," Gareth barked as he got back on his stallion, the horse's nostrils flaring as he whinnied and stamped.

Bleakly, Lucas asked, "The other kingdoms have been compromised?"

Gareth whipped his reins, his horse reared, and they were off, answering Lucas's question. He spurred his horse on after the others, hooves thundering the ground, the wind whipping his hair. Riding the horses that hard would be tough, especially in the heat of the day. It was already warm, too warm to be considered comfortable. Lucas took a deep breath in, his thighs aching, his ass numb, when he peeked ahead at Gareth's wide frame. A seed of worry had planted itself in his gut. It wriggled and wormed, threatening to bloom into fear at any moment.

Three days—after bypassing a small forest, hills, and the village of Redcol—Ivory's Kingdom was in sight. It was a familiar place for Lucas, the city where he studied, learned, fought, and defended. The kingdom he ran away to after his father's death.

He knew the streets like the back of his hand. He knew a few people even better, and everyone knew of him. It was home in a way, yet it wasn't.

A smile tugged at the corners of Lucas's mouth as he reminisced about the times he had come here with his father. He was young, no older than eight or nine, when Cesar brought Lucas along to pick out a gift for his mother. *It's for our anniversary,* his father had said and winked. They had gotten a few things that day—a necklace, a new dress, and a crate filled with red clay blocks. Elana had been thrilled with her new supplies and smothered them in kisses.

To the west, woodlands covered a small portion of Alucard's Region and spread into Wolfgang's. Lucas's old Professor Cadmus Locke lived in those woods, or at least the last he knew, he did.

Despite having been here a little over a month ago, it felt different, unknown to him. The buildings of stone, wood, and concrete were the same as Lucas remembered. The cobblestone streets, however, lie bare and desolate. Houses, shops, and inns were abandoned. Everyone had been sent to a familiar location— Pich went to canvas Cytor, Lycn to the Kingdom of Phoenix and Ntesal, and Barbus to Liotkin. Also, having been to Anddulia, Lucas couldn't believe how, in just a few days, maybe a week, the kingdoms had fallen.

Gareth spoke of the message Malice left on the monolith when they had stopped to rest that night. There were no signs of life in Ntesal, Liotkin, or Anddulia. If he were to make it in time, he would send the residents of Ivory to Alucard's Kingdom and Cytor, if they would listen to him, that was, and defend the city. *Seems something turned out all right.*

"Malice also said to turn back," Gareth had informed the Unit, irritation worsening his already stern expression.

"Will we?" Barbus asked.

"No."

And that was the end of it. Lucas liked the sound of leaving the rest of the mission to Malice. He was capable enough. *Never back down from your duty, son. Once you say you'll do something, do* it, his father's voice resonated in his skull.

Something clenched Lucas's heart ever so gently, just enough to cause discomfort.

There was a sweet smell lingering in the air, almost like spoiled fruit that festered in the sun. It wafted with the wind, then disappeared.

Eventually, they reached the castle's courtyard. Vibrant gardens encased fountains on either side and statues were scattered across the grounds; a painting come to life. However, the castle of white adorned with blues, greens, and purples stood out like a scarecrow in a meadow.

Lucas felt calmer the closer he got to the castle, the sound of hooves a steady melody of clacks, his eyelids growing heavier by the second.

The Unit entered the courtyard, following the stone path. A black mass was propped against the rails on the castle's front steps. Holding his fist up, Gareth motioned for the Unit to halt. He dismounted, the others mirroring their leader. The mass became clear. It was Malice, his shoulder against the dark metal barrier, his head of white down. Lucas contained his laughter, clenching his jaw to do so. They had been racing to get here while Malice was snoozing the days away. *Lucky bastard.*

Gareth didn't find it as amusing. The knight stomped forward and up the stairs until he was standing directly in front of Malice. Down to one knee, Gareth grabbed his shoulder and shook him. Lucas yawned, his vision gradually hazing.

"Malice," Gareth said, his voice almost a mumble. Malice didn't react, so Gareth shook him again. "Malice!" That time, he raised his voice, briefly snapping Lucas out of his state of exhaustion.

"Pich!" Lycn yelled as he caught Pich. Lycn—legs probably weak from weariness and travel—fell to his knees with a thud, arms holding onto Pich's body.

Lucas fumbled to get his feet out of the stirrups, the heel of his boot stuck. Gareth stood and whipped around, swaying. *He's about to fall.*

Finally, jumping down from his horse, the world spun in complete disorder, making Lucas's stomach twist. Someone shouted and the sound of boots on stone succeeded it. Lucas managed to take a step. His legs had gone limp. He crashed, yelping as all his of weight bore down on his knees. The pain cleared the fog in his head for a second. Lycn was doubled over, Pich and Barbus had cushioned Gareth's fall.

Everything went black.

Lucas opened his eyes, his face pressed against the rough, warm stone. He lifted his head and surveyed the undulating world around him as he used his arms to drag himself forward. Lycn was right there. Maybe he could shake the beastman awake and have him hightail it back to Alucard's Kingdom with Pich. Fingers reaching for Lycn's motionless body, Lucas cursed himself as his eyes fluttered closed, his limbs refusing to cooperate any longer.

King's Duty
XIV

Thud! Corgan groaned and rolled to his side, squashing the grass beneath him. Magnus blinked sweat from his eyes, popping his stiff shoulders.

"How… does Sir Gareth… keep up with you, your majesty?" Corgan panted.

"He trains more than you, Corgan, that's how." The ocean glimmered on the horizon, catching Magnus's attention when the wind picked up. It was cool, refreshing, goosebumps appearing on his dark, freckled skin.

The royal knight grunted, lurched, and got to his feet, brushing off his dirt-stained pants. Corgan was a bit shorter than Magnus, but wide, his gut rounded from alcohol, black patches of hair on his chest, stomach, shoulders, and back.

"Let's go again," Corgan said with a nod of determination.

Magnus shook his hands out and swayed on his feet a bit, leaping forward. Corgan reeled, dodging Magnus's punch. Swiftly, the knight hunkered down, moved into Magnus's guard, and jabbed his sternum. Magnus caught his fist, gripped it, yanked him, and elbowed his face. A nasty crunch sounded, blood squirting like a fountain from the man's nose. His eyes screwed shut, his free hand waving at Magnus as if he were waving a white flag.

Magnus didn't stop.

Left knee to the gut, fist to the ribs, Magnus wailed on Corgan until the knight was on his back, covered in blood and bruises. He held his trembling arms out in front of his face.

"Enough," he sputtered, a slight whistle to his words from the gaps in his teeth—said teeth white pebbles in the grass. "Please, your majesty, you won."

Out of breath, Magnus relented, then kneeled beside him. "I apologize," he said, jaw tensing. Corgan laughed or coughed. Magnus couldn't tell as he placed his hands on his core.

Magic flowed from Magnus into Corgan. The bruises faded and after a few minutes, his teeth regenerated.

"Neat skill there, your majesty," Corgan said, a smile on his face. "I was worried my nose would never be the same. Pretty sure you broke it there."

"I did."

Redness surrounded the knight's already broad nose, blood drying and cracking on his skin. Magnus extended his hand, hoisting Corgan to his feet, the sun baking them like loaves of bread.

What came over me? The crimson splattering the grass and Corgan's body was spilled unnecessarily. Magnus knew that, yet he didn't stop. Heat spiked through his chest. He knew, however, that it was more than his father's blood inside his veins that had him on edge.

"Want to move on to weapons or magic, your majesty?" Corgan asked, sweat gleaming on his skin.

Magnus quirked an eyebrow. "You still want to spar with me after what I did?"

Corgan shook a hand and exhaled. "No harm done, least no permanent harm done. I should've stayed on my toes, fought properly. That's my fault for underestimating you, your majesty. Sir Gareth has trained you, I should've known better."

"Gareth has only taught me defensive measures, my father taught me the rest," Magnus said, the heat in his chest worsening at the mention of his father.

"Oh…" Eyes moving around aimlessly, Corgan scratched his head, probably unsure what to say or if he should say anything at all.

"Let's use magic. It's been a while since I've done that."

After a dip of his head and a smile, Corgan turned on his heel and walked a suitable distance from Magnus.

Gareth had always told Magnus that if he needed to know anything, it was to protect himself. If any fighting needed to be done, Gareth would do it or by the knight at his side. Holister, Magnus's father, had viewed the matter differently. *If you are to be king,* Holister had said, *then you will know how to fight. If you are to know how to fight, you will learn how to kill.* In hindsight, Magnus couldn't disagree with his father. Not anymore.

A wielder's core housed more than one element—Corgan could use metal and earth magic.

Hand at his side, Corgan pulled something out of his pocket. A grey cube, perhaps, Magnus was too far away to see it clearly. With his opposite hand, the knight forged himself a sword, swinging it around to get a feel for it. *Always ready… good.*

Magnus did the same, light pouring from his palm as he shaped it into a common sword, more warmth enveloping him. His use of the four main elements was limited. Magnus could move rocks the size of a child, move a tub's worth of water, create a bonfire, and control enough wind to get a sail going. Nothing extravagant like Malice could. *He's extraordinary, though, no sense in comparing my abilities to his.*

When Magnus came out of his thoughts, Corgan had disappeared. His eyes widened, darting all around until he spotted the knight gliding across the plains as if he were on ice. A wall of earth erected at his side with a rumble and Corgan used it to launch himself toward Magnus.

In a heartbeat, he was there, sword glinting above his head. Magnus spread his feet and took the strike head-on, grunting at the force of Corgan's blow. The longer they stayed like that, the more Magnus's sword of light bit into Corgan's blade, melting the metal. Smoke, a thin squiggly line, rose between them. Corgan pushed off and landed on his feet.

They circled one another, swords raised, until the knight attacked, swinging left and right. Magnus parried every blow. Their blades would kiss, a silent hit that sent tingles down Magnus's arms. It'd been a while since he fought like this. He fell into a rhythm with Corgan, defending, attacking, watching how Corgan used the earth beneath his feet to his advantage.

The initial attack was the first and last time the knight expelled a substantial amount of magic, probably meant to land a solid blow before the fight actually started. Magnus couldn't blame him. They had begun before noon, and Magnus kept his winning streak well into the evening.

The sky was golden, reds and oranges bleeding into the clouds, birds and bugs singing. Sweat dripped down Magnus's skin, tickling his back. Corgan huffed and puffed, hands on his knees. He was his own rain cloud with the amount of precipitation he was producing. As he stretched his burning muscles, Magnus took in the surrounding area—there were divots, patches of dirt, and small pillars of smoke billowing toward the sky from their sparring session, though few and far between.

"Thank you," Magnus said once it seemed Corgan regained some composure. At least he wasn't wheezing anymore.

"No problem, your majesty. Glad to be of service," Corgan said politely, his face and torso red from spending the day in the sun. "But can we return to the castle now?"

Magnus blinked at him, realizing they had only eaten breakfast, and chuckled under his breath. "Yes, I'm sure you're famished after the day we've had."

"And you aren't?"

"I am. So much so that it hurts." His stomach twisted and gurgled in response, as if to agree.

Together, they walked toward the castle in the south; the stone piercing the sky like a jagged white mountain. Along the way, they collected their discarded shirts, both waited until they were on the castle grounds to put them on again. Magnus wanted to cool down a bit longer. He assumed Corgan did as well.

It had been a month since Unit One's mission started and just a few weeks ago, Malice had returned. It was a brief visit. He had flown here, landing on Magnus's balcony, wings of night whooshing, to collect a letter for the nobles of Ivory's Kingdom. A warning that if they were to continue down the path they started, they would join the Kingdom of Phoenix, and that was a guarantee.

The Price of Decisions
XV

Part II

All who are seers are blind, but not all who are blind are seers.

Around his wrists and ankles, Barbus could feel a cold, thick cuff. With the slightest movement, the chains jingled. The stabbing in his core explained his lack of sight and, based on the details of the mission, it wasn't a stretch to believe the more intelligent voidents the king spoke of had captured them. It was out of character to attack so boldly and so soon. He wouldn't've guessed it, that was for sure. He assumed these voidents used deadly nightshade, didn't know how, but that was the only thing he knew that could knock someone out.

Must be why I'm tired, about ready to fall asleep if I don't think of something.

The last time he'd been this blind, he'd been a boy. The ability to see magic was intuitive for most seers, except for him. The elder that raised Barbus alongside all the other misfits and orphans in his home village taught him about a different type of sight.

A seer's magical flow was a bit different from normal. As magic flowed up to the head, it followed the curve of the skull and back down. For a seer, the magic split off into, then out of the eyes. Magical energy connected to magical energy; a seer could see the flow of magic in people, animals, plants, and bugs. The elder cackled and said that, of course, one cannot see what had been killed or what had never been alive. Whatever humor the elder thought was in her lesson, Barbus didn't get. Regret pinched his heart at the thought of her. She was dead; had died soon after he left Zeldine's Region.

A sound, like rock scraping against rock, echoed off the walls. Barbus looked to his left. His jaw dropped, but he quickly closed it. Standing there was a mass of swirling colors—red, blue, green, white, brown, and black clustered and warped like a maelstrom. So, he wasn't completely without sight, just in a room desolate of magic.

It walked forward in long strides until it stopped in front of him.

The only times he had ever seen something, or someone, with that many colors housed in their magic was when he was in the presence of his highness, Magnus Castine, or Malice Reap. But even then, there was a difference between light and dark magic. Light magic was just that, light. His majesty's magical energy was a mix of pastel colors that nearly had a glow to it. That thing was just a mass of darkness. *A voident, huh?* Its magic so closely resembled Malice's, it was almost uncanny. However, Malice's magical energy was controlled, steady, and refined as it flowed through his body. This voidents magic was as chaotic as the sea during a wicked storm.

The voident's thin arm moved, its hands holding something when it stabbed his shoulder. He flinched and jerked away. *Was that a needle?* A burning sensation seeped and spread down his arm and up to his neck.

"What did you do?" Barbus asked. Silence. Clenching his jaw, he ran over a list of poisons that Pich had told him about. Pich liked to ramble, and he liked to listen.

There were two that came to mind, hogweed and burn hazel. Both caused a stinging and searing sensation. If boiled, burn hazel could be incredibly beneficial. Tasted like shit, though.

The burning spread fast, too fast it seemed, like fire racing inside his veins. He ground his teeth to keep himself from screeching in pain. The voident moved backward as if it wanted to enjoy the show from afar. If that were the only thing injected, the burning would be it. The effects of the poison wouldn't get much worse. Barbus had to suffer through it until the poison wore off.

His stomach started to churn and cramp. *'Course, that's not all.* The voident must've mixed bloodroot and hogweed. He felt lightheaded as his tongue retreated down his throat. Drool dribbled from his mouth, onto his beard, then on the floor—he heard the drip of it hitting the ground. He heaved and spewed stomach acid. The pressure made his eyes water as he coughed violently.

The mass of swirling colors watched him intently. *Sick bastard, enjoyin' watchin' me spew my guts.*

How long had it been since Barbus started vomiting? His body convulsed, and he gagged, but there was nothing left, all the bile his stomach produced on the floor. The voident had left some time ago.

Although his body was sore and strained, the burning in his veins had lessened. He brought his head up slightly, a scream penetrating the walls. Who was it? Who would be awake after a hefty dose of nightshade? Gareth would be, he was resilient, and his muscles helped with the poison, just as Barbus's fat helped him. He listened closely, but no more screams flitted to his ears. Just thinking his name brought Barbus back twenty years when they had first met, a welcomed memory to keep his mind off the pain and nausea.

It was a stormy night. Barbus was running through the empty streets of Anddulia. His legs were burning, and every wheeze brought a stabbing pain into his lungs. Blood, hot, almost boiling, dripped into his eyes. His entire body was bloody and beaten, though. The howling wind and thrashing rain seemed louder than the booming thunder. Though nothing could smother his haggard breaths.

Something he knew not to do was look behind him, yet he did. No one was chasing after him. He slowed down as he came around a corner. A crack of lightning shot across his path, forcing him to stop dead in his tracks. Barbus, panting, wiped the rain, sweat, and blood off his face and hunkered down, readying himself for another fight.

"I think it is about time you stop running, Ahenobarbus Narine," a deep commanding voice called out before he cracked his chains against the ground once more. The hairs on Barbus's arms raised from the static.

Barbus, righting himself, laughed dryly. "Why?" he asked. "So, you can throw me into a cell?" Barbus hawked and spat. "I'd rather fight you here and die than rot in prison!"

Gareth studied him for a long while, eventually collecting his chain, the metal links scraping the stone. "Become a royal."

Barbus reeled as if he had been slapped.

"Leave the life of petty crime behind and do some good for once."

"You think I wanted this life?" Barbus snarled.

"A part of you, yes," Gareth said as he clipped his chain into the holster on his hip. "But I know you do it more for the money. Tired of living life at rock bottom?"

"Damn right I am!" He eyed the man, offended the royal would get comfortable enough to let his guard down so quickly. "And I'll be damned if I have to start all the way at the bottom again, just to what? Put on a smile? Make the people feel at ease?"

Gareth chuckled under his breath and took a step closer. "If you agree to come with me, I could talk to the king and have you start as a Royal Knight rank E," he offered. "You will not be able to get any higher without a bit of work, I must admit, but this should do for now."

It was certainly worth considering, but Barbus was more concerned about the deal going belly up. Many *comrades* sold him out for a few coins. That was how he had gotten into that mess in the first place. Yet again, from overhearing chatty royals, he knew the pay was good.

He sighed, "Fine." Barbus cracked his neck and rubbed it down like it was sore—it was. "Don't expect me to get all chummy with you!"

Gareth shrugged. "I'd suggest getting a little friendly."

Barbus raised a suspicious eyebrow.

"I am the one referring you, meaning the king will most likely put you in my Unit. You know how it goes. You bring in a stray, you have to look after it, right?" He laughed as Barbus made his way to him, cursing and grumbling.

The rest was history. In the rearmost of his mind, the memory was still a fond one. Especially now, as Barbus faded in and out of consciousness, it even made him chuckle a bit.

"Gareth"

There was a thick, milky white fog all around. Gareth could not see a meter in front of him. Shuffling forward, he kept his hands out, sweeping from side to side, his breathing as controlled as possible.

A hand came from behind and squeezed Gareth's shoulder. He whipped around, but no one was there. His eyes darted for a moment. He turned, the white fog becoming grey. It continued to blacken as he took one step back, then another, and sprinted the way he came. The darker the fog became, the harder it was to breathe.

Gareth stopped, the fog completely black. He choked and gagged, the fog now like sludge sticking to his airway. Dropping to his knees, he could not tell if his vision was fading or if he was even awake.

From the left to the right, the walls, the floor, and the ceiling were all earth. Lifting his head, panting from the nightmare, his head throbbed as he tried to remember what happened. Gareth had felt tired soon after entering Ivory's Kingdom, the steam he had fizzling out bit by bit. The Unit had fallen victim to the same drowsiness. He had caught a dizzy spell, Barbus had caught him, and that was the extent of his memories. He had been captured but where was he taken, by who, and why?

After realizing he was alone and wondering where his comrades were, Gareth jerked his wrist, but something jangled and kept his arm from moving. He looked up, a cold cuff shackling him to the wall clamped around his wrist. His ankles also had cuffs around them, a chill seeping into his bones from the icy metal. As Gareth tried to yank himself free, a sharp stabbed pain raked his torso, taking his breath away. Instantly, he recognized the pain. His magic had been drained while he was asleep. New questions flooded his mind.

How long had he been out? Were the others alive?

There was a sudden rumble, then a blinding orange light spilled into the room. Gareth flinched and groaned. Quickly, he whipped to the entrance, his eyes fluttering as they adjusted to the light. No one stood in the rectangular doorway. Gareth swiveled his head, his eyes going as wide as a full moon, his breath hitching.

A creature of black, smoky wisps flaring off its body, peered at him. It was thin, lanky, and tall, perhaps taller than a giant if it were to stand up straight. There was a pitch-dark void where the mouth, nose, and eyes—where the face should have been. Three jagged horns came from the top of its head like a poorly carved stone or a chipped blade.

Its head tilted from one side to the other, as if viewing a strange animal. The voident righted itself and Gareth followed, his head almost completely back. He swallowed the dry lump in his throat.

"You were out for days," it drawled.

Gareth shuddered at the sound of its voice. It was a scream echoing off the walls of a chasm, metal scraping stone.

"You are the second to awaken amongst your companions." It slid one foot in front of the other, taking a step.

Gareth's mouth opened, but nothing came out.

"Do not try to speak."

How could he not? He had questions that needed answering. "W-w-wh-hat… did-did you do t-to-to them?" he stuttered and choked.

The voident stared silently for a few seconds. "The same thing we did to you."

We?

"And they will get the same treatment you'll be getting." Suddenly, the voident was close, black embers bouncing off Gareth like bristly petals. "I don't play favorites." It slinked away, "Not yet anyway," then walked out, and the wall slid shut behind it.

What the hell is that thing talking about? Gareth tried to think of anything that stood out prior to and soon after entering Ivory's Kingdom. The streets were empty, the lamps unlit, and the sun was strong, but the breeze carried a nice, sweet fragrance that made the heat bearable. The smell lingered in his mind, and he got a sudden whiff of it again. What was the scent, a poison of some sort? His thoughts squeezed his brain, forcing his eyes closed as he winced. That was a mistake. His eyelids became lead when he attempted to peel them open, to no avail.

Hours must have gone by since the voidents' visit. He fell in and out of sleep, waking up from nightmares over and over again yet his cell was always empty.

The wall thundered open and a different voident walked in. It was broader, muscular; the horns coming out of the sides of its head like a ram's, curled and ribbed. Reaching the middle of the room, the wall closed, and the voident held its hand out. A flame burst in its palm, painting the room in golden light.

It lumbered to Gareth's left side, uncuffed his hand, and froze. *Did it grow a third arm?* Slowly turning its head, the voident peered at Gareth. He shivered.

"Brace yourself," it rumbled.

One hand went under his arm, just below his armpit, while the other clutched Gareth's wrist. He tugged his limb, but the voident kept a powerful hold. Gareth struggled to wrench his arm free of its grasp. He knew what was about to happen and would rather have his arm sawed off than what the voident was about to do.

"No." Panic gripped his heart, squeezed it. "Please." It felt like his breath was stolen. "I am begging you." What else could he do but plead? "Do not do this." His voice trembled. The voident ignored him.

His skin, every muscle, ligament, and tendon were snapping like string. The bone ripped out of its socket as the voident towed his arm. His shoulder popped. He grunted in pain, clenching his jaw so tightly he thought he might break a tooth. A warm flow of blood slipped from his mouth onto his chin and down his throat. The voident continued to pull and pull and pull. His elbow and wrist snapped and cracked. He screamed. A wet tearing noise filled his ears. Then the world went black.

Gareth glanced to his side to see his majesty scribbling something on the table, both sitting at a desk in the library. Magnus was a boy, no older than eleven or twelve. His face was soft and somewhat pudgy. Suddenly recognizing the outfit Magnus wore, Gareth flinched back in his seat, surprising the young prince.

Magnus looked at Gareth, his eyes big and round, and asked if he was okay. Gareth nodded, despite wanting to shake his head no. He peeked at the clock on the table.

He wanted to send Magnus away. Tell him to put his studies down. He could return to them later, but his body did not listen. Instead, he leaned closer and pointed the mistakes out on the paper, explaining how they were wrong. Magnus sighed, nodded, and fixed the equations.

Gareth woke with a start, the chains jingling from his abrupt movement. Frantically, he whipped his head to the left, his arm attached to his shoulder. He glanced around, feeling as if his mind was playing tricks on him. It was not. Dried pools of blood stained the dirt beneath his arm and the walls. It had been yanked off, then reattached. Why? How? Was the other voident waiting beyond the corner to heal him? Time passed when his arm began to burn and throb. It was reattached, but the damage had still been done and he did not have the magic to regenerate it. At least he still had the limb; better than seeing his arm on the ground rotting. He sighed.

Lycn, Lucas, and Barbus were tough, thick-skinned, and durable. Each one of them could take a beating. Gareth knew, if anything, those three would survive, not unscathed, but being alive was better than being dead.

Pich, alternatively, was small and thin. Their body could barely handle a lightweight bow specially made for them if they hadn't practiced for a bit. He cursed himself, regretting the fact that he had not trained Pich the way he should have. He should have made them do resistance, strength, and combat training, everything a normal royal would learn. Why had he not? To recall his reasoning was futile between the pain in his arm shooting into his chest and the ache of his core.

"Lycn"

In a box of earth, *a wonderful way to wake up*, Lycn could smell the soil and stone, the musk of mold or mildew, the stench of blood that wafted into his cell often enough. He moved his arms, the chains jingling, a reminder that he was shackled to the wall. A pain lanced across his midsection, taking his breath away. Another reminder that whoever captured Unit One was smart enough to drain their magic. He groaned. He was waiting—had been for what seemed like hours—for someone or something to arrive and was tired of it.

There was a smell in Ivory's Kingdom, bittersweet and out of place that Lycn should have known was suspicious. It was almost intoxicating, compelling him to take deep breaths, feeling the relaxing effects of whatever was in the air. *How foolish.* If Pich were here, they would know what was in the air once Lycn explained the smell. Even if he didn't, he was sure they'd know anyway based on the effects. He sighed and started counting his heartbeats, since it was the only thing he could hear aside from his breathing. Then his ears twitched. Soft footfalls were coming closer before they stopped and the wall burst open with light, blinding Lycn.

"Ahh, if it isn't the little wolf boy," someone said as they drew near. *Coyote, actually.* Earthy blood and bitterness filled the dungeon, making Lycn's nose crinkle. "Glad to see that you're awake."

"What the hell do you want?" Lycn snarled when his sight finally returned to him.

In front of him stood a creature of pure darkness, black wisps like embers shooting off its body and horns. His blood stopped momentarily, his breath becoming as thick as mucus and catching in his throat.

"To hurt you," it said. "Simple enough, isn't it?"

"Fuck off." Lycn had a hunch that asking this thing questions would get him nowhere.

"I'd rather not."

"Then let me go and I'll fuck off." Pich never liked his potty mouth, so he stopped cursing in front of them. Lucas got a good laugh out of it for months. Eventually, he accepted it and stopped teasing him, *the bastard.*

"Tempting, but no." The creature, which Lycn assumed was a voident, stalked across the room, its body gangling, limbs thin and bony. *Does it even have bones?* "I'd much rather hear what you sound like compared to the dark elf."

That was Sir Gareth? Guttural screams woke Lycn up hours ago, but he thought they were a trick his mind was playing on him, a cruel jest, a delusion from his weariness.

"I'm not much of a screamer," Lycn said, fear gnawing at his mind like howlers devouring their prey. Howlers left nothing behind. They ate bones and all.

"You always scream."

As its hand rose, one finger grew and thinned into a needle-like blade. The tip pressed into Lycn's forearm, he watched its finger sink into his skin like a knife to soft butter. He set his jaw.

It stopped, dragged its finger across to the nook of his arm, down, lengthwise back, and up. The voident sneered while peeling the rectangular slab of flesh, uncovering the throbbing red fibrous muscle beneath. Lycn ground his teeth and held his breath, his head snapping toward the entry. The hallway was glowing orange, the smell of burning linseed oil filling his nose for a split second before iron did. Blood steadily oozed down his bicep to the floor—drip, drip, drip. It throbbed, seared, the pain a constant pulse through his arm. Lycn started chewing on the inside of his cheek, giving him an alternative source of pain to focus on.

"Nothing?" the voident voiced with what seemed to be genuine disappointment. "Too bad. Guess we'll have to keep going until you give me what I want."

Fuck. I should've just screamed, got it done and over with.

A numb fuzziness encased Lycn's body like a woolen blanket. His vision was hazy, everything a blur or spinning. It all hurt, burned as if someone pressed a cattle brand into his skin. Repeatedly. The voident had taken several slabs of flesh, some it ate. Though Lycn didn't know how, since it didn't have a mouth or a face, it was just a void. But it did, none too silently either. It sounded like a hammer pounding on fresh, bloody meat right off the animal. Bile mixed with the blood on the ground now because of it. If Pich were here, they would have been able to heal him.

Gareth had brought Pich in for training one day. They were short and scrawny, reminding Lycn of a delicate flower that could lose all of its petals if the wind blew too hard. They were out of place, like a rose in a bed of weeds.

Since Gareth focused on teaching Pich to use the bow and arrow, Lycn was partnered with the biggest brute in the kingdom. A bear beastman that everyone called Iron Fist. He dodged every blow except one, and that earned him the beating of a lifetime until Pich stepped in. They had stones for standing up to a beastman twice their size, stronger than a dozen men with a temper that could rival a dragon to boot. Gareth stopped the royal from going berserk, giving him a few broken bones while Pich healed Lycn. He grumbled to no end though and Pich slapped him upside the head for it, too. *Shut up and sit still, so I can heal you!* they had told him.

Lycn thought it was ironic to be facing death while thinking of his lover and smiled a wry thing. He had only heard others talk about it, seeing your life flash before your eyes as death breathed down your neck. Thinking of loved ones left no room in your mind to think of anything else. Apparently, it was true, and he didn't mind. Didn't mind one bit.

"Lucas"

Fire had been the reason so many revered Lucas at Everest Academy. Fear, however, hid in the hearts of his peers. Professor Cadmus hadn't feared him.

After weeks of pleading, Cadmus had agreed to spar with Lucas a few times before the seer and a knight visited the academy. The tall dark elf, a scar running across his face, invited him to join the royals in Alucard's Kingdom soon after Cesar's death. Lucas had agreed. He couldn't stand to be anywhere near the place where his father had been murdered. Nor could he stand the contempt in his mother's eyes whenever she looked at him.

Cesar was of average height, a little taller than Elena, but his body had years of training engraved in his large muscles. He had chestnut brown, curly hair, and freckles from being in the sun too much. His square face would only soften when his smile grew big and goofy. Although his hands were calloused and scarred, they were gentle and loving. He would tell story after story about his adventures as a knight, and Lucas loved them.

A few years ago, reports of people dying in the same manner his father had had come in; a spear of ice through the back. They were rare, but Lucas caught wind of it anyhow. From eyewitness reports, the person responsible for the killings, including Cesar, was a half-blooded dark elf with long black hair spewing nonsense about god and judgment. Not so soon afterward, Lucas ran into his father's murderer by chance in the streets of Alucard's Kingdom.

Six years after Cesar's death and his blood still boiled at the thought of Kuro's face. If only he could have killed them right then and there, he would have.

As much as he was glad Malice killed them during the Games, Lucas wished he had been the one to send Kuro to hell.

Grabbing onto the chains, Lucas struggled to pull himself up, and kicked his legs around, trying to break free. He dropped, the chains clinking. The tip of his shoes knocked something over as his body dangled. It sounded like a stick hitting the earth. He was out of breath and his muscles ached. It wasn't the first time Lucas had awoken, but it was the first time he'd stayed conscious for more than a few seconds.

The wall opened in front of him. He flinched as a voident waltzed in.

"Where are the others?" he shouted and blinked till he could see properly. The voident stood before him. It was big and bulky, its body as black as night and its face even darker.

"Close," its deep voice boomed.

Now that there was light, Lucas was encased in rock, a pile of wood beneath him.

"HA! You think I'm scared of a little fire?" His lips flared, baring his teeth. Lucas held strong, unwilling to let the sweat building in his fists be known or the trembling of his legs be noticed. *Stand proud when fear threatens to consume you,* his father once told him.

"You may not be." The voident stepped away and lifted a hand. "But that will not save you from the pain." In a quick motion, its hand circled, collecting fire, throwing it at Lucas's feet. The wood caught aflame, sending embers into the air.

That's fine, I can handle this much. Heat quickly reached the soles of his feet, flames licking at his boots. He lifted his legs, knowing he wouldn't be able to do it for long, but he couldn't help but delay the inevitable. Then, moving closer, the voident pinched the bottom of his shirt. A flicker caught, creating a flare of ginger. The fabric singed around the voident's fingers, turned red, and sparked.

The pain was bearable at first. Fire spreads though and consumes even faster. Scorching heat burned his throat and his lungs, breathing now a joke. He could smell his own burning flesh, and his stomach churned. The blaze beneath gripped his pants, gradually climbing up. His pain came out in bursts of screams. The voident had left soon after igniting his shirt, closing the wall behind him.

Lucas tried to yell, but his throat was far too burned. He couldn't breathe from the dark grey smoke trapped in the room.

He was going to die.

He didn't want to die.

Suddenly, the pain was gone, and Maryjane's corpse flashed in his mind, Joseph as well. He had grown so much since the last Lucas saw his little brother. Lucas wondered if they had the same thoughts, only to realize that no one was coming to save them. Had Cesar panicked as death took him? Or was he calm when he accepted his fate? How frightened were Maryjane and Joseph in the end? How was Mother doing? Did she know about Joseph's death? Was she dead, too?

Something as cold as ice splashed down onto Lucas. He couldn't see, couldn't hear either. More ice washed over him, waves of pain surging through his body as if the voident were toying with his nerves directly.

Stand proud when fear threatens to consume you.

But what about pain, father? You never told me how to handle the pain.

"Pich"

Their head had been throbbing for a while, a constant squeezing of their brain that made Pich grimace often. The room was blurry enough without their glasses. Being alone in a dark room made of earth didn't help, and that was about all they knew about their location.

Pich had gone over the archive of poisons in their head a million times since they woke up. Someway, somehow, whoever captured Unit One had managed to get deadly nightshade in their systems. If Pich had to guess, they'd say it was airborne, dust perhaps, in Ivory's Kingdom, which also meant this was a trap from the beginning. They cringed at the burst of pain in their skull and took a deep breath, attempting to calm their racing thoughts.

"Quite the thinker, aren't you?" a voice drawled from the corner.

Pich jerked, their eyes darting to the rightmost corner in front of them, the spot a few shades darker than the rest of the room. "Who are you?" they asked, their voice pinched from the dryness of their mouth.

"Valken." Valken, whatever it was, peeled itself from the wall, strode toward Pich, then stopped—its proximity intensified the stench of mold. "You should be asking what I am."

Pich swallowed, rather glad the creature was a blurry mass of darkness. "What… are you?"

"A voident," Valken hissed.

Voidents? I didn't think we would run into one when they were so elusive in the kingdoms, let alone be captured... but why were we captured? It goes against everything we know about them.

"You are weak compared to the others," the voident said. "Fragile, like glass. I like breaking glass—the sound is delightful."

"Why did you kidnap us?" Pich ignored the growing disgust and fear in their gut, like spiders crawling up Pich's airway, spinning webs to prevent their fall.

Valken tilted his head, more of a jerk, an uncontrollable spasm. "Because someone wants to meet your leader."

Gareth? But why? "How is he involved with the likes of you?"

It went silent, Valken as still as an undisturbed pool of water. A heartbeat passed, then another and another. Valken's hand encased Pich's lower jaw, a squeak of a gasp escaping their throat, eyes wide, heart pounding like drums in their chest.

"With the likes of you?" he repeated, malice dripping off every word.

He squeezed until Pich's jaw snapped. They screamed, tears burning their eyes when Valken pinched the tip of their tongue and cut it out. Blood gurgled in place of a wail, wetness streaking Pich's cheeks. Burning heat pulsed from their face and mouth.

"I liked that sound. The sound of glass breaking." Pich could hear the smile in his tone, the desire, bile lurching into their throat.

The voident drew his arm back and punched Pich's gut, forcing all the wind out of their body in a single wheeze. Pain bloomed in their abdomen. Again and again. Valken wailed on Pich. Their screams were nothing but air escaping from their lungs as their body thumped against the wall behind them. It wasn't long before he started laughing, a vile cackle ringing in Pich's ears.

Eventually, out of breath, Valken stalked out of the dungeon, the wall rumbling open and close. Pich dangled from their shackles, their body in agony like they had never felt. If only they would pass out, as unlikely as it was, since they hadn't so far. If only they had decent regeneration skills, the pain would be tolerable or short-lasting, or both. Pich was a bit envious of Malice's regeneration and he was smart to learn how to heal beforehand.

Did he know… that we would be captured?

Every doubt Lycn had, every worry and complaint. Were they all true? Were they fools for going along with Malice, Pich even going as far as to defend him? If Malice knew, so did the king, which meant the king approved or thought of the plan in the first place.

Malice stood at the center of the dungeon, his green eyes peering at them with an ethereal glow. Pich jolted, pain lancing through them. Then they blinked him away. *The pain is making me delusional.* They laughed and it almost instantly became a cough that was hard to stop. Once they did, they closed their eyes again and leaned their head on the wall. *We made a mistake. Trusting Malice was a mistake.*

"Malice"

The heads of nobles speared in front of their very own castle; the sight would have been poetic if it weren't expected. Magnus wanted that kingdom gone, anyway. It was a win-win for him and Malice. He'd like further confirmation of who speared the nobles, though. It was better to have the facts than to go off of guesses alone.

The wall grumbled, rock grinding on rock. Malice's ears rang. A voident sauntered in, then stopped before Malice.

"How are you awake?" it asked in a low tone.

"I have a resistance to poison. Deadly nightshade was a frequent treat for me when I was younger," Malice replied evenly, borderline sarcastically, which earned him a snarl.

"Don't give me that tone!"

Malice blinked and sighed. "Where is he?"

"He?" the voident echoed. "Cas? In the hallway."

"Where is *he*?"

"Riddles!" The voident threw his hands up and reeled. He paced, his feet making a padded noise as if he were wearing fur socks. "I hate them. Always talking in riddles, you fickle things!"

Not the brightest, I see. "Zephyrus," Malice said shortly. Zephyrus was the first name that came to mind, as doubtful as his being the culprit was. Dead men couldn't command the living. He would try Lazarus next.

The voident halted, his arms frozen, when he slowly put them to his sides and turned to face Malice. "You know our commander?"

It... was him... Zephyrus is alive?

"How?" The voident rushed in close, a gust of air following his movement. "Who are you to him?"

"Someone you should fear, but are too ignorant."

There was a twitch in the voident's jaw. Malice caught his gaze for a split second—what he assumed was the voident's gaze, anyway. He cuffed Malice's chin, the tips of his fingers turned long and sharp like a blade. The voident pried Malice's mouth open, grabbed his tongue, and cut it out. A wet thump from it hitting the floor followed. Malice's head lowered, blood pouring from his gaping mouth.

The voident cackled a high-pitched, jarring melody.

Malice did too, cutting the voidents short, his own voice deep and humorless.

"I drained you of your magic," he snapped.

"You did."

"How are you regenerating?" The voident slammed his fist into the wall beside Malice's head with a booming crack. "You are a human, a weak race—a pitifully weak race."

"Human?" Malice almost laughed again. "Far from it, but you'll find that out eventually, I'm sure."

I need confirmation. The Unit can hold out for a month, but no longer. Magnus agreed to that as well. Sooner the better, of course, but... we'll see what happens.

The Price of Decisions
XVI

Part III

Screams carried about the dungeons. Often.

Unit One had been stuck down here long enough for Barbus to recognize each voice that rang in his ears. The first was Gareth. His was deeper and gruff, almost like a howl from an old wolf. Then it was Lycn, his voice a bit nasally like he'd fallen ill. Lucas's was higher than Lycn's, usually cut short, followed by the wretched stench of burnt flesh. Finally, Pich's. Their voice was the highest, the most feminine. Although, theirs sounded more like abrupt shrieks, probably because the skinny voident liked to use'em as a punching bag.

Barbus managed—honestly, surprising himself—to count the days or nights. It helped that the big one stuck to a schedule. Once a day, the voident would pour bugs and water down his gullet.

A month had passed. Which certainly gave Barbus plenty of time with his thoughts, too much time if you asked him. He never thought the quiet was something he would come to dread, but it did, and right now, it was quiet. The sound of his heart pumping blood and poison through his body and his strained wheezes was sickening.

Every now and again the voidents would talk, their conversation muffled beyond the thick earth walls, their tones sharp and angry. *Not seeing eye to eye then, eh?*

Taking as deep of a breath as he could without hacking, Barbus let his head lean against the cool, rough stone behind him, sending shivers down his spine. His arms throbbed in a hundred places from the injection sites, his body heavy as if filled with sand. Though, perhaps that was all the ale curdling in his stomach. A smile touched the corners of his mouth. *Ale or beer would be nice. Hell, I'd even go for a nice stein of chicha.*

A cry of pain, Lycn's, echoed, reaching Barbus's ears over his labored breathing. He was used to it—his stomach no longer churned, and he no longer winced at the sounds of his comrades, his friends, getting tortured. Instead, he thought of anything else. Helen, his lover, one of the doctors at the castle. The young royals training their hearts out at the coliseum, the knights teaching them, guiding them. He missed being there, watching the sprouts grow into fine warriors. That was something he and Pich had in common: the love of teaching. Though they'd wanted to teach the next generations of healers and doctors, it was why they became a royal.

And that was why they weren't trained properly. *Gareth's too soft.* It wasn't just Barbus who thought better of not training Pich. Everyone in Unit One had. They should've learned the basics, learned to protect themselves. Both were stubborn about the subject. Pich and Gareth were two peas in a pod sometimes.

Barbus was content with teaching how to throw a good punch, one that would put someone clean on their ass or simply knock them out. *Aim for the nose or jaw,* he told the royals. *Everyone tears up if they're hit in the nose and you hit the jaw just right, they'll be seeing stars.* Most had nodded their agreement, probably from personal experience. Marris, one of Barbus's closest friends, certainly helped with that one. He chuckled, which turned into a wet cough, phlegm, and blood splattered on the floor. His beard too, he was sure.

How much longer till they get bored of this? Will we ever be set free? Perhaps it'd be better to die here. Sure sounds nice right now. To rest without pain.

"Malice"

Despite it running through his body, Malice wasn't fond of darkness. He much preferred the light. It repelled many things.

The sounds of distant chatter grew after a time. Valken and Cas were arguing again from the sounds of it.

"Our orders were to keep them alive," Cas growled.

Valken's practices had become rather intense as of late and relentless at that. He wasn't giving the Unit enough time to breathe or regenerate a fraction of their injuries. Malice wouldn't be surprised if they had made nice friends with death because of Valken's antics. *Makes my job that much harder though.*

"Yes, and they are."

"Barely!" Cas snapped. "You are making things much more difficult than they need to be." He took a deep breath and released it, the sound a low rasp.

"Aww," Valken mocked sympathy. "You poor pup. What can you do? You're at the bottom. A dog who must obey or you will be put down."

Malice could imagine Cas turning somewhere else, unable to say anything.

"I follow Commander Zephyrus. Not you."

Valken scoffed.

"If he says we are to kill them, then that is what we will do. If he says to keep them detained and unable to fight back, then that is what we will do. Or I will do it alone."

Silence loomed in the corridor. Valken rushed past the door, fists clenched, obviously seeking Pich to relieve some anger.

Soon after, Cas entered the chamber. "You do not have to pretend to be asleep. I know you heard everything."

"I didn't know you had a set on you." Malice brought his head up, grinning. "Good for you."

Cas grumbled and walked closer, whispering, "He will arrive soon." The voident left, closing the wall when he stepped into the hallway. *A loyal mutt till the end.*

*

The quiet disturbed by yelling and loud crashes, booms, and thuds, Malice looked to the wall when it burst open, sending hunks of earth across the room. Valken stood in the new entrance, shoulders in rhythm with his heavy breathing. Behind him on the floor was Cas, limp and motionless.

"What has you so upset?" Malice asked.

Valken marched over and slammed Malice's head into the wall. Crumbles of dirt fell to the ground, followed by a thin stream of blood going down Malice's spine.

"You are a pest! One that is not needed," he said through what sounded like gritted teeth.

Valken's hand empaled Malice's chest while the voident pulled him away from the wall. He removed something, wetness tearing, a coldness quickly filling Malice. In his hands, Malice's heart pounded, the ichor dripping to the floor. He crushed it. Blood and chunks of flesh exploded, sloshed, plopped. The voident's arm retracted. Malice hung from the shackles in the wall.

Valken turned. "That is how you get the job done," he mumbled and stared at Cas, who was still doubled over against the wall.

Bones cracking, reforming, and breaking through skin as the chains on the walls stretched beyond their limits, snapping. The sound reverberated off the chamber's walls. It had been a long time since he assumed his true form. His limbs felt foreign. He moved his jaw, it popped. The bones in his legs ground together, the flesh moving with them until his legs were that of a goat's. Malice wiggled his first set of fingers, the tips now black claws. The second set reached to feel his chest where Valken stabbed his heart out. *Not the first time someone's done that.*

A long, dragon-like tail swung low from side to side behind him. The movement was strange to Malice, as if someone else was controlling his tail with a string. He tried to spread his wings, but they were too big for the room, the wing thumbs scraping the ceiling. Eventually, all four of his eyes settled on Valken.

The voident hadn't moved and would be statuesque if it weren't for his entire body shaking. Malice watched for a moment longer, fear emanating from Valken like steam from a teapot.

There was a certain… thrill about watching a monster tremble.

Malice grabbed Valken by the neck, his fingers wrapping around and overlapping his thumb, lifting him so they were face to face. "If Zephyrus is coming, I'll be leaving." Valken flinched at his words.

"Ugly, aren't I?" Malice remarked.

Valken laughed awkwardly, but it just sounded like he was choking. "I'm glad we eradicated the devils," he said, his words strained. "Such revolting creatures don't deserve to walk on this planet."

Malice considered Valken. If he stared long enough, his mind would eventually put a face to the black canvas that stared back at him. Eventually. "You missed one." He smirked, crushing Valken's neck, a single mushy snap.

Absorbing the darkness that made up Valken's very being, Malice was surprised a voident, a creature of darkness, could forget so easily who Malice was.

That was Valken's final mistake.

"Cas"

Cas was stiff when he woke, so he dragged himself into a better position where his back was against the wall and his legs were out in front of him. *One hit and I was out... Pathetic*. Hoping Valken moved on, he glanced around and flinched. Malice stood with his shoulder braced on the smoothed frame, which Cas could have sworn was jagged. The paleness of his bare body almost glowed in the torch's light. Malice looked like an angel, the exact opposite of what he was.

"Awake now?" Malice asked, calmly, Valken nowhere in sight.

"Where—"

"Dead," Malice answered without giving him a chance to ask the question.

He pushed off the wall and started down the corridor when he stopped and turned toward Cas. "Fetch me some clothes, will you? I'm a bit chilled."

Cas stared at Malice, sighed, and got to his feet. His orders were to help Malice until the commander arrived. Although, even if those were not his orders, he'd still listen to Malice. A gut-wrenching feeling told him that Valken died a miserable death. Unless Cas wanted to face the same fate, he would do as he was told. *One master to the next.*

At the end of the passage was a staircase that spiraled into a supplies closet in the castle of Ivory's Kingdom. Cas followed it to the ground floor while Malice walked in the opposite direction.

*

The eerily quiet hallway was long enough to have six chambers, one for each member of the Unit and Malice. It was wide. He could extend his arms out to his sides and not touch either wall. There were two torches in metal holsters on the wall, shedding enough light to see both ends of the hallway. The dungeons were hastily made, hours, maybe a day or so, before Malice made it to Ivory's Kingdom. Lack of skill and carelessness probably had more to do with it than lack of time.

Close to the wall, Malice glided his hand on the rough texture of the earth, his nails leaving thin lines as he went. He came to a halt, jerked his hand across the wall, and it opened. About ten meters from his chamber was Lucas. The smell of smoke, burnt flesh, blood, and other bodily fluids was overwhelming. Malice's nose scrunched up as he scowled at the limp body hanging from the ceiling. Lucas's skin was charred, blistered, and raw. He doubted any scavenger would want to feed on what was left of the elf.

Somewhat out of breath, Cas came running up from behind, a pile of folded cloth in hand. "Here," he panted as he gave them to Malice, "your clothes."

Malice took them and slid into the underwear, a white blouse with ruffled sleeves, dark green trousers, then a pair of the same-colored green slippers. Cas glanced around Malice, recoiling when he saw Lucas.

"Go get more supplies." Malice buttoned his shirt and stuffed the excess into his pants.

"Pardon?"

"Clothes, sheets, blankets, pillows, food, water, and medical supplies. Put it all into a trunk or two and meet me in front of the castle," he elaborated. He kept the voident alive to use him, not to have him stand around with his head up his ass.

"… All right."

One hand out, lying flat, palm side down, Malice's fingers sliced the air. The chains snapped and Lucas slipped into a bed of air. He walked into the hallway and gently placed Lucas on the ground. The right side of his face had been ripped to shreds and overcooked. His mandible and cheekbone was showing amongst blackened frays of skin. His eye was gone, melted at some point, his ear too, which was little more than a mound on the side of his head.

Beside him, Malice knelt and tried to feel a heartbeat. It was there, but it was faint and slow, his breathing strained. Malice noted the most severe of burns, his leg where the bone poked through the skin, and his misshaped torso that looked to have been trampled on.

Ten meters down, Gareth wasn't any better. Across his chest and back were long slashes—red, bloody, and swollen—from a whip that went as deep as bone. His wrists, elbows, and shoulders were like knots of wood. Quickly getting him down from the wall, Malice placed Gareth beside Lucas, then ventured into the next chamber.

Barbus was pale, his stomach nothing but a flap of loose skin from all the weight he'd lost. His eyes were sunken into dark sockets. Sweat dripped from every pore, making his bruises of black, red, blue, and purple shine. Barbus's nails were blackish green, signs they had been torn off repeatedly. Up and down his arms and neck, bruised red dots spotted his skin where Valken had injected poison. Malice gently felt the angel's torso, arms, and legs. There were little to no other injuries.

Lycn's chamber had a horrid, rotting smell. Malice didn't know which he preferred, Lucas's burnt flesh or Lycn's decay.

Pus, yellowish and green, dripped from a discolored wound seemingly carved out of his right arm. Lycn's skin was mottled, hot to the touch. Malice pressed his fingers to his wrist, his heartbeat rapid. Once he was down from the wall, Malice did a once over the rest of his body. His injuries mirrored Gareth's. No injection sites.

Lastly, Malice went into Pich's dungeon. Feces and urine were strong in the air as well as the metallic tang of blood. Their entire body was black, blue, and yellow, swollen to where Malice could hardly recognize the fairy dangling from the shackles. Their stomach was bloated, probably internal bleeding. However, Pich truly was only beaten. There were no burns, injection sites, or patches of skin missing, nothing but damage caused by a fist or foot.

Malice noticed pinkish-red masses on Pich's back when he unshackled them, dingy brown bone at the center of the wounds. Valken had snapped their wings from their shoulder blades.

The Unit was in awful shape, worse than Malice predicted. Valken did a number on them. It was no wonder Cas was throwing a fit. All on beds of air that were raised a meter above the ground, Malice carefully brought them up the staircase into the closet. Once on the main floor, he swiftly got everyone out of the stairwell and gently placed them on the green marble.

Malice whirled and headed to the closet, moved both hands up in a circular motion, thrusting them down. The earth thundered beneath his feet and soon the stairwell he was staring into collapsed. As he spun on his heel, Malice lifted the Unit and started toward the front entrance.

*

As ordered, Cas sat on the front steps of the castle with two leather-covered trunks at his side. He had searched all over the castle for clothes, sheets, pillows, food, and medical supplies. There were plenty of clothes, so he filled one trunk with them while sheets and pillows stuffed the other. The food he found was moldy, bug-infested, or half-eaten by vermin.

In the southern wing of the castle, Cas collected bandages, thread, needles, gauze, and alcohol and placed them on top of the clothes in the first trunk. There was not nearly as much as he expected to find, but there were two clinics in the kingdom that Malice could get supplies from.

A shadow suddenly approached him. Cas jumped to his feet and whipped around. It was Malice, five bodies floating behind him.

Before he had the chance to say anything, Malice demanded, "Follow me," and strode toward the gates.

He watched the Unit float past him, one by one, then quickly fumbled to grab the trunks and follow along.

Cas walked through the empty streets, the bittersweet smell gone. Zephyrus had come up with the idea to use deadly nightshade and spread it around the kingdom. The sky was bright blue, small white blobs moseying by. Summer had begun as the cicadas screeched and the birds whistled. The breeze brought a hint of salt from the ocean in the north, woodland, and lush green grass.

Close behind Malice, Cas stalked the small forest, the trees spread out, rays of light breaking the shade apart. It was loud with bugs and other critters. A little way in, a clearing was visible. Upon getting there, Malice placed the Unit down about five meters apart. He pointed Cas toward the middle of the glade, and he lumbered over to put the trunks down.

Meanwhile, Malice put his hands out to his sides, then brought them up diagonally, but stopped above his head. From his movements, slabs of earth erupted around each person to form a hut. The hut was wide enough to fit four people and was about three meters tall.

Cas watched Malice bring up the back walls of each hut all at once, amazed he had the energy to do so. *Valken and I had drained their magic frequently. He should not be able to do that.*

Abruptly, Malice turned and marched toward then beyond Cas. The demon stomped his foot, creating a circular crater for a fire pit.

"Leave for now." He glanced over his shoulder. "Return when Zephyrus arrives."

"Is—" Cas looked to Malice. "Is that all?" He expected to be put to full use, threatened, or perhaps killed like Valken was.

"Unless you want to collect firewood while I'm gone, yes, that's it," he said in a level tone as if he had lost all interest in Cas.

"For letting me live," Cas bowed at the waist, "I shall help in any way possible until my commander comes." He had little choice, considering his orders from Commander Zephyrus.

Help Malice, the commander said.

Why? I thought you wanted him dead. Cas had questioned.

I want you to keep an eye on him. To do that, you need to let him use you.

If he refuses?

Insist, Zephyrus hissed, *and bring him to me when I tell you.*

Malice's eyebrow jumped. "If you wish to be helpful; go to the clinic in the southwest while I ransack the one in the east." He walked into the woods the way they came.

Cas trudged to the shade of the trees and sank into it. He resurfaced in the clinic, the room dark and stuffy. It hadn't taken long to fill a few crates of medical supplies—gauzes, potions of some sort, needles, bandages, and so on. Whatever he could fit in the crates, he took and returned to an empty, tranquil glade. As he placed the crates next to the trunks from the castle, he glanced over the huts and decided to go collect firewood, maybe find some food while he was at it.

The sun rode low in the sky, casting long shadows across the forest floor. Cas trekked back to the opening, four fish, two squirrels, a toad, and a few rabbits, branches and sticks in hand. He tossed the wood inside the pit and sent a flame to its center. After a second it caught ablaze, and Cas plopped beside it.

The number of crates increased by two and they were spread out instead of stacked, the latches flipped up. A wooden bucket sat beside the crates. Sheets had also been hung on the front of each hut. He turned to look at the bonfire, picking up a fish, merging his hand into a sharp blade, and fileting, then gutting it. He did not need to eat, but he knew Malice would have to at some point.

When the moon shone brightly above the canopy of trees, Malice had finally emerged from one of the huts. If Cas recalled correctly, it was the beastman's hut. He was resilient and, in the first week, had quite the mouth on him. *Everyone breaks at some point.* Almost two weeks in, he had begged for the one named Pich. Just a glimpse of them was all he needed, he had told Cas.

Valken had planned to accommodate his wishes by putting all the royals into one chamber. He wanted to witness the pure horror on their faces as they watched Valken torture their comrades.

If he could have, Cas would have retched. He wanted to and almost felt a need for it.

Bucket in hand, Malice dropped it by the trunks, then came to sit by the fire. Blood and grime stained his clothes. The smoke and discarded animal skins barely masked the stench wafting beside Cas. The voident plucked a stick from the ground and handed Malice a rabbit. He took it, started peeling the meat off the body, eating it.

"You're more useful than I thought," Malice said in between bites, startling Cas. "Your friend did a number on them, by the way." He peered over the flames.

"We were not friends," Cas said, disgust thick in his tone. A smirk teased Malice's lips. He grunted and turned the other way. "That demented fool deserved death long before you gave it to him."

"Hmm." Malice swallowed. "I'm sure he did."

Finishing his last bite, Malice tossed the stick into the bonfire and extended his hand for another. Cas gave him the toad next, expecting a flare of his lip or a glare that could kill. Instead, he took it, tore one of the hind legs off, and wolfed it down. *Not picky?*

The question Malice had asked Valken resonated in Cas's ears. *Where is he?* Once his tongue regenerated for the fifteenth time, Cas thought, he had asked Cas the same question.

"How did you know about Zephyrus?"

Malice spat out a piece of bone, his thumb wiping the corner of his mouth. "The way he killed the people of Phoenix."

Cas jolted, his posture stiffening. *He has known for that long?*

"He's never liked nobleman or monarchs, for that matter. Anyone of a higher status he hates with a passion." Malice's eyes sliced through the fire to Cas. "That's why their heads were on spears, yet the townspeople weren't."

Even Cas had no idea his commander held such a great disdain toward noblemen. At the time, he thought Zephyrus's actions were to send a message only Malice would understand. As true as that may have been, there were more personal feelings involved than Cas could have imagined.

"My instructions are to help you until he arrives," Cas said.

"You will leave when I tell you," Malice replied bluntly and took another bite.

"I do not follow your—"

"This time you will, or poor Zephyrus will be down another dog."

Cas, swallowing, chose to remain silent until Malice finished his meal, rose, and headed for the beastman's hut. He knew when to keep quiet, a skill taught to him some time ago.

Bright and early, Malice came out of one of the shelters, throwing an empty bucket at Cas, and returning to the hut he stormed out of. Cas took it as a command to fetch more water from the pond. When he returned, pushing the sheet out of his way, Malice rushed to Cas, snatched the pail of water, and went to the next royal. He noticed the second bucket lying on its side near the trunks. Cas scooped it up and hurried to the pond to refill it.

Midafternoon came around, and Malice sent Cas into the kingdom. He was to retrieve whatever was left behind in the clinics. He was also ordered to find a teapot, cups, towels, cloths, and soap. There was not much left at the clinics to grab as Malice and Cas snatched most of the supplies. He located a teapot on someone's porch and found everything else in the same house. *Lucky find.*

Malice had hauled himself away in one of the huts, an empty bucket lying on the ground. Cas laughed dryly to himself, thinking Malice was going to get the most out of using him.

Well into the night, Cas had lost count of how many times he had run back to the pond. He was starting to think it would be drained before those royals could walk again.

The moon was almost full, and by tomorrow it would be. Everything not touched by the fire's ginger light was bathed in pale blue. The ground was cool, damp with dew, yet the air was warm, almost dry from the summer heat.

Malice came out from the last hut, a bit of sweat glistening on his skin. As he walked toward Cas, he noticed the muscles Malice had were gone, his body now gaunt. His cheekbones were prominent, and his eyes were sunken into shallow dark pits. A bit of guilt made his heart throb. Cas put his hand to his chest. *I did not know I could feel guilt.*

Cas handed Malice a steaming fish after he sat down. It was surprising how much energy Malice had, physically, mentally, and magically. Cas recalled how much of a process it was to drain Malice's magical energy. His taunts were thought to be a tactic to delay the inevitable or to instill a bit of fear in Cas and Valken. They were both sorely mistaken. He laughed at himself, temporarily catching Malice's attention.

Malice tossed the bones and stick into the bonfire and extended his hand for another. Cas obliged, handing him a squirrel.

Once the food was gone, Malice reclined, one arm supporting him, and gazed at the inferno. He had used quite a bit of the supplies they had gathered from the clinics. Continuously, Malice threw out vials, jars, even syringes while he worked on the Unit.

"I am surprised you know so much about medicine," Cas said to break the hush. Usually, he liked the peace and quiet but something about Malice's silence gave Cas's body a prickle sensation.

"I learned from the fairy," Malice said and used his chin to point at one of the huts, "but mostly from my brother, who came from a long line of witch doctors and healers."

Cas did not expect Malice to carry on with the conversation. "What do you use the most of?"

"The medicinal herbs," he said, cracking his neck. "It's what I'm most familiar with."

"Herbs?" Cas cocked his head a bit. "What you use to make food flavorful?"

Malice smiled. "Yes, and no. There are certain herbs used for medical purposes, some for cooking, and some used for both."

"Which ones are you using? What are their purposes?"

"Knit bone is good for wounds, to stop heavy bleeding, and some say it helps mend broken bones." Cas listened intently.

"Willows Bark is a pain reliever but, unless I grind it up, they can't have it until they can chew. The secretion aloe vera creates is good for burns. Echinacea leaves are used to fight infection and bring down swelling. I can brew them into a tea which makes consumption easier."

That's why he wanted the teapot.

Malice altered his posture, switching one hand to the other. "Catmint helps the smaller things: stomach aches, breathing, nausea, and so on." He waved his free hand dismissively. "I grabbed burdock, which reduces fever and also helps with infection."

"Do you plan to use the other medicines as well?"

Malice nodded. "I plan to use everything at my disposal as long as the Unit can tolerate it. Their regeneration will have to take care of the rest."

"Do you know how to heal?" he asked but shook his head afterward, answering his own question. He had watched Valken skin Malice, cut his limbs off, yank bones out of their place and through the skin, yet he didn't have a single scratch when Cas saw him naked in the dungeons. It was impossible to have that high of regenerative capabilities and be able to heal at the same time.

"A little, enough to repair a broken finger, close small wounds."

Cas's head perked. *I stand corrected.* "You are quite impressive."

Malice said nothing in return, his expression unreadable. He suddenly rose, brushed his pants off, and headed for the elf's hut, disappearing behind the white sheet door.

Cas sprawled across the soft grass, wondering when Zephyrus would come. The last thing he had heard from the commander was that he would come soon.

He gazed at the bright stars above that avoided the light of the moon. The nights were louder than the day sometimes as owls and crickets talked endlessly into the darkness and small animals skittered all around, rustling in the foliage. Wolves, perhaps coyotes, would howl to make their presence known. The fire cracked and sputtered, shooting dancing embers into the sky.

Whatever the commander's orders were, they were to be followed absolutely and without deviation, but something tapped at the back of Cas's mind. It may be flawed, but this was his first time tasting freedom, and it was very sweet.

If there were options presented to him, would he stay with Zephyrus, or would he side with Malice? Which monstrosity would he go to?

Cas lurched upright, glanced at the huts, a light inside one of them casting a shadow of Malice's arms and hands moving around. He was hard at work, but why? What drove him? Cas noticed the way he had looked at them, the lack of emotion in his eyes, the way he chose to escape only when Valken tried to kill him instead of a month ago. Malice cared not for his comrades, so what drove him to go that far?

What drove *Zephyrus* to go that far?

These two, Cas sighed as he stood, *are much alike, I think.* Since Malice had eaten all the food, he figured it was time to go hunting.

"Gareth"

Something cold and wet dripped, then gently rubbed against his forearm, waking Gareth up. His eyelids were heavy, but he forced them open, anyway. A blurry white blob was above him. He blinked a few times, Malice eventually coming into focus. He concentrated on Gareth's arm. There was a thin red line where a nasty gash used to be, brown string crossing from each side, tying it together. Malice was cleaning it up with a damp rag, which he expected to hurt but did not.

"Why—"

Malice stopped what he was doing, put his arm under Gareth's head, lifted it, and guided a small amount of water into his mouth.

"Drink first," he said as Gareth closed his dry mouth and swallowed. The cold water rushed down his throat. He felt it hit his stomach like ice. It was not much, but at least it was refreshing.

"I gave you something for the pain, so you shouldn't be feeling much of anything."

Gareth started to wonder if Malice could read his mind.

"I'm surprised you're conscious." Malice looked at Gareth when he picked the cloth up again and continued to clean the freshly stitched wound, his eyes falling on Gareth's arm.

"So am I." He wanted to chuckle, but that would probably hurt too much. "How is everyone else?" At least he could listen for now. His throat was sore and scratchy, which made it hard to talk, and his chest throbbed with every breath he had to take.

"Barbus was poisoned to hell."

Gareth screwed his eyes shut and turned his head away. The voident Cas told him as much, but a part of him had hoped it was a lie.

"I'm not sure what he was given, so I can't administer any medicine. It could kill him. He has to ride it out before I can alleviate his pain. As for his other injuries, I'm treating them the same as everyone else." Malice slung the rag over the side of the bucket, grabbing the already threaded needle.

"Lycn's right arm is infected, and he's in sepsis. The medicine is helping, but I'll still need to amputate."

His words hurt more than the needle piercing his chest, pulling the string through, and tugging the wound closed.

"Lucas was cooked then iced repeatedly. I doubt his skin will recover its sensitivity. Burns cover most of his body while his ribs and leg were broken. His regeneration skills are high, so his injuries aren't as bad as they could have been." He paused, tugged the thread, tying it off.

"Pich will not survive."

Gareth whipped his head toward Malice, a sharp pain shooting into his neck, his eyes gone wide.

"Pich's regeneration is that of a child's and their wounds are too extensive. Even if someone as good as them were to come in the next hour, they would not survive more than a month at best."

Gareth's jaw clenched as he glared at the pivoted ceiling. Despite Malice being as gentle as he could, he felt the pinch and pull of the needle going in, then out, as he closed the next wound on his chest.

Malice went on, "Valken's favorite was Pich, so they got the brunt of his anger and frustration. Most of their bones are broken, they have bruised and punctured organs, internal bleeding, amongst other things about which I don't know. They're a mess no one can clean up anymore."

He made quick work of stitching the x-shaped slashes from shoulder to shoulder, rib to rib. After putting the thread and needle down, Malice dunked the cloth into the bucket, rang it out, and tended the wound.

"Perhaps if it was a week ago, there might have been hope, but it's too late."

Gathering his supplies, Malice left as tears stung and swelled in Gareth's eyes. Grief was an oppressive weight on his entire body.

The Price of Decisions
"First Sword"

Malice had cleaned, sutured, and medicated the Unit over and over till the sun rose. To heal, the Unit needed to be in better condition to receive Malice's magic. If they received it now, their bodies could shut down.

"Go to the pond," Malice told Cas as he pushed the white sheet out of his way. The sun blazed, taking his sight a moment to adjust. "And stay there for an hour."

Cas stared at him, hands twitching when he shifted, grabbed the buckets near the fire, and lumbered into the woods.

He waited, counted to ten. Then he walked to the trunks, sat on one, and crossed his legs. Eyes had been following Malice for some time now, he could feel it in the tingling of his nape.

"I'm impressed," birds squawked in response, "you tracked me all the way here, so stop playing with the birds in the treetops and come down," he said and smiled.

A gentle thud sounded behind the huts alongside some leaves falling to the ground. From the shadows emerged a short beastman, features like a bear. Her rich brown skin made the tans and creams of her clothes stand out. She strutted toward Malice, her black, tight curls bouncing slightly. In front of him, she bowed to one knee, her head down.

"My liege," Eunice said. "My tracking skills are second only to yours. It's why you've kept me around for so long." She looked up at him with eyes almost as dark as her hair and her hand went to the leather satchel, keeping it pressed against her hip. There were a few more wrinkles around her mouth and creasing her brow than two years ago.

Malice wagged his finger, telling her to rise. "True, to some extent. Your quick-wittedness matches mine. It keeps me on my toes."

"Thank you."

Holding his hand out, Malice asked, "What have you brought for me?"

She moved her satchel, flipped it open, and grabbed papers, handing them to him. On top of everything was a letter sealed with red wax. "Reports, mostly."

Setting the papers on the trunk beside him, Malice used his claw to cut the envelope open, pulled the letter out, and began reading. Meanwhile, Eunice's head swiveled, taking in the glade. The pit had a small kindle going with animals on sticks to one side of it, and a teapot. A little behind the two trunks were somewhat empty wooden crates of medical supplies. Eunice's nose crinkled at the smell of blood and other bodily fluids—her sense of smell was at least twice as sensitive as Lycn's. Even without heightened senses, Malice could smell it, too, and it was vile. Once she heard about the Games of Retribution, Malice assumed she had made her way to Alucard's Kingdom then tracked him by his scent.

"The region is doing well," Malice said after a long silence and handed the letter back to Eunice, who put it in her bag. "The kingdoms and cities seem to be recovering slow but sure."

He took the stack of parchment from the trunk and skimmed through those as well. When was the last time he had glimpsed over letters and documents like this? A task so mundane brought a host of memories.

"If I may be so bold." Eunice dug in her satchel and found a jar of ink and a feather pen.

"You may."

She kept them in her hand until he was ready to use them. "We have all the help we need, but cannot start until you pick a location."

He was silent, diligently reading the contents of each page.

"I would like to propose that we rebuild on top of the ruins of the kingdom. It will be symbolic for the rebirth of a better nation."

"Are you suggesting we tear down my brother's monument?" Malice asked flatly, as his eyes remained on the sheet of paper.

Eunice stiffened and, after a moment, spoke, "Not at all. I apologize for even thinking of such a thing." She neither liked nor disliked Kiran before the incident, but afterward, her hatred toward him flourished like a blossom in spring.

"Hmm." Malice placed a paper on the trunk. "If we are to build a new kingdom, do it elsewhere. That pile of stone, wood, and ash will stand for a different reason."

"May I ask what that is, my liege?"

Malice held out his hand when he finished reading the abundance of parchment, Eunice quickly got blank sheets and handed them to him. Her other hand was still out, the ink and pen sitting in her light-skinned palm.

"I want it to fill many with fear—fear of me and what I will do. But I also want it to fill many more with might and pride for the region they protect, knowing I will have their best interest at heart." Malice dipped the quill of the feather into the raven black-ink and scribbled something down.

"Soon, I will step out of the shadows. I have saved the region in my grandfather's name, now," Malice handed the ink-stained paper to her, "I will rule in mine."

"If that is what you want, then I shall happily oblige." She inclined her head, a smile creasing her cheeks. Documents folded, Eunice gently pushed them into her bag and swiveled it to her side.

"Is that all?" she asked.

"How quickly can the kingdom be built?"

"As quickly as you want it."

"It needs to be finished by the Kings Summit."

"It shall be done."

He briefly considered his first sword. "Why did you track me down?"

Eunice stiffened, her eyebrows jumping. "You are a hard man to communicate with, especially when I hadn't a clue of your whereabouts until recently, my liege," she said.

"And you thought it best to track me down, leave your regency behind to whom?"

She swallowed. "… Hyacinthia, my liege. She offered so that I might find you and have the chance to talk to you face to face."

"About what?"

"The nobles are gunning for your throne," she said. "They say that you have been gone for too long, long enough to forfeit your crown on the principle of abandonment."

The letters, of course, said nothing about this. Why would they tell Malice their intentions when they needed him out of the way? Malice sighed into his hands, running them through his short, filthy hair. *Gods, I need a bath.* "They do not trust me."

"No."

"They never have, so what difference does it make… but I need them to stand with me this time around." *It'll be better in the long run if they do.*

"Would you like me to send for Priscilla?"

Malice smiled. Eunice always did catch onto his ideas before he needed to voice them. "Priscilla is a name I haven't heard in a while. How is the old bat?"

Priscilla Wheelock was the oldest servant in Hordes Kingdom prior to becoming an elder. The bag of skin and bones certainly enjoyed using her title to the fullest. He chuckled to himself.

"Alive, amazingly enough," Eunice said in a lighthearted tone, a smirk resting on her lips. "She's enjoying having young men feed her."

"Still?" Eunice nodded and Malice cringed a bit. "Have her readied for me. I'll be returning a week before the summit."

The smirk on her face vanished, and she nodded. "Yes, my liege."

Uncrossing his legs and rising, Malice gazed down at the short beastman, memories flooding his skull. "I look forward to the next time we meet."

Eunice bowed, one hand going over her chest. "As do I." She turned and walked into the woods.

Her silhouette disappeared beyond the foliage. Malice was sure she would have asked an abundance of questions. *What are your plans? Why are you here in Alucard's Region? Why are you caring for injured people?* And so on. She had never been one to go out of her way to learn of his plans, either out of lack of curiosity or want to preserve her sanity. Perhaps both.

Malice had left her in charge of running Hordes Region while he was away, and it seemed she was doing a fine job. It was nice to see her again. After spending most every day with her for nine years, he missed their daily banters.

Even so, Eunice's loyalty, useful as it was, may be the death of her.

The Price of Decisions
XVII

Part IV

Malice drew a line of fire from his index finger and thumb, pinching both sides. The cloth tied just under Lycn's shoulder would stem blood circulation while showing him where to cut. With his mangled arm resting on Malice's leg, Malice tugged the thread of fire through his arm, tissue and blood sizzling. Smoke rose and slightly clouded his vision as the smell of burning flesh and rot filled the hut. He gave more strength to cut through bone then muscle and skin.

Lycn's arm rolled off his leg. He grabbed it and threw it outside. Before he could stitch it up, he would have to grind the bone down so he could pull as much skin over the wound as possible. Malice created a knife, the blade fine and short, and began to chip and smooth the bone.

As he threaded brown string into the eye of a needle, he heard a thud and crackle from Cas, throwing something—the arm most likely—into the pit of flames.

Malice stretched as much skin from all sides into the center, sewed the wound closed, and cleaned it. When it was sufficient to his liking, he lifted Lycn's head, opened his mouth, and guided echinacea tea down his throat.

Bandages now wrapped around Lycn's shoulder, collarbone, and chest. Malice left, taking his supplies with him.

His nostrils flared at his own funk. He was covered in sweat, grime, blood, and other bodily fluids. Most of which weren't his own. The pond nearby didn't have the clearest of water, but it was deep enough to submerge completely, and he was sure the water would be warm from the sun.

At the trunks, Malice set his bucket of supplies down and glanced toward the campfire. Cas suddenly stood, head pointed skyward. A few seconds had gone by when he finally looked at Malice.

"He is here."

So much for my bath. Malice, sighing, stalked to the closest shadow of a tree. Cas hadn't moved.

"What are you waiting for?"

"I'm curious to know what you are doing?" Cas said.

"We're traveling by shadow unless you want to walk to the castle."

Cas hurried over. "I did not realize you knew how to travel with the shadows."

Malice sank, the shadow darkening, consuming his and Cas's bodies. It was tricky at first, learning at the age of ten, but there were trickier things he had learned at that age.

They rose into a dim closet. Cas took the lead, guiding Malice to the second floor, eastern wing of Ivory's castle. Pine green, white, gold, light oak, birds, and florets crawled up the molding and décor—the same few colors were everywhere his eyes landed. Green started to look volatile.

They passed many closed doors, paintings of scenery in between them. On the side tables, spaced every two doors, were vases of dead, wilted flowers, their shriveled petals dark brown on the floor. A thick layer of dust covered the surfaces and when passing a window, the stagnant dust sparkled. Stale musk sat heavy in the air.

Cas hastened his pace to reach the last door on the left and open it. Warm light painted the green and white rug spanning the width of the room. The lounge had plenty of seating throughout the space. To one side, cabinets held glasses, goblets, and chalices as well as ale, wine, and mead, amongst other alcohols. Long windows let in the brilliance of day on the back wall. A chandelier made from antlers hung from the center of the ceiling with three lanterns off the ends, none lit.

Malice noticed a head of long, smoky white hair sitting in front of the mantle, not moving an inch. Surprise and relief washed over him. *He truly is alive.*

"Zephyrus"

The door opened with a quick squeal, then closed, the knob jingling. The blaze in the hearth crackled as the deep, jagged scar down his face and what was left of his marred arm ached. Zephyrus rose and turned. The rustling of his sleeveless blue kimono was the only thing that made sound save for the fire. Malice silently crossed the room while Zephyrus's crimson eyes followed him.

"How nice of you to carve out some time for me, Malice," he said bitterly. So vividly did Zephyrus remember coming home after months to his mother, father, and sister, all dead, rotting. The smell returned to him, twisting his gut.

Malice raised an eyebrow and glanced over his shoulder. "For you, Zephyrus, a bit of my time is worth sparing," he sneered, returning the attitude.

"I apologize for my subordinate, Valken. I would have punished him accordingly, but you took care of that for me."

Valken was a nuisance before he was of any use. The very reason he sent the voident to capture the royals and Malice was because he had hoped Malice would kill him. Without cause or permission from Lazarus, he couldn't just kill anyone he wanted.

Unlike Malice.

Reclining in the chair, Malice put his feet up on the table. "He was rather annoying. I'm sure you knew that, though." The way he talked, his tone, was more cynical than it had been eight years ago.

"Indeed, he was." Zephyrus walked in measured strides to the table. "I heard about your feat in the Games. It would be impressive if I didn't know your past."

He smirked. "I'm sure it would be. Even more so, considering it did its job exceedingly well."

Zephyrus's eyebrows twitched. "What is that supposed to mean?"

"Did you think it was just to show that I was alive and well?"

"You meant to catch my attention?" *That can't be true... he couldn't have known I was alive.*

Malice replied with a glance, his eyes so cold they could freeze the entire room.

A shiver ran up Zephyrus's spine. He hesitated and leaned against the table. After their duel almost eight years ago, Zephyrus dragged himself into the nearby forest where Lazarus saved him. *He's bluffing... he has to be.*

"We're both here for something Malice, tell me what you want."

Malice chuckled, obviously amused he was able to get under Zephyrus's skin. "I want to make a deal."

Zephyrus inclined his head, teeth grinding.

"I want you to leave my region alone. For good."

Zephyrus scoffed. "I haven't been in Hordes Region since you ban—"

"Alucard's Region is mine," Malice said flatly.

Zephyrus startled upright. *Since when? How long have Malice and Magnus been betrothed?*

"My kindness is wearing thin, Zephyrus. The next time I see you or your goons in my region, there will be no kindness left to give."

For a time, Zephyrus stared into Malice's unyielding gaze, the floodgates of his mind opening, filling every bit of space in his skull with memories. Rumors traveled like a rat, reaching every royal in Hordes Kingdom, including Zephyrus. Malice refused to deny what he had done eight years ago, guilt as plain on his face as words in a book. Eventually, he cleared his throat and opened his mouth.

"And you want to fight me to the death? Because the scar on your face and me taking your arm wasn't enough for you?" Malice said before a breath could even leave Zephyrus's lungs.

Zephyrus's eyes twitched. "No. It wasn't. A fight to the death means one must die, yet you let me live." No matter how one-sided it was, Malice was challenged and did not uphold the traditions of a duel.

"I wounded your pride?"

"You did more than just wound my pride, Malice. I want revenge!" his voice boomed off the walls, his chest rising and falling at a steady yet fast pace, heat pulsing in rhythm through his body.

"Why not just kill me now?" Malice asked.

"And go to war with both Alucard's and Hordes Region? Possibly the entire continent?" Lazarus needed time. He was still recovering his forces after Malice wiped out over ten thousand voidents when his kingdom was destroyed. "I am not that stupid, but I could ask you the same question. You had your chance to kill me."

Malice shrugged. "Who saved you after our duel?"

Zephyrus narrowed his eyes on Malice and answered hesitantly, "… Lazarus."

"Killing you would mean I would have to kill Lazarus. Killing Lazarus would start a war Vinyamar couldn't win. So why don't we both do our sides a favor and prolong the inevitable?"

"Fine."

He rose, the chair scraping against the floor, and approached Zephyrus. "A proper duel in exchange for a cease-fire."

Malice stopped. He was close enough for Zephyrus to see the ring of golden brown encasing his slit pupils, feel the weight of Malice's presence bearing down on him. A proximity that made Zephyrus's stomach turn. Yet something ached, something deep inside him. Whatever it was, it reminded him of the times they had laughed together.

"Do we have a deal?"

"We have a deal," Zephyrus said, his voice coming out much weaker and softer than he wanted.

"Good." Malice stepped backward. "Then the first snowfall of Alucard's Region, the oasis we came across as kids in Mutuwa." When he approached the door, Malice turned around. "And tell Lazarus my greetings." He left with a smirk on his face, slamming the door.

Lazarus saved Zephyrus eight years ago, healed him, taught him the ways of war and leadership. Zephyrus had been kept busy, which forced Malice to the catacombs of his mind. The want for revenge dried his throat as if he swallowed buckets of sand no matter how many he killed for the voidents cause. Nightmares of his kin plagued his dreams, Malice standing over them, their blood staining his hands. He had thought he started anew, but the past had a chokehold on Zephyrus, one that seemed inescapable.

Malice had made himself known in Alucard's Region at the Games of Retribution. Nothing was going to stand in his way. Not this time. Not when Malice was there, ripe for the killing.

The voidents he attached to several royals returned to him in the spring, reporting their findings when they did. The king had plans to send a Unit on a mission to gather information on him and his footmen. Malice was to join them. It was like music to his ears!

"Damnit!" Zephyrus grabbed the closest thing, a chair from the long table, and threw it across the room. It crashed into the wall and clattered to the ground, leaving holes and cracks. The web of Malice's schemes caught Zephyrus just as well as he caught Malice.

Cas inched away from the door, his hands stuffed behind him. "Is there a problem?"

Zephyrus jerked his head to the voident, eyes shining with anger. "I was a fool," he hissed. *Once a fool, always a fool.*

What did I just agree to?

Pacing the room, Zephyrus regretted everything.

Malice was different. Too different from the boy he knew eight years ago. That wasn't the boy he had talked to as equals, despite their social differences. What had happened between then and now?

Revenge kept him going, fueled him, led him to this point, but now that he was here, what could possibly make Zephyrus move forward, to carry out their agreement? Death was no longer a possibility. It was not something in the back of his mind, or an unlikely consequence. It was certain if he fought Malice come winter.

If.

He could run, but where? He could hide, but Lazarus would find him. He could rescind his words, but would Malice let it go? Would Malice let him live as if it had never happened? As if the lives he had taken were not people at all but cattle, birds, or even ants. Not if he and Magnus have joined hands. And Lazarus, he needed time. If Zephyrus were to revoke his word, what would happen?

I need to see it through. I chose this path to walk down, chose not to leave it. You reap what you sow.

"Malice"

Malice didn't think Zephyrus was alive after their duel. He had followed a blood trail into the forest the next day, and it stopped at the base of an oak tree. Nothing but a small pool of dried blood had remained. He assumed howlers had gotten to Zephyrus. The beasts, besides their gut-wrenching howl, were notorious for eating everything: organs, clothes, bones, excrement. A part of Malice had hoped that he was miraculously saved, perhaps even by Kiran, who lived in that forest. He had eventually let go of the notion, of course.

And yet, that was what had happened. However, Malice wouldn't have guessed that Lazarus was the one who saved Zephyrus.

That brought the question of why, but Malice could easily make a guess. Lazarus wanted someone under his thumb and in his debt. Permanently. Who better to target than a revenge-hungry child with nothing to return to?

As he entered the glade from the tree line, Malice smiled to himself. The Games of Retribution were meant to make a scene, not one big enough to alert the other rulers, but big enough to catch the attention of a few predictable shadows.

Malice peeked inside each hut, his smile dying. His bath would have to wait. Lycn had woken up, frantic in his absence, the blankets thrown about, and a few wounds reopened in his struggle. The pain most likely sent his body into shock, and he lost consciousness.

As Malice treated the wounds—again—Lycn called out to Pich in his sleep. He glanced at Lycn's troubled expression. It might be best to combine his and Pich's huts, since he couldn't be with Lycn at all hours of the day. Nor did he want to. If he were to wake up again, seeing Pich next to him would probably calm him down. Malice sighed, annoyance gnawing at every corner of his mind. Lycn sure liked to make his job difficult, injured and comatose or not.

*

Awake when Malice entered his hut, Gareth was deep in thought from the look of his furrowed brow.

"Are you in pain?" Malice asked as he knelt beside Gareth. He could hold conversations and stay conscious for a short time, but his body was feeble from weeks of torture and malnutrition.

Gareth glared. "I am basically a filleted piece of meat with all these wounds." His sharp tongue made Malice chuckle before he grabbed a small sack out of the crate. He dumped bark into the palm of his hand.

"Willows bark," Malice said and pushed his other hand underneath Gareth's head, carefully lifting him. "It's more potent than ginger and catmint, but you'll have to chew it."

Gareth nodded, opening his mouth, so Malice could place the bark on his tongue. He started chewing the tough slab and puckered when Malice placed his head down again.

While Gareth was chewing, Malice explained the other's situation. When he was done, the bark turned to mush, and Malice moved on to his next patient.

*

Hands on Barbus's sternum, Malice focused on injecting a small stream of magic into his core. Healing was the process of giving an extra hand to what was already there, fanning the flames to strengthen them. If regeneration alone helped with the majority of injuries, healing took care of the rest.

Even though it had been a week since coming to the glade, Barbus suffered from fever, cold sweats, extreme waves of pain, and vomiting. Malice checked his pulse, his fingers pressing behind and underneath his mandible. It was weak, but better.

Barbus convulsed. Malice quickly turned him over to his side, grabbing the bucket, and placing it in front of him. He heaved and retched everything Malice had given him that day. After a time, Malice laid Barbus's head down, propping a pillow behind his back. If he were to puke again, at least he wouldn't turn over and choke on it.

*

Lucas responded to the pain each time Malice peeled the dead, charred skin from live flesh, which was a painful, tedious procedure. Malice had to do small sections at a time to keep from overwhelming his body.

Lucas's regeneration was better than Malice had expected, as most of his lesser burns were almost completely healed. The broken bone in his leg, after Malice reset it and put a splint on it, mended quickly. However, maggots squirmed where bone had penetrated the skin. They were small and hadn't eaten much, so Malice had easily flushed them out.

Lucas jerked awake, his left eye jutting all around, surprising Malice. He tried to move and sit up, but Malice held him down by the shoulders.

"Lucas," he said as gently as he could, "you're safe, but you need to remain still." Lucas fixated on Malice, his chest rising and falling rapidly.

The elf stared into his eyes, pleading with Malice, fear a quivering light in the sea of blue. Eventually, Lucas calmed down and relaxed into his makeshift cot.

Malice thought it best to stop the treatment. Tomorrow would be a good day to start healing sessions. If it helped the severe burns, Malice wouldn't have to peel off the dead skin, but if it didn't, Lucas would have a lot of pain and suffering ahead of him.

A refreshingly warm breeze hit Malice as he stepped into the glade. He closed his eyes and took a deep breath, enjoying the smell of grass and flowers as it reminded him of the times he would stand on the balcony with Magnus. When the wind dissipated, he cracked his neck, set his crate of supplies by the trunks, and turned to face Lycn's and Pich's huts.

He raised his hands, then slowly brought them down diagonally and out, the walls of the huts coming down. The sheets were let go of and dropped to the ground. Sliding his feet apart, Malice stretched his arms out to either side of him, forcing them together. The slabs beneath Lycn and Pich moved closer until they were next to each other. Now that they were an arm's length away, Malice thrust his hands into the air, erecting the walls once more. He gathered the two sheets and tied the edges of one side of each sheet together. The walls and peak of the hut opened a sliver so Malice could stuff the edges in, creating a door.

Warmed by the sun, the water was perfect. Malice's foot sank into mud as he stepped into the pond, cringing at the goop between his toes. He quickly dove and swam toward the center, where the water was the deepest. When he resurfaced, he couldn't reach the ground and bobbed in and out of the water.

He brought his fingers up to touch his ear, the smoothness of the lobe as strange as ever. He had left all his jewelry with Magnus. The teardrop earring he received over fifteen years ago still glistened as if it were brand new.

He came home after his first Kings Summit and shoved the earring through his lobe. Annabeth, his caretaker, was shocked and had scrambled to his aid. When he was older, Malice had a silversmith in Hordes Kingdom make a silver stud to match. The second set of earrings was a gift from Kiran for Malice's coronation. The last set, a simple pair of black studs, was once his mother's.

Malice let himself sink, the water engulfing his head. Small fish swam past him, and weeds tickled his feet. The moon was an undulating shard of white underneath the surface. He stayed under for a few minutes, allowing Magnus to overtake his thoughts.

Malice missed him, missed his touch, his smile, his voice, everything… more than he thought he would.

The night Malice returned from the knight's barracks in the northwestern sect of the castle, he and Magnus had talked for hours. When he didn't know, but at some point, they had both fallen asleep and woken up in each other's arms. Magnus was warm, his shirt slipping open to reveal his freckled chest and a feather necklace, his hair tousled. Malice had stayed there, the sun rising lazily above the horizon, enjoying the comfort of Magnus's arms wrapped around him. He yearned for it, a deep ache throughout his body.

Having soaked long enough, Malice swam to shore. He grabbed the cloth and two jars of soap sitting on top of his pile of clothes beside a folded towel. Then he went back into the water to scrub himself—he needed it.

To feel clean, at least somewhat clean, after so long, gave Malice a surge of energy, a weightlessness to his limbs. As he dried himself on the pond's bank, the bliss was ebbed by thoughts of the Unit. Soon, everyone would be able to bathe themselves. Their stench was growing more horrid by the day. Dry enough, Malice dressed, collected his used things, and started toward the glade.

The Price of Decisions
"Letting Go"

Searing, aching pain emitted from his arm into the rest of his body. Lycn groaned and turned his head, peeling his eyes open. Although hazy, his jaw dropped when he saw a stub where his right arm used to be. He wanted to scream, yet nothing came out. He tried to sit up, only to crash down. An explosion of pain made his head feel light, his vision blackened, and his stomach jumped into his throat.

Lycn gasped to catch his breath. Warm light seeped through the sheets in front of him, but it was dim inside the hut anyhow. He glanced to the right one more time. Pich was lying beside him. Time froze for a second. The pain was gone, replaced by the need to be by Pich. Lycn yanked the covers off, pushed himself up, and crawled to Pich's left side so he could pull them into his embrace.

They were warm, their heartbeat faint, but Lycn could feel it all the same. Relieved, he brushed their hair from their forehead and kissed them. Pich's skin was black and blue and in many places swollen as if thousands of bees stung them. Lycn didn't care. They were alive. He squeezed Pich a bit tighter, glad to be holding them in his arms again. Tears swelled in his eyes as his bottom lip quivered. A warm trail of wetness stained his cheek and nose. His fingers glided over the grooves of their spine as he caressed their back. They had lost so much weight, it pained him more than his injuries did.

"Please," he whispered, kissing their forehead again. "Please fight. We're almost home, just a little bit longer and we'll be home." He didn't know how true those words were, and he didn't know if Pich could hear them, but if they could, he hoped the words gave them just a little more strength to keep breathing.

All it took was a few years for Pich to wiggle their way into Lycn's life and make themselves a spot that would leave a gaping hole if they were to leave. Pich had filled his days with life when they were mundane. For the longest time, he felt stuck in the same pattern, doing the same things day in and day out. Then Pich came along, throwing everything out of balance. Life was too difficult to imagine without them, and he refused to try.

Songbirds whistled and tweeted as Lycn sluggishly opened his eyes. A bitter cold suddenly hit him, causing his entire body to shiver. He wiggled his arm out from under Pich and sat up while looking around for another blanket, ignoring the throbs of pain in his midsection.

He noticed Pich, the purple hue of their skin. Their stillness. Shifting, Lycn placed two fingers under their jaw to feel a pulse.

There was none.

"Pich?" he heard himself mutter. Their body was as cold as snow. Something gripped his chest, pushing and squeezing it at the same time. It didn't make any sense—they were fine last night.

"Pich."

They were breathing and their heart was beating. All Lycn could do was cling to hope, right? He couldn't breathe, his vision blurred and doubled. Tears fell and sobs escaped his mouth.

Lycn hated how Malice was right. He hated the voidents who captured them, hated the king who sent them on this mission, that Malice waited so long to save them. He even hated Pich for leaving him like this, for not letting him get the chance to say goodbye or tell them how much he loved them. He stared at his dead lover, nothing those creatures ever did compared to the aching and stabbing pain in his heart. Lycn wailed until his voice went hoarse, but even then, the tears kept flowing.

Later in the afternoon, it had rained. Malice pulled the sheet back, his hair and clothes dripping wet. Lycn clung onto Pich as Malice walked closer and bent down in front of him, his expression neutral, as if he couldn't care less.

"Why," Lycn forced through his sobs, "would I ever give them to you?" his voice was tremulous, brittle.

"Because you don't have a choice," Malice said bluntly and placed his hands under Pich's body, waiting for Lycn to let go.

Up close, Malice was haggard too—his skin caked in filth, his hair short and scraggly, a darkness haunting his sharp features—but that was the least he deserved.

Eventually, Lycn released Pich's body into Malice's arms and he left. Lycn's hand reached for them involuntarily, bitterness tainting his blood. The sheets flapped closed.

Why is he fine? Why does he get to walk around and feel the sun? Why does he get to return to his lover, and I don't?

"Malice"

Malice returned to the glade, the rain worsening. Around the steaming firepit sat Lycn, Lucas, Barbus, and Gareth. Nearly two months had passed since the start of their mission. The Unit had spent a month in captivity and a few weeks in the huts. None of them were in any condition to travel long distances, nor were they able to move around a lot, yet here they were, sitting around a quelled blaze, wearing miserable expressions on their faces.

At the edge of the glade, Malice stood and looked to the sky, to the white flashes in the dark clouds, before considering the broken people in front of him. Broken was an understatement.

Each one of them seemed deep in thought, reminiscing about the times they had spent with Pich, thinking about all the things they could have done differently. Seeking someone to blame for Pich's death, for everything, including their shortcomings.

That someone will no doubt be me.

*

Malice flew above the land in search of a smaller village, a stable, or a farm close to the forest outside Ivory's Kingdom. The Unit could be left alone for a short while and Malice wanted to take in some fresh air. Just outside of Redcol, Lucas's hometown, was a paddock. He landed a little distance away and walked into the wooden stables, mostly occupied by horses— leather, dung, and hay, a strong stench. A stout old man cleaned and trimmed a horse's hooves at the far end.

Malice approached the working man, tears streaming down his face. When the stable master gave Malice his attention, he rambled, explaining—loosely—the situation he was in.

"Tears don't work on me, lad," the old man said with a grunt.

Malice paused, straightened his slightly hunched posture, and wiped the tears from his eyes. "Shame."

"And I ain't got horses to give unless you've got the coin to pay for 'em."

"Would you deny a direct order from the king?"

"'Course not, but he ain't here now, is he?" The stable master's beard wiggled with his mouth as he switched hooves, the horse nickering.

"Sure he is, or must I flaunt my status?" Malice mused, then tilted his head. "I could just kill you and take your horses." *If I truly wanted to piss Magnus off, I would've done so already. It would certainly be easier.*

The old man, stiffening, audibly gulped. He sighed, wiped the sweat building on his brow, and set the horse's hoof down. Hands on his hips, he leaned backward until pops raked his spine.

"Fine. You can take my own, Charge and Ember, sisters," he said, pointing toward two stalls behind Malice.

They were beautiful, both had warm auburn coats and a white underbelly. The mare with a white stripe down her face was called Ember and her sister Charge, since she liked to charge those of which she wasn't fond.

"Men, mostly," the stable master said. "'Cept for me."

"You can do a bit of work for me, though. Since you ain't payin'," he added when he hobbled past Malice.

"Why not," Malice said. He wasn't exactly excited to return to the glade just yet.

The stable master showed Malice around to the other side of the paddocks where a wagon, used for transporting bales of hay to local farmers, holds, and villages, sat. The two unloaded the hay, stacking it against the stables. It was a quick job between the two of them. The stable master was quite strong for his age.

Inside the paddock, as Malice went to the horses, the old man grabbed a leather bag and handed it to Malice by the strap. It was stuffed with carrots, the mare's favorite treat.

Carrot in hand, Malice lured the horses out and around to the wagon and, with a helping hand from the stable master, hooked them up to the wagon.

Ember and Charge were feisty at first, as the stable master had warned. Once Malice gave them a carrot and a few pets, they calmed down. He hoisted himself onto the wagon's bench, paused and climbed down.

"Did a boy named Joseph happen to have a horse?" Malice asked. Being outside of Redcol reminded Malice of the Trading Festival and of Charles. *He was an abominable human.*

He flinched at Joseph's name, his deep socketed eyes falling to the grass. He breathed deeply for a few moments and glanced at Malice, nodding.

"May I see it?"

He nodded again, this time slower, as if he were apprehensive.

Malice followed the stable master until he stopped in front of a horse, its coat a leather brown while its mane was black.

The stable master patted the gate of the stall solemnly. "Here he is," he said. "Finbar is what Joseph named him not long before he…" he trailed off. "But why are you concerned with him, huh?" He suddenly turned defensive, his wrinkled face scrunched.

"I'm with his brother, Lucas." The stable master's jaw fell ajar. "If the colt doesn't have a mount, perhaps I can take him to Lucas. He could use a new ride anyhow."

Malice approached, reaching his hand out for Finbar to sniff. He stroked the bridge of the horse's nose. Considering how small that wagon was, he wasn't sure if the entire Unit and the trunks would fit. Being cramped would do them no good on the journey back to Alucard's Kingdom. *Beggars can't be choosers… neither can thieves.*

Silent for a minute, the stable master caught and caressed his long, white goatee.

Finally, he said, "All right." He looked Malice in the eyes and held his arm out. "I'm choosing to trust you not because of your person, but because I want this horse to be with someone Joseph knew, his kin."

Malice went to take his hand when the stable master clasped his forearm and held it, Malice returning the grasp. It was a traditional greeting amongst warriors in Zeldine's Region, which made sense now that Malice got a closer look at the old man's snaggleteeth and his ever so slightly green skin. Although mixed with very little orc, he was probably raised with their traditions and values.

The old man slid the iron rod from the latch and opened the gate. Finbar cautiously padded out as the stable master grabbed a bridle and reins hanging on a thick nail behind him. Malice gently pet Finbar to keep him calm, the stable master fixing the bridle in place.

"I'll meet you outside when I bring you a saddle," he said, shooing Malice outside, to which he obliged.

He tied Finbar's reins to the wagon's front, so he could trot beside it. When he climbed in and sat down, the stable master waddled toward him and put the saddle in the wagon's bed. He backed away, nodding his farewell. Then Malice was off with a whip of Embers and Charges reins.

A month after Pich's death, Malice felt the Unit could handle the journey to Alucard's Kingdom. The timing of their return would be on schedule, about three months from start to finish.

The early morning sun peeked through the trees, warming what the night had cooled. Dew lay thick on the foliage around and in the glade while the bird song was loud but calming. Finbar, Charge, and Ember grazed around the edge of the glade, ears flicking in whatever direction a noise came from, occasionally bringing their heads up to look before returning to the supple grass.

Malice sat on a blanket in front of the blazing fire, the heat making his pale skin flush. The clay teapot over the flames whistled, so he pulled it off, grabbed a cup, and poured the echinacea tea.

Heavy stomps rushed across the glade. Malice put the teapot and cup down at his sides, glancing to his right.

Lycn bolted toward Malice, fist balled at his side, face bunched with anger. His honey-yellow eyes darted to the teapot near Malice. The beastmen picked it up and dumped the hot tea over Malice's head. *Good thing I can't feel pain.* Steam rose all around him, a sweet scent filling his nose.

"Lycn!" Gareth yelled from his hut as he stepped out just in time. "What are you doing?" He gimped over as fast as he could.

Lycn ignored Gareth, his breathing heavy and strained, pain pinching his expression. Summoned by Gareth's shout, Lucas and Barbus emerged from their huts. Barbus stopped and leaned against the earth walls while Lucas went a little further, halting.

"You act so high and mighty," Lycn snarled. "Do you feel good about yourself?" His voice quivered as he spoke, "I don't care what Sir Gareth says or the king; you planned all of this, didn't you?"

Gareth recoiled, his eyes going wide.

"How else would you explain this damn mission? You knew exactly where to go after the Kingdom of Phoenix, exactly who it was that captured us. That's why you asked Pich to teach you how to heal, isn't it?" Hatred coated every single word that spilled from Lycn's mouth like sap on bark.

"What kind of deal did you strike in exchange for killing those voidents? Was it letting Pich die? Was that it? Say something!" Lycn finished, huffing as Gareth's hand fell limp to his side.

"What nonsense are you spouting, Lycn?" Gareth asked quietly.

Malice pushed himself to his feet, his skin and clothes getting sticker as the tea dried. "I'm surprised you were the first to figure that out. I was sure Gareth would have gotten to the conclusion sooner than anyone else."

Gareth shifted, his expression taut.

"Bas—"

"I made a deal. Not to sacrifice Pich, but myself instead. Pich died because of your leader's unwillingness to train them properly." Malice stared at Gareth. "Perhaps if they had been more experienced, more battle-hardened, they wouldn't have died."

Gareth winced and slouched even further, his gaze falling to the grass as if he were too ashamed to look anyone in the eye.

Malice could only imagine how *helpful* Pich was. When the battle was over, he was sure Pich excelled at healing the Unit. Before and during the mission, they were no doubt a liability. And the fault lay solely with Gareth as their leader.

Malice would never have allowed Pich's powerlessness— their inability to protect themselves—to hinder a mission such as the one they went on. He would never have brought them along in the first place if he were their leader.

"The king," Lucas had made his way closer to the pit, eyes darting between Gareth and Malice, "will not stand for this. It doesn't matter if you nursed us back to health, you—"

"Who do you think approved of this plan in the first place? God?" Malice was the one who stepped away this time, his temper flaring in the depths of his chest, a sudden burst of heat that lingered. "The king knew everything—that we would be followed, captured, and tortured."

Barbus almost slipped off his hut, but caught himself and raced toward the heart of the glade. "Did the king know about the Kingdom of Phoenix and all the others?" Barbus stopped beside Gareth, and grabbed the dark elf's shoulders, shaking him upright.

"Of course he did. But you're mistaken about something." Eventually, Lucas came to stand beside Lycn and his Unit. "The other kingdoms are fine. Phoenix was the sole sacrificial lamb."

"You lured us into that trap?" Lycn's bunched fist trembled. Lucas moved closer, putting his hand on his chest to hold him back.

"Why?" Barbus had collected himself after he cleared his throat. Gareth was looking at Malice again, though his disposition was still miserable. "None of this makes sense, lad."

Malice flopped into a seat of air and crossed his legs. "I knew someone had to oversee this region, and I was betting on someone who wanted revenge. Turns out I was right," he said impatiently, his irritation getting the better of him.

"Voidents are sensitive, always itching for a kill. Their leaders are no different. One kingdom was sacrificed but had they known what our intentions were—and use your brains a little here—do you truly think they would have left the others alone?" If only they knew about the inner workings of the Kingdom of Phoenix, they'd be grateful to rid this region of it.

"What is the deal you made?" Gareth cut in, his body caved in on itself with grief, shame, and betrayal, Malice assumed.

"In exchange for leaving this region alone, all I have to do is fight the one behind our capture. Zephyrus."

"That's it?"

"Yes, it is."

"Why have us go through all of this?" Lycn pushed past Lucas, forcing the elf to stumble forward when Gareth caught his arm and righted him.

"It was the only way to ensure success." Malice rose and swiftly closed the distance between him and Lycn. "Had we done it differently, war could've broken out. One none of you could win, even if you survived their onslaught."

Malice was toe to toe with Lycn, staring up at the anger burning in Lycn's eyes. He grabbed the beastman's jaw, yanking him down, his face now lower than Malice's. Where it should be.

Lazarus may be recovering his forces, but that didn't mean he wouldn't try to start a war if Malice pushed his buttons just right. It was better that both Zephyrus and Lazarus thought Malice was a few steps behind them before he struck the truce. There was nothing either side could do now.

"Besides, I wanted to see just how much the strongest Unit of Alucard's Region could take." Malice tilted his head. Lycn's knees buckled, and Malice forced him to the ground. "Apparently not much." Malice threw Lycn to the earth, expression twisting when he landed with a thud.

Glaring at the others, he went on, "The king did not order me to bring you all from the brink of death, I did that of my own volition, and this is the thanks I get?" At his side, Malice's fingers twitched. "You corner me to find out the truth, but if you had waited, the king had full intentions of telling you upon your return."

Calm yourself. His hand relaxed, as did his tone. "Don't worry, the king will tell you about our plans, more than what I chose to share."

Malice whipped around and picked the teapot up alongside the cup and started toward the trunks. "We leave at dusk, so I suggest you start moving."

In silence, everyone worked to make it seem like they had never stayed in the glade. The blaze at the center turned dirty sheets, clothes, and pillows to ash.

The first of the two trunks held what was left of the medical supplies—bandages, a few herbs, syringes, needles and thread, and scissors. Malice had used everything else from the clinics. As the flames grew, Malice deepened the pit and threw in empty vials, sacks, and crates. The second trunk had clean clothes, blankets, and a few pillows. At a lazier pace, the journey would last a week, a week and a half at most. It wouldn't be too difficult to hunt and gather food during that time.

Barbus and Gareth were the first to finish cleaning their huts out. After Malice slid the trunks to the head of the wagon, the two men climbed in and sat down. Both looked haunted, their faces long. Lycn struggled without his dominant arm, but he eventually trudged from his hut, throwing sheets into the campfire along the way, and to the wagon where Gareth helped him up. Lucas also had a challenging time adjusting to partial blindness. Regeneration brought his eye back, but the fire had scorched it bad enough to keep his sight from returning.

Malice grabbed the saddle from Redcol's stable master and hurried to Lucas, who had flung a pile of clothes into the pit. He handed Lucas the saddle, nodding toward the colt across the glade near the wagon.

"His name is Finbar," Malice said. "Your brother's horse."

With a grim expression, Lucas ventured closer to his brother's mount. Carefully, he introduced himself, gently petting the horse's head, neck, and sides, examining the horse. Finbar was a fine animal—a Hackney, tall, lean, and elegant, suited and bred for pulling carriages. Then he put the saddle on Finbar's back, released the straps, pulled the tie strap, and fastened it securely. Finbar remained calm during the entire process, probably used to having been saddled and mounted by Joseph.

Malice turned toward the huts and plunged them into the earth. As he passed the fire, he swung and closed his fist, quelling the blaze. Sliding his foot across the grass had closed the pit. Lucas trotted up beside the wagon, patting Finbar, when he came to a stop.

The atmosphere was intense and cold, but there was a longing to go home.

Malice secured the back of the wagon and walked to the driver's bench, climbing into it. He grabbed the reins and whipped. The wagon rocked into motion. Ember and Charge whinnied, their heads bobbing, as they trotted into the woods, and the wheels squeaked softly.

The forest was lush with greenery, birds hopping in the trees, bugs chirping all around while a gentle breeze moved the foliage. It reminded Malice of Mutuwa and the oasis he had discovered when he was seven.

Soon, the Unit was out of the woods, the warm sunlight hitting them with its might. Lycn gasped. Malice peeked over his shoulder at the gravestone.

Pich Conwrath, Royal Knight rank B,

A healer who helped hundreds, if not thousands,

A friend to many, a lover to one,

With a smile that could light the darkness,

Upon their death, even the sky mourned them.

The wagon rattled from the horses, quickening their pace. Malice had wanted to bury Pich and leave it at that, but he thought of what Magnus would have done and created a tombstone. Behind him, Lycn sniffled while everyone else was silent, the grief dense and oppressive.

Accepting The Price
XVIII

Magnus sat in his study, leg bouncing under the desk, the heel of his shoe clicking against the marble floor. The three-month mark had passed days ago, yet Unit One hadn't returned. A restlessness crept down to his bones, making them itch.

He hoped that any day, any minute, any second Malice would walk through the door, followed closely by Gareth, Barbus, and Lucas, then Lycn and Pich. All in good spirits, all intact. Magnus knew that wouldn't happen, no matter how much he hoped it would.

He had ordered the patrolmen around the kingdom and castle to be on high alert for Unit One's return. So, now all he could do was wait. Magnus reclined in his seat, drawing his hand over his face, weary from lack of sleep. His thoughts rarely ceased, and he couldn't get comfortable in a bed that felt as vast and empty as the ocean.

Deliberate heavy knocks came to the door, startling Magnus out of his thoughts.

"Enter."

It was almost the middle of the night. Most servants and royals were resting or finishing up the last of their duties. He pushed himself upright. The doorknob squeaked as it turned, and the door swung open. Rising from his chair with his hands on the desk, Magnus's breath left him, his eyes wide, his heart pounding in his ears.

"Malice?"

He had thinned out, his face hollow and his eyes sunken into dark pits. The sun had kissed his skin, dirt stained his hands. His white hair that almost touched the tip of his nose was now short, his forehead mostly bare.

"Not who you were expecting?" Malice stepped into the study, closing the door behind him. Magnus watched as Malice came to sit in front of his desk, his mouth hanging open.

"It was a good thing I left my jewelry behind," Malice gestured to his left ear, "I feel as though they would have gotten destroyed."

Still at a loss for words, Magnus had started to shuffle around the desk when Malice put a hand out, stopping him.

"I have much to report. You should sit down for now." He looked at Magnus, an exhaustion in his dim green eyes that he'd never seen. Magnus grimaced and sat back down, nodding for Malice to begin.

A heaviness sat on Magnus's chest when the details of the mission were out in the open. He included everything the voidents did to Unit One, their injuries, and how he treated them. The only thing he did not mention was what they did to him, but Magnus let it slide.

Pich was sweet, Magnus thought, and one of the best healers in the region. Their love—need—to teach was an attribute that was scarce and one that would not be replaced easily. It saddened him to know they were gone.

At the same time, the mission had worked, relieving the tension in Magnus's shoulders. The region would be safe from the voident's grasp long enough for Magnus to think of countermeasures and put them into action.

Not even Malice could have predicted Valken's intense desire to cause others' horrific pain. If he had, they both would have planned the mission a bit differently. Nevertheless, the other kingdoms were untouched and would remain that way for quite some time. Phoenix was also no longer a concern, no longer able to pawn people off as if they were goods at a market. The objective had been reached, and that was what mattered.

"Royals take an oath," Malice said after a few minutes of silence. "They are prepared to die for their regions and kingdoms. Pich knew the risks."

Magnus glared at his desk, knowing the truth in Malice's words.

The possibility of losing Unit One altogether suddenly hit Magnus like a slap in the face. Lucas, Lycn, and Barbus could retire knowing their king had deliberately put them in harm's way and Magnus would have no grounds to stop them. Even Gareth might leave the life of a royal behind him. Magnus buried his head in his hands and closed his eyes, his brain throbbing. Perhaps that would be for the best.

"They won't retire."

Magnus's head shot up.

"Gareth has bottled his rage for now, but if he wants to release it, he'll stay. As for the others, they all have a reason to continue fighting."

He knew Lycn's, Barbus's, and Gareth's reason to stay. Lucas might stay out of principle, but that was doubtful. His parent's legacy could only tie him down so much. Magnus knew the chances of them staying were as equal as them leaving.

Magnus relaxed a bit, his shoulders drooping.

"Your decision was the right one. Everything comes at a cost. It wouldn't have mattered what you chose to do in the end. Something would have been lost," Malice added, his voice hoarse from talking so much.

"I know," Magnus said. "This was one of the best outcomes I could have hoped for. The Unit is alive, and you're home." *Save for Pich*. He could not hold Malice's gaze.

"But?" Malice prodded for more.

Magnus sighed. "But it does not lessen the doubt, the concern, or the burden that now rests upon everyone's shoulders."

"You're right, it doesn't. I apologize for the sacrifices made. Perhaps they were unnecessary, but what's done is done." There was little remorse in Malice's tone.

Magnus shook his head. "There's no need for you to apologize. I've known that some situations require a necessary evil, and this was just one of them." He leaned his head into the tips of his fingers. "I still do not see a course of action that could have ended with the same result, or better." Both needed to be dealt with, delaying war, and stopping the Kingdom of Phoenix from trading any more innocent lives.

"Neither do I."

They sat in silence, each breath draining Magnus's worries. The news was sudden and a lot to take in at once. He was being emotional, thinking too much about the subject. Overthinking leads to doubt, anxiety, things that would cause him to falter.

After a few more deep breaths, Magnus felt as though he were levelheaded again and glanced at Malice. It was as if Malice was absorbing every inch of Magnus, his eyes steadily moving across his person. A subtle warmth grew in his chest.

"I missed you," Malice breathed.

Magnus's eyes widened for a split second before he smiled, the warmth expanding. "I would be lying if I said I didn't miss you, too."

A grin spread across Malice's lips as he closed his eyes and reclined his head back. "I'm glad."

Magnus's smile faded and his eyebrows twitched. "When was the last you slept?"

"Almost three months ago."

Immortal races don't need as much sleep as mortals— demons, angels, fairies, elves, and dark elves could go without for months, years if they didn't use magic whatsoever.

Magnus was tired as well, mentally exhausted, partially because he had quickly grown used to sleeping next to Malice. Magnus pushed his chair out and stood, his eyes on Malice.

"Let's go."

Despite perching an eyebrow, Malice obeyed.

"We're going to bed," Magnus clarified.

A soft chuckle escaped his mouth as he followed Magnus to the door, into the hallway, and up to the third floor. The sound castle was dim, the only light coming from the windows via the moon, painting the floors in icy blue. Magnus, peeking over his shoulder, extended his hand behind him, and Malice took it.

Magnus didn't want to speak. Although there were many things to be said, he simply wanted to enjoy Malice's presence again.

As soon as they got to Magnus's bedchamber, they collapsed onto the mattress, the softness of it giving to their weight, the frame squeaking in protest. He drew Malice into his embrace, his arms wrapped tightly around Malice, his head tucked against Magnus's chest. With a hand gently caressing the space between Malice's shoulder blades, Magnus breathed. He just breathed.

Eventually, tears surfaced in Magnus's eyes. Why he cried, he didn't know, but he let the salty drops stream down his face. *That's a lie. I know why these tears flow.* He kissed the top of Malice's head, his hair tickling Magnus's nose.

"I love you," he whispered.

Malice was immobile, his body relaxed in Magnus's arm, his chest rising and falling at a slow, steady pace. It wasn't long before Magnus gave in to his own tiredness.

Swallowing against the dryness in his throat, Magnus's eyes blinked open. He moved, causing Malice to stir in his arms. Magnus stared for a while, awestruck, and smiled widely. He was sure he looked goofy as all hell right now, but he didn't care and squeezed Malice, taking in his scent and warmth as if he had never done so.

The sun was on Magnus's backside, a dampness sticking his clothes to his skin, telling him it was already late morning. Checking the clock on the hearth's mantle had confirmed it. Begrudgingly, Magnus wiggled out from under Malice, careful not to wake him, then sat on the edge of the bed. He stretched and yawned. *I need to check on the Unit.*

The halls were busy with servants, maids, butlers, and royals. Each carried linen, trays of food, empty plates, or a bucket of supplies. Magnus, after dressing himself in a white silk shirt and forest green trousers, walked into the long corridor toward the grand staircase leading to the lower floors.

The infirmary was a large room of white and had windows at the opposite end on the first floor. Ten beds on either side had curtain dividers in between, and all but four were empty and untouched. Gareth, Lycn, Lucas, and Barbus rested on their cots.

Two healers stood beside one another, going over the supplies in the cupboards while the doctor, Helen, looked at some notes. Magnus dismissed them with a nod of his head, and the three of them bowed, scampering off as fast as they could.

Magnus grabbed a wooden stool from the side of an empty bed and put it in front of the Unit. They were in as bad of shape as Malice described them. Gareth was the first to notice his king after the door closed. He pushed himself upright. The blanket fell off his chest, uncovering the scarred lacerations which were the color of Boysenberries, puffy and scabbed. He was skinny now too, the combination of his height and muscle gone, making his appearance gangly. His distant gaze, although understandable, stung.

Magnus took a deep breath and said, "Malice knew Charles was involved with the voidents, but he didn't know how specifically." His voice was steady and monotonous, eyes locked on the front courtyard of the castle. "In order to draw them out, he caused a scene at the Games. Upon your return from gathering information, Malice told me there was a good chance the four of you had been marked. Unsure, we agreed on a code during the first briefing."

Magnus glanced over the Unit. Everyone regarded him with anger, disgust, sorrow gleaming in their eyes, drawing their expressions taut.

"If he were to keep silent, then none of you were marked but if he were to say anything at all—"

"It meant they were," Gareth finished his sentence, his voice slightly hoarse.

Magnus nodded. "After he confirmed voidents were attached to your shadows, we went back and forth, idea after idea, for over a week until we landed on this one. There was one gamble that would determine the course of the mission. It, however, meant sacrificing a kingdom."

Lycn glowered at Magnus. "Did you choose the Kingdom of Phoenix because of its small population?"

"I did." Putting his hand underneath his thigh, Magnus guided his leg over the other. "There was more to it than that."

Lycn's eyebrows softened from their furrowed state.

"The Kingdom of Phoenix was corrupt. The nobles were involved with the trading of slaves."

Lycn's mouth gaped.

"I had been trying for the past year to work against them, to stop the trades, and to fish out the leader of the operation."

"So… you killed them?" Lycn breathed, his voice brittle, eyes reddening.

"I did it to set an example. The other nobles knew of Phoenix's corruption, some admitted they had been tempted because the pay-out was good. One kingdom in particular was of great concern to me."

Lucas swallowed, opened his mouth, and spluttered a cough. "Ivory's Kingdom," he said as a statement, somewhat surprising Magnus. "I… noticed a change in the nobles when I was there in the spring. They were nervous and in a rush to see me out of the door." He breathed sharply, a flash of pain washing over his face. "I didn't think it was because of slaves or money."

Lycn's head whipped toward Lucas, his expression still drawn with shock and pain. He turned to Magnus. "Are you saying that I missed such… such vile acts? That the nobles were trading slaves right under my nose?"

Magnus had sent Lycn to the Kingdom of Phoenix because he knew the streets better than anyone else. In hindsight, it was a mistake.

"I am, and you did," Magnus said shortly, and moved on. "How the people were killed would confirm whoever had been following Malice. When he saw the nobles and royals beheaded and speared, displayed in the castle's courtyard, he knew Zephyrus was the one behind all the attacks. He's one of the commanders overseeing the region with quite a sizable warband."

They had intended it to be Lazarus, expected a few others as well, and made plans accordingly, each different. Lazarus and Zephyrus had apparently become two peas in a pod since Zephyrus's exile.

He turned his attention to Gareth. "Knowing you, Gareth, would send him to the other kingdoms because of his speed, Malice agreed to go when, in reality, he never did. Instead, he came here." Gareth's eyes went wide, and he turned away, his brow furrowing, jaw clenching. For a moment, Magnus thought he saw tears swelling in his silver eyes.

"Once I had given him the letter he needed, he went to Ivory's Kingdom and told the nobles what happened to Phoenix. Malice persuaded them to keep themselves in check, then helped evacuate the people, dividing them between here and Cytor." It was easier explaining things to them than he had anticipated, perhaps because they were too distraught to react or argue.

"Helping the people move gave the voidents enough time to plant their trap before Malice returned and your Unit arrived."

Relief to finally share his reasoning with Unit One washed over Magnus, but something else took its place, something that pricked his veins like a thorn.

"Why?" Barbus muttered. "Why was it necessary for our capture? Our torture?" Barbus lazily moved his head, though Magnus couldn't tell if his pure white eyes were on him or something else. "Why didn't you tell us?"

"It wasn't necessary," Magnus admitted. "But look at how you all coped. None of you tried to escape or fight against the voidents. Malice told me about the habits of Valken and Cas. You had chances and you could have made opportunities, but you did nothing long enough for those openings to wilt, to die, forcing Malice to save you." Magnus ran a hand over his face, releasing an exasperated breath.

"Escaping should have been your top priority. I expected the strongest and most capable Unit in Alucard's Region to at least make the effort." The shock drawn on Unit One's faces tore at Magnus's heart as if claws had scoured down his chest.

"I didn't tell you because not a single thing could go wrong, or war could have potentially broken out," Magnus said.

"Potentially?" Gareth repeated. "Malice talked about this war, but it does not explain why you sacrificed so much."

"I was looking at the bigger picture." Magnus uncrossed his legs and stood. "A few thousand, compared to a few *hundred* thousand, is expendable. War with the voidents when we are not prepared, even if it was just a fraction, was too big of a risk. A bucket of water does not compare to the ocean, Gareth. Besides, as Malice said, I wanted to see how weak my royals had become." This was the time to address said weakness and cut it out like a tumor before it was too late.

"Now we have months to prepare, to plan, to get stronger until the voidents can be held back no longer. This region will not fall while I draw breath and if that means that blood must be spilled, and pain must be felt, so be it."

Magnus considered his men, fists bunching at his sides, disappointed they could not see the bigger picture. He turned on his heel, grabbed the stool, and placed it beside the bed he got it from, marching to the door.

Magnus stopped in his tracks. "I will offer the four of you a choice. You can retire as honorary knights of the region, and when the time comes, you will be protected. Or—" He glanced at the Unit through their reflection on the door's window. "You can fight. Let it be noted that if you choose to retire, any action taken against the voidents will be treated as an act of treason. You will be arrested and imprisoned."

He sighed, guilt weighing his shoulders, and added, "Despite all that I have said, I acknowledge how hard you've worked, and I am sorry that Pich could not be saved. They were remarkable in their craft and a valuable healer to the region… I do expect an answer when you can walk freely around the castle."

Magnus left the infirmary and went the way he came, his head floating like he had too much to drink. As king, he could not afford to think about individuals all the time. He must think of his region as a whole entity. Up the stairs, Magnus trudged and told himself, for the greater good, a few lives lost, and a few feelings hurt was a measly price to pay.

Upon returning to his chambers, Magnus looked forward to sleeping in the same bed as Malice again, but Malice was up and half-naked, changing near the closet. Magnus slammed the door shut and rushed toward Malice.

"Good morning," he said with a smile as he shifted to face Magnus.

Magnus yanked the shirt from Malice's hand and pulled him into his arms. The warmth of his body bled into Magnus, melting his frustration. Malice wrapped his arms around him and squeezed as if at first he was hesitant or confused. His hands gripped Magnus's shirt while Magnus nuzzled his head against the crook of Malice's neck and shoulder. They stayed like that, enjoying one another's embrace, until Malice pushed him away.

"Have you talked to the Unit yet?" Malice asked.

Magnus frowned. He didn't want to have to talk about this so soon, but the resolution in Malice's eyes brought words to his lips, anyway. "I did," he said shortly. "None were too pleased with you or I, understandably so."

"Is there something else bothering you?"

"They're divided." He glanced toward his balcony doors, the vibrant garden below swaying gently. "Unit One is no longer a team, a family. They sit together, but they no longer share a bond. They're no more than strangers now." In the past, Magnus could stand beside them and feel trust and warmth, the same kind you would get from a family.

"They were separated." Malice gave a gentle squeeze to Magnus's hand. "They heard one another but were subjected to something a little different. It wouldn't surprise me if they all felt alone, as if their comrades could not understand what they've experienced. If we had stayed a few more days, I feel that Valken might have moved everyone to the same cell."

"That's torture in its own right, especially for those who are close."

Malice nodded. "I can't say for certain, but there's too much history between them for everything to fall apart now. It'll be difficult, I'm sure, but I think their bond, in time, will reforge itself." His eyes were tender and his voice soft.

Magnus took a deep breath, "I'm sure you're right," and exhaled. Shaking his shoulders, Magnus pushed the Unit out of his head then eyed Malice's person. "Before you get fully dressed, you need to bathe."

Malice, dumbfounded for a split moment, broke out into laughter. "Do I stink that badly?"

"A bit, yes, but look—" Magnus grabbed his arm and gestured to the streak of mud crackling his skin.

"You have a point."

"Come," Magnus said as he led Malice from the closet to the door beyond the hearth next to the balcony and opened it, dragging Malice behind him.

A white porcelain soaker tub lay in the middle of the room, a vanity was on one side while an open shower was on the other. The shiny tiles were square slabs of white marble, and the walls were the color of a peach. A golden chandelier with crystal teardrops hung from the tall ceiling. Long windows stretched across the far wall, matching the balcony.

Still pulling Malice, Magnus stopped at the shower. The faucet squeaked when he turned it. A steady stream poured from a steel spout high on the wall. Malice stripped his pants and underwear off, since that was all he had managed to put on. He stepped into the water.

Magnus turned and walked to the vanity cupboards to get soap, cloths, and towels. He draped the towels over the edge of the bathtub, and set everything else on the floor, swallowing his jittering nerves. He undressed. It wasn't like this was the first time he had seen Malice naked.

Wet and naked, on the other hand… *keep your thoughts in check.*

Magnus came up from behind Malice, handing him soap and a dark green washcloth. Malice, smiling, stepped away so that Magnus could rinse his body.

It had been three months since Magnus last saw Malice. He peeked over at Malice, who had his back turned, admiring his slim hourglass figure and ivory skin. Only his arms and face were slightly tanned, leaving faded lines around his neck, shoulders, and biceps.

As he washed his own body, Magnus noticed a mole centered on Malice's spine. His eyes lifted to Malice's nape, his hair covered most of it. Magnus swept the white strands out of the way, unveiling another mole in Malice's hairline. Absent-mindedly, he let his finger slip down Malice's spine, stopping in the middle to touch the beauty mark he found earlier, going all the way to the base of his spine where Malice's tail grew from.

"Magnus."

Magnus suddenly snapped his hand to his chest, heat flushing his cheeks.

"Sorry, I—" Malice turned, the front of his body covered in soap. "Um…" Magnus's eyes caught and followed a cluster of suds slithering down Malice's chest, then abs and further down…

"Enjoying the view?" Malice asked with a devious smirk. Words caught in Magnus's throat while his head felt like it was on fire. Malice chuckled, shifted his chin to the side, and gave Magnus a peck on the cheek.

Malice's green eyes traveled up and down his body, snapping Magnus out of his trance and allowing him to regain some composure.

"Are you?" he asked, his thumb caressing Malice's cheek.

"How could I not?"

Malice's hungry gaze ate him whole. His heart fluttered. Magnus's lips tingled as he remembered the sensation of Malice's pressed against them. Every breath shared between moans and gasps was like honey, rich and sweet, a caress to his ears. Malice's cold hands had explored his body, shivers raking his spine.

Retreating slightly, Magnus put his hand down. "We shouldn't." Worried that he might give in, Magnus didn't look Malice in the eye. "You need to relax, recover from these past few months."

"A kiss won't hurt… or do I have to beg?" Malice said, his tone playful.

As entertaining as watching Malice beg would be, Magnus shook his head. "No more than a kiss."

"We'll see."

Malice kissed Magnus, his lips damp from the water. They were tender, one after another, and made Magnus's head go blank. Their kiss deepened, their warmth becoming one. Still, Malice was slow, his tongue moving languidly, his hands staying put on Magnus's chest. *Why?* He was usually so desperate, starving, impatient with his kisses. Magnus didn't mind taking his time, but he came to enjoy how Malice would smother him.

"Gods, I've missed you," Malice breathed into Magnus's mouth.

... Damnit.

Magnus, wrapping his arm around Malice's waist, tugged him closer, their bodies pressing together. Malice gasped in between kisses. *That's what I like to hear.* Faster, harder, until he became breathless; that was what Magnus wanted. He missed the proximity, the indulgence.

At some point, Malice slipped down to his neck, his lips gliding over Magnus's wet skin, leaving sparks of excitement in his wake. Magnus's eyes were closed, his head tilted back, the heat from Malice spreading throughout his body.

His eyes opened as his head jolted. Malice had gotten to his knees, his hands gripping Magnus's upper thighs.

"May I?" he asked in between kissing Magnus's waist and hips.

Magnus gazed down at him, biting his lip. He wanted this, he wanted this more than telling him no. *But Malice needs to rest...*

"As long as you're not pushing yourself, you can do whatever you please." Magnus brushed Malice's hair, tucking strands behind his ear. *Yet again, when hasn't he done whatever he pleases?*

Malice smiled. Magnus flushed and looked away. The warmth Malice's mouth provided enveloped him. Magnus shivered when Malice withdrew, his hands creeping to the back of his thighs. His tongue danced around, feeling every inch of Magnus as his head moved steadily to and from. Magnus swallowed, then let out a low groan, his hands entangling Malice's wet hair, his arms following the rhythm of Malice's bobbing head. One hand glided down Magnus's thigh, caressing his smooth skin on the way up.

When Magnus peeked, Malice had two fingers in his mouth, his other hand stroking him. Magnus had never seen Malice appear so erotic, his cheeks red, his eyes filled with desire, and his own cock starving, twitching with excitement. He pulled his fingers out, thin strings of saliva following and breaking. His nails were unevenly short on those two fingers now.

"What… happened to your… nails?" Malice took Magnus to the hilt while teasing and slipping a finger into his body. He gasped, gripping Malice's hair.

Malice swallowed often, his throat clenching while his tongue relentlessly pestered every inch of Magnus, his legs trembling every time. Unhurried, his finger went in, squirmed, retreated, and thrust in again. Magnus focused more on the front, thinking his backside wouldn't give him much pleasure anyway, and so far, it hadn't.

Not long after, Malice glided a second finger in. Something sent a wave of sparks through his body. Every thrust made him quiver, an unrelenting heat coursing inside. His head grew fuzzier and fuzzier.

"Malice," he moaned. "Wait, please…" Malice's tongue teased Magnus one final time as his fingers quickened.

His knees buckled when Malice stroked his cock with his warm, slippery hand. His mouth kissed wherever it pleased, now that it wasn't enveloping Magnus's cock. Twitching, Magnus gasped, pleasure surging.

As he rose, Malice ran his lips against the trail of Magnus's hair, loosely defined abs, plump chest, collarbone, and neck until they were face to face.

Magnus was out of breath, his body still tingling and shivering. Malice's curious hands feeling every inch of his skin didn't help.

"Let's finish cleaning up," Malice said.

Magnus grabbed Malice's shoulders and slammed him into the wall, bringing his mouth to Malice's. It wasn't enough. Three months of going without Malice's touch; Magnus didn't realize how much he had missed it, how much he had longed for Malice's kisses, his fingers, his voice, everything.

Hot breaths escaped between them as Magnus kissed Malice, hard. One hand teased and played with Malice's chest, the other glided down his torso and stroked him. Malice moaned, his hands going up and down Magnus's muscular arms. Away from his lips, Magnus kissed Malice's cheek, his ear, his neck.

"Magnus." His breath tickled Magnus's jawline and ear, his hips thrusting into Magnus's hand.

His moans were deep and velvety, but raspy, and close to a growl when they lowered in volume. As Magnus felt himself harden again, he took Malice's hand in his and rubbed their cocks together. Malice groaned and let his head drop. Magnus looked at him, sweat and water one and the same now. With his free hand, Magnus gripped Malice's hair and yanked his head back, biting the base of his neck. He thrust his hips fast and hard, feeling himself against Malice. Magnus kissed the spot he made before the mark disappeared.

Their moans filled the bathroom whenever their lips parted. It was like Magnus was high. The entire world vanished around him, and the only thing filling his thoughts was Malice.

"Call my name," Malice whimpered, making Magnus quiver.

"Malice." He rested his head on Malice's shoulder, shuddering with every twinge and surge of pleasure. "Malice."

Malice moaned, holding onto Magnus's arm, his nails biting into Magnus's flesh.

"Malice," he continued, picking his head up, eyes focusing on Malice's face as it contorted in ecstasy, a flush to his cheeks, his eyes half open.

Malice orgasmed, twitching, his voice soft and drawn out. Magnus groaned, his body tensing, sparks racing from his groin to his fingertips.

They stood against the wall, sweaty and out of breath. Magnus was glad they were already showering. He caressed Malice's cheek; it was hot to the touch, a glint lingering in his serpent-green eyes.

"Now, let's finish bathing."

Accepting The Price
"Divide"

The clear night sky had an abundance of stars as Gareth walked to the king's study. He paused at the top of the stairs to catch his breath and wipe his damp hands on his pants.

Knocking on the door, Gareth waited for a response. A part of him hoped Magnus was elsewhere, so he did not have to confront him, but it was not enough to make him walk away.

"Enter." The king's voice filtered through the door. Gareth collected himself, turned the knob, and stepped in.

The king glanced at Gareth, to the papers in his hand and put them down, giving Gareth his full attention. "Is it all right for you to be walking around like this?" he asked, gesturing to a chair for Gareth to sit.

He nodded. "I am a little winded from walking up the stairs but fine otherwise," Gareth admitted, and sat down.

"What brings you here, then?"

"I took an oath," Gareth steeled his nerves as he looked Magnus in the eyes, "to protect the land and its people. I do not plan to step down because of the loss of a life or a few more scars etched into my body." Pich was another person he wished to protect. Instead, he coddled them. Not that it made the grief and guilt any less raw, agonizing.

He frowned, thinking about Magnus's explanation in the infirmary. After he left, the air was dense and uncomfortable.

Gareth could only withstand the suffocating atmosphere for so long. When the doctor returned, he asked if they could retire to their chambers. She agreed on the condition that a guard was placed outside their room in case they should need anything.

"I do not agree with your course of action." Hesitantly, Gareth questioned, "Did Malice force you to adhere to that plan?"

Magnus's expression suddenly went sour. "Are you implying that I can't make decisions for myself?"

"Malice is strong, stronger than you or anyone else that I know. I would not be surprised if he threatened you to get what he wanted." Gareth went on, ignoring Magnus's worsening mood, "I do not think you would trust him so easily. It does not matter how long you've known him, the rumors about Malice, they are all true. He has confirmed that much."

"Gareth."

"He is manipulative, cunning." Gareth's eyebrows furrowed. "He killed his kin for his selfish desire. What makes you think he would not—"

"GARETH!" Magnus shouted as he slammed his fists onto the table. Gareth flinched.

"You have no right to doubt Malice the way you are! He saved your lives, not because I ordered or asked him to, but because he felt responsible. Have you no gratitude or grasp of the situation you were in?"

"How could I when he was the one who put us there in the first place?" Gareth's anger was getting the better of him, he knew this was no way to talk to his king. "I have known you your entire life, Magnus, and you have never acted this way. How can I not suspect the one thing that has changed?"

"You know the version of me you created long ago. An image you refuse to let go of now that I am grown." Magnus stood abruptly, pushing his chair back and almost knocking it over. "You only see the change because I stopped hiding. I am not kind nor gentle. For the greater good, for the bigger picture, lives are expendable. I have more important matters to worry about and if you will not support me the way the right-hand man of the king should, then you will be replaced!"

The king glared down at Gareth, his breathing heavy. "You have no right to undermine my authority. I am the king, the ruler of this region, not some child you need to pamper and it's about damn time you start seeing me as such."

Speechless, Gareth slouched in the chair. Magnus retook his seat and collected himself.

"You and your Unit will take the next week off."

"What?"

"For the next seven days, you will rest and recuperate. At the end of the week, you will be reexamined. If you are determined fit to return to your daily duties, then you shall, if not, you will wait another week."

Gareth leaned closer to the desk. "But Magnus—"

"If you do not pull your head out of your ass, you will be demoted and someone more qualified will take your place." Magnus calmed his voice down, but anger still burned bright in his eyes, wrinkles forming between them, his features mirroring his mother's.

Gareth's mouth gaped open, a sudden sharp pain stabbing his chest.

Magnus took a deep breath, his expression softening. "I need a right-hand man that will help me, support me, and offer sound logic. I need someone who will be my shield, my sword, or my horse at any given time, not someone who sees me as a babe who needs their hand held. Am I understood?"

"..."

"Am I understood?" the king repeated.

"... Yes."

"Leave. If you have anything more to say, save it for the end of the week."

Gareth slowly rose from his seat, stumbled around the chair, and walked out.

The door creaked when Gareth opened it, the smell of stale linens and musk flooding his nose. Everything was as he left it, his bed perfectly made, his books and decorations organized on his shelves. Before he closed the door, the guard, wearing a full suit of silver armor, peeked in, their armor clinking.

"Would you like me to call a maid to clean your room and change the sheets, sir?" the guard asked, their voice guttural.

"... No," Gareth said in almost a whisper as he closed and locked the door.

It felt like Magnus had betrayed him and it hurt like hell. How much of their relationship was a façade? How long had Gareth been the only one thinking that they were more than a king and his right-hand man? That they were friends?

Gareth stomped to the bookcase, grabbed, and flung everything on the shelves, one by one. Books he'd never read but kept anyway because they were gifts. Knives in intricately designed sheaves never to be used in battle. Trinkets and charms he'd received from grateful citizens or from those he'd saved.

They crashed into the wall and banged on the floor. Papers scattered as he slammed stacks onto the floor or threw them across the room. The clock on his mantle splintered, and the glass exploded into hundreds of pieces. He kicked one armchair over and flipped the other across the room. Both crashed with loud rattles and thuds.

His breathing was ragged. The guard outside pounded on the door, the knob jangling as they tried to turn it, asking what was wrong. He gave no response and grabbed the back of his desk chair. A breathtaking pain lanced through his torso and stopped him from throwing it. He collapsed to the floor. Gareth hunched over, gasping, cradling the tender scars on his chest.

"Sir Gareth!" the guard shouted as they beat on the slab of wood. "Are you all right? Please unlock the door before I break it down!"

"No!" Gareth struggled to say. "I am fine."

The guard paused for a moment. "But sir—"

"Damnit, I said I am fine!" he growled, hurling the closest thing near him at the door and winced. The guard spoke no more.

After a time, Gareth got to his feet, staggered and limped to his bed, crawling under the dusty covers with a crinkle of his nose. The dark room was now quiet, the space as stagnant as when he first entered. Head buried in the pillows, Gareth could smell remnants of his soap in a flat sort of way.

The anger had subsided, and all that remained was defeat. He turned to his side, his ribs and chest throbbing, so he turned to his back and stared at the ceiling. Then his eyes closed, and he could remember the day the previous ruler, Holister Castine, died alongside his wife and youngest son.

It snowed that day. Magnus studied in the castle's library while Gareth corrected the mistakes on his worksheets.

Gareth knew, as the sun was setting, the prince was eager to visit his mother and brother.

Despite her marriage to Holister, Vesh lived in the western district of the kingdom where the houses were small, and the people were none too friendly. She was a prostitute, became heavy with child out of wedlock. Holister feared his authority and image would diminish if the public knew. She had fought hard to see Magnus in spite of the late king. Padma, Holister's youngest son, was like the dirt beneath his shoes. While Magnus was whom he planned to pass the region on.

After letting the prince go and realizing he had forgotten his cloak, Gareth remembered taking his time on the way to her house, chatting with people and royals alike. He did not want to spoil Magnus's time with his mother.

Eyes opening, Gareth wished he would have run after Magnus to save him from the scene he would walk in on and save him from his fate. He tossed, ignoring the pain screaming in his torso, and screwed his eyes shut, trying to fall asleep. Forget about the day, forget what had happened over the last seven months. Just for a little while so the nightmares could cease.

When was he ever that lucky?

Clear as day, the moment he had walked into Vesh's home painted the back of his eyelids.

Vesh laid on top of Padma's corpse, both beaten in the kitchen's walkway. In front of the table near the sink, blood pooled around the king's body from the holes in his chest. The prince stood beside his father's corpse, expressionless. Ichor dripped from the kitchen knife still in his hand, multiple bruises blooming on his face and neck.

Holister had a nasty habit of drinking himself into oblivion and taking his frustrations out on Vesh, and when he came into the picture, Padma.

Gareth had assumed Magnus had walked in on his father beating his mother and, induced with rage, had killed his father. Gareth had never asked for details. And the prince never spoke about it either, never dared to cry in front of anyone. He stood tall at their funerals and chose one of the elders to step in as ruler until Magnus was old enough.

Perhaps it was when Gareth would find Magnus sobbing into his pillows late at night that he started thinking differently. That he wanted to fill a void Magnus's father had left and become someone the prince could cry in front of, so he did not have to hide.

What changed? After all these years, Magnus felt he needed to hide his true self from me.

Gareth saw the sense in Magnus's words tonight. He viewed the king the way he had when he was a boy, someone he needed to protect. Like Pich. That scene—blood so heavy in the air, alcohol adding to the pungent odor, the despair in Magnus's eyes—however, would forever be engraved in Gareth's brain. He doubted he could change the way he saw the king because of it.

He would try, though. It was the least Magnus deserved.

"Magnus"

"I am the king! I am *his* king!" Magnus paced from one end of the room to the other while Malice sat on the edge of the bed, watching him. "Gareth has served this region for three generations, starting with my grandfather. He watched my father grow, yet never treated him how he treats me." Magnus glimpsed the smirk on Malice's face and rolled his eyes. He was too frustrated to be amused by his antics tonight.

"Gareth is much like an old dog, he's stuck in his old ways," Malice said. "Although difficult, it's not impossible to teach an old dog new tricks."

"I know." Magnus waved his hand toward Malice.

"After tonight, I think he will change."

Magnus stopped in his tracks and turned on his heels. "And why is that? Because I told him the truth?"

Malice shrugged. "It might make him realize the error in his ways. You are too kind sometimes and it shows with how you've let your royals become lax."

Magnus's jaw clenched, his brow furrowing even deeper. "Not every region needs to train their royals to be killers, Malice."

"Right now, they do."

No argument came to Magnus's mind. What did come to his mind was that Malice was not the one Magnus was angry at, yet he was taking his frustration out on him. Who else would listen to a man's rant with a smile on his face?

Taking a moment to recompose himself, Magnus eventually sat beside Malice on the bed, sighing. "What if he retires after this?"

"He retires. There are others that can replace him," Malice said.

"They can't and they won't. Gareth was even more important than Pich to this kingdom. Losing him... isn't a card I'm willing to put on the table."

"Do you really think he would retire?"

"He could."

Malice laughed, a humorless grunt. "Doubtful. He's spent fifty years serving this region. Do you genuinely think he would give that up, walk away from his people, his home, all because the two of you fought?" He looked at Magnus, his expression thoughtful. "If he does anything at all, he might step down as your right-hand man, but he will not stop being a royal. You'd probably have to kill the man before he retired."

Magnus huffed, his irritation as potent as it was when he stormed in here soon after Gareth left the study.

Gareth's entire life, as Magnus knew it, was to protect and serve Alucard's Region any way he could. Many royals revered Gareth, sought his approval, his tutelage. Magnus lost count of the times someone had asked if they could be put in his Unit. To lose Gareth meant to lose the morale of over half his forces, a hit he couldn't afford with war on the horizon. Gareth wasn't just a pillar, he was a part of the foundation for the royals.

Perhaps with the changing times, someone needs to take over the position of right-hand man and give Gareth a break.

He leaned closer and rested his head on Malice's shoulder, staring at the grim, empty hearth over the back of the couch.

"You're calm," Magnus muttered, feeling a slight twitch from Malice. "I've never seen you let your emotions take over. Everything you do seems calculated a thousand times over."

Malice chuckled softly. "Is that how you see me?"

Magnus didn't respond.

"I suppose that's the case now." Malice tilted his head, so it was resting on Magnus's. "But when I was younger, there wasn't a thing I wasn't angry at."

"Really?" Magnus couldn't imagine Malice ever losing his composure. Then again, he couldn't imagine him having a tail either.

"I was angry I became a ruler. Angry at my brother for using me. Angry at you, my father, my mother, my subordinates. I was angry at myself, most of all."

"Was there a reason behind it?"

"Of course." Malice lifted his head. "I never wanted to become king. I had planned to hand the throne over to Kiran or Zephyrus."

Magnus shot up. "Zephyrus?" he repeated. "Why him?" Out of the two, Kiran seemed to have been the better option based on what Malice had told him.

"He was ambitious. Someone who wanted change and was willing to go the distance for his people. He was the perfect candidate, and he wanted it too."

"Until he challenged you and was banished," Magnus interjected. Malice gave him an approving glance. "What about Kiran?"

"Kiran was happy to be my regent, happy to give advice when needed, and that's all he wanted." He spoke so warmly about Kiran, as if his brother had never betrayed him.

"I had my reasons. Some better than others, but," Malice leaned onto the bed, his arms supporting him, "I learned to put a cap on my temper. It's not gone, just well managed."

Magnus smiled wryly, pushing himself off the mattress. Whatever temper he meant, Magnus had yet to see it. At least, to the extent Malice was referring to.

"How about we retire for the night?" There was quite a bit left on his mind, but most of it was already done and over with. No point in dawdling on the past.

"Doesn't sound like a bad idea." Malice got up and followed Magnus to the closet. After handing Malice a set of nightclothes, he undressed.

Time Heals All
XIX

Morning training began after running, just like any other day. After Malice left, the routine returned to what it was before spring, and Ida was with her group again. Training had become slow, mundane, and predictable.

At the edge of the coliseum, under the shade, Ida stared at one of the closest instructors, Sir Vinney, a Royal Knight rank S. Despite his bulky body, he was nimble; she would rarely hear his footsteps, almost like Malice. She sighed, then took a swig out of her waterskin while she waited for the others to finish running around the arena.

Malice's training was difficult, unpredictable, and he never gave her a chance to get used to one thing before moving on to the next. The king, over the last few months, had lit a fire under the instructors and, as a result, the regimen had changed, but compared to Malice's, it was still easy. Too easy.

As if her thoughts summoned him, Malice appeared in the open space at the center of the arena. He wore a white oversized shirt, the collar and sleeves ruffled, the bottom tucked into dark blue trousers. He actually wore shoes today as well. Ida, glancing around, quickly made her way to the center of the arena.

His eyebrow flared. "You've grown," he said, a smile tugging at the corners of his mouth. "You were as tall as my nose. Now we seem to be the same height."

"You should have expected as much from a giant," she remarked.

Malice gave a slight nod of his head.

"You've had three months to improve." His tone changed. It was harsher, colder. "Show me the process you've made."

He was right. Over the past three months, Ida not only went on smaller missions throughout the kingdom—mostly finding and arresting criminals—but she also trained at the royal's barracks. On quite a few occasions, she'd lost track of time, and only realized when the sun blinded her.

Once Ida put some distance between her and Malice, she hopped twice on each foot. "So, which will it be? Water? Fire?" She cracked her neck from one side to the next.

I don't mean to sound cocky, but—"I'm sure I could defeat your air golem now." Ida shook her hands out at her sides.

She froze.

There was no golem, and Malice was putting his hands up, popping his knuckles one by one.

Ida swallowed the abrupt lurching of her stomach, then smashed her fist into her open palm, doing it to the other hand as well. Malice had waited patiently in a loose, wide stance.

Over the course of her training as a royal, Ida learned to recognize a certain gleam in someone's eyes. Malice was hungry for a fight, but so was she. Three months of essentially fighting against herself, Ida couldn't push down the excitement bubbling to the surface. She also couldn't wait to slug him a good one across the face. *I've been waiting a while to do that.*

Clouds of dust rose, swept away by the breeze, as training started around them. Ida was the first to strike, using her smoke to propel her. She wrenched her fist and swung at Malice's face. He pushed her hand to the side. The momentum allowed her to swing her leg up. The heel of her foot nearly grazed his nose as he reeled. With him leaning, it would be easy to knock him off balance. Ida, instead of letting her foot down, rocked forward, stomping her leg in front of Malice. She rammed her elbow into his gut. He used the back of his hand to keep it from being a direct hit, though. A sweep of his leg took Ida out while he grabbed her head and slammed it into the ground.

Ears ringing, Ida's vision doubled as Malice receded. "Long distance," he said when Ida eventually got to her feet.

Two black throwing knives appeared in both of his hands. He threw them all at once. Each was a blur of speed. Arms to her side, Ida dropped, grabbed a bow of smoke, and stood. An arrow nestled against the bowstring and in her fingers when she drew it to the corner of her mouth. She let go. The arrow whistled toward Malice's heart, and he evaded.

Malice threw more knives. Ida parried the ones she could keep track of with an arrow, the airborne projectiles meeting to create a plume of dark grey. The rest, she dodged.

They kept their distance from one another, using the wide space at the center of the arena to their advantage. Retreating too late, she yanked the bowstring back, a knife grazing her cheek. Blood dribbled down her face and she wiped it off, then dashed around him. She held onto her arrow until Malice turned. The arrow was nothing more than a flash of slate grey. Of course, Malice caught it before it struck his eye and crushed it, the smoke billowing out in all directions.

He smiled. "Mid-range." A spear, longer than his body, appeared in his hands.

He's evaluating everything.

Ida dropped the bow and arrow, letting it dissipate. She extended her arm and grabbed a staff of smoke—she wanted to put what Sir Lycn had taught her to use. It swirled in her hands so she could get a feel for it. Their weapons clashed, making a noise as if padded. Malice thrust his spear, aiming for Ida's gut, but she avoided it somehow. She used the staff to launch herself up and over Malice. After landing on her feet, she turned and jabbed his back in an instant. Simultaneously, he swung the spearhead around, slicing the staff. It never had the chance to hit. Ida scrunched her nose, thinking her choice of weapon was poor against a spear.

"Sword."

A long sword materialized in place of the spear. It resembled Sir Lucas's in a vague sort of way. He, stepping forward, drove it down. Ida brought her own sword up, catching his attack head-on. It was heavy, the blow numbing her arms, straining her shoulders. She shoved him off and dove in, not wanting to give him the chance to strike again.

Malice caught her assault with the edge of his blade. He swerved, driving her sword into the ground. Stepping closer, Malice brought his knee up, slammed it into Ida's ribs, pain sparking her vision, and released her sword. She cradled her side briefly. In a cleaving blow, he brought his sword down. Ida braced her sword with her arm against the dull side. Their blades connected, an instant rush of corrosive pain expanding within her arms.

They held position, Malice carefully observing Ida, and Ida observing Malice.

He was relaxed, not a single sign of distress. The black from Malice's nails traveled just below his knuckles. Conversely, sweat dripped down Ida's skin and soaked her shirt as she tried to breathe without wheezing. She rammed her shoulder against her hand, forcing Malice off, allowing her to break away. Then she got low, both hands gripping her sword.

"Add a shield," he said, darkness spilling from his hand and forming a wall of black on his right arm.

Ida's confidence wavered for a split second. She wasn't all that experienced in shield work. Shields made it hard to move, plus they were big and clunky, at least the ones on the rack were. Nevertheless, she jerked her arm, creating a shield of smoke, a condensed storm cloud.

His sword sliced through the air, a whistle, and Ida propped her shield up. The blade struck hard. If the sword were metal and her shield iron and wood, her ears would be ringing. Plunging forward, she stabbed blindly and felt the pressure of his sword on her shield die. She shuffled backward, letting her guard down to check on Malice. He wasn't in front of her anymore.

Instinctively, she slid her arm out of the strap and slung the shield over her back. A blow connected, sending her tumbling forward. The shield disappeared in a fog. Ida caught herself and flung her gaze toward Malice. A pleased look rested on the demon's face.

"Dagger," he said, the sword and shield now two daggers, each the length of his forearm. They differed from the ones Sir Gareth usually had in his holsters; one side had a jagged edge resembling a poorly drawn lightning bolt, the other smooth.

Perspiration trickled into her eyes, Ida wiped it and readied herself. She threw her right arm down, bringing it up with a dagger in hand. Black wisps, like embers, shot out from Malice's blades. The black on his hands now went to his wrists.

She wondered what it meant but didn't linger on the thought—didn't have time to.

Cautiously walking around him, circling him, Ida waited. Malice's sharp green eyes moved, and she rushed in. She whipped the dagger up diagonally; it scraped against one of his blades. The other came from the side, aimed at Ida's ribs. She receded and ducked simultaneously, swinging her leg out to sweep him off his feet. He jumped. Ida got to her feet and went to bury her dagger in his stomach, but one of Malice's daggers blocked the path of the blade.

When his feet touched the ground, swiftly, he moved away, a smile on his face. He froze, which made Ida think they were done. Then he rushed her. She reeled, panic seizing her muscles momentarily. He was fast, gliding around to Ida's backside as if he were floating. Dagger swinging with her, Ida spun on her heels. It met one of Malice's blades. He regarded her as if he were impressed and smirked.

The daggers vanished, and Malice put his hands up. "Hand-to-hand combat."

Ida grinned from ear to ear. Her fists were speedy and intense as they pummeled Malice's forearms, protecting his face and chest. She attacked relentlessly, small bursts of magic aiding her strikes, making them harder, faster. She bounced, bringing her leg around. Malice caught it and slammed her into the dirt. She padded the impact with a blanket of smoke before racing toward one of the groups. Creating a wall of smoke, Ida jumped and used it to propel herself toward Malice. She flipped herself, her foot bearing down on his head. When he sidestepped, she landed, the loud boom catching the attention of the closest royals.

Ida rose, put some distance between her and Malice. He rushed in, his fist a heartbeat from connecting with her jaw. Just barely, she dodged, but his other fist punched her side. She skidded across the dirt and dropped to her knees. The hit stole her breath, tears burning her eyes.

Ida turned back to Malice. He was already on top of her, his foot not even a hand's width away from the side of her head. She flattened herself to the ground as much as her flexibility would allow and his foot coasted over her. Ida rocked forward, scrambled to get to her feet, then charged.

A few hours went by when Malice called an end to their spar. Ida was dripping with sweat, her lungs burning like they never had. Random spots all over her body ached and throbbed from Malice's blows. Luckily, she had also worked to improve her regeneration these past few months.

For a second, she couldn't believe she missed getting beat every day. Still, something about working hard and being challenged made the bruises worth it.

Ida looked at Malice, who glistened in the sunlight, dirt staining his white shirt. He was fine otherwise—of course he was. Ida, however, knew she would be sore tomorrow and laughed to herself as she reached for the waterskin on her belt. *This is what you wanted.*

"You did good, Ida." Malice approached, giving her a nod of approval. "Your development is quite impressive."

It was rare for Malice to give out compliments like that. Ida cringed. She might just prefer his riddles over the peculiarity that just left his mouth. She couldn't help the small smile on her lips as she wiped the wetness off her face with the inside of her collar.

She had seen the improvement, but she wanted to feel it. No one here in the coliseum could put up enough of a contest for

Ida to feel anything besides boredom. Instructors weren't allowed to spar with royals unless it was under special circumstances, like Iron Fist. She'd heard rumors about him when she first started training. Apparently, he was some big brute who didn't know restraint until Sir Gareth gave him a personal lesson. Iron Fist retired after the humiliation of losing to a knight was too much to bear.

"That's all for today," Malice said. He swiveled and walked toward one of the gates, snapping Ida back into reality. "We will spar from here on out, so prepare yourself," he added.

A whistle penetrated the sounds of training, which signaled the last movement of groups. Despite the exhaustion tugging at her limbs, excitement conquered it, and Ida quickly joined her group.

"Barbus"

Barbus's room provided little relief. Stale dust had replaced his smell, and his bed no longer held the same comfort it used to. Barbus sat on the edge, the wooden frame squeaking a bit, and ran his hands over the soft fur blankets.

More often than not, he would wake from a dead slumber, gasping for air as his throat felt like it was closing. Sometimes, his eyes would open to see a figure standing in the corner of his room watching him. He would try to sit up or move his legs, but was paralyzed. The figure always noticed when Barbus awoke, and it would slither to his bedside. Fear squeezed his heart and lungs while his head spun. Then the figure would be on top of him. So close, he recognized it—a voident. The voident's head moved and contorted, stretching beyond its limits, engulfing Barbus.

That was when he would wake, finally able to move his body, and frantically search the room.

The poison, as if it never fully made its way out of Barbus's system, wanted him to suffer in more ways than one. Barbus's appetite never returned. It was a struggle to force himself to eat three meals a day. Usually, after an hour, his plate would finally be empty, but once he tried to stand, his stomach would do backflips and somersaults. Afraid of losing all of his hard work, he would stay put until the food had settled in his gut.

Before the mission, he hated tea. The flavor of bitter leaves never ceased to disgust him. Now, perhaps because of the herbal medicines Malice gave him, tea had become pleasant, especially with a cube of sugar and a dash of milk.

A white porcelain teacup sat on the surface of the dresser against the wall in front of him. The tea was probably cold now. It'd been a minute since he made it. He wasn't quite ready to drink it, anyway.

Barbus thought of the coliseum and resuming his training. He would need to regain the muscle he lost somehow. Besides that, he enjoyed teaching the little sprouts. He wondered how much they had improved in the last three months, and how much he would have to catch up in comparison.

If he were to be honest, the idea of using his magic terrified him. Any of the poisons he was given could have done permanent damage to his core.

More than that, the pain of having his magic almost completely gone was engraved in his mind and body. What if he were to overdo it? The fear of getting hurt was never this strong. He got off easy compared to Sir Gareth, Lucas, and Lycn, and at least he was alive, unlike Pich. He had no right to complain when things could have been much worse, yet the dread was deep and unyielding. The option to retire was tempting, more so than he would have thought, considering Sir Gareth refused to leave. Barbus rolled over to his side, unsure of what to do with his own cowardice and indecision.

"Lycn"

Life with one arm was both easier and harder to adjust to than Lycn imagined. He got used to dressing himself and bathing, but he would have to reteach himself how to write and wield his staff. It was strange. At times he felt as though he still had an arm and would reach for something, his shoulder twitching or wiggling in response.

If Pich was alive, they could have helped heal his arm before Malice chopped it off.

After dinner, Lycn walked into Pich's room. Very few plants were alive, most wilted, flies hovering over the corpses of succulents. A smell like moldy bread hit Lycn, and he cringed as he strode to the bed.

The room couldn't stay like this. Not if Sir Gareth wished to continue leading a Unit. He would need this room cleared for Pich's replacement. A Unit must have at least five members to be deployed on missions outside the kingdom, so until Pich was replaced, Lycn wouldn't be doing much.

He plopped down on the edge of their bed, looking at the shelves above their desk. Their books and other medical and healing supplies would be handed off to the king in hopes he would have the new and old generations of healers learn from Pich. It was what they would have wanted.

Tears suddenly swelled in his eyes, his vision of the desk blurring. Big drops fell to the floor, one after another. He closed his eyes and cried quietly into his hand. Lycn thought he had let go of their death enough to stop crying over them.

Pich's screams haunted his nightmares. He would dream of them getting tortured despite having never seen it. Thick dark circles under his eyes could attest to that. It was a constant switch between anger like a storm, toward the voidents, toward Malice and the king. And guilt like shackles for not doing anything for Pich.

Lycn stood, wiping tears from his cheeks, although he was sure they were stained and his eyes red. He headed to his room between Lucas's and Pich's, and closed the door, remembering how Pich had scolded him about not collecting anything aside from his old, battered staffs lined against the wall. His room was so bare they could hardly tolerate it, and it drove them mad. Not much interested him enough to start a collection. Pich pouted when he had said that. Their face suddenly lit up, and they ran to their room, returning with a scroll. It was tarnished; the edges frayed and torn.

"What's this?" Lycn asked as Pich handed him the scroll.

"A map!" they declared, unable to hide their excitement, their wings fluttering.

"… A map?"

Pulling the end of the string, it untied itself, and Lycn unfurled the parchment over his bed. At the top, in fancy writing, it wrote *Yeager's Region*. In the right-hand corner was a compass and in the middle was the region of dwarves, a hot, dry chunk of land.

"I found this lying in the street when we went on a mission to help the royals in Yeager's region," they answered the question on Lycn's mind. The safest routes to each city and kingdom were marked along with every forest, river, and stronghold, as few as the forests and rivers were.

"Start collecting maps." Pich had a sparkle in their eyes. It made his heart pound violently against his chest. He was sure Pich could hear the rhythm of it, too.

He nodded. "All right."

Now, a few years later, he had a chest as tall as his knees full of maps. He had started snatching a map at every place he went to. The new maps had cream-colored parchment, the old were tan and stained with tea, dirt, and other mysterious things. They may not be recent or accurate, but he had a map of every kingdom, region and one of the entire continent. To Pich's credit, it was fun collecting them, comparing the new to old, region to region. Lycn would sit next to Pich and think of reasons for the placement of a certain kingdom or criticize it.

Lycn stared at the chest full of maps, wondering if he would even enjoy his hobby without Pich here. *Do I want to find out?*

When morning came, Lycn grew tired of the four walls surrounding him. Once Barbus invited himself, Lycn went to the coliseum for a change of scenery.

It was busy, royals shouting, getting thrown about, weapons clashing, magic roaring. It was organized chaos the way Lycn saw it. Barbus had brightened as he watched a group in the corner attack their instructor. The only knight gutsy enough to do that was Marris, an angel specializing in hand-to-hand combat. If Lycn didn't know any better, he'd say Barbus and Marris have a thing for each other, but any time it was brought up, they both denied any romantic feelings for one another.

After a pat on the back, Barbus strutted to Marris's group. Lycn didn't wait to see her reaction before he turned his attention elsewhere.

At the center of the field, Malice and a tall girl with oat-colored locks sparred—Ida was her name. They both had swords. Malice's was as black as night while Ida's was grey like smoke from a fire. He had forgotten Malice started mentoring a royal prior to the mission.

Malice's movements were fluid, easy, no strain could be seen. His skin was untainted by what the voidents had done to the Unit. Those monsters probably didn't do anything to Malice.

Lycn hawked and spat, his blood boiling, but watched as they traded fast and furious blows.

Malice and Lycn locked eyes, startling him into looking away. He snuck a glimpse just as Ida swung her sword, cutting Malice's arm off in one clean motion. The limb fell to the ground, the sword of darkness dissipating, blood splattering the dirt, yet he didn't even bat an eye.

Ida hesitated, Malice said something, and she continued to fight. She rushed in, ready to deliver another heavy blow. An arm of black holding a sword grew from Malice's shoulder, blocking Ida's attack.

Astonished, Lycn's hand went to his shoulder, feeling the bumpy scars underneath his fingertips. He had seen many other royals after losing a limb do that—not as quickly or efficiently as Malice, albeit—so why he hadn't thought of it till now was a mystery. He glanced at his shoulder, and at Malice, who was staring at him. In a breath, his arm regenerated, bones sprouting anew, fibrous tissue encasing it, then flesh, and the two went on.

Bedroom door slamming, Lycn paced from one side of the room to the other, an excitement he hadn't felt in months making him restless.

He wondered if this was Malice's way of showing pity, a way to fight. In the same manner, someone could create an object like a hammer, a pen, a sword, Lycn could materialize and manipulate an arm of magic. With that, retiring was off the table. Although it would take a while, Lycn could avenge Pich and make sure their sacrifice wasn't in vain. Losing his arm was a temporary setback, another hurdle to jump over after scaling a mountain.

Time Heals All
"Mask"

Someone knocked on the door, five heavy thuds. Gareth stood on the other side, solemnly, his broad shoulders slumped, and his expression haunted. Lucas turned, leaving the door open, and walked toward his room.

"I don't have an answer yet, if that's what you're here for," he said, his bare feet padding on the cool marble floor.

Retire or stay and fight; the options presented by the king were clear. Lucas was tired. The will to fight was long gone, leaving a cold emptiness in the cavity of his chest.

"That is not what I am here for," Gareth sighed. "I do not blame any of you for not wanting to stay, if that is what you choose." He continued to follow Lucas, stopping at the door to his room. "I am here to give you something."

Lucas turned to face his former leader. "Give me what?" he asked, his tone short.

"I did not tell you everything about the day your brother died... I did not tell you everything that Cadmus had done."

Lucas grimaced. He didn't want to talk or hear about Joseph any more than he did about Cadmus.

"He grabbed the necklace around Joseph's neck," Gareth talked anyway.

Joseph didn't have a necklace. Maryjane had one, though.

"He placed it on Joseph's stomach with a message."
Gareth looked miserable as he retold the story, or maybe he had
the first time, and Lucas refused to see it. *"Give this to his
brother, Lucas Knightridge."* From his pocket, Gareth presented
a sunflower pendant, a string for a chain bunched in his hand.

It came back to him, like a wave crashing on the shore.
Joseph had bent down and ripped that pendant off Maryjane's
body before running away. Lucas took the necklace, hesitantly,
the metal warm from being in Gareth's pocket.

"Do with it what you will." Gareth frowned, clenching his
fists at his sides. "I should have given this to you long ago, as
well as the news of your brother's death. I know the two of you
were anything but close, but you were still blood, and you should
have heard from me immediately."

"I am sorry, Lucas." Gareth bowed, straightened, then
left, giving Lucas no time to formulate a response before the
door clicked shut.

For days, Lucas had stayed in his room thinking of his mother's
face when he appeared on her front doorstep, only to deliver
devastating news. He left soon after Joseph ran off. Lucas
figured that if he were to go anywhere, it would have to be
somewhere their mother wouldn't know to search. The only
person who came to mind was Professor Cadmus, and it turned
out he was right.

Would Joseph have returned with Cadmus had he arrived
moments earlier?

What's done is done, he told himself. There *'s no changing
the past.* Yet he couldn't get it out of his head.

Lucas looked in the mirror, disgusted, horrified by what
stared back at him. The burns on his face left him blind in his

right eye, his teeth bare, and his ear a mound of flesh. Thinking of what the people he would try to save would say, how his comrades and his friends would look at him, made his heart drop to his stomach.

He requested his meals brought to him. He wasn't ready to face anyone else besides the Unit, but even they were difficult to face.

Some places on his body, where the scarring was most intense, were numb. He had tried sticking a needle into his skin, pushing it down until his fingertip hit flesh and drew blood, but he felt nothing.

The only thing that didn't seem to change was how easily he fell and stayed asleep, but it had become difficult to wake up. Lucas told himself it was nothing to worry about.

A voice in his head would tell him otherwise. *Deadly nightshade runs through your veins, if you fall asleep, you'll never wake again. You're poisoned*, it would say. It was false; it had to be. That didn't keep fear from embedding itself like roots into his body, keeping him from falling asleep too often or too deeply.

*

At the end of the week, Lucas visited the castle doctor Helen, Barbus's lover. The horrified expression on her face, when she saw him enter the infirmary, flashed against his eyelids whenever he closed his eyes. He couldn't blame her. Lucas had the same reaction when he saw himself in the mirror for the first time after coming home.

Helen cleared him to resume his normal duties around the kingdom, provided he took it easy. His core was severely damaged, as was everyone else's. Except for Barbus's. Evidently, Malice knew to focus on his core rather than his external injuries because of the poison and healed his core. It irked Lucas when Helen told him that, but it made sense. Had Malice neglected the Unit's physical condition, they would all be dead.

Before Lucas left, his examination finished, the doctor handed him a note and said, "I'm sorry I can't do more for you. I truly wish I could."

There's a craftsman named Yahui beyond Alucard's Kingdom to the north, on the coast. He left a week ago and should be back within two days. I cannot tell you more, but when you get there, you'll know.

What is that supposed to mean? As the wind blew off the ocean, Lucas gripped his cloak and tugged it across his chest. It was getting late, the day bleeding into night. He glanced at the note in his opposite hand. *I'll know when I get there?* He regretted waiting till he returned to the barracks to read it. In his defense, he just wanted to leave. The weight of the stares from the servants in the halls and from Helen was crushing. He hadn't caught his breath until his bedroom door closed and he had sunk to the floor.

Through the tall swaying grass to the edge of the cliff side, Lucas strolled. The dark water crashed against the rocks of the cliff, white foam rocking at the currents whim. The breeze was constant here, and he took in the salty mist. To the east, he could see the outline of Cytor, a coastal city known for its fish and sails. Pich grew up on the outskirts of the city, helping with their family farm and clinic.

Again, he looked around for anything he had missed.

Behind him was a small forest of oak and cedar trees. Directly to the north was the start of the royal's barracks. He could see the outline of the houses against the setting sun.

Sighing, Lucas turned back to the sea, enjoying its beauty, and accepting the fact he was sent out on a wild goose hunt. He wasn't angry. It had been too long since the last time he ventured outside the kingdom for reasons other than a mission. The quiet hum of bugs and splashing waves soothed his mind of worries and dread.

"Looking for something?" a voice, sleek and breathy, interrupted the quiet.

Lucas whipped around, his heart skipping a beat. The person behind him was shorter, the tall grass brushing against their hips. Their dark hair had a purple tint. A white cloth hung from their two small horns, obscuring their face. Their loose baggy clothes hung off them except for the thick red rope around their waist that seemed to keep everything from falling off.

The demon said after a moment, "Are you Lucas?"

Lucas stared at them, holding his fur cloak closer to his person. He nodded.

"Great, I'm Yahui." *This is Yahui?* He sauntered toward Lucas, who moved out of his path, letting Yahui pass. "Come on, pretty boy. I got a mask to make, don't I?"

Pretty boy? Lucas, gathering his courage, cautiously fell into his step.

At the cliff's edge, Yahui slid his foot across the grass. Now in a wide stance, his hands shot up into the air, stopping just above his head. The ground thundered, caved, and split open, uncovering a staircase. Yahui motioned for Lucas to follow him.

In the darkness, Lucas lifted his hand, a mini blaze bursting from his palm.

"Oh," Yahui drawled. "Fire magic. Very useful, pretty boy."

"Don't call me pretty boy." It might have been true in the past. Lucas knew he was on the handsome side, but now there was a reason he wanted a mask.

"You *can* speak." Beyond Yahui, warm yellowish light began filling the stairwell, and a flat surface was emerging. "But I call it how I see it, pretty boy." He shrugged and stepped into the space.

"Welcome." Yahui gestured with wide open arms to a cave.

There was a window built into the side of the cliff, the ocean right outside, sparkling from the last bit of daylight. There were two couches, one bright red and the other adorned with fur hides in front of the window, a table between them, a rug underneath. A single bookshelf shrouded Lucas's view of one side of the room. Closer to him, against the wall, was a table covered in an assortment of stuff—glasses, vases, masks, thread and needle, jars of ink, and more. A collection of everything.

A bar spanned across the wall to his left, bottle after bottle of alcohol sat on open hanging shelves behind the counter like a tavern. Everywhere his eyes landed, there was something new and out of place.

On almost every surface was a partially melted candle. Yahui walked around to light them. After the third or fourth candle, Lucas flicked his fingers, sending flame to all the candles he could see. Yahui stopped, glanced at Lucas, and chuckled.

"Thanks for the help, pretty boy. Now come along."

The way he spoke was alluring to Lucas. In a way, it was similar to Malice if he wasn't as sinister and cold as he was.

He trailed after Yahui, his footsteps echoing off the walls in loud clacks. A little shop was behind the shelf that obscured Lucas's view at the entrance. Stacked on the floor were wood and metal. Scissors, string and rope of all colors, beads, various-sized chisels, and a mallet were scattered on the surfaces of the space. Near the furnace in the corner, a vent leading up and through the stone, was a dresser with more tools and supplies sitting on the top.

Yahui pointed to a stool he pulled out, the legs scraping against the floor. "Sit so I can get your measurements, pretty boy."

Obediently, Lucas sat down, watching as Yahui grabbed a rolled cream-colored paper strip, black ticks on the edges. He came back to Lucas, unrolling the paper before measuring his head. First, the length, the width, and lastly, the circumference.

Lucas glanced at the table again. There was a wood carving knife used for paring, whittling, and cutting. Beside the knife were several types of gauges and different-sized rifflers. If he had all that, then he probably had a leather thumb guard as well, or at least he should. His father had told him how easy it was to cut yourself, and if you were unlucky, cut the whole finger off.

Now that he was closer, Lucas could see an old anvil, the edges smooth, rust starting on the top, next to the right side of the furnace on the ground. The dresser must hold all his tools— hammers, tongs, swages, and forging bits.

Lucas admired all the masks displayed on the shelves. Some were colorful, with bright pops of scarlet, indigo, or even gold. Some resembled animals like a fox or owl. One mirrored a frog. There were a few at the top that illustrated a ghastly creature, three eyes, horns, flat teeth, two tusks protruding from the bottom lip, and a big, flared nose. The lines carved into the wood exaggerated the creases of its face; it looked sickeningly happy.

"It's said," Yahui said quietly close to Lucas's ear, startling him, "those are what devils were like before they went extinct."

Yahui bounced to the other end of the table, "Done," and searched for some paper and a stick of graphite to write Lucas's measurements down. A few seconds later, Yahui pushed the paper further onto the table alongside the graphite, hopped up, and sat on the edge, his hands resting on his leg.

"I like to get to know my customers a bit," Yahui said and pointed to the right side of his face. "Tell me how you got that scar, pretty boy."

Straight to the point, huh?

The doctor had asked too, but Lucas's stomach twisted, and his tongue retreated down his throat when he thought about it. She was sympathetic and dropped the subject for his sake. Yet here, he felt relaxed. For whatever reason, Yahui made him feel at ease, something he hadn't felt in months.

Lucas opened his mouth, and everything poured out like a waterfall. He fixed his sights on Yahui's demeanor, searching for signs of discomfort or anything really to make him stop, but he listened to Lucas's rambling, intently at that.

When he finished, light no longer shone through the window and the cave had a chill in the air. A heaviness he didn't know was there lifted off Lucas's chest. He took a deep breath, smelling the wood, metal, and salty stone all around him. The sound of waves filled the silence, the gulls a muted cry.

Lucas didn't know what to do anymore.

"I'm sorry," he said at last, "for telling you... so much." He looked away as heat rushed to his cheeks. "I started... and it all... just... came out." At this point, he expected Yahui to say something with a pretty boy at the end.

Yahui started laughing out of nowhere when he jumped down from the table. Lucas glowered at him. Nothing he had said was funny.

"You certainly know how to make someone pity you!" He continued laughing, holding his gut as he leaned forward.

Grinding his teeth, Lucas got off the stool. "I did not come here for pity!" he snapped and stormed out of the shop, shame sinking into the pit of his stomach. *Why did I even bother opening my mouth?*

Footsteps rushed behind him and Yahui grabbed a hold of his hand. "Sorry," he said while trying to catch his breath. "I didn't mean it like that."

Lucas snatched his hand back. "I didn't tell you to get a free mask either."

"That's what I meant."

Lucas scoffed and turned, irritated with Yahui, and irritated that he even wasted his time coming here.

"Wait, wait."

Lucas stopped and turned.

"I'll make you your mask, but I won't do it for money."

Brow raised, Lucas eyed him suspiciously. "What do you want?"

"Stay with me tonight."

Lucas's jaw dropped, and he stared blankly at Yahui.

"Not like that," he corrected himself, although he was clearly suppressing a smile and failing. "It's been a while since I've had company, someone to talk to, so just stay the night, won't you, pretty boy?"

There it is. "As long as you don't do anything… that's fine."

Returning to the barracks didn't feel right at the moment, anyway. His room was foreign, like nothing in there was his. He had already told the king he would stay and fight, but he didn't want to be in the barracks anymore, nor did he want to stay in Unit One.

Yahui held his hand up. "I swear it. Besides, pretty boy, I like consent." He snickered when Lucas's face flushed and he spun, stomping into the other room.

"Lycn"

Out of breath, Lycn caught himself with his arms on the floor. Sweat dripped off his nose, one drop after another. Pain pulsed through his core, so he dispelled his arm of air, a small gust of wind prickling his skin. He sat back, pushing his wet hair away from his face as he swallowed against the dryness in his mouth. He grabbed the waterskin from his bed and chugged. Water spilled from the corners of his mouth, further soaking his shirt. The warm water wasn't all that refreshing, but it quenched his thirst immediately, and he finally took a deep breath.

After a few seconds, he got up and sat on the mattress. He looked at his stub for an arm, wiggled it, and was satisfied. Barely a week had passed from when Lycn started creating an arm of air, using it for everyday tasks like writing, eating, carrying, and lifting things. Helen said he was fine, healthy for the most part. *Take it easy*, she firmly told him. It reminded him of Pich whenever he would injure himself.

Yesterday, he had begun retraining his body, building the muscle he lost while maintaining his arm for as long as he could. Half an hour was the limit without pain. He'd learned the hard way what happened when he overused his magic while the core was recovering. Spent the rest of the day in bed and still woke up to a sore core this morning. Lycn smiled wryly to himself. He should have taken the doctor's warning a bit more seriously.

Eyes moving from one worn and battered staff to the next, leaning on the wall, Lycn recalled the king's speech in the infirmary. From what he'd heard, everyone in Unit One stayed. Lycn didn't question Sir Gareth, he was the king's right-hand man after all, and Barbus would follow him anywhere. His loyalty toward Sir Gareth ran deep, like tree roots in the earth.

Lucas, on the other hand, he was sure was going to quit. Lucas was once a force to be reckoned with, but now he seemed as fragile as a wilting flower. *Pathetic. He should have retired.*

Cracking his neck, Lycn stood and stretched his arm to the sky, then headed out of his room into Pich's. All their belongings had remained untouched since his return, except for some crates he brought here a few days ago, fully expecting to clear the room. He couldn't bring himself to do it then, and he had to force himself to do it now.

The few plants that were alive over a week ago were now dead, just like the rest. He sucked in a breath, held it, let it go. He grabbed a crate from the stack and set it on the desk. Each time Lycn plucked a book from the shelves, he would stop, examine the cover, turn it to the backside, and place it in the crate.

A sense of foreboding quickly filled Lycn. It felt wrong to put their possessions in crates and clean their room because if he did… that meant Pich was truly dead, and they were never coming back. Their existence would slowly fade from everyday life, and that scared Lycn.

He pushed the feeling down, which made him lightheaded and a little nauseous, and continued putting Pich's books into the crate. Soon he moved onto the surface of the desk, where journals, papers, and more books were scattered across it. Anything pertaining to medicine would be handed over to the king, everything else either burned or given to Pich's kin.

Once he set the crates in the living room, Lycn plopped on the couch. With a burst of air, his arm disappeared. He stared at the hearth and felt detached from the world as if he were on an island while the mainland was in the distance. He could see its light, yet it couldn't reach him.

He wondered when Pich would be replaced and by whom. Before that, he wondered if Unit One would stay the same or if everyone would be placed in different Units. Either way, Lycn would continue to move forward with or without comrades. He needed to make Pich's death mean something, and he knew they would want him to remain a royal to do so.

The Kings Summit
XX

The dining hall was lively with knights fresh from patrol, just waking up, winding down, or getting ready to head out. Servants dashed between the tables, catering to the royal's every whim; more food, more alcohol, play some music, so on and so forth. They looked like busy bees, not that Gareth helped to ease their hurried feet.

He toyed with the bottom of his chalice, his finger gliding over the smooth metal. Beside him was Barbus, his face delirious from alcohol. Corgan was drunker still. Lycn was too busy stuffing his face to drink, and Lucas had yet to be seen. Gareth sighed when a shadow fell over the table.

"Is this seat taken?" Magnus asked, and the table hushed.

Gareth shook his head. "No. Please, sit," he said, waving his hand to catch a servant's attention. "Have some food and drink while you are here." A servant nodded, scampering off to the kitchen. The king's appearance brought bitterness to his mouth, as if he ate unripe berries.

"Thank you." Magnus smiled as he sat down.

Gareth glanced from his drink to Magnus, realizing they hadn't been this close in weeks. Guilt caused a lump to form in his throat.

"It's not often you join us." Corgan wiggled in his seat, his face flushed, and his words slurred. "What's the special occasion?" His eyes, half closed, lazily moved from the king to Gareth. "Did ya have a fight?" he hiccupped.

Magnus chuckled humorlessly. "No, nothing like that." The servant appeared, poured the king a cup of ale, and left just as quickly. "I came to eat."

"And?" The knight eyed Magnus suspiciously.

"And to ask a question." The king's clothes shifted. Gareth was not looking at him though, instead, his eyes were glued to the deep blue tablecloth.

"Are you my right-hand man?"

Gareth's head jerked and spun, his eyes wide. He met the king's calm expression. Shock rippled through the table as Lycn, Corgan, and Barbus exchanged glances. Gareth did not expect a question like that, not in ten years, or fifty or even one hundred.

He had been attending the summit as the king's right-hand man for over thirty years and had no intention of stopping now.

"I will be your right-hand man until the day I take my last breath, your majesty."

Magnus considered Gareth for a while, his lilac eyes steady. "Good," Magnus eventually said and stood without having touched his drink. "I expect you to be ready in two weeks for the Kings Summit."

"Of course."

The king nodded, then turned to leave.

"What about dinner, your majesty?" Barbus asked.

"I've spoiled the mood enough. Besides, I'm not hungry." Magnus smiled, continuing on his way.

The king was fast on his feet, no one could protest his leaving. The red cape, lined with black fur, flared behind him as he reached the door. Gareth stared at his back, an ache tugging at his heart when the doors closed. They had not talked since the night after the Unit returned from the mission. He had seen the king many times from a distance in the corridors, the dining hall, the garden, with Malice, but he had never gone out of his way to talk to him. He could not find the words to say, more like he could not choose the right ones.

Corgan hiccupped. "So… ya did fight!" He slammed his goblet on the table, the contents on its surface jumping, a smirk resting on his lips.

"Shove it!"

Sometimes it seemed his pride would not let him apologize for his actions. Sometimes it seemed he did not know how. Gareth blamed it on the fact that Magnus had seemed busy these past few weeks, running around like a chicken with its head cut off. He told himself he would apologize when he found the time for it. Magnus took the initiative because he was most likely tired of waiting.

The king was not the only one who had a lot on his mind.

He glanced between Barbus and Lycn. The state his Unit was in had been like a haze over his mind, a boulder disrupting his thoughts.

Lycn was determined, a fire blazing under him again. His hair had grown out some, his muscle mass gradually increasing, while the color returned to his skin. He talked more, had a better handle on his temper.

Less than a week ago, he stumbled upon Lycn taking crates of books and papers to the southern wing of the castle. Gareth was shocked and proud at the same time to see that Lycn was able to use magic to replace his arm. As he walked past, Gareth glanced inside the crates, noticing the contents inside belonged to Pich, and knew what Lycn was doing. Ever since, Lycn's head had been clear, as if getting rid of Pich's things enlightened him.

Barbus was also putting weight on, but Gareth doubted he would ever get that big gut again. Although, with the amount of alcohol he was consuming, he might. His personality changed, too. He was not as carefree and lighthearted. There was a darkness surrounding him now, an aura of solemnity. When he was training at the coliseum, teaching the royals, Gareth could see a glimmer of who he used to be over three months ago. Similar to Lycn, he was not spending as much time with Unit One. If he was not at the coliseum, he was with his lover Helen or spending a short time with Gareth.

Gareth had only seen Lucas at the coliseum training, wearing a mask of red and gold after he was cleared for duty. Their interactions were brief and to the point.

The old Unit One was dead, and it died alongside Pich.

*

After eight days of travel, Gareth and Magnus finally made it to the edge of Dun Raik. Not an hour from the ominous forest was the kingdom of Liotkin, a city wealthy in minerals from the mountain it resided behind.

The arrow carved in the trunk of an elder tree pointed to a relatively straight path leading to the Barren Circle. Gareth helped Magnus out of the carriage and stretched his taut limbs. He'd much rather travel on horseback. It was faster, and he would not be so stiff. The carriage, however, held their belongings for the next week while attending the Kings Summit and the Celebration of Peace three days afterward.

Adjusting his layered clothes, far too formal for his blood, Gareth scanned the wall of trees that was Dun Raik. Supposedly, wyverns, bears, howlers, and even basilisks dwelled within the darkness of the forest. *What a farce.* The trees were too close together to allow such enormous beasts to scratch an itch behind their ears, let alone hunt, sleep, or breed as they would need to.

The king waved off the bench men on the royal blue, gold-trimmed carriage. Magnus looked regal, handsome. Gold shimmered on his clothes, hung from his ears, and decorated his hands. Each step made his cape flow, the deep saturated greens and greys of his outfit complimenting his rich skin tone. How he could wear as many layers in the dead of summer as he was, bewildered Gareth. He felt close to death in this heat.

Still, Magnus's demeanor seemed to have brightened since the day they left. He was brooding and snippy. Gareth assumed it was about Malice not joining them on their travels. It was shocking to hear that Malice would attend the summit after seven years, even more so when he had declared he would have nothing to do with the rulers and stormed off.

Out of the corner of Gareth's eye, something moved in the shadows. He stepped in front of Magnus, acting as a shield, static surrounding his hand. He stared at the tree line and concentrated on any noise.

It was silent.

A dark mass slithered around a tree. Gareth's heart stopped, his breath caught in his throat. *A voident? But why?* His hands trembled, his joints locking up.

"Don't look so scared."

All the fear melted into rage when Malice emerged from the trees in all black. Gareth, grinding his teeth, moved away from Magnus, a light tremor to his hands yet.

Malice's clothes were sharp, dapper, everything perfectly tailored to his body. Gareth noticed he had a fuller figure than the last he saw him. It seemed he had gained all the mass he had lost during their month of captivity and then some.

"I would say it is nice to see you again, but I think it would have been better if you had stayed gone," Gareth grumbled when Malice walked past him to Magnus.

"It's a good thing I'm not here for you." Malice smiled deviously back.

Gareth, clicking his tongue, saw no humor in his remark.

Stopping in front of Magnus, Malice bowed, his cloak of midnight kissing the ground. He brought Magnus's hand up to his lips. "Shall we get going?" he asked.

"Yes," Magnus replied after Malice released him.

Gareth felt out-of-place watching them and a little disgusted, if he was being honest. *Out of all the people in the world, you had to fall for Malice.*

"I'll take the lead to light the way," Magnus said and walked past the trees into the forest. Gareth, then Malice, fell into Magnus's stride behind him.

Almost immediately upon entering Dun Raik, the moss created a thick, spongy layer their feet sank into. Magnus lifted his hand, a glowing white ball illuminating the path and the immediate vicinity. Malice did the same, a flame now dancing in the palm of his hand. The moss quieted their footsteps, but nothing else. Birds tweeted and screeched, howls bounced off the trees, and twigs snapped underneath heavy feet. Mushrooms of all types—tall, short, spotted, and clustered—were everywhere.

The deeper they went, the more a certain type of fungi appeared, a glow mushroom. During the day, the small mushroom gave a faint blue glow, but at night, the blue light breathed life into the forest. Flowers were few and far between, the ones that could survive with little sunlight were strange, their shape reminiscent of a bird with a long, thin beak. However, there was an abundance of huge leafy plants falling over the path and hiding tree trunks from view.

"Where did you learn to manipulate your magic to create limbs?" Gareth broke the silence in a low tone. Malice didn't answer, so Gareth assumed he wanted more of an explanation. "Lycn saw what you did during training one day. Ida cut your arm off, yet you continued with an arm and sword of darkness."

Those who had lost a limb, if they evaded infection or fever, retired, thinking themselves useless. A few, however, figured they could magically recreate that appendage as if it were an effortless task and they were sorely mistaken. It takes too much magical energy to sustain the limb for long. Fighting or otherwise.

Malice grunted and answered, "It's protocol in Hordes Region. Learning to fight without a limb is a must if you are to become a royal."

"Sounds cruel." Gareth looked over his shoulder. The dancing shadows on Malice's face gave no hint of emotion.

"Maybe so, but," he said, "it allows royals to continue fighting, complete the mission, or to keep their lives and their comrade's lives intact if the need should arise."

"It might be a good idea to implement that into our training regimens," Magnus said, somewhat surprising Gareth. "As long as a healer is nearby, they can reattach it."

"… If you think it is necessary."

Gareth disagreed. Healers would make sure no permanent damage was done, but that would not alleviate the pain. He knew that pain and he knew it well. Excruciating. Mind-numbing. All his reason and will, gone in the face of the pain he experienced at the hands of the voidents. To become proficient at it, royals would need to have their limbs severed again, and again, and again, and then a few more times for good measure.

There were options to strengthen the royals, ensure their survival, and Gareth did not believe pain was one of them.

Not wanting to speak anymore, he let the sounds of the forest fill his ears once more.

"Magnus"

A gust of warm air carrying the smell of soil and stone rustled the trees, indicating the end of Dun Raik. It was noon when Magnus, Gareth, and Malice stepped into the Barren Circle. Their feet crunched the gravel and dirt. At the center of the Barren Circle was a massive castle. Six points, each taller than the last, towered over the land and trees. About half of the castle had collapsed or had been destroyed centuries ago, long before the founding rulers claimed their thrones. The sky above was clear. Clouds, bugs, animals, even mighty beasts like howlers and onyimyths avoided the circle. The temperature never changed in the Barren Circle, either; it never snowed or rained. There were no signs of life no matter where one looked, hence its name.

As Magnus and Gareth ventured forth, Malice stopped. Magnus peeked at him and waited, which forced Gareth to pause as well. Malice stared at the trees for quite some time.

Gareth narrowed his eyes in the same direction. "Do you know what he is waiting for, your majesty?" he asked.

"I don't," Magnus said softly. He focused on Malice rather than the trees he was staring at.

Minutes went by and Malice started walking slowly toward Magnus and Gareth, a grin resting on his face. Still searching the edge of Dun Raik, nothing jumped out to Magnus.

"Were you waiting for someone?" Magnus stayed a little behind Malice, eyeing his demeanor.

"You will see."

Magnus's eyebrows twitched. He didn't like being kept in the dark, especially when Malice had always told him everything.

The castle had a few cracks at the base, but nothing more. It had remained nearly untouched since its discovery a millennium ago. The entrance of the castle was a tall archway with swirls and shapes carved into the stone around the edge. Great stained windows, murals of meadows in full bloom, painted the inside with red, blue, green, and yellow. Emerald floors and pillars had long since lost their intense shine due to dust and dirt. A giant marble statue stood at the center of a winding staircase leading to the upper floors. The creature was similar to an angel, yet its features were too different to be called one. Perhaps it was an archangel. Magnus once read about the archangels, their culture, language, and where they inhabited, though not much.

Again, Malice stopped, but this time, he turned his back to the archway. Gareth and Magnus waited just outside the entry.

Eventually, hurried footsteps sounded beyond the castle and a short beastman appeared. Her clothes were as black as Malice's, save for the brooch of Hordes region insignia—three horned skulls, a sword through the middle—pinned to her left breast. Her dark hair was interwoven with a red string and tied into a bun. *This must be Eunice, Malice's first sword.* Magnus had never met her in person, but he spoke often about her in his letters. After briefly looking at Gareth and Magnus, Eunice bowed, lowering her head.

"My liege," she said, "I apologize for making you wait," rose, and met Malice's gaze.

He smiled, nodding toward the castle's entrance. "Come, we have a few things to discuss before the summit begins."

Malice went inside, Eunice on his heel, Magnus and Gareth following.

"Do you know her?" Gareth, whispering to Magnus, leaned down and over.

"That is his first sword," Magnus answered, his tone matching Gareth's, "Eunice Baklav."

Gareth grunted but said nothing else.

The inside of the castle had furniture, empty vases on tables, dusty bookshelves, and worn faded rugs. The stair railing, the handles, and knobs, even the crown molding and fixtures were all a weathered gold. Throughout the many floors, there wasn't any décor. The castle would be like walking into a museum, rich with history, if there was more to see that would share secrets of the past. Instead, it felt cold and empty, like walking through a deserted alley.

While trudging up the stairs, Malice and Eunice talked.

"Is it finished?" Malice looked down at Eunice for a split second. His eyes had moved to Magnus in that second. Magnus twitched, and Malice turned around.

She nodded. "Yes, my liege. Construction went off without a hitch and finished faster than expected."

"Good." There was satisfaction in Malice's tone as he moved on to the next topic. "Have you been able to gather as many as I thought?"

"No."

"I see," Malice sighed. "Many are too apprehensive yet, I assume?"

Eunice fished something out of her pocket, whatever it was crinkling when she found it. "Unfortunately, my liege." She handed him a piece of folded paper as they rounded and started up the second flight of stairs. "However, they can be won over."

Reading the letter, Malice huffed, crumbled the paper, and handed it back to Eunice. "Of course. I half expected this." Eunice shoved the letter into her pocket. "Are the preparations in order?"

"Yes, my liege, just as you instructed."

"You've done well."

Magnus couldn't get a grasp on their conversation and was hoping the summit would reveal some of it, while the rest, Malice would tell him subsequently. After months of no secrets, suddenly having them felt like a stab in the back. Magnus adjusted his shoulders a bit, his cloak uncomfortable now.

A thought entered his mind. *Isn't this... what I did to my own royals?* He shook it off. *It is, but it was necessary.*

The third floor, where the summit was held, was a wide-open space with a single long, dark oak table near the windows on the left side. The space to the right of the staircase was even emptier, only a couch and coffee table at its center. A metal chandelier caught shimmers of the light, creating patches of white around the room. Glowing particles floated without direction.

Magnus and Malice were the last rulers to arrive.

A right-hand man or first sword stood behind almost every ruler. Two were in armor, while the others dressed the same as Gareth and Eunice, casual in a sense.

No one was surprised by Malice's presence thanks to Magnus's constant communication with the rulers, but most seemed unsettled by his appearance, a sudden tension in the air. Malice and Magnus took their seats at the head of the table opposite of Caroline, who rose from her seat, stunned, mouth hanging open, her eyes on Malice.

"Malice?" the Queen of Jared's Region said hesitantly. Caroline was the face of kindness and humility. Her green eyes were the exact opposite of Malice's, warm and tender. The gold pendant lying on her bust stuck out against the white of her dress.

Malice scanned the room, probably taking in how little the rulers had changed over the past seven years. The biggest difference was that Leontios now sat where his father Anselm had all those years ago.

"Caroline," he replied indifferently.

A faint smile grew on her face. "I can't believe—"

Yoon Woo slammed his hands on the table, the ruler next to him flinching. "You have some nerve showing your face here!" he shouted. "You, who is neither king nor noble, have no right to sit with us today. No matter what Magnus has said!"

King of Braxton's Region, the land of giants in the south, Yoon Woo. The lines on his face were deeper than last year, proving how much he frowned. He wore the same outfit every year; his white hanbok with red spider lilies embroidered at the bottom. A black, transparent Bok hid his bun of grey hair on the top of his head.

Magnus's expression hardened, his jaw clenched, a single spasm of muscle.

"What makes you say that?" Malice asked.

"Your kingdom—"

"Is standing proud and is prospering quite nicely," Malice said in a chiding tone. Magnus caught a glimpse of a smile creep onto Eunice's lips, pride adjusting her posture.

Caroline fanned her hand toward Yoon Woo, telling him to calm down. It was not as if the rulers didn't know Malice was coming. Magnus knew Yoon Woo was going to be like that. He also expected Ko to do something similar, yet he sat there, silently glowering at Malice. For now.

"What happened to your kingdom in the first place? We all thought you were dead." She glanced at Magnus, who had only said that Malice was alive and planned to attend the summit. No matter how hard she or any of the rulers pressed for more information, Magnus would not tell. Even if he had Malice's permission to do so, he wouldn't have.

"What I do in my Region is none of your concern," Malice's tone was dry. "And obviously I'm still alive, otherwise I wouldn't be here, would I?"

Caroline recoiled, as if his words hurt her.

Decimus cleared his throat and rose to gather everyone's attention. "Although there are many things to talk about, there is one that stands above the rest." His deep brown eyes darted from ruler to ruler. "These creatures," he waved his hand like he was trying to remember something, "… voidents, they call themselves."

Everything Decimus, King of Cain's Region, wore was white save for the gold straps across his chest holding his fur-lined cape on his shoulders. His clothes were sharp, and the surface smooth.

At least Magnus wouldn't have to explain what voidents were, or Malice. Though he doubted Malice would give a straightforward answer just for the hell of it. He smirked at the thought.

Basia nodded with a grunt, the gold chain from her nose ring to her earring moving too. "Aye. No matter how many we kill, more just keep comin,' the stubborn bastards. We're no closer to findin' their objective than when they first started appearin' either." Her eyes, glaring at everyone in the room, were dark, almost black. Even in the sun.

"Ha, please," Thorn chimed in, his gruff voice, thick with accent, echoing off the walls. "Isn't it obvious?"

Basia turned toward him, a thick eyebrow raised.

"They want battle! They want to kill, for blood to be spilled. It's as simple as that." Thorn leaned into his chair, head tilting up. The sunlight caught his ear, making the line of gold running down his lobe sparkle. The dark elf on Caroline's left was rugged, his short, oiled-back hair peppered with grey. The once white cloak slung over his shoulder was nearly black from the blood of his slain enemies.

"They are not difficult to execute," Violet, Queen of Yeager's Region, said calmly. "But they are persistent and simple-minded." Her dark mass of hair covered her eyes ever so slightly, just enough to be unable to see them.

Surin Raelle shrugged, his layered garments shifting. "They remind me of a dog doing a trick to get a treat." He added, voice hinted with disgust, "Killing seems to be the reward."

"Even so," Basia rocked her seat, the legs clicking on the floor, "I've killed every voident that's crossed my path, even went out of my way to find'em. Doesn't seem to matter one bit, though."

"Voidents are creatures of darkness. Darkness is infinite." Magnus put out one hand, then the other, pushing his fingertips together when they met. "If the source—the creator—continues to thrive, they won't stop. No matter how many you kill."

"Who is their creator and how can we kill it?" Basia said, a wicked grin slanting her eyes.

Malice and Magnus exchanged a look before Malice said, "Their creator is the god Coatliris."

It went silent for a moment, Malice's words hanging in the room.

"There is knowledge scattered throughout the continent, left behind by our ancestors, and shared from those who were alive centuries ago about Coatliris and the voidents," Surin said, pushing his coral hair back with webbed fingers, the gills on his neck flaring.

"What are voidents?" Violet asked, her voice monotone. "Yes, they are creatures of darkness, but what makes you think their existence is so closely tied to Coatliris?"

"They're vestiges," Decimus was, surprisingly, the one who answered. "Fragments of the god whence they were born."

"If that's the case," Leontios, scowling, arms crossed, said, "why don't you three know much about them?" He directed the question toward the eldest rulers in the room, Caroline, Thorn, and Valentine. Both elves were well into their four hundreds, while the fairy was in their mid-three hundreds.

"I have heard tales, but nothing more," Caroline admitted. She too had an accent, her mouth somewhat closed, and her pronunciation of vowels was odd. Thorn nodded at her statement.

After shifting in their seat, Valentine said, "I've known about them since I was a babe. My people have always loved the tales of gods, devils, archangels, and the past species. We celebrate and re-tell their stories often." Their soft voice was melodic, angelic, and soothing to Magnus's ears.

"As have we," Violet said. "Some still worship the great deity that is Coatliris, and generations ago, all of my people worshipped the god. Voidents, however, were not a part of the history we knew."

"The idea of a god and its visages has simply died off over the years. Had the founding rulers not perished, perhaps the continent would know more." Surin's blue eyes swept across the table.

Valentine rubbed their sun earring as they spoke. "What do you suggest we do?" Their expression turned grim. "I cannot sit by any longer watching my people die like this." They appeared genuinely hurt, as if someone ripped their heart from their chest. They've always been a bit more sensitive.

Valentine Ezhil, Ruler of Florence's Region, sat across from Thorn. Faires wore very little clothing or nothing at all, at least for those raised in Florence's Region. They were kind enough to wear a thin, translucent fern green robe. To match the gold necklace falling over their collarbone and shoulders, there was a gold strap on their waist, keeping the robe from slipping open.

"Prepare," Malice said vaguely, a grin teasing the edges of his mouth.

The wolf beastman Ko growled with clenched fists on the table, clearly having no patience for Malice. "For what?"

"For war."

Caroline's posture stiffened. "War?"

"Against the voidents," Magnus answered. "It's the only way to draw out Coatliris."

Leontios, King of Oakens Region, laughed wryly. "What makes you think a god exists?" He leaned forward, bright red eyes narrowing on Malice. "If it does, why hasn't it shown itself?"

"I find this rather intangible myself." Valentine's expression was somber, but their voice remained soft. "Sure folklore, myths, and stories all say that gods once roamed the lands—I have read just about every tale in my region, and I love celebrating the possibility of their past existence—but where is the proof that one still lives today and that it is not just a legend?"

With a sound argument, no one could refute it.

"That voidents are running around killing people should be proof enough when ten or so years ago, they weren't so active." Valentine gave Magnus a dubious look, their thin hand stroking their earring.

Magnus went on, "When the founding rulers met their demise, what do you think could have killed them? The war of species was a fresh scar on the land. Things may have calmed down, but it was not enough to stop Coatliris from waking and killing the rulers as the rulers subdued the god and the voidents."

"A sacrifice was made six hundred years ago, one that stifled the voidents and tired out Coatliris," Malice said, one black nail picking underneath another.

"If you think, after hearing all this, the sacrifice made by the founding rulers was enough to hold them off forever, you'd be a fool. The voidents do the legwork for decades if not centuries before Coatliris emerges." His voice was cold but his gaze slicing up and across the table was even colder. Magnus's skin bristled.

"To do what, exactly?" Surin questioned, his scales glistening in the afternoon sun.

"Kill off most of humanity. In the process, causing species to go extinct." Magnus recalled the journal in his study left by his great-grandfather Alucard. The only entry he had ever written about archangels was in that journal, and so was half a page of information about Coatliris—the material Malice had cross-checked with Hordes' records before the mission.

"Humanity was once plentiful with diverse species." Malice raised his hand to eye level, "One by one, they were extinguished," and snapped it shut. "Now there are only twelve when there used to be twenty, fifty, perhaps hundreds of races."

"The possibility of voidents attacking our people," Leontios glanced at Magnus and Malice, "while lacking cause, is far-fetched. What reason do they have to kill us off and why now?"

Leontios was the youngest ruler, aside from Malice. All over his tan skin were pale blotches, the one masking most of his face and scalp, resembled a skull. Black tattoos covered his chin, neck, shoulders, and back, all meaning something different. Magnus wasn't educated enough in barbarian culture to recognize those differences and their meanings.

"Does it matter?" Malice asked.

"I don't think so, lad," Basia chimed in, her grin revealing more of her silver and gold decorated tusks. "History says enough. They mean to hunt us for sport. We'd not be standin' here if it weren't for the foundin' rulers. Reason be damned when they're at our front doorsteps lookin' for blood."

It wasn't often Magnus agreed with Basia, she usually let blood lust influence her decisions, but he did in this case. Sitting around talking about why Coatliris wanted Vinyamar's inhabitants dead would get them nowhere.

"Just know, now that they have started to move," Malice said, his deep voice resonating, "they won't stop until most everything's been wiped clean."

Yoon Woo grunted, his shoulders tensing, and his expression full of disdain. "You sure know a lot, Malice."

"You seem to be the epicenter of these events as well." Ko glared at Malice from across the table. "Yet Hordes Region remains untouched. Perhaps the land is cursed from years of disgrace walking across it."

Magnus felt a flare of heat rise from his stomach to his chest. Ko could try to hide his scorn for Malice a little better. Behind Malice, Eunice's eyes widened, the corners of her mouth twitching. *Is she… holding back laughter?*

Malice regarded the King of Wolfgang's Region with little emotion, then he flashed a smile. "They fear me more than they fear death." Ko's expression hardened. "Whatever is mine, they will avoid like the plague the best they can."

"You can say that with absolute certainty?" Decimus looked at Malice, skepticism written across his face, and gestured to the table. "What evidence do you have? For all you know, voidents could be attacking your people as we speak."

"Over a month ago, I temporarily and falsely claimed Alucard's Region as my own." His green eyes glazed over the table. "Not a single blade of grass has been touched by the voidents since."

He paused. "Do they fear death or complete annihilation? Unlike the rest of you, Magnus and I have something voidents would rather not face."

"Oh?" Thorn mused, elbow perched on the table, his eyebrow perked.

"Had Magnus stepped forth, made himself known as a threat, they would have relented all the same."

"Light," Magnus peeked at Malice, a memory rising from the depths of his mind, "expels the darkness. Killing a voident would be simpleton's play for me. Malice can control darkness, so killing would be just as easy for him. They know this, they also know that we stand together. Between the two of us, death is the least of their concerns."

"It helps that I destroyed one of their warbands two years ago," Malice said plainly. "From which they are still recovering."

Frost suddenly bit the air, and the room went uncomfortably silent. Magnus let the feeling of satisfaction wash over him. Watching a few rulers writhe in their seats was a reward he didn't know he wanted to see.

"If this war is as inevitable as you say it is." Surin readjusted his collar, pulling it out and down, exposing all four of his gills. "We need to strategize. The time we have left needs to be used wisely, whether they show up at our doorstep or from our backside." Surin gazed over the rulers as he rolled his shoulders and raised his chin ever so slightly.

"You're right." Malice smiled. "And I wish you the best of luck."

Magnus snorted and instantly put his hand over his mouth and looked away. Eunice did the same, her hands trembling at her sides, her lips pressed tightly, and her eyes screwed shut. Gareth, however, was less than amused, a scowl almost as intense as Ko's on his face.

Dumbfounded, Surin leaned forward, his hand out. "You... won't help?"

"No."

Leontios stood, knocking his chair over, and slammed his hands onto the table. Decimus and Surin snapped toward him. "Why trouble yourself by warning us if you refuse to help further and see it through till the end?" His triangle earrings jingled as his head moved and anger scrunched his face. "You would abandon your own people? For what?"

"Don't whine, Leontios, you're a big boy. Deal with it. I have things to do and places to be." Malice set his back against the chair, arms folded over his chest.

"What's more important than Vinyamar; your own continent?" Leontios pressed, his face scrunching up even more.

Leontios jumped off the table when Malice's attention came to rest fully on him. "Allow me to tell you again: That is nothing any one of you need to know. What I choose to do is my business and mine alone. The only time you will be informed otherwise is when you're important enough to be told."

Malice saw the rulers as little more than pawns, easily manipulated and replaceable from the board. That he made as clear as glass. Magnus shifted in his seat. Something about Malice's tone... was exciting. He swallowed the feeling in an instant.

Thorn suddenly leaned closer to Caroline, whose eyes glistened. "Huh?"

"What happened to you?" she said louder, her face twisting with pain. Magnus raised an eyebrow, confused by her outburst. She acted like they were close when Malice was a child. "This... this isn't you."

Malice tilted his head. "It's not?" He swiveled to Magnus. Magnus returned his inquisitive gaze and shrugged. "I wonder, who am I then? A child that you so desperately want to pity?"

Caroline flinched, a tear running down her cheek.

"Were you so blinded by what you thought of me I no longer look the same to you? Am I acting too far out of your imagination?" Malice went on, his tone just as playful and mocking as it was.

"Get over yourself, Caroline. You saw whatever you wanted because the truth wasn't to your liking and now you're forced to come face to face with reality." Malice smiled. "Pathetic really. A grown woman acting like a child whose toy was taken. If only I had enough shits to give, I would humor your pity party."

"Malice—"

"No matter what you all choose to do," Malice cut off Thorn's protest, "war will come when snow falls upon the land. Honestly, I couldn't care less what you do."

Malice leaned over, whispered, "Pretend I said something," and kissed Magnus's ear. When Magnus smiled, giving a quick nod, heat lingering on his ear, Malice stood and stepped around the chair in one swift movement, Eunice fast on his trail.

Magnus glanced over his shoulder. He watched Malice's frame grow smaller until he turned around the bend and could be seen no more.

The rulers were awestruck, especially Caroline, whose entire world, apparently, had come crashing down on her. Malice had a way of seeing through people, getting under their skin, and getting a rise out of them. A part of Magnus wondered if he did it on purpose or if it was an unconscious practice.

He sighed heavily into his hand as it drawled over his face. At his side, Gareth was distraught, angry, his fists shaking at his sides.

"I think Surin has the right idea," Magnus said, catching everyone's attention except for Carolines. "We should discuss preparations and counters while we have the chance."

Surin gave a plastered-on smile, which Magnus assumed was supposed to be reassuring or a way of thanking him. He rose and started talking.

The Celebration of Peace
XXI

Gareth stared at his outfit spread across the bed, a bit shocked Caroline did not call off the celebration after what happened at the summit. He supposed that would be too many people to disappoint and she would not have been able to handle that.

Stripped down to his underwear, Gareth pushed his arms into the white shirt with a crumpled collar, put his wine-colored trousers on, and tucked the shirt in. He grabbed the black leather belt, slid it through the loops, and tugged, buckling it. After clipping the dark red triple bow to his collar, he threw the matching long-trailed coat, gold roses traveling up from the bottom over his shoulders. Gareth walked to the full-length mirror on the wall beside the dresser and fixed a rose brooch to one side of his coat with a wheat gold strap going to the other to keep it on his shoulders.

He never thought such nice, regal clothes suited him. This outfit chosen by the king was no different. The feel of the soft silk shirt against his skin was strange, the scars on his chest made it even stranger. The tidy, brightly colored coat did not match his strong-featured face and rough hands. He ruffled his plastered hair until it was a mess. One hand stayed to play with a patch of white hair, the other dropping to his side. The pale birthmark was barely visible when he was a babe—or so his mother had told him. Having spent so much time in the sun, the mark stood out now.

At the very least, he wanted to wear one comfortable thing tonight. Gareth glanced down at his boots, a good number of the scuffs and scratches older than Magnus, and slipped his feet into them. Although he wasn't happy with the king's choice of clothing, it was not like Gareth could have done better. With a quick pop of his neck, he headed for the door. The dark stained slab of wood creaked open. He sidestepped and closed it, leaning back into the small area between his room and the kings.

The walls of Hoovers Inn's fourth floor were painted a light ivory green, gold spades running down to the baseboards. Candle fixtures and lamps holstered on the walls drowned everything in the warm light. The crown molding matched the dark cherry wood floors and doors. He took a quick peek down either side of the hall, noticing only a few more rooms on both sides.

The fourth floor had the biggest, most luxurious chambers for the wealthy who liked to stay here. The innkeeper, a squirrely man, always insisted that the king and his right-hand man stayed in these rooms, free of charge, despite their willingness to pay and despite their willingness to be put in different rooms.

Gareth hadn't waited long before Magnus's door opened, and he walked out. His shirt was a deep plum purple while the puffed-out sleeves were translucent until reaching the helm on his wrists. The white corset had gold loops and string that went slightly over his snow-white pants. His cloak of dove feathers, brushed with a thin coat of wax, gleamed in the light as it trailed behind him. His red hair was loosely styled, much like how Gareth usually had his hair. Gold painted his lips and cheekbones and decorated his fingers, earlobes, and neck.

"You look…" Awe stole his words for a second. "Truly stunning, Magnus."

Magnus scanned him up and down, then grinned proudly, his shoulders set. "As do you." He patted the side of his arm. "I'm glad I picked your outfit."

"Of course you are."

"Shall we get going?" Magnus asked, nodding toward the opposite end of the hall.

Holding his arm out for Magnus to take, Gareth let the smile that had been tugging at the corners of his mouth win. "We shall."

Beyond Dun Raik—which shone blue from the glow mushrooms—into the brightly lit circle, home to an enormous castle, Gareth and Magnus walked side by side, watching as people, wore their finest clothes or nothing at all, filtered through the trees. Bowls of flame on posts lit the entire Barren Circle, music and talk a buzz growing louder. The castle itself had lamps, jars of fireflies, and candles to combat the darkness of night.

There were too many reddened faces to count when Gareth and Magnus entered the bustling courtyard. Almost instantly, Magnus was pulled aside. Gareth grabbed Magnus's arm, anchoring him when he noticed the one pulling and let go. Caroline embraced Magnus and started a conversation too quiet for Gareth to hear.

The bustling mass in front of him made Gareth groan. The thought of dancing tired him out despite not having moved an inch. People gossiped, they always gossiped. Someone lost their farm because a disease killed their livestock. An affair produced a bastard son. Malice's newly built kingdom floated to Gareth's ears. A magnificent city, they had said before the words faded. The knight peeked at Magnus when he kissed the queen's cheek, and she did the same, then glanced over her shoulder. Gareth tried to follow her gaze, but failed. Caroline waltzed off, smiling.

Their eyes met. Magnus nodded and smiled, to which Gareth returned the gesture. As he struggled to get back to Gareth, Magnus suddenly frowned, noticing something near the entrance of the courtyard. This time, Gareth spotted who or what was there. Ko Wolfgang, a wolf beastman with multicolored fur, glared at Magnus. Gareth glowered as well, despite knowing he could not see him.

Hand raised, Magnus pointed at his palm, mouthing something like *I'll be back*, Gareth was sure. He nodded, and Magnus walked away.

Tune and chatter filled the square alongside laughter and cheers. On stages opposite the double-arched entrance, lyres, harps, drums, and flutes played joyful, upbeat melodies. In the shadows and halls, a handful of couples explored one another's bodies. Others smoked while some seemingly wanted to get away for a moment. Against the walls were tables of food ready to be feasted upon and alcohol to wet the pallet. Festivities were spread throughout the Barren Circle and the first and second floors of the castle.

Gareth shuffled through the crowd, eventually getting to the tables of drink in gold chalices and goblets decorated with jewels. He grabbed a cup, swirled it as he sniffed the air like a hound. At first, he thought to sip it slowly and enjoy the flavor, but when he got a taste of the ale's sweet fruitiness, he downed the whole cup.

The alcohol warmed Gareth's body from the inside, sweat starting to dampen his skin and make his head feel almost as light as feathers. Magnus was still trapped with Ko in the shadows, both wearing stern expressions, Ko's first sword a glimmer of armor at his side. He sighed, turned, and grabbed another chalice, guzzling it down. He was too sober if the events of the Kings Summit weighed on his mind as heavily as they did.

He hadn't a clue about half of the things Malice and Magnus spoke of. The two went back and forth as if it was natural, as if they had done it a thousand times. Voidents were nothing new, but all that talk about the god went over his head. It was a fairytale, had to be. Perhaps voidents were simply a long-lost race, angry with humanity for forgetting about them.

That sounded more like a fairytale than the gods.

Either way, it frustrated him that Magnus refused to tell him anything until the summit had concluded. The night of, when they returned to the inn, Magnus explained all he knew about the voidents. At least, Gareth hoped he had.

A giggle came from beside him, then a hand crept up his arm. He turned his head, making sure not to do it too fast.

"A little thirsty, are we?" a plump fairy barely clothed had asked. She looked at him, her rose-pink eyes shining in the warm orange light.

He glimpsed her empty cup; the rim stained the same color red as her lips. "Seems like we are."

She grinned, slid her hand up Gareth's torso, and gripped the gold strap across his chest. She yanked him down to her level. "Find me when you feel like leaving," she whispered into his ear. Like static, her warm breath caressed Gareth's skin and lingered after she let go. She walked away, hips swaying and wings fluttering, a new goblet in her hand.

Maybe it was the alcohol talking or the sudden discomfort his clothes brought, but Gareth had to stop himself from following the fairy. Instead, he watched her short stature disappear in the crowd and peered at the archway where Magnus and Ko were deep in conversation.

"My, my," another voice, deep this time, breathed from behind Gareth.

He whipped around, almost smashing right into the table and losing control of his cup. Luckily, a bit of wine had spilled on the ground rather than himself or the jerk in front of him. Gareth glared up from the dark red puddle on the stone, frowning. Malice had a rather amused look on his face.

Three clear markings over top of each other on Malice's forehead seized Gareth's attention. One was familiar as it was the one Magnus received the day of his coronation—a straight black line, a curved one above it, and a dot representing a person. Alcohol disrupted his thoughts. He could not recall the meaning. Then a *V* with a line across it that seemed like blood, though dried and cracked now. The third resembled a tent of four somewhat curved lines in white. Malice wore clothes as black as night, glinting gold claws decorating the back of his hands and fingers. His orange-kissed hair appeared trimmed, accentuating his sharp face.

Gareth put a bit more space between them. "Nice of you to finally show yourself." Eyes skyward, the half-moon was well above the tree line now. "Took you long enough," he said.

"Aw." Malice pouted his lips a bit. "Did someone miss me? How sweet," he said mockingly.

"Absolutely not."

Gareth scanned Malice from the top of his head to the tips of his shoes. Now that the shock had worn off, he noticed something off about his demeanor. It was as if he was proper, like a king, a ruler, and not just some brat. He stood a bit straighter because of it.

Gareth poked at his forehead and asked, "Did you get re-coronated or something? Didn't know that was a thing," he said the last part into his half-empty cup. The alcohol hit like a sack of rocks, and he puckered.

Malice laughed under his breath. "Something like that." He picked up a chalice, eddying the wine until it tempted the rim. "It's what happens when you step out of the shadows into the light, I suppose." He tilted his head at his drink.

"It's almost like being away from home for decades and returning out of the blue. You have to reintroduce yourself in a way," he said and returned his sights to Gareth.

"How does it feel to bask in the sun again?" Gareth asked. Malice's eyebrows shot up.

Staring for a few heartbeats, a humorless grin spread across his lips. "Bittersweet, like wine."

Gareth raised his goblet. "Cheers to your misery, then." Malice clinked his cup against Gareth's and the two of them chugged their wine till it was gone.

"You should go after her," Malice nodded in the direction the fairy left in before he set his drink down and grabbed another. Gareth also reached for another cup, but Malice blocked his hand.

"Trying to get me to leave?" he asked, knowing the urge to go after her was getting stronger by the second. Malice shrugged and said nothing, his hand still hovering over the chalice.

He sighed, "Fine," and threw up his hands, "I will go, but if anything happens to Magnus—"

"You'll have my head on a silver platter?" Malice inquired, cocking his head. "Good luck with that."

Grunting, Gareth smiled, checked on Magnus, who stood across from Ko, and turned, setting off to find the fairy. He doubted she had gotten too far or left. *I deserve to let loose, to give in to my desires... right? I've earned it.*

"Malice"

Malice shifted toward the table of alcohol, more irritated than tired. He licked his teeth and set the cup down.

The feast held in honor of his return was unnecessary and a waste of time. Over the past three days, he was reminded of one of the reasons he hated kingship. Malice reached up and glided his hand over one cheek to the other. He had smiled so much he thought his muscles would tear.

Malice spun on his heel and leaned against the edge of the table, gazing at the mass of gleeful faces dancing at the center of the courtyard. Lushes stumbled about with friends at their sides, and rulers blended in amongst their subjects. Roasted meat, fruit, and alcohol scented the subtle breeze. A few stray eyes met Malice's briefly, then words exchanged behind hands, openly, or directly into another's ear. Talk of his kingdom, no doubt, or his appearance. He didn't exactly fit in with such a cheerful gathering. *I look like death incarnated. As Eunice so kindly told me,* Malice snickered.

It was different here; the excitement toned down compared to Hordes Region, where his people were ready to burst with joy.

Just beyond the stage, Malice spotted Basia surrounded by women, men, and everything in between. She was more popular than he would have thought, considering how intimidating and burly she was. A dark elf fed her grapes off the vine when she turned her head while a human sipped from a goblet. They leaned forward and kissed Basia, dark red liquid pouring from the sides of her mouth.

Malice landed on Valentine in the corner, hiding in the shadows, chatting with someone, a chalice in their hands. They laughed, putting their hand on the chest of whoever they were talking to. Even from this distance, Malice could see their face and neck turn strawberry red.

Decimus and Surin stood by the tables of food, both absorbed in their discussion. Those two were as thick as thieves, had been for as long as Malice could remember.

If the other rulers were here, they were not in the courtyard. Malice couldn't imagine Violet or Yoon Woo enjoying the celebration. He thought the same for Ko, but near the entrance of the courtyard, where the shadows were their darkest, Magnus was talking to him. Malice frowned. Neither had a pleased expression on their face. Ko grumbled something and stomped away. Magnus stayed glaring after him, then let his shoulders drop a bit.

As Malice took a step forward, a big hand clamped down on his shoulder, dragging him into the dancing circle. He didn't realize the music had changed. The melody was fast-paced now and so was the dance following it.

In a series of spins and twirls, Malice and a robust orc danced on the outer edge of the circle. The orc's green skin was greener around his eyes and ears, and he stunk like a tavern, yet he was light on his feet and his touch gentle. They faced opposite directions, their right hands pressed flat together while their left was behind their backs, and the two cantered clockwise, then counterclockwise.

"Thanks for the dance, pretty lady," the orc said as he bowed and spun to meet his new partner and start all over again.

No wonder he was gentle with me.

Malice's next partner was a demon, her face obscured by a deer mask. She wasn't much shorter than him, but she was clumsy on her feet, missing beats, stepping on his toes. The demon seemed familiar. He looked down at her, the memory of a woman he'd met long ago suddenly flashing in his mind.

Hyacinthia?

It wouldn't be a problem if she were here since Eunice and Malice had returned to Hordes Region the moment they exited the castle. Eunice happily stayed behind as well, said she'd much rather spend the time with her wife.

"Why are you here, grandmother?" he asked quietly, his voice a soft rasp. Hyacinthia flinched, whipping her head to the side when Malice was flung deeper into the dance. She vanished from his sight, and he let it go.

The people around Malice were blurs. The music quickened once more as he changed partners, almost at the center of the dancing circle. He was glad this dance was about to end. A good swig of wine would cure his parched mouth and gullet, and the headache growing behind his eyes.

Again, Malice spun around and was caught while catching his next dancing companion. It was Magnus, his beauty in the warm light leaving him speechless for a time. The glisten in his eyes as they met Malice's, the gold shimmering on his lips and cheekbones—Malice couldn't tear his eyes away, but who would want to?

Magnus smiled. "I see you got wrapped up in this, too." Tightening his grip on Malice's hand, Magnus tugged his waist close.

"More like dragged." Malice chuckled a bit, his irritation melting like snow in the spring.

In the heart of the courtyard, they stopped dancing. Magnus's expression said that he had many questions he wished to ask. Malice would be more than happy to answer them, just not now. Not as the music turned to a hum and the people around them disappeared. Not as Magnus's warmth bled through Malice's clothes. Not as his hand traveled up and caressed Magnus's face before he nuzzled into it. He would talk after their lips touched and parted. They would talk after the greed of wanting more subsided.

Magnus's eyes were half closed for a split second. He looked around and grabbed Malice's hand, yanking him from the court. They weaved around people and the gap they left in the dancing circle was filled with elated faces. Magnus stopped at a table of food and started laughing when he cupped Malice's face, his thumbs rubbing his cheeks. He pressed his forehead into Malice's and mouthed something Malice couldn't make out, then righted himself again.

"I know where Caroline stashes the alcohol," Magnus said abruptly, a wild grin on his face.

"How?" Malice raised an eyebrow.

"Every now and again, I offer to help." He gestured to the courtyard. "Last year I followed a guard to the second floor into a cellar where there were crates upon crates of alcohol."

Malice smiled. "Shall we dance the night away with a bottle of wine in our hands?" he asked, entwining their fingers.

"Couldn't have said it better myself."

In the western wing on the second floor of the castle was a dimly lit cellar, labeled crates of alcohol stacked almost to the ceiling. Malice carried one of those crates so Magnus could lead the way to the fourth floor. Door after door, moonlight painted the floor and walls in a wan sapphire. There was a spiral staircase at the end of a long, quiet corridor. They scaled it, and Magnus opened the wooden latch, took, and slid the crate of wine across the stone floor, then climbed the rest of the way up. He offered Malice his hand and hoisted him up.

The tallest of the six towers oversaw everything. The noise below was almost mute, the air crisp. Clusters of stars in blue dust avoided the moon's light. The edge of Dun Raik was in sight, a dark, hard line meeting the softer shadow of land. In the distance, somewhere in the forest, an owl hooted. It reminded Malice of his old castle, the balcony he would go to every now and again to clear his head, escape from the life of a king.

Malice opened a bottle of red wine, taking a long draught, the earthy herbal wine going down smoothly, and propped himself on the wall of the tower. On the edge beside Malice, Magnus looked down at the glowing courtyard, his expression drawn taut as if his head were a whirlwind of thoughts and questions. It probably was.

"Did you get re-coronated to gather more forces?" Magnus asked. "To win those who were doubtful of your determination?"

Malice pushed off the wall and handed the bottle of wine to Magnus. "I did. Despite the fact that I never gave up my throne or power, there were quite a few who were concerned over whether I was truly here to stay or if I would leave when the going gets tough." As he peered at the bustling party, Malice chuckled. "Hypocritically speaking, that is exactly what I plan to do."

"Sincerely speaking, that's not at all what you plan to do."

Malice shrugged, a smile still on his face. "You have more to ask, don't you?"

"... Why didn't you tell me about Eunice?"

"I didn't think she was of concern," Malice said. "Besides, she didn't want to come, so I didn't think she would show." The scowl on Eunice's face when Malice invited her was hilarious, admittedly, but enough for him to believe she wouldn't attend the summit.

There was a lengthy silence between them, one that settled on Malice's shoulders like lead.

"I don't like that you kept me in the dark," Magnus finally said and turned to face Malice, the bottle of wine in his hand. "Compared to you, I am a child, ignorant and naïve. You have planned so much, everything it seems. I wouldn't doubt if you knew which kingdoms were to fall by the end of the war, but I don't know these things and I want to."

He swallowed. His eyes darted to the courtyard, then back to Malice. "I thought when you had returned that there would be no secrets between us."

Malice's eyebrows twitched. "There won't be. I have no good reason for keeping these things from you." He tried to produce a reason for not telling Magnus, yet nothing came to mind.

"Ask me anything."

"Where did you go the day I left for the summit?"

"I was here, in the Barren Circle," Magnus's eyebrows shot up, "collecting my things from the library to bring into the new kingdom." He had stored all important documents in the library underneath the castle before Hordes Kingdom was destroyed. It was the safest place of which he could think. It was also the only place he knew no one else, besides Magnus, knew existed.

Magnus took another swig of wine, some liquid dripping from the corner of his mouth, staining his shirt. He sighed heavily and turned away from Malice. "Now I truly feel like a child."

"Why is that?"

"I got so frustrated over the smallest of things. For a moment—" he hesitated, his brows furrowing. "I thought you were distancing yourself from me, that you would… disappear again."

Malice laughed, though he did so unintentionally. Magnus shot him a glare. "Me? Distance myself from you? Ludicrous. You've no idea how long I just wanted to be in your presence again. How many times I stared at nothing as I replayed the times we spent together in my mind, waiting for the chance to see you again."

Magnus's glare gave way to awe. His beautiful eyes were wide, and his gold-painted lips parted ever so slightly. Malice's heart fluttered, a chill racing through his body, and it all went numb. The moment he received Magnus's final letter crept from the corners of his mind. It was the storm that had capsized the boat, drowning the sailors, and leaving nothing when the seas calmed.

When Magnus set the bottle down and moved closer, Malice pushed the memory away. Magnus's warm hands glided down Malice's arms, lacing his fingers with his, bringing his hand up.

"Dance with me," Magnus said. He led them around the rooftop, their feet and the barely audible hum of music below falling into sync.

"Why do you wear a feather around your neck?" Malice asked. He no longer wanted to talk about himself.

Magnus, letting go of one of Malice's hands, plucked the feather out of his shirt and held it up while turning it in his fingers. "It's a tradition for angels to keep one of the feathers they shed during their first flight." Malice studied the feather of tan, white, and brown.

"My mother followed underneath as I flew over the plains, yelling and cheering me on. When I came down to land, I didn't know how. If it weren't for my mother catching me, I would've crashed." His eyes were downcast, his mouth a harsh line.

Malice had heard a great deal about Vesh and Padma from Magnus's letters. He wished he could have met them.

Tucking the feather into his shirt, Magnus smiled, the sadness vanishing, as he and Malice continued to dance.

It was well past midnight, the moon hovering over the western side of Dun Raik. Magnus and Malice talked endlessly, the conversation shifting from topic to topic.

The two of them now lay on their backs, star gazing, empty wine bottles all around them. The celebration beneath was still as rowdy as it was when he first arrived. Malice would bet any amount of coin that the cellar on the second floor was nearly empty, if not completely.

He sat up, a little sad he had to leave the ground, when the cold stone felt nice against the burning of his skin. Magnus followed, his face flushed from the wine. He stumbled to his feet and offered a helping hand to Magnus, hoisting him up. Magnus brought his hand to Malice's head, brushing his hair out of his face. Then his finger slid down to Malice's collarbone. The coldness of Magnus's hand against his hot skin made Malice shudder.

"Magnus," he said in a deep, raspy voice. "Do you fear me?" Magnus's eyes went wide.

"No." Magnus stepped forward, closing the little distance between them. "Your beauty, your power, have never been things I fear."

Malice's head cleared momentarily. The intensity of Magnus's eyes was something he couldn't look away from, as if it were forbidden to do so.

"I fear you will leave me behind, force me to watch you disappear beyond the horizon. I fear you will not let me stay by your side."

Malice smiled and closed his eyes. "As good as it is to be feared. From you, at least, it feels good to be loved."

"The moment you told me your name, I was ensnared in your trap. Even when you let me go, I couldn't help but search for you, long for you. Then you came back, and I had fallen so much deeper." He grabbed Malice's face, cupping his cheeks in his hands. "How could I be scared when I'm so completely infatuated with you, Malice?"

Malice's mouth parted in awe, his eyes wide as his ears became hot. He placed his hands over Magnus's and drew them off his face, cracked a smile, and laughed. Those who had loved him grew to fear him, detest him. It was something Malice expected from everyone, including Magnus, at some point. Yet here he was, telling Malice that he was infatuated with him.

"Magnus." A gentle breeze carrying the scent of moss, booze, and food swept through, pushing strands of Magnus's hair out of place. Malice carefully tucked them behind his ear. "I love you. Even before I knew what it was, I loved you. I loved you when you told me it was wrong, and I loved you when you wanted to hate me."

Magnus blushed, his eyes sparkling from the moonlight, his hands reaching for Malice's.

"I am," Malice heard the softness in his voice, surprised that it was his own, "so helplessly in love with you."

Lust
XXII

Hoovers Inn was a big concrete building with cherry wood beams and iron balconies on the front of it. A hearth, however, welcomed visitors with warmth, and a café wafted coffee and freshly baked pastries. The innkeeper gave Magnus and Gareth two rooms on the fourth floor, refusing to let him pay, as he had done every year.

Magnus and Malice, holding onto each other, stumbled as they ascended the stairs to Magnus's room. The innkeeper stayed behind them. Before they reached their door, he darted ahead, unlocked it, and waited for Magnus and Malice to enter before closing it behind them.

Magnus looked at the door, giggling, "What a funny man." His words were slightly slurred together.

They swayed and shuffled to the bed. Magnus fell onto the mattress, bounced a little. The room was dim, light from the streets and the moon soaking through the curtains. Malice wobbled around the bed to one of the lamps on the side tables—multiple jars on both of them—and climbed over to the other, the room lit. His shoes clacked on the green marble floors as he came back to Magnus, who was attempting to undress.

Malice watched, his green eyes steady on Magnus's flimsy fingers that were trying to undo the buttons of his shirt and corset. The dammed things were slipping from his fingertips as if they refused to be separated from the soft material around them. Eventually, Malice crouched down, sliding his hands in place of Magnus's.

"Let me help," Malice said and focused on the buttons, somewhat struggling himself—his nails kept getting in the way. His eyes narrowed when finally, the corset was unclipped, and the shirt hung open.

Malice gently tugged the corset from Magnus's waist, tossing it to the floor, his eyes fixed on his body. Magnus swallowed, wriggled out of his shirt, and let it rest behind him.

Just today, Malice was coronated, his clothes ornate, hidden detail of his region scattered about his attire; flowers embroidered in the fabric of his cloak, skulls stacked in vertical lines on his corset and neck piece, swords at the helms of his shirt and racing down the sides of his pants.

Magnus twirled his finger around, telling Malice to turn, and he did, his back now facing him. The cape, neckpiece, and lastly the corset, Magnus uncuffed every layer, Malice shrugging them off as Magnus helped pull them. With a wiggle of his shoulders, Malice's blouse fell to the ground.

His back was muscular, more so than the last Magnus had seen him shirtless, smooth, and warm, almost hot to the touch. Magnus traced the knots of muscle with his finger, landing on Malice's beauty mark. This was his second time facing it. Magnus got up and kissed his spine, his lips leaving smudges of gold.

"You look good in gold," Magnus noted when he glanced down at the golden claws decorating Malice's hands. Though he looked good in everything… or nothing at all. The thought of

Malice naked reminded Magnus of when they bathed together after the mission, the paleness of his wet skin, the curve of his waist and hips, the delicate nature of his hands moving across Magnus's body. Every sensation returned to his mind vividly. He shivered.

Malice turned too quickly as he reeled a bit, Magnus catching him by the arms. Malice smiled. "You look good in everything."

Magnus snorted a bit. "Tell me again," Magnus whispered and drew Malice even closer, leaving no space between them.

Malice raised an eyebrow, his eyes a dull glaze from the wine, his tone playful. "Tell you what? That I love you?"

Magnus nodded.

"I love you."

"Again." His heart pounded in his chest.

"I love you."

Malice repeated those three words like a chant, his voice deep and soft, each time causing Magnus's skin to prickle as he kissed Malice's neck. They were slow pecks, his lips pressing against the warmth of Malice's smooth skin, gold stains left in his wake.

"How long must you ignore my lips?" Malice asked, index finger trailing up from Magnus's torso to his collarbone to his chin.

Magnus smirked, tilting his head up. "Not long." He kissed Malice, his hands gliding from Malice's hips up to his arms, guiding them around his neck and shoulders.

Malice was exceptionally warm, most likely because of the alcohol. Opening his mouth, Magnus tasted the bittersweet wine on Malice's tongue as if he had just taken a sip of it. The sounds of the city settled, a low murmur of activity. Malice removed his arms from Magnus's shoulders so his hands could explore. His breath was heavier, drawn out, a raspy moan from the back of his throat filling Magnus's ears. Malice barely let Magnus catch his breath between kisses, their bodies squishing together.

Magnus pulled away, his chest rising and falling almost in rhythm with Malice's, heat fogging his mind like a cloud in summer. He brushed a few strands of hair that had gone loose out of Malice's face.

"Malice," he breathed. "There is no need to rush."

Malice's eyebrows twitched, then he nodded. "You're right… but kiss me anyway," he said and lured Magnus into another kiss. This time he didn't rush, the movement of his tongue more deliberate, his breath controlled.

Magnus's fingertips traveled tenderly along the curve of Malice's spine, against the muscles that would twitch every so often. He moved to Malice's torso. His muscles were firm, hard when flexed from years of diligent training. Magnus had watched how he trained a few times, watched the sweat bead on his skin and slip to the floor as he forced his body to remain absolutely still in poses Magnus could do, probably, but he would be as shaky as a leaf.

Magnus let his lips trail down Malice's neck, along his prominent collarbone, to his abs, his knees on the cool wood of the floor. He kissed the space between his groin and navel, the white hair fine and soft. Malice gasped.

"I never repaid you for what you did to me," he said, his voice breathy and quiet. Already unbuttoned and somewhat opened, Magnus hooked his underwear with his thumb, pulling Malice's pants down.

"You don't have to," Malice said while twirling a lock of Magnus's hair around his finger.

Magnus stared at the path of whiteness on Malice's lower torso, reminded of the light dusting of snow that came every year before winter would truly descend.

Locking eyes with Malice, "You don't want me to?" he asked.

Until now, it had been a game of restraint, but was there really a need for that anymore?

So many times, he had watched Malice undress, the pallor of his skin glowing in the light, and stemmed the urge to watch it flush from the heat their bodies shared. More often than not, it was just the two of them, talking. And as much as he could comprehend the words spilling from Malice's mouth, he could not ignore the sound of his moans whenever it returned to him. So many times, he had noticed juice shimmer on Malice's lips after eating, been reminded of his mouth around his cock, and craved the feeling of it again.

The memories fueled the desire pulsing through his veins, waves of summer heat washing over him.

Malice brushed Magnus's hair back. "I never said that." He tilted his head. "I just don't want you to do something because you feel you have to. I want you to want it."

Magnus chuckled as he gripped Malice's cock in between his thumb and index finger, kissing it down to the hilt. Moving his head, Magnus sucked, then leisurely glided down Malice's shaft and retreated, Malice groaning. Every movement of his head and mouth, every swirl of his tongue, was an emulation of what Malice had done to him. Those he had slept with wanted to get in the king's pants so badly that they refused to let him do much of anything. He went back and forth, hoping his sloppy technique would provide some enjoyment for Malice.

His cock was hard, twitching when Magnus withdrew for air. Malice's breathing had quickened a bit, his ears and cheeks a little red. Although, Magnus wasn't sure if that was from the alcohol or pleasure.

Magnus swallowed Malice as much as his mouth and throat would allow. He gasped as Magnus's throat clenched. *At least he likes it, or perhaps my technique isn't half bad.* He wondered how Malice could take in all of him without gagging. Tears stung his eyes as he moved, his rhythm much faster now.

Gripping his hair, Malice moaned. Magnus paused briefly. That wasn't the first time he had heard Malice moan, but it certainly was not that loud or pronounced. A single shiver ran down his body before Malice toppled onto the edge of the bed, one arm catching himself, the other catching the back of Magnus's head.

The stiffness in Magnus's pants made them uncomfortable. He gripped Malice's thighs, his head becoming fuzzy.

Legs trembling, Malice pushed Magnus's head away. Magnus closed his eyes and turned simultaneously, warmth splattering his face. After a second, Malice released Magnus's hair, got off the bed, and wiped his face clean.

Magnus grabbed his hands and kissed his palms. "It's fine." Malice seemed disappointed, as if he were upset that it ended so soon. It was rather adorable and humorous.

"Get on the bed," Malice commanded when he glanced down at Magnus and smirked. Something changed. His eyes were steady, hungry, and his demeanor fierce.

The bed creaked as Magnus pulled himself onto the edge while Malice padded to the nightstand on the right, grabbing the longest of three bottles. He came around to the foot of the bed, the bottle in Malice's hand filled with oil. He pushed Magnus down, his plump chest giving into his fingers, his hand sliding down to Magnus's trousers where he uncuffed them. Sharp eyes fixated on Magnus's, the vibrant green shimmering in the lamp's light. Malice gently pulled his pants and underwear off, throwing them across the room.

Despite his gentleness, Malice seemed impatient, like it was taking everything to stop himself from devouring Magnus. He felt a lump form in his throat and swallowed it.

Pushing one knee up against his body, Malice put the other leg over his shoulder. His eyes slithered down. Magnus's body flushed as he looked away, too embarrassed to watch what he was about to do.

"Tell me if you want to stop," in between giving pecks to Magnus's calf, Malice's voice was kind and caring.

He grabbed the jar, and it popped open. The cold oil made Magnus flinch, the smell of lavender and honey wafting toward him. His hands started trembling, so he balled them into fists, pressed them into the blankets. Anxiety had settled in the pit of his stomach. He'd done this to others, but no one dared do it to him and he had never asked for it.

When his leg was moved from Malice's shoulder, Magnus opened his eyes. Malice solemnly let go of his other leg and straightened himself, letting Magnus sit up.

"I told you," Malice said quietly. "I don't want you to do something because you feel you have to." He lovingly caressed the side of Magnus's head, "I want you to want it," and moved forward to straddle his legs.

"I apologize for scaring you," he said, guiding Magnus by the jaw into a kiss.

His lips were soft and warm. They parted, leaving a need for more. Gazing into Malice's eyes, feeling his breath caress him, Magnus remembered the first time they had kissed, and the desperation in his hands as they explored his body. The desperation behind his every action, as if he'd never get the chance again. A similar look showed in his expression, but it was tempered.

Magnus wanted to bring it back.

Their lips collided and opened, their heavy breaths hot, their tongues mingling without a sense of hurry. Malice bit Magnus's lip as he tilted his head up. Magnus gasped. One of Malice's hands started fondling his chest, his finger teasing his nipple. Before he could say anything, Malice rushed in, his kisses inexorable.

Five snaps, one after the other, came from their left. Magnus didn't know what it was and didn't care. It was subtle over the sounds they were making. Malice stroked their cocks together, slow and tender, his hand going over every twitchy vein. Magnus's nipple was already hard and sore from his teasing, but the pulsing heat was better than he thought it would be. Malice allowed Magnus to catch his breath, moving his lips down to Magnus's neck and shoulder.

The oil in between them and their hands made wet squelching noises, the lewd sound alluring now that he could hear it over their moans. He twitched. Magnus grabbed and squeezed Malice's shoulders, his voice drawn out, the pleasure flowing through his body like a rising tide.

"Malice," Magnus moaned in his ear and suddenly he stopped, leaving Magnus's body spasming and the sparks of pleasure dying. He blinked, mouth hanging open.

"Why… did you stop?" he asked. Malice turned his head away from Magnus's shoulder, a devious grin on his gold-stained lips.

"I want you to want it," he repeated. "I want you to need it so much that you beg me to fuck you." He chuckled softly, kissing Magnus's neck as he did.

That's what he meant? Malice grabbed both of his knees after pushing Magnus onto his back and pressed them to his chest.

"Wait, a moment." Magnus wiggled to see beyond his knees. Malice's warm breath hit him. He shuddered.

"Can't you just use your fingers?" he pleaded with a slight crack in his voice. Malice ignored him, plunging his tongue deep inside. Magnus threw his head into the bed, gasping, his heart beating in his ears. *Did his tongue just get longer? How?*

"Your tongue—" Magnus said, a groan consuming the rest of his words before they could form.

Malice squirmed and wiggled inside. He dragged it out, gradually, leaving Magnus shivering.

"Does it satisfy you?" he asked, licking the corner of his mouth, smiling.

Magnus's entire body felt as if it was engulfed in flames, he was so hot. "Just use your fingers."

Silent for a moment, Malice tilted his head. "Is that what you truly want?" His eyes stayed on Magnus's. "Because I don't think it is. You like my technique and how I move inside you, don't you?"

Magnus blinked.

"I won't continue unless you answer me, my king."

Sighing, Magnus tossed his head to the side and bit his lip. He reluctantly met Malice's unwavering gaze once more. "I like it," he said, his voice hushed.

Malice shoved his tongue in, moving it erratically, leaving nothing untouched.

"Please," Magnus begged into the sheets. His ass was up, his chest buried in the bed, and his hands tangled in the blankets.

They had changed positions, but that was a while ago now, he thought. Malice's tongue was still inside him, jerking all about while he played with his cock, his thumb teasing the tip. Peeking toward the balcony, the first rays of sunlight colored the curtains.

"Let me come." Every time he was on the brink of orgasm, Malice would rein him in. Alcohol no longer muddled his mind. Instead, ecstasy took over, numbing his reason and drowning him.

"I want you to fuck me. Please." The rise of pleasure he had felt so many times was coming again, surging to the surface. "Please." Magnus stifled his voice in the sheets, hoping Malice wouldn't notice.

"Good boy."

Magnus's cock pulsed, his body trembling and spasming, his moans long and breathy but muffled.

His head was blank even as Malice brought him up by the shoulder, turning him around so they faced each other. Then, bracing Magnus against him, Malice reached for the oil and poured it over Magnus's lower back.

The cold snapped Magnus into reality and he inhaled. "You tease." He allowed Malice to maneuver his legs and body since his strength was gone. Magnus was sitting on his lap now, hovering over him.

"More," Malice uttered, a growl at the back of his throat, and nipped Magnus's ear lobe. He started squirming underneath him, the oil making Magnus slippery. "Give me more."

The choice words that first sprang to his mind died. Malice begging… was something Magnus might get addicted to if Malice did it any longer.

Magnus reached behind him, arched his spine a bit, and gradually sank onto Malice. When he could go down no further, he let go of the breath he was holding, Malice shuddering underneath him. It was almost suffocating how deep he was.

Malice was careful, his pelvis moving in purposeful thrusts. The sensation wasn't pleasurable, but it wasn't painful, and Malice was patient—for that, he was grateful, since it gave him a chance to adjust to Malice's length—his head against Magnus's chest.

As he slid out, he grazed something that made Magnus shiver uncontrollably for a split second. He looked at Malice, confused, when Malice smiled and licked his lips. Magnus knew that smile.

"Wait," he said, his nerves clawing at his throat. Malice did.

"Would you like to stop?" he asked.

Magnus shook his head and exhaled.

"Then," Malice kissed his chest, "what would you like me to do? Tease you? Change positions? Ram my cock inside you? Or would you like it if I were to receive you instead?" He dragged his tongue along Magnus's skin, kissing it down to his nipple, his teeth scraping against him. Magnus shivered.

"You know what I want," Magnus answered. *Please, don't make me say it aloud again.*

"I do, but I want to hear it, nonetheless."

"... Be as rough with me as I was with you in the shower."

He grabbed Magnus, lifting him just enough so he could move his legs out from under him. "As you wish," he said, gripping Magnus's ass as Magnus wrapped his arms around Malice's neck.

Malice started pounding Magnus. Their skin smacked together with every thrust, the bed squeaking in unison, and sounds Magnus never knew he could make were pouring out of his mouth. He wondered if those in the rooms next to them could hear him moan. If Gareth could hear him. Magnus unwrapped an arm from Malice's neck and covered his mouth, hoping it wasn't too late to keep his voice down.

Frowning, Malice stopped moving and kissed the back of Magnus' hand. "Every time you withhold your voice from me," Malice said, "I'll stop."

Reluctantly, Magnus moved his hand away from his mouth and wrapped his legs around Malice, grinding into him. "Fuck me."

A mischievous grin appeared before he started thrusting mercilessly into Magnus. He was faster and harder, his hips moving differently, bursts of pleasure crashing into Magnus's body.

Face to face with Malice, Magnus found watching his expression contort in ecstasy, intoxicating. To see someone who was usually controlled, unbothered, and calm, disheveled, and begging for something, Magnus felt drunk all over again. He shuddered and tugged Malice into a kiss, their hot breath becoming one, saliva spilling from their mouths, creating a sloppy mess. His body smothered Malice, their chests slipping against each other from sweat. Malice cursed under his breath as they parted lips, panting, his voice getting raspy.

"Magnus," Malice said, letting his head fall onto Magnus's chest, "You need to get off."

Magnus felt it too, but didn't want to move just yet. He enjoyed watching Malice squirm underneath him. Then he rose just in time as he orgasmed, his back curving. Malice immediately stroked Magnus's cock until he convulsed and shuddered.

They stayed like that for a time, Magnus straddling Malice, panting and damp. Magnus, glancing to his side, smiled at the brightness of the window. The sounds of a busy town were like a hum beyond the walls.

"How long till we have to return?" Malice asked, a bit breathless yet, disappointment underlying his tone.

Magnus thought for a second. "Tomorrow."

After kissing Magnus's forehead, Malice got up and went over to the dresser, opening every drawer until he grabbed small cloths to clean himself and Magnus.

Magnus stayed on the bed, reaching behind him, and wiping Malice's semen off his back. It was thick and sticky as he rubbed it in between his fingers, pulling them apart every now and again.

The few lovers Magnus had had paled in comparison to Malice. He looked at Malice's reflection in the mirror, staring at his face, gold shimmering in random places. He must've brought quite a few people into his bed seeing how good he was. Magnus frowned. A flicker of jealousy stirred, and he got up, grabbing the bottle of oil that somehow stayed on the bed.

He walked to Malice and quietly set the bottle of oil on the dresser as his other hand crept up Malice's arm and shoulder. He was warm and sweaty, scented with lavender from the oil. Closer he stepped, so they were skin to skin, his hand traveling around to Malice's front.

"I thought you would have wanted a break," Malice said.

Magnus shook his head, his hair tickling Malice's neck. "How could I leave this divine feast standing in front of me alone?" he said before his teeth grazed the bend of Malice's shoulder and the base of his neck. Though truth be told, Magnus didn't know when they could indulge in each other's presence like this again, so he wanted to savor every moment.

He grabbed the oil and poured it over Malice's backside. With one hand, he squeezed and pulled Malice's cheek, the other teased him. As he shoved his finger inside, squirming it out, Magnus pressed himself against Malice once more. His body molded to Malice's, their sweat gliding and mixing. He was sure Malice could feel his poorly controlled breathing and his heart pounding in his chest. In slow, deliberate thrusts, Magnus rubbed against Malice, unsure of how much longer he could restrain himself.

Hands gripping the edge of the dresser, Malice moaned softly when Magnus added another finger and kissed his neck, played with his chest. He was getting restless, his patience wearing thin. Magnus shoved a third finger in, surprising Malice, and he gasped. He wondered how Malice could wait so long, how he could continue to tease someone without losing composure.

Magnus sucked and kissed a spot on the top of Malice's shoulder, retreating just in time to see a red mark vanish. That happened last time, too. He removed his fingers, turned Malice around, and just as quickly lifted him onto the dresser. Malice raised an eyebrow. Magnus kissed him, deep and hard, the head of his cock pestering him.

Malice reeled, wet lips glistening. "Where'd all this confidence come from?" The tip of Malice's nail dragged along Magnus's delts, his expression a mix of amusement and yearning.

Magnus paused and looked away. "This is what I know. I've never… been on the receiving end." He wouldn't have been against the idea if it were ever presented to him, but he wasn't entirely comfortable with it, either.

Until now, with Malice.

"Was it good?" Malice asked.

Head snapping up, Magnus locked onto Malice's gaze. "Yes, of course it was. I would have told you to stop if I didn't like it."

Malice shifted, leaning slightly to kiss his ear. "I'm glad."

Breath tickling Magnus, he shuddered. "… Are *you* all right with this?"

"Do you think I'd still be sitting here if I wasn't?"

"I suppose not, but let me know if you change your mind." Experiencing penetration first-hand, Magnus knew the discomfort that came with it as much as he knew the pleasure that came afterward.

"I doubt I will," Malice chuckled.

Their conversation was short and sweet before their lips locked together again. And that was fine. They could talk later.

Malice slipped his warm tongue into Magnus's mouth, his moans escaping in between breaths. Magnus guided his cock into Malice and thrust. He groaned, gripping Magnus's back. Not too fast, but not too slow. Magnus kept his pace consistent. The dresser creaked like the bed and hit the wall, a steady beat of thuds.

"Faster," Malice moaned as he tried to wiggle his hips back and forth, opposite to Magnus's thrusts.

Magnus forced his hands underneath Malice, hoisted him up, turned, and stomped to the bed. Carefully, Magnus laid him down, put his hands on Malice's knees, and rammed himself deep inside Malice. Magnus retreated sluggishly, then roughly slammed into him again.

Magnus enjoyed the view below him, Malice twitching, squirming underneath him as his cock drove him mad, his claws gripping the bedsheets, his rich voice filling the room. It was better than he could have ever imagined.

Gods, he's beautiful.

Malice brought his arms up and wrapped them around Magnus. "Harder." His fingers sank into his skin, the tips of his nails pressing down like the tip of a needle on either side of his spine.

Magnus put Malice's legs over his shoulders and supported himself with his arms. Malice appeared ravenous, starving for more. He asked for it and he shall receive it.

Deeper, harder, he shoved his cock in and slid out. Malice tightened and clenched down on Magnus, and he gasped as pleasure exploded and overwhelmed him. *He's incredible.* Magnus couldn't peel his eyes off Malice. He had said it earlier, but he truly was divine. He couldn't get enough of him. The way his sweat-soaked hair stuck to his shimmering skin, his deep moans raspy and desire-filled, his slender, muscular body shivering. *And I did that to him.*

He moved down after switching positions, his chest pressing against Malice's back. "I love you," he breathed.

Every fiber in his being longed for Malice right now. He was happy, giddy, excited, intoxicated with Malice, an insurmountable pleasure consuming him. *He's mine as much as I am his. How did I get so lucky? What did I do to deserve this? I don't even care what I did. I'll bask in him for as long as possible.*

Silent Goodbye
XXIII

A warm gentle breeze came from the open balcony windows, making the curtains flow, the smell of freshly baked pastries, grass, and rock filling the room. It sounded as if the door clicked when Magnus took a deep breath and allowed his eyes to flutter open. Malice wasn't beside him, and then he was with a silver tray of food and tea. He set the platter down before gently brushing tousled hair out of Magnus's face. Malice kissed his forehead and smiled.

"Good morning," he whispered.

Magnus propped himself up, sliding to sit against the headboard, the wood cold against his bare back.

"Good morning." Magnus smiled, his eyes wandering Malice's body as if it were a map. His hair was a mess if he had ever seen one and gold covered his skin, either in streaks from sweat or smudges from Magnus's lips, memories of their bodies entwined, bringing a rush of heat to his veins.

Magnus picked up a strawberry and took in the contents of the tray. Peeled and sliced peaches were next to bowls filled with steaming oatmeal sprinkled with cinnamon, sugar, and blueberries. A small pitcher of orange juice and a teapot, a small jar of sugar cubes, and honey beside it. On the edge of the tray were four slabs of toast. Dark blueish purple jam coated them. The slices of ham were also steaming.

Malice poured them both a cup of hot black tea. From the smell, it seemed to be Kamin tea from Florence's Region in the south, slightly fruity, and full-bodied yet smooth. Coffee was too rich for Magnus's blood, too bitter even with sugar. The first time he drank some, he nearly bounced off the walls for hours until he crashed.

"I'm still amazed you can walk silently," Magnus said after swallowing and grabbing a peach slice. Although now that he was thinking about it, Malice made sound the night of the celebration when they returned to the inn. Undoubtedly because he was drunk.

Malice took a sip of tea, then set the cup down. "It's an unconscious habit now, but it was difficult to keep up at first," he said, plucking a blueberry from the oatmeal and popping it in his mouth.

"You keep an extremely thin layer of magic underneath your feet, right?" Magnus closed his index finger and thumb, trying to leave barely a hair strand of width between them.

Malice nodded. "It's a technique all assassins know. Your royal knight, Vinney, was it? He should know how to walk silently." A bit of blackberry jam got on his upper lip. Magnus wiped it off with his thumb, Malice's lip soft and supple.

"He does." Thumb to his mouth, the jam was sweet.

When Magnus glanced at Malice, he was staring, his body very still before he took a deliberate bite out of his toast.

After the tray was empty of food, Malice went out to the balcony to take in the fresh air. The golden light of morning made his white hair almost glow.

The clock ticked on the dresser as Magnus went over the details of the summit. He would give aid to the other regions if necessary, but as he told his fellow rulers, he would protect his own first and foremost and that they should do the same. Everyone had agreed.

Four months to prepare for war was not a lot of time and there was so much to do it felt overwhelming. In just a few hours, everything would become hectic between training, informing his nobles, creating shelters, building battlements, and so on.

One of the biggest issues, Magnus thought, was the lack of healers. More than just a handful of royals lost their interest in the practice after Pich's death. With Pich's books and journals, Magnus would have to force his royals to at least learn the basics. If Malice could do it, they most certainly could.

He tilted his head against the headboard and released a long, drawn-out breath, the tension in his shoulders fleeing.

Malice, stretching, walked into the room, his eyes going from Magnus to the clock on the nightstand. His expression soured a bit as he went to the opposite side of the bed, crawled onto the covers, and laid his head on Magnus's thighs.

"I must return to Hordes Region," he said in a level tone. "I have much to do."

Magnus smiled or tried to, but he found it difficult. "I know." He reached over and grabbed Malice's hand, giving it a tight squeeze. "We all do." He glanced outside to the bright blue sky as sparse white fluffs floated southward.

"I must prepare myself and my royals for the change about to crash down on us. Time is limited but, it will be enough." At least, he hoped it would be. Magnus peeked down at Malice, his eyes focused on their hands and interlocked fingers.

"Our company will be short," Malice said. "The nights will get longer as winter settles in, though."

"You plan to visit me at night?"

"Is that a problem?" Malice looked up through his long eyelashes. He was calm, lethargic even, like a cat.

"… No," he answered hesitantly. "I just thought you would be too busy. I don't want you putting more stress on yourself if you don't have to." Was he reassuring Malice or himself? At this point, he didn't know, but he didn't want to let go yet and tightened his grip on Malice's hand.

"Besides, I'm too slow to make it to Hordes Region without having to turn back right away."

"Hmm," Malice grumbled. "I'll arrive at dusk, and I'll make it to the kingdom around mid-morning."

"You don't plan to come every night, do you?"

"I'm not particularly fond of the idea of not seeing you as often, so I'd like to."

Magnus knew he was fast, but he didn't think he was that fast. Hordes Kingdom and Alucard's Kingdom were at opposite ends of the continent, like two ends of a string, they couldn't be further from each other. If Malice were to fly from his region to Magnus's, spending the entire night here, when would they sleep? Or get the work that wasn't done during the day finished? As much as Magnus appreciated the gesture, it would be too much.

"I'll help where I can while I'm here if you need it," he said. "But if I'm being honest, I'd much rather keep you up at night doing other things." A smirk now rested on his lips.

Magnus snorted. "I'd rather spend our time doing anything but work if it can be helped."

Heartbeats passed, silence settled between them, and Malice's smile faded. He was unusually quiet for a while, his expression blank until he eventually said, "What did you and Ko talk about the night of the celebration?"

Magnus, a bit surprised, glanced down at him. "He warned me, said that I would come to regret siding with you."

"How so?"

"He said that you're dangerous."

"I am," Malice said.

"That you're cunning."

"I'm inclined to believe that as well."

"… That you would come to betray me."

"…"

Anger flashed on Malice's face, a ripple of muscle in his jaw, his hand gripping Magnus's briefly. "I would never do such a thing."

"I know," Magnus said, his tone gentle. And he did. He believed Malice would never betray him, if not for his own experience, for the love they share.

"I would never impose that feeling on you," Malice added, something in his tone that Magnus couldn't quite recognize.

Magnus's heart strained, a subtle throb behind the cage of his ribs. Many had betrayed Malice, the first being his own mother. Vendetta, the former Queen of Hordes Region, attempted to kill Malice many times, but she was simply the first on the list. Magnus reached across his lap to caress Malice's head, twisting a lock of Malice's hair around his finger.

"We argued for a short while," Magnus said. "Until he realized that my mind could not be changed. I will stand with you for as long as you allow me."

Eyes closing, Malice brought Magnus's hand to his lips, his breath hitting his skin. "As I with you."

Sitting up and shifting, Malice moved forward, gently pushing his lips into Magnus's. Their mouths parted, and slowly, greedily, their kiss deepened. Malice seemed desperate, like this was their final kiss. Magnus would have liked it had the kiss not felt like an unspoken goodbye. Like the past few nights together were their last. Still, he savored every gasp and the breathlessness they shared, until no more time could be spared.

Proposal
XXIV

From the kitchen to the living room, Ida paced and chewed her nails. She wore her finest clothes that she'd bought the day before yesterday for the Ceremony of Royals.

A week ago, during training, a servant from the castle handed out letters from the king. Ida had also received an envelope sealed with dark blue wax in the shape of a sun. Impatiently, like many others, she ripped it open and read the contents. Ida would receive a higher rank, but the letter said nothing else. At first, the excitement was overwhelming, but it didn't last long as anxiety descended into the pit of her stomach.

Now Ida waited for Laci, who liked to take her sweet time getting ready. Finally, after what seemed like hours, she came hopping down the staircase. Her outfit was far too simple for the amount of time it took for her to put it on. An open-chested shirt with thick silver edges, diamonds, and snowflakes in the corners of the collar. Over her shoulders, silver cuffs clipped a white shawl onto her shirt. A dark grey wrap decorated in the same diamonds and snowflakes on Laci's shirt was around her waist. Her pants were the grey of her wrap, her boots black.

Ida looked her friend up and down, rolled her eyes and, turning to the door, scoffed.

Laci stomped toward Ida. "What's that reaction for?"

"It took you that long to dress yourself?" She scowled over her shoulder. "We might be late because of you." Being late for training was one thing, being late for the Ceremony of Royals was another.

"Oh please," Laci sounded exasperated. "You're too stressed about this. You're getting promoted. What's there to worry about? Shouldn't you be celebrating?"

Laci was here not for the glory that came with the title of royal, she was here for the money. Laci was from a poor family, barely having a roof over her head for most of her childhood. She told Ida she didn't want to live like a pig stuck in a pen, taking whatever it could to survive. Not because it wanted to, but because it had to. Money was as good of a reason as any other in Ida's book, but her lack of care sometimes grated on her nerves to no end.

Ida knew she was right as they reached the door and rushed out. Red, orange, and yellow leaves covered the ground, crunching under their feet. The air was crisp and refreshing. She had been worrying over her rank for the past week. It affected her work because she couldn't focus. Her mind constantly ran back to her promotion. But why was she getting promoted? Ida asked herself that time and time again. She had gone on local missions in Alucard's Kingdom and was training just like the other royals. Nothing she had done over the past two years warranted another promotion, at least not in her mind.

Ida marched on while Laci struggled to keep up with her pace.

Eventually falling into her stride, Laci said, "You look nice, you know."

Ida considered Laci, her eyebrow raised. She wore a leather cross lattice top, a single gold diamond on her bust. The brooch she received when she became a royal guard was pinned to her left breast, over her heart. Fitted black pants and dark maroon belts sat on her waist and hips, holding her sword and waterskin. Her worn boots came above her knees, the straps going from the inside to the outside flapping as she walked.

"You do!" Laci insisted. "It's not often you look… presentable."

Ida couldn't help but smirk because, once again, she was right. Ida was usually covered in sweat and dirt or wearing armor on patrol. She bumped her shoulder into Ida. Smiling, Ida returned it.

The castle's front courtyard had rows of dark wooden chairs. Laci patted Ida's shoulder, gave her a wink, and sat in the back where most seats were empty. Chatter echoed throughout the courtyard. Too many conversations drifted into Ida's ears for her to discern any topics. The castle loomed over her, more than she remembered from last year. She had always seen the castle's gold, white, and blue exterior from afar, admiring it from the outskirts of the kingdom, hoping one day she could set foot on the castle's grounds. She was not disappointed when she did last year. Banners waved on either side of the grand doors, the region's insignia, a sun with three sets of wings and an eye at the center.

Down the middle aisle to the front row of chairs closest to the grand marble steps, Ida somehow felt out of place, like eyes pierced her bones whenever they landed on her. Her throat became scratchy and her mouth dry. The aisle was getting longer the further she walked. Sweat dampened her palms, Ida bunched them at her sides so no one would see.

The six royal knights of rank S stood on the stairs, three on each side. Sir Gareth was positioned at the bottom of the left side, Lady Marris to the right on the stair above. Sir Arthur, then Sir Vinney and the last two, Ida didn't recognize. One was slim, almost bony, and aloof. Their skin was pale like they hadn't seen the sun for decades, their cheeks and eyes hollowed in a blueish-grey color. Their clothes—a long-sleeved shirt and trousers—were black, slightly baggy, and the simplest of the knights standing on the stairs. The other, standing on the right top stair, was a short woman, a dwarf with pale brown curly hair. She seemed kind, like she couldn't hurt a fly, but the battle axe reflecting the sunlight on her back suggested otherwise. She wore leather from head to toe, wrapping around her body in different directions.

Ida took one of two open seats when she reached the first row. The ones beside her greeted her, returning their attention to the front of the castle.

The arched double doors stayed closed for a while until they suddenly parted for the king. His clothes were lavish, adorned with various blues and gold while his cape, flowing behind him, was as black as a raven. Resting on his brow was a crown of gold feathers, eyes within the feathers. Each step the king took, the louder Ida's heart pounded in her ears.

She sucked in a breath, held it for a moment, and let it go. In her lap, she picked at her cuticles, then peeked up. She flinched. Even if it was brief, she thought she and the king had locked eyes, and that he had smiled. He probably smiled at everybody sitting in front of him. *Get it together.*

King Magnus stopped on the last step and looked upon his subjects, an air of grace about him. Behind the king, a servant followed, trying to stay inside the king's shadow until they reached Sir Gareth, handing him a long reddish-brown box. They bolted inside the castle. The courtyard went silent. He gave a short and sweet speech, although Ida hardly caught any of it.

With a courteous smile, the king started calling the royals in the front row. Her leg bounced like it didn't know how to do anything else. A royal got to one knee, their head lowered and rose. After Sir Gareth opened the box the servant gave him, the king secured a brooch to their left breast underneath the others.

Ida tore her nails down to the bed.

All the knights wore pins. Sir Gareth had four, Lady Marris six, the slim one had ten. Each brooch represented the promotion and the rank they received. Royal Guards received silver badges, Royal Knights got gold. The rank also determined the design of the brooch. Glancing down at hers, Ida pushed it up with her thumb. Two feathers crossed each other, a sword down the middle, and an eye at the center, the silver as shiny as the day King Magnus pinned it on her.

The person next to Ida rose, taking her attention off her brooch, and marched to the king, bowing before the last step.

"Yosef Clarkson," the king announced, "Royal Guard rank D is hereby promoted to rank B." The courtyard erupted into applause and cheers as it had for all the others.

After taking his seat, the person to Ida's left was called upon. "Yennefer Clarkson." Ida peeked at the guard, only now seeing the resemblance between the two. However, Yennefer looked a few years older. "Royal Guard rank A. You have been promoted—with the recommendations of many knights—to a Royal Knight rank E." Her brother huffed, folding his arms over his chest, while everyone else hooted and hollered.

Dainty clouds passed over the sun, a salty draft caressing Ida's skin. She shivered. Yennefer took her place next to Ida, fondling the new shiny brooch on her shirt. Except for the fact that it was gold, the design was the same for a rank E Royal Guard. Ida, assuming that was the one she would get to, swallowed the dryness in her mouth, not that it helped.

She was the last to be called, and her mind was racing. She knew what to expect, yet she didn't at the same time. What if there was a mistake, and she was about to be demoted? Or completely dismissed? Ida's stomach dropped, a sudden wave of nausea hitting her, the world spinning.

"Royal Guard Ida Ravish," the king said at last.

Ida took a deep breath, hoping it was enough to gather her senses and not make a fool out of herself. She rose, each step forward like walking through thick sludge until she bent down to one knee. Something about the king differed from last year. His presence wasn't as warm or kind. He felt… intimidating… like Malice.

"You have achieved a magnificent feat, Lady Ida." Ida kept her head down as her eyes went wide. "Not only have you gained compliments from nearly every knight,"—Despite being on the ground, her knees felt like they would give out any moment—"you have caught the eye and earned praise from a fellow ruler."

Whispers washed over the crowd. Nothing she could make out, but she knew exactly who he was talking about. Everyone that had been in the coliseum while she trained did too.

"Therefore, Ida Ravish, you are hereby promoted to Royal Knight rank B."

At first, the crowd was stationary and quiet like the calm before a storm. Ida couldn't believe her ears.

"Rise," the king said in a low tone.

She stood, the shock refusing to wear off. He smiled when Ida met his gaze and pinned the brooch to her shirt just below the first one. As he leaned forward, the difference in their heights became non-existent thanks to the stair he was standing on, and whispered in her ear, "Malice is expecting great things from you."

He said one more thing, "He is also looking forward to a change in your answer the next time you meet." He pulled away, clapping with the rest of the royals.

Not knowing what to say, Ida dipped her head and started toward her seat. On the right side of the aisle, a few familiar faces caught her eye. Sir Barbus had his fingers in his mouth, whistling. It was a surprise to see that he had lost his gut, even more of a surprise to see that Sir Lycn had lost his arm. She was glad both seemed to be doing well and were training again. Sir Lucas sat beside Sir Lycn, his face covered by a deep red mask, a coin-sized sunflower embedded in the forehead like a third eye. It was simple and framed his face perfectly. From the back dangled red beads, silver stars, and a tuft of red string at the bottom. He was quieter now, more reserved. It was as if he and Sir Lycn had switched personalities.

Ida sat down and Yennefer punched her shoulder, grinning, giving her a thumbs up. She smiled her thanks, but her mind was elsewhere.

Malice had said nothing the last time he was here a few days ago, so she thought he didn't know about the ceremony. That prick was probably wearing a devilish smirk right about now, wherever he was. The corner of her mouth curved slightly, then fell as she sighed.

All the anxiety that curdled her gut; what was it for? Nothing felt different. Matter of fact, she felt underwhelmed, expecting some sort of excitement to spark a fire in her, get her blood flowing. This was an achievement not even Sir Gareth had accomplished at her age—Ida should be swelled with pride and joy, yet something was lacking.

I'm greedy, both she and Malice had proclaimed months ago. Staring at her open palms, callused and dirt-stained, she wondered if this wasn't enough for her. If it wasn't, what else was there to grab onto?

I should just be content with this. It's more than I could have asked for, anyway.

"Almost as soon as I returned from the Kings Summit," the king said, snatching Ida's attention, "the training regimen changed drastically." His voice and face were stern as his gaze swept the courtyard.

"If you had questions, they were shot down or ignored. But now, I'm going to answer them. Unless you have been living under a rock, you should have heard by now about the voidents and their attacks."

There was a subtle tingle growing in Ida's hands, slowly traveling up her arms.

"They only stopped because of a deal made by another ruler. The truce, however, will only last until the first snowfall. On that day, war will erupt across the entirety of Vinyamar."

Murmurs and gasps spread like wildfire through the crowd. The knights on either side of the king, however, seemed unbothered. They must have been briefed about it beforehand.

"We are going to fight. Fight for our family, for our friends and lovers, for our land."

Anticipation fluttered in Ida's stomach.

"The training regimen I implemented is similar to the greatest fighting regions on the continent."

Ida wondered if Malice extended a helping hand in the creation of the new regimen. Some techniques being taught closely resembled a few of the things Malice had already shown her, so it would make sense.

"We have little time, but I have faith in my royals. We will rise with the times. We will charge the enemies and emerge victorious!"

Royals jumped from their seats, cheering and yelling battle cries. Ida remained seated, keeping a close eye on the king, watching his face relax into a small smile. He turned up the stairs and vanished within the castle while the knights gave orders, directing the chaos.

Now that the ceremony had concluded, it was tradition to feast in the castle's dining hall. Last year, Ida had felt as though she wasn't worthy enough to set foot in the castle, so she left before anyone could drag her along.

As she looked at her palms once more, excitement surged from the tips of Ida's toes to the top of her head. More than it ever had. This was what she wanted, a chance to be triumphant, to go headlong into battle and win, to prove herself. The missions she'd had thus far were simple, easy. But now, she thought she knew why Malice advocated for her promotion. Change was imminent and someone would have to be a fool to let themselves get caught up in the swirling tide of it all. Ida was no fool; Malice taught her that much. The opportunity given to her would not be taken lightly.

*

It had been a month since her promotion and winter had started to bare its fangs.

Sluggishly, Ida opened the door to her barracks and closed it, rubbing her hands together. The kitchen to her right and the dining room to her left were empty, the house silent. In front of her were the stairs leading to the second floor of rooms. To either side of the stairwell were even more rooms. Striding into the dining room, the wooden planks squeaking under her feet, Ida thought a good draught of wine would warm her right up.

Not much had changed since becoming a knight simply because Ida had yet to be put in a Unit. The biggest difference— one she liked quite a lot—was that royal guards now greeted her. The other change was where she was posted in the city, the western district of Alucard's Kingdom. Houses were shabby and small, the people wearing rags or close to it. Crime was more or less the same. Petty squabbles to break up, thieves thinking they could outrun her, a few fistfights that were uncalled for.

Boring, in other words.

Ida went to open the glass curio cabinets, eyeing the chalices and bottles of alcohol, when a sound drifted to her ears, and she paused. After a moment, she realized what it was, cringed, rolled her eyes, and headed for the stairs. High-pitched moans and creaks sounded from one of the rooms on the first floor—she supposed that was one way to warm up.

Her armor clinked up the stairs, her wet leather shoes squeaking. It had snowed today, but the snow was too light to stick, melting as soon as it touched the ground. Luckily, another perk of becoming a knight was that Ida could afford some more woolen breeches and tunics at the start of winter. She had tossed out the old raggedy ones.

As she approached her room, an unease crept up her spine, into her mind like a spider. Ida halted in front of her door, placed her hand on the knob, a knife of smoke forming in her other. Exactly three heartbeats went by when she opened the door, pitching her knife.

Malice sat on the edge of her head, head cocked to the side, her knife in the wall behind him. She scowled.

"What are you doing here and how did you get in?" she asked, a slight growl in the back of her throat.

Malice hadn't shown himself in a month. The demon was bulkier, his hair longer, shaggier, a smirk on his face.

"What a greeting," he mused. His voice was as deep as ever; unnatural compared to his stupidly pretty face.

"What do you expect when you're uninvited?"

Malice shrugged. Ida stepped in, closing the door behind her when Malice flicked his finger to the candle on her dresser, casting the room in a deep shade of orange.

"Answer me," Ida demanded.

"How has your life been as a knight? Are you satisfied with your position?" he asked, his tone sleek.

"Is that why you're here? Why don't you get to the point?" She wasn't in the mood for his riddles or small talk. She wanted out of her armor and into that small warm bed Malice was currently sitting on.

He dipped his head, the smile never leaving his lips. "Fair enough. I have a proposal for you, Ida."

"Go on."

"My regent is needed elsewhere. She's a fighter, not a diplomat. With the upcoming war, I need her on the front lines."

Ida raised an eyebrow. "And this involves me how?"

"I think you would be a fine replacement. A permanent replacement, actually," he said, dropping the smile.

She just stared at him, head blank, unable to comprehend the words that came out of his mouth. "Why?" Ida said after a moment.

"Because Hordes Region needs a change of pace. It needs a ruler that won't become drunk on the power of the crown. That won't become complacent simply because they are immortal." Malice crossed his legs. "A ruler that can provide heirs, generation after generation. Someone that can and will make strides to improve their realm whilst they still live because they know one day death will take them whether they want it to or not."

Ida wasn't a noble and didn't have a mind for politics any more than his current regent apparently did, but it made sense. Immortals don't have to worry about a natural death, so they become content with their respective expertise. Ida had seen it many times with older knights. They'd become arrogant, thinking no one under half their age could give them so much as a scratch. And every time, Ida watched as that same knight nursed a bruised ego alongside a bruised face.

A question remained.

"Why me? I'm not of noble blood, far from it. There are plenty of mortals out there who would be more than happy about sitting on your throne. Why give it up yourself? Don't you like being king?"

Malice grunted a laugh and said, "I never wanted to be king, either. I've always wanted to hand the crown over as soon as I could. I can't just pass it on to anyone though, now can I?"

Ida frowned, crossing her arms.

"I want you to take my place," Malice continued, "because I've trained you."

"I won't become your puppet," she snarled.

"I don't expect nor want you to. I've trained you not to control you, but so you can fight alongside your subjects, stand beside them rather than above them. Besides, you're right. You're not of nobility or royalty, your blood won't win the people over, but if you could show them you are on their side, now more than ever, you will earn their loyalty and respect."

Ida studied Malice, searching for the double-edged blade this offer surely was because every word coming from his mouth was an absurdity that she was… in fact, considering.

No matter how tempting the offer was, she didn't like it. "To become queen just so you can run away from your responsibilities, all the while making a fool out of myself. You can shove the proposal up your ass."

Malice had no reaction, expressionless, stationary, eyes steady on Ida's. "My regent would teach you the ropes so you would not make a fool of yourself. And what if I'm running away? Is that so wrong?" he asked, his voice dead.

"My answer is still no." Ida adjusted her shoulders, unfolding her arms, and stood straighter, looming over Malice. As grateful for his teachings as she was, she would not become more of a pawn than she already was.

After several tense minutes of silence, Malice sighed and rose, the top of his head coming to Ida's eyebrows now. "Fine, but the offer will remain for the unforeseeable future."

Refusing to utter another word, Ida watched as Malice turned, sauntered to a corner of her room, and walked into the wall, the shadow extending from the house to consume him, before absorbing back into the wall.

Mouth ajar, Ida blinked at the shadow Malice vanished into, flabbergasted. She had never seen magic used in such a way. Perhaps it was exclusive to him, since he had dark magic.

Ida shook her surprise off and stripped her armor, the metal clunking when it hit the floor. Then her bed screeched in protest to her flopping on it. *Was this what his majesty meant at the ceremony? How ridiculous... I can't become queen, especially if it means I would replace Malice.*

But... if it wasn't Malice who was offering, would I have said yes? Should I have said yes even if it was Malice's throne I'd be taking?

No. She shouldn't have. Ida refused to be anything like Malice, a rotten king who killed an innocent boy in the streets. She refused to play by his rules. Besides, his interest would eventually shift to someone else, and he'd leave her alone.

Queen Ida... sounds... sort of nice.

The End…
XXV

In the midst of Mutuwa, was an oasis Malice found before showing Zephyrus when they were kids. It became a meeting place where the two of them had talked, more like Zephyrus rambled endlessly while Malice listened. They had sparred here, hunted, fished, and sometimes they had sat in the glade and stared at the bloated clouds.

A single claw-like cavern split Mutuwa in two. Within the cavern was a pool of brackish water, sea dwellers swimming carefree. Above the water were ledges and caves. Most were home to creatures and beasts like wyrms, massive worm-like reptiles with daggers for fangs. Being right off the sea, the air always had a briny mist flowing between the trees. Bright green leaves, twisted vines, and thick moss covered the ground, dangled from branches, and obscured tree trunks. Blossoms in colors Zephyrus didn't know existed, bushes soft and thorny, and plants with leaves twice the size of his torso were abundant throughout the forest.

Zephyrus stood glaring down at the clear water in the cavern, watching fish play a game of tag. His reflection rippled from their movements, but he could see the scar on the left side of his face going into his hairline all the same.

It'd been eight years since Zephyrus was banished—eight years since he had been in Hordes Region let alone this close to Hordes Kingdom—yet he remembered it like it was yesterday. The look on Malice's face was seared into his memory. His tone and words echoed constantly in his mind like a chasm. His left eye twitched, the scar throbbing.

Uncomfortable with the image staring back at him, Zephyrus turned and walked from the cliff's edge to the tree line. The cool shade stung his skin. He closed his eyes, breathing in the familiarity of Mutuwa—salty moss, wet soil, and a hint of blood. He had thought of returning to this forest, returning to Hordes Region many times, but the memory of his family haunted him, and the aftertaste of his banishment was pungent enough to keep him away.

"Reminiscing the past?" Malice dodged a tree branch as he stepped into the open. His white hair and black clothes contrasted the vibrancy around him while his smooth, indifferent tone was irritating, like nails on a chalkboard.

"Don't talk as if we're familiar with one another." Zephyrus glared. "It's disgusting."

Malice's eyes twitched. "That's a bit harsh, don't you think?"

"For a murderer? A monster? Not at all."

He stopped no more than fifteen meters in front of Zephyrus. "I didn't kill your family." Malice tilted his head. "I think you know that, but the one who did is already dead—I killed them—so who better to blame than me?" His long, bony hands gestured to his chest. "Your desire for revenge was left unfulfilled. A thirst that is hard to quench, isn't it?"

Zephyrus laughed dryly. "It's a thirst like none other." The breathtaking scenery lost its luster, the life of the forest drowning in a cold grey.

"But you've never had to wait to satisfy your craving, have you?" He glared at Malice, his face unchanged. "Whatever you wanted, whenever you wanted it, you had it. A simple snap of your finger," Zephyrus snapped his finger, "and you were prepared to jump in haphazardly while someone stood close by to save you."

He remembered the training grounds in Hordes Kingdom. He'd watch Malice get hurt, but someone was always quick to heal him, so he could continue sparring.

"I never got the chance to be so reckless, Zephyrus."

Stunned, Zephyrus licked his lips into a grin. He knew that tone, heard it many times, as a matter of fact. Before his armor was perfected, Malice was temperamental, especially towards his siblings—the ones who had built the foundation of corpses he now sat upon.

"How does it feel to peel your mask off?"

"Disgusting. Vile," he replied instantly. "How does it feel to watch my mask fall and shatter?"

"Incredible. Euphoric, even."

The two stared at each other. Leaves rustled in the breeze, the distant sound of rushing water calming to an extent. This type of banter reminded Zephyrus of the times he called Malice a friend, causing his skin to crawl.

"If we are to fight," Malice said after a while, "is there truly a need to hold back?"

Horns grew from his head as another set of eyes split and opened above his cheekbones. His legs changed to those of a goat's and a second set of arms sprouted from his ribs. The color of Malice's skin became a muddied reddish color. Huge black wings stretched to either side of him, folding up. The sounds curdled the bile in Zephyrus's stomach—Malice's bones were breaking, grinding, his skin tearing, muscle fibers snapping, then regenerating.

Zephyrus gulped, his lip flaring when a chill ran through his veins. He had never seen Malice's true form, nor had he seen any other demon look like that. Demons and angels could only control a few aspects of their appearance, yet Malice had changed everything.

Blood running cold, Zephyrus averted his eyes. An unsettling feeling made the hairs on his neck and arm stand on edge. The last time he had felt such an unnerving fear was when he pissed Lazarus off for disobeying an order. His entire body had trembled before the voident… this was different.

"You're right," he forced beyond the lump in his throat. From the stub of his left shoulder grew an arm of darkness. His hands and feet turned into claws and forelegs sprouted from his back—bug-like traits from his half-blooded father.

"Eight years I've waited to kill you," he growled. "Your reign is over, Malice."

Darkness flowed around Malice's hands. "Quite the contrary." He smiled. "It's only just begun."

Zephyrus bolted, striking Malice with all four arms. He caught everyone when Zephyrus yanked him forward, bashing his knee into Malice's chin. Malice's grip loosened just enough for Zephyrus to jump away. Black rope around his wrists that led back to Malice caught his eye. Malice wrenched, and Zephyrus came flying toward him. Using his open set of hands, Malice caught his shoulders while driving his fist into his stomach, forcing all the air from Zephyrus's body. Not giving him a chance to breathe, Malice punched his face, making him stagger backward, tears stinging his eyes. Then he kicked Zephyrus's chest, his sternum cracking, hurling him through the forest until he slammed into a tree trunk.

Birds screeched and scattered above. Malice was quick to launch his next attack. Zephyrus dodged to the side as a boulder crashed into the tree he landed on, gasping at the waves of pain. The tree cracked, snapped, and toppled to the ground.

Swinging his arms in a circular motion, a wall of black split the earth. Malice moved to the right, evading the piercing wall. It was enough to distract him, at least.

Memories flooded Zephyrus's mind like high tide. They used to spar until their limbs were numb, then talk as if the world around them didn't matter, as if Malice hadn't already spilled blood, as if Zephyrus didn't fear those bloodied hands and what they might do to him.

Zephyrus sprinted behind the wall of darkness and his foreleg snatched Malice by the neck. He kicked Malice's side, and, concurrently, Malice broke his foreleg in half with an ear-piercing snap. A hiss of pain escaped Zephyrus's clamped jaw. Malice flew into the cliff, the boom echoing, plumes of dust obstructing Zephyrus's view.

Abruptly, he soared from the haze of dirt. He was so fast Zephyrus didn't have time to react. Malice grabbed Zephyrus by the shoulders, his claws biting deep into the flesh. They launched into the sky. Malice threw him to the ground. The earth met Zephyrus with a harsh embrace, a blast of debris enveloping him, his back screaming in pain.

Zephyrus flipped onto his side when Malice crashed, making the ground cave and crack even more. He swept his legs around, catching Malice's. Zephyrus, grunting, knocked Malice to the forest floor and pinned him. His legs wrapped and squeezed Malice's neck and one of his arms while his forelegs restrained two of his other wrists. Hardening his grip, Zephyrus yanked Malice's arm from his shoulder. The sound of flesh ripping and bones cracking was gut-wrenching.

Somewhat free, Malice thrashed, threw Zephyrus off, and got to his feet. One spurt of blood sprayed the ground, then stopped. Every breath was a struggle as Zephyrus watched Malice's arm regenerate. Muscle quickly encased bone, skin enveloped muscle. He spat at the ground.

"I knew you weren't a demon," he shouted, glaring at Malice. "Demons don't look as repulsive as you."

He had a suspicion in Ivory's Kingdom. The way he had recovered from a month of nonstop torture was too far-fetched for a demon. Or any of the twelve species, for that matter.

Hand on his shoulder, Malice rotated his newly regenerated arm. "And?" he asked, his cold eyes meeting Zephyrus's. "You traded your lava magic for darkness. I could sense it the last we met, and your arm is confirmation."

Zephyrus flinched. His eyebrows furrowed deeply, his nose scrunching up. Darkness flowed and consumed his shoulder, soaking up the light without reflecting anything. Malice's aura changed, the atmosphere around them becoming dense and unsettling.

"You would let it consume you rather than fight me with your own strength?" Malice asked, disappointment rich in his tone.

"This is my strength!" Zephyrus snapped. "This has become my power! Now we are on even grounds."

Eyes raking Malice, "Does that scare you?" he leered.

"No. But it does scare you." Malice crouched, and leaped forth, black flowing around his hands like foam around a dog's mouth.

Zephyrus reeled, dodged the sweep of Malice's claw when something struck his ribs, breaking them, taking every ounce of air from his lungs. He crashed into the cavern, the rock rumbling, and fell. An icy wall shocked his system as he plunged into the water, chunks of earth falling close behind. Zephyrus swam to the surface, avoiding the rocks sinking to the bottom, his arm and lungs burning.

Malice flew down, picked him up, and raced to the sky. In mere seconds, they were above the canopy of Mutuwa, giving Zephyrus no time to struggle as Malice's wings thrust himself downward, flinging Zephyrus up at the same time. Malice sent him to the ground.

He collided with the earth, the warmed dirt swallowing him. Everything went pitch black. A single wave of agony pulsed through him.

Zephyrus's eyes snapped open. Then he was gasping, crawling his way out of the hole. Malice landed a few tens of meters away, debris shooting in all directions.

"You're outmatched, Zephyrus. Always have been," Malice said, stalking toward Zephyrus, who was desperately trying to escape as he dragged his body against the grass. Just one second. That was all he needed to regain some strength. No, to simply get to his feet.

"Give up."

He stopped and dug his nails into the dirt, failure keeping him down. "... No," he heard himself say. The darkness from his arm crept onto his torso and neck, the sensation like walking through a spider's web. "I'm not finished yet!" Arms trembling, Zephyrus pushed himself upright and turned to face Malice.

One step after another, Zephyrus and Malice walked toward each other. They charged. Zephyrus clobbered Malice, thick spikes of darkness on his knuckles, bones in Malice's face crunching. Malice stiffened his fingers and stabbed Zephyrus's neck. His eyes went wide, but he stayed put. The pincers on Zephyrus's forelegs gouged Malice's eyes out, and they both took a few steps backward.

Blood spilled from Malice's eye sockets onto the grass and soil with a slosh. Zephyrus held pressure on his neck, a crimson river running down his body, soaking his clothes. He began choking on his blood. Malice had already regenerated. Red streaked his face like war paint. Zephyrus concentrated on his neck, and he stopped choking as the wound closed.

Then Malice was on top of him, his palm inches from Zephyrus's face. He regressed, amazingly enough, and darted into the forest, using the trees as cover.

He knew there was a gap between their skills, but he didn't know the difference was like comparing a kindle to the sun. It wasn't like this when they were children. Zephyrus had a chance when they were children—beat him time and time again before Malice had come into his own. Zephyrus wasn't game for Malice to hunt when they were children.

Zephyrus zigged and zagged between the trees, hoping to lose Malice. Even if it was only for a second. A wall of darkness erupted in front of him. Feet digging into the earth, Zephyrus barely stopped himself from slamming into it. He surveyed the forest. Malice was nowhere in sight.

A claw reached from the darkness, and Malice grabbed Zephyrus from behind as he hauled himself out. It was a mistake taking his eyes off the wall.

Panic seized Zephyrus's thoughts. His hand transformed into a blade, he cut Malice's arm off. Zephyrus shot forward, brushing Malice's appendage from his shoulder, turned on his heel, extended his hand, and closed his fist. Darkness encased Malice and crushed him until nothing was there.

Zephyrus, sucking in shallow breaths, focused on the sounds around him; the subtle noise of waves smacking the beach and cliff sides, the howling wind, the rustling of trees.

"You didn't think you could beat me at my own game, did you?" Malice's deep voice said from behind him.

His vision went black as pressure squeezed his head. He felt his consciousness slip away from him like sand through his fingers.

*

Eyes fluttering open... *Am I... alive?* The blue sky seemed too serene to be real, too bright. He moved his head to one side. No one was there. He turned to the other side, where Malice stood over him, watching. Malice's form was normal. He appeared human again. A reflection of the friend Zephyrus once had stared down at him. Dirt and blood caked his skin. His clothes were torn but there were no bruises, cuts, or other injuries. Glancing back toward the sky, the sun was an intense white circle, blinding Zephyrus.

Blood bubbled in his throat when he groaned. He hacked and red sprayed the ground. It was only then did he realize the right side of his body was gone. Zephyrus's legs were gone as well, as if a beast had mangled them. His guts, fleshy pink, red, veiny, and pulsing, spilled over onto the ground. Some were sliced open, while most were squashed.

Malice stomped and sat on a square hunk of earth. "Surprised you're still breathing?" he asked as his eyes raked what was left of Zephyrus. "It's the darkness. Once I take it out of your body, you'll be dead." His tone was level, irritatingly level.

Zephyrus tried to speak only for blood to catch in his throat.

Malice shrugged like he knew Zephyrus's question. "I thought you'd like to talk a bit more before death takes you."

Zephyrus's chuckle was a gurgle of thick fluid, pain shooting across his torso. He spat out a big, dark red clot and took a breath.

"I only have one question for you," he lied.

The metallic taste coating his tongue and the ringing in his ears was like a ticking clock. He had many things he wished to say, to ask, and he wanted to hear Malice's response to everything. He wanted to know why Malice had never denied Zephyrus's accusations.

"What would you do," Zephyrus sucked a breath in, the forest growing dim, "if the world were to come crashing down around you?" He glanced over at Malice.

He already knew the answer to the question plaguing his heart. It was because Malice felt as though he was guilty, even if he wasn't.

Malice skimmed over the battered land, the aftermath of their battle, returning his dead eyes to Zephyrus. "I would sit on my throne and revel in the glory of its destruction." A smile curved the corners of his mouth.

His answer was funny, terrifying, and expected.

Malice brought his hand up and let it hover over Zephyrus's core. It was like he pulled a stitch out of the skin after the scar had healed. There was no pain, just the sensation of something leaving.

Mutuwa gradually became silent.

Malice finished quickly. There must not have been much magic left. Anticipating him to have departed by now, Zephyrus was pleasantly surprised to see that Malice had stayed.

You were right. Zephyrus wanted someone to blame, and that someone was Malice. He wondered what would have happened if he let go of his hatred. If he had spoken with Malice before challenging him to a duel. From the beginning, Zephyrus knew he didn't kill his family. Nevertheless, he let rage consume him.

As the edges of his vision faded, so did Malice, and for a split second, he wished Malice would save him again, give him another chance at life.

I hope you gain your throne, that you can watch the world burn and that you burn with it, so I can see you when you're done.

... Before The Beginning
XXVI

It was fun at first, fighting Zephyrus, getting lost in the motions, reminding Malice of when they were kids. Until the darkness corrupted him, made him go berserk. The fun had disappeared, so what was the point of drawing the fight out? Malice sighed and got up after one final look at Zephyrus. His crimson eyes dimmed and glossed over.

A spot next to Kiran waits for you.

In the stillness, crows had gathered above, cawing. Howlers would come soon as well, amongst other scavengers.

Malice took in the damage of their battle. The land was destroyed as far as the eye could see, trees knocked down or flung about, blood staining the earth beneath his feet. A good portion of Mutuwa, in a sense, was now barren.

From the shadows of the trees, slow, loud claps echoed. Legs of black took deliberate strides into the open. Lazarus had finally shown himself. He had to bend almost completely at the waist to dodge branches. His body was lean, not nearly as bulky as Cas's. There was one thing that set him apart from all other voidents, however.

Lazarus had a face.

The voident stopped at the shadow's edge. His eyes swung from Zephyrus to Malice. "A marvelous show," he dipped his head, "I was truly entertained."

Malice wasn't interested in small talk this time around. "Why inject him with dark magic when you knew his body was not meant to handle it?"

A body was only meant to handle the magic with which it was born. Infusing a different element was like ingesting poison. One could get used to the effects, but that didn't mean the damage stopped. Even more so if it was light or dark magic.

"To kill you." He tilted his head, the spiral horns on top of his head catching leaves. "Obviously that didn't work, but," he smirked, "I tried." Lazarus's voice wasn't deep, but it was malevolent and daunting.

"Although," he continued, "I don't appreciate you killing my son."

"Don't start playing at emotions," Malice said.

Lazarus threw his hands up and took a step forward. In just a few strides, Lazarus stood in front of Malice. He bent down to Malice's height.

"What is your deal, hmm?" He tilted his head to the left and the right like a bird. "If you wanted to start something, you should have known that Zephyrus wouldn't have been enough." Lazarus closed his fingers until there was a small bit of space between his thumb and index. "He is too small of a fish to cause such a commotion."

Malice nodded. "You're right, he is."

Lazarus tipped his head again. "Then why?"

"Because he led you to me."

The air went frigid, and Lazarus cautiously took a step back. His loose facial features appeared concerned. "I didn't realize you were looking for little old me," Lazarus said, his smile controlled, gesturing to himself. There was an edge to his voice now—the same tone he had before Malice killed his forces.

"You're," Malice glanced at Zephyrus, back to Lazarus, "a big enough fish, you see."

Something clicked in Lazarus's mind. "You want to start a war!" he proclaimed with a snap of his fingers. "Don't you?"

He sluggishly stalked around Malice like a hyena circling its prey. "That's too bad. You no longer have any ground to stand on. No trade to make. Nowhere to run. Nowhere to hide." Lazarus, slithering his hands around Malice's shoulders, moved in close. "Today is your last Malice Reap," he whispered in his ear.

"How disappointing," Malice said abruptly. "When I was younger, when we first met, I was scared shitless of you. My bones would tremble in your presence," Malice admitted. Of course, he was ten years old when they had first met.

"You have either fallen a great distance, Lazarus…" Malice cocked his head up, "or I have risen too high to see you as anything more than an ant."

In a lurching motion, Lazarus gripped Malice's neck, picking him off of the forest floor. "You insolent brat!" he snarled, "I should have killed you on that mission!"

Malice clawed at the voident's hands, face turning red as he gasped for air and chunks of black flesh went flying to either side of them, dissolving. Moments of struggle passed when Malice's neck snapped and squished out between Lazarus's fingers like firm clay, his body ultimately falling limp.

Lazarus was breathing heavily, Malice dangling from his grasp.

Malice's head popped up, magic leaking from every pore on his body, and the voident, gasping, dropped him. Lazarus stumbled backward and fell, his body freezing, his chest heaving. Malice smiled. *So easy to trick. You never change, do you, Lazarus?*

That mission was Malice's first. The Squad he was assigned to had abandoned him in the nest of enemies. Malice had killed that day—seven mercenaries, to be exact. Lazarus showed up, offered to save him if Malice, then guided him home. It was later that Malice had figured out he was saved for the sole purpose of killing. He had a talent for it, as Lazarus had told him.

"Do you," Lazarus wheezed, "have any… idea of what… you're about… to do?"

"I'm going to start a war." Malice crouched in front of Lazarus. "Just like I did in Forli and Ragar."

The voident, with a ghastly howl, broke free of Malice's intimidation and barreled toward him. However, a wave of his hand forced Lazarus to a dead halt.

Malice shook his head, clicked his tongue, "Tch, tch, tch," and rose. "Did you forget something, Lazarus?"

Twisting his wrist, Malice jerked his fingers up. Lazarus's body lurched to the sky and stopped a meter above the ground.

"Have you forgotten what you're made of?"

Lazarus stuttered, "I-i-i-im-im-impossible!" then shouted, "We killed the only two species able to do that thousands of years ago!"

"I am from the Reap, Valor, and Apostolov bloodlines, mind you, the closest to our ancestors. There has only been a handful of generations since our ancestors went extinct—since you killed them." For a moment, Malice could have sworn Lazarus went pale. Even if he didn't, his body trembled like a leaf in a storm, which was just as good.

"I am what you tried so hard to get rid of. Even Zephyrus realized what I was before you did." The last bit of Lazarus focused on Malice. "I am a devil." His body vanished.

Voidents were connected to their commander. All those under Zephyrus and Lazarus would have felt their death no matter where they were on the continent.

War was so easy to start, yet so difficult to put an end to. Amid battle, bloodshed, chaos, and loss—it was the concentration of tragedy that would bring out a god. Malice had tested the theory he got from an old elf he met when he was nineteen. It proved to be an effective ploy on Forli, using war to lure out the god of fertility and love, Tushuni. Malice had killed it before he returned to Vinyamar prior to the new year. It had been a little slower going with Asaselil, the god of earth and wind, on Ragar, but patience was a virtue.

The warm breeze caressed Malice's face as he looked down upon his region, his wings whooshing. He took a deep breath, enjoying the fresh scent of water and the forest. It was peaceful, the blue sky housed white, voluptuous clouds that drifted southeast and carefree birds that rode the wind. His kingdoms and cities were scattered across the land, grey blotches against a green canvas.

Soon, all would fall into anarchy, while Malice would be elsewhere in a land free of war. When the time came, there too, he would watch the continent crumble.

Acknowledgements

Writing The Black Throne started in a multitude of mini notebooks filled with characters, rules, world-building ideas, and chapter plans. Of course, eighty percent of those ideas were scratched and tossed into the trash. Rightfully so with some of them.

Eventually, notebooks turned into docs. Soon after, I sought beta readers, and boy, did I get the reality check I needed! Without them, The Black Throne would not be what it is now. From the bottom of my heart, I want to thank the future authors on BetaReaderio and Critique Circle. Not only did you read the terrible first drafts and give me excellent advice, but you also allowed me to read yours and offer my amateurish guidance. Both of which helped me grow as a reader and a writer. I also want to thank my very supportive family. Whether it was my dream of becoming an artist or experimenting with my identity, I was supported and loved.

I want to send my gratitude to the authors who inspired me the most. John Gwynne, Holly Black, and C. S. Pacat. The mix of war, politics, romance, and action tickled my brain in such a delectable way. Of course, the author who ignited my love for reading, thank you, Cassandra Clare. I know it's silly, but without their books, I wouldn't have fallen in love with writing.

Finally, a simple phrase is all that is needed sometimes. This is one of those times. To all who have read this book, thank you.

Instead of going on about stuff I've already mentioned, I will share three facts I've yet to make public.

1. I named my two dogs after book characters. My eldest, a black lab mutt, is named Magnus after Magnus Castine from my own stories! However, I'll admit, I initially got the name from *The Mortal Instruments* series. Anyone a fan of Magnus Bane? My Alaskan husky is named Laurant after Prince Laurant of Vere from the *Captive Prince* trilogy. I have to say, the characters in which they're named fit their personalities exceedingly well! 2. I have a flare for the dramatic… in architecture and design, that is. I would love a gothic-style Victorian house, black, gold, and deep royal blue themed with accents of my favorite colors (lavender, sage or forest green, sunset orange, etc.) throughout. Ah, that would be heavenly. 3. Outside of writing, I love to cook. Though, I do follow a recipe most every time. Rarely do I make the same thing twice because I love trying new foods. One thing I hate is bland food. My food has to have more than salt, pepper, and paprika (sorry, not sorry, white ancestors).